Take A Chance
On Me

Chapter One

God was punishing her.

It was the only logical conclusion. Madeline Donovan had done the unthinkable, and now she had to pay.

Sister Margaret had warned her time and again, but she hadn't believed.

Well, today she was a believer.

A bead of sweat slid down her spine as she took another painful step, wincing as the blister that had formed on her pinky toe half a mile back rubbed against the strap of her four-inch-heeled sandal.

Of course, she could take the shoes off, but then she'd be forced to walk barefoot on a deserted highway in the dark. Seeing as she was on the Lord's bad side, keeping the heels on was the safe bet.

The wind whipped, swirling around her like a mini tornado as another car zipped past at eighty miles per hour. Stupid Southern-belle curls, long transformed into a tangled heap, flew into her face and blinded her. She pressed closer to the bushes lining the two-lane road. Best not to tempt fate by walking too closely to motor vehicles.

Her dress caught on a wayward branch and she ripped it free. The sound of the tearing fabric seemed to echo down the highway. She sighed with satisfaction. The damned thing's destruction was the only bright spot in an otherwise miserable day.

Off in the not-too-distant horizon, peeking through the trees like a beacon of hope, a red neon sign blazed in the night sky. The word BAR blinked, winking at her, making her mouth water, urging her on. She'd been following the sign since her car broke down, and it got closer with every anguished step.

Tightening her grip on the small purse, her fingers dug into the tiny crystal beads. She had fifty bucks. More than enough to plant her ass on a stool and get drunk. Maybe not the smartest choice, given her situation, but she'd stopped caring about smart the second she'd pulled out of that parking lot.

All-too-vivid images of this afternoon filled her mind while sweat, already dampening her temples from the humidity and the long walk, trickled down her hairline.

What had she done?

This morning she'd had no idea she would take this kind of drastic measure. There'd been no sense of impending doom, no inner knowledge of what was to come. All she'd woken up with was an upset stomach and the complete certainty of where the day would end.

It hadn't included walking down a dark, unknown highway in the dead of night.

Now look at her: one act of desperate panic and she was stranded in the middle of Illinois farmland. Well, punishment or not, she would make it to that bar.

With her gaze trained on the red sign, she took another determined, torturous step toward salvation.

What felt like an eternity later, Maddie threw open the door. Adrenaline alone had kept her going for the last quarter

Take A Chance On Me

A Something New Novel

JENNIFER DAWSON

ZEBRA BOOKS
KENSINGTON PUBLISHING CORP.
http://www.kensingtonbooks.com

ZEBRA BOOKS are published by

Kensington Publishing Corp.
119 West 40th Street
New York, NY 10018

All Kensington titles, imprints, and distributed lines are available at special quantity discounts for bulk purchases for sales promotion, premiums, fund-raising, educational, or institutional use.

Special book excerpts or customized printings can also be created to fit specific needs. For details, write or phone the office of the Kensington Special Sales Manager: Attn.: Special Sales Department. Kensington Publishing Corp., 119 West 40th Street, New York, NY 10018. Phone: 1-800-221-2647.

Zebra and the Z logo Reg. U.S. Pat. & TM Off.

First Mass-Market Paperback Printing: February 2014
ISBN-13: 978-1-4201-3425-4
ISBN-10: 1-4201-3425-6

First Electronic Edition: February 2014
eISBN-13: 978-1-4201-3426-1
eISBN-10: 1-4201-3426-4

10 9 8 7 6 5 4 3 2 1

Printed in the United States of America

To my husband,
who supported every crazy idea I've ever had.
I still remember everything about the day
I met you in the library,
from your 100-percent-success-rate pickup line,
to the Elizabeth Arden card I wrote my number on.
It's been twenty years and you're still the best thing
that ever happened to me.

And to my mom,
my biggest cheerleader,
who truly believes I can do anything.
Everyone thinks their mom is the best,
but in my case,
it's true.

mile. Her dress was torn and streaked with dirt, but she'd finally made it.

Maybe God hadn't abandoned her after all.

A warm gust of humid air and probably a few mosquitoes followed her into the nearly empty bar. She'd have bites tomorrow, but she wouldn't think about that now.

No. She'd think about that, and everything else, later.

Frozen, she panted for breath so hard that she was surprised her breasts didn't spill out of the strapless dress. She gave it a hard tug to be safe. No use adding flashing to her list of transgressions.

Tangled, hairspray-sticky curls covered her back and neck like a sweaty blanket. She was thankful she didn't have a pair of scissors or she'd be tempted to hack it off. This day had been disaster enough; she didn't need to add bad hair to the mix.

She sucked in a lungful of beer-laced air and glanced around the ancient, dimly lit bar. Worn paneling the color of driftwood baked in the sun too long looked as old and tired as the male patrons sprinkling the tattered landscape. There wasn't a female in sight.

A trickle of alarm slid down her spine. Maybe she shouldn't be here alone.

The thought flittered away when her attention fell on an empty stool. She'd be fine. Growing up with three older brothers had made her well schooled in the art of self-defense, and these guys seemed more interested in their drinks than in her.

Besides, she couldn't walk if her life depended on it.

The bar loomed straight ahead. Its old, faded panels and black countertop could serve on any this-is-where-alcoholics-come-to-die movie set, but to her, it was nirvana. The distance to the stool grew exponentially the longer she stood on feet pulsing with pain. She gritted her teeth. It was only a few tiny steps.

She could do this. She'd already done the impossible.

She took one hobbled lurch, then another, until she was finally right where she wanted to be.

With a weary sigh, she plopped onto the round, cushioned stool. A slow hiss of air leaked from the seat as it took her weight. She closed her eyes. Heaven. She might never move again. An air-conditioned breeze brushed her overheated skin, and she just about groaned in sheer pleasure. Dropping her head into her open palms, she luxuriated in the pure joy of sitting.

She'd made it. The pressure on her feet eased to an insistent ache. She was safe. For the first time since her car had died, she allowed the fear to sink in. She wanted to lay her cheek on the cool laminate counter and weep in relief.

"What can I get for you, Princess?" a low, deep voice rumbled.

Maddie's head shot up and a man blinked into focus. Her mouth dropped open. In front of her stood the most gorgeous man she'd ever seen.

Was she hallucinating? Was he a mirage?

She blinked again. Nope. Still there.

Unusual amber eyes, glimmering with amusement, stared at her from among strong, chiseled features.

She swallowed. Teeth snapping together, she tried to speak. She managed a little squeak before words failed her. A hot flush spread over her chest. Men like this should be illegal.

Unable to resist the temptation pulling her gaze lower, she let it fall. Just when she'd thought nothing could rival that face.

Shoulders, a mile wide, stretched the gray T-shirt clinging to his broad chest. The muscles in his arms flexed as he rested his hands on the counter. A tribal tattoo in black ink rippled across his left bicep. Oh, she liked those. Her fingers twitched with the urge to trace the intricate scroll as moisture slid over her tongue.

For the love of God, she was salivating.

Stop staring. She shouldn't be thinking about this. Not now. Not after today.

It was so, so wrong.

But she couldn't look away.

Stop. She tried again, but it was impossible. He was a work of art.

"You okay there?" The smile curving his full mouth was pure sin.

That low, rumbling voice snapped her out of her stupor, and she squared her shoulders. "Yes, thank you."

His gaze did some roaming of its own and stopped at her dress. One golden brow rose.

Before he could ask any questions, she said, "I'll have three shots of whiskey and a glass of water."

His lips quirked. "Three?"

"Yes, please." With a sharp nod, she ran a finger along the dull, black surface of the bar. "You can line them up right here."

When he continued to stare at her as if she might be an escaped mental patient, she reached into her small bag and pulled out her only cash. She waved the fifty in front of his face. "I assume this will cover it."

"If I give you the shots, are you going to get sick all over that pretty dress?" He leaned over the counter, and his scent wafted in her direction.

She sucked in a breath. He smelled good, like spice, soap, and danger. She shook her head. What was wrong with her? She was *so* going to hell.

She pushed the money toward him. "I'll be fine. I'm Irish. We can handle our liquor."

"All right, then." The bartender chuckled, and Maddie's stomach did a strange little dip.

He wandered off, and Maddie released a pent-up breath, trying not to stare at the way his ass filled out his faded jeans. Never mind the flex of powerful thighs, the lean hips, or the—

Snap out of it.

What was wrong with her? She had bigger things to worry about. Her car was dead. She had no clothes. She'd made a huge mess of her life. And she was spending the only money she had on booze.

She couldn't afford to add impure thoughts to her rapidly growing list of sins. She needed to pull it together. She'd drink her shots, figure out a plan, and be on her way.

To where? She hadn't a clue.

The future stretched before her like a blank, empty slate. Fear and panic bubbled to the surface. She'd never been on her own. She wasn't sure how to go about it. It was sad, considering she was twenty-eight, but true.

A new thought worked its way through her muddled brain, breaking over her like the dawn of a new day: she was free. Free in a way she hadn't been in too many years to count. She could do whatever she wanted. There was no one looking over her shoulder, no one watching her with worried eyes. Maybe she'd have a chance to breathe and remember the girl she'd been before her life had gone to hell.

Before she could think too much about it, the gorgeous bartender returned. He lined up three shot glasses and tilted the bottle with a flick of his wrist. In one fluid pour, the smoky amber liquid filled each glass to the rim. "Bottoms up."

She picked up the small glass and downed it in one gulp. The alcohol burned as it slid down her throat and hit her stomach, warming her in an instant. She reached for the next shot and downed it, too. Muscles that had been tight for years loosened, and her shoulders returned to where they belonged, instead of hovering at her ears.

The alcohol rushed through her veins at Mach ten, and

too late she remembered that she hadn't eaten. Not her brightest idea.

Oh well, that was the theme of the day.

The bartender stood over her, his watchful gaze burning a hole into her. She didn't need to look up to sense his questions. She took a sip of water and tried not to fidget.

In record speed, the whiskey did its work, with her brain going a little fuzzy and the world turning a little brighter. With each passing moment, her situation seemed less dire. She could do this. It would be an adventure.

And what adventure was complete without eye candy?

Said eye candy still hovered over her, making her skin prickle with awareness. Unable to resist the pull of him, she gave up.

It didn't hurt to look, did it? Raising her head, she met his amused eyes and smiled.

He smiled right back. "Let me guess, you haven't eaten."

"How'd you know?" She traced her fingertip over the edge of the empty shot glass.

"I'm astute that way."

Tongue-tied, she picked up her water again and took a long gulp, draining it. The ice clinked as she placed it on the chipped counter.

"Thirsty?" he asked, in a low voice that vibrated in her belly.

She straightened and tried to look proper. "It's important to stay hydrated when you get drunk."

He laughed. "And why the rush to get drunk, Princess?"

"Stop calling me that." The scowl she'd intended died halfway to her lips.

Another meaningful glance at her attire. "If you don't like being called a princess, maybe you shouldn't wear such a sparkly dress."

"I suppose you have a point. I'm normally more of a jeans and T-shirt kind of girl." The last shot of whiskey sat in front of her, and she took a little sip. A drop of alcohol clung to her lower lip, which she licked.

His gaze tracked the movement, eyes darkening to burnished gold.

The tip of her tongue stalled mid-swipe and retreated to press against her teeth.

Was something happening here? Appreciating the view was one thing, but she needed to be good. She'd been good for a very long time and now wasn't the time to break her streak. Maybe the alcohol was playing tricks on her, making her imagine things. She gave herself a tiny mental shake.

"What's your name?" he asked.

He was a stranger. She shouldn't tell him her name. She shot back. "What's yours?"

Again, the corners of his mouth twitched. "Mitch Riley."

She sighed. Well, now he'd been forthcoming so she had to tell him hers. "Maddie Donovan."

He held out his hand. "It's nice to meet you, Maddie Donovan."

She slipped her palm into his. His grip was warm and sure, and a tingle raced along her arm. She snatched back her hand as though she'd been burned.

"Hard day?" he asked.

"You could say that."

"Wanna tell me about it?"

"No thank you."

"Don't you know you're supposed to confess to your bartender?" He reached for her empty glass and filled it with fresh ice and water before placing it in front of her. "Drink this."

She frowned. She'd had more than enough of people telling her what to do. She wasn't about to take orders from a stranger, no matter how gorgeous. "You're kind of bossy."

"Proper hydration was your argument." He moved down

the bar and returned with a bowl of pretzels. "Here, eat these."

Brows drawing together, she stared at the bowl full of tiny brown twists. Once upon a time, she hadn't let anyone push her around. "What if I don't want to? What if I want more whiskey?"

More liquor wasn't a good idea, but now she had a point to make. Sure, she'd wobble if she got up, but she had something to prove and alcohol fueled bravado.

A crooked, boyish grin slid over his lips. She suspected it was designed to disarm her, but it failed miserably. He placed the flat of his hands on the bar. "If you want more whiskey, you'll eat first. I don't want you knocked on your ass."

She blew out an exasperated breath. "What do you care?"

"It's a nice ass." He peered over the bar to evaluate the body part in question. "From what I can see, that is."

Just to be defiant, she picked up the rest of the shot and downed it. "I'll have another."

He pushed the bowl toward her. "You'll eat pretzels. They're good for soaking up alcohol."

"What about 'the customer's always right'?" she huffed and crossed her arms. Was she being ridiculous? Maybe, but who was he to make decisions for her? She'd had enough overbearing men to last her a lifetime. From now on, she called the shots. And if she wanted more drinks, then by God, she'd get them.

Maddie looked past him, her vision skipping around the bar. A blond, surfer-looking guy sat in a corner booth with papers scattered over the table's surface, perusing them with obvious interest. She pointed to him. "Maybe I need to tell your boss you're refusing to serve me."

A deep, amused rumble. "You can't get higher than me, Princess. I own the place."

Deflated, her shoulders slumped. "Oh. Well, never mind."

He pushed the bowl again until it was right under her nose. "Eat some pretzels and drink some water while you tell me what kind of trouble you're in."

With her spine snapping ruler-straight, she asked, "What makes you think I'm in trouble?"

He gave her a slow, meaningful once-over. "Do I look stupid to you?"

No, he didn't. All the more reason to stay away. If she could walk, she'd leave, but for now she was at his mercy. Between the buzz in her head and her swollen, aching feet, she might never move from this stool again and be forced to deal with his bossiness forever.

"I had car trouble. I broke down on Highway 60 a couple of miles back."

His lips curved down and his golden eyes flashed. "You walked?"

"What was I supposed to do?"

"It's the twenty-first century. Where's your cell?" He scowled as though she'd done something wrong.

How could she know she'd need one? She held up her tiny purse. "It didn't fit."

His gaze flicked over her. "What's with the dress?"

Not wanting to say it out loud, she toyed with a piece of the fabric and said, "What, this old thing?"

"Cute." His jaw hardened into a stubborn line. "So?"

Denial was pointless. The dress fell from her fingers. "I ran out on my wedding."

Chapter Two

"Was this before or after 'til death do us part?" Mitch asked the tipsy bride swaying on the stool. He'd shove those pretzels down her throat if necessary. Irish or not, if she didn't get food in her stomach, she'd be sick.

Green eyes flashed as brilliant and blinding as the crystals covering her overflowing wedding dress. "Before. I'm horrible, but not that horrible."

Good. He'd learned his lesson where husbands were concerned. No matter how appealing the woman, he wouldn't make that mistake again. "I take it this was a rushed exit."

"If you must know, I climbed out the church window." She placed a hand over her forehead and squeezed her lids shut. "My mother is going to kill me. She'll never forgive me."

Interestingly, there was no mention of the guy she'd ditched at the altar. "I'm sure she'll get over it."

Lashes fluttering open, she shook her head. "You don't understand. I'm twenty-eight. All her friends' daughters are married. Half of them have kids, and the other half are pregnant. I've been with . . ." She leaned in, her eyes darting around the room. ". . . *him* since I was fifteen. I'm past due."

Family expectations were something he could relate to.

Not meeting those expectations, even more so. "I'm sure she wants you happy."

Maddie straightened. "Ha! She wants me married. Period. End of story."

The last thing he wanted was to talk about her abandoned wedding, but he figured his job as her bartender required at least a cursory question. "Do you want to talk about it?" He placed his hands on the counter, hoping he passed for disarming.

The corners of her mouth pulled into a deep frown as she pushed an empty glass toward him. "About that shot."

Okay, no talking about the wedding. Fine with him. He'd rather argue about pretzels. He pushed the bowl under her cute little nose. "I believe I laid down the law on more shots. You don't like it, there's another bar about ten miles from here. The rest of the town is dry."

Chin tilted in defiance, her knockout, heart-shaped face scrunched up in concentration as she tried to stare him down. Too bad for her—he could do this all day.

Several moments ticked by before she conceded with a long, put-upon sigh, followed by an adorable pout. She picked up a handful of pretzels and shoved one in her mouth. "Happy now?"

"Yes, and you'll be even happier when you can sit upright."

"I can sit fine." The satin on her princess dress rustled as she teetered, belying her words. The veil she wore fluttered around her face, the white a stark contrast to the deep red of her hair.

Grinning, he reached over the bar and flicked the filmy fabric. "No chance to remove the veil, huh?"

She jerked back, hand flying to her head to pat the fluffy tulle, complete with tiara. "Ugh! I forgot."

He leaned into the counter. "You certainly know how to make an entrance, Maddie Donovan."

"What?" She smiled, the corners of her mouth a little shaky. "I'd think all the runaway brides would come here."

He popped open the cooler and grabbed a Bud. "Do I sense a new advertising slogan?"

"Put your picture on a billboard and you'll have to beat them away with a stick. No slogan necessary." A bright red flush staining her cheeks, she clapped a hand over her mouth. Her eyes were wide with what he suspected was horror.

He laughed, startled to hear how rusty and unused it sounded. When was the last time he'd been this engaged in a conversation?

She peeled her fingers away. "Did I say that out loud?"

"'Fraid so." It had been a long time since he'd flirted, but he hadn't forgotten how. It had been even longer since he'd felt anything but numb. And numb wasn't the word that came to mind when he looked at the runaway bride.

"Ignore me." She held up one of the empty shot glasses. It swayed in her fingers. "It's the booze."

"If you say so, Princess."

Those green eyes narrowed. Her gaze traveled over his face and body as though he were a suspect in a lineup. Trying to keep a straight face, he twisted the cap off his beer and tossed it without looking at the trash can. To his surprise, it was damn hard. He'd smiled more in the last fifteen minutes than he had all last year.

Finally, she glanced around his sad, sorry-looking dive. "Um, what's your current slogan?"

"Bar."

"I think you can do better," she said with utter seriousness, then popped another pretzel in her mouth.

She was such a cute little thing. Petite and small boned, she looked as though she might float away in that huge dress.

"I like to keep my business plan simple, catering to bikers and alcoholics."

Once again, she glanced around. "Mission accomplished. Although I don't see any bikers."

"There's a festival over in Shiloh."

Auburn brows drew together. "And I'm where, exactly?"

"Revival, Illinois, population 2,583." He'd recognized the city on her the second she'd walked through the door. "You're about four hundred miles south of Chicago. How long have you been driving, anyway?"

"Since about twelve-thirty."

He calculated the math, scratching his temple. "What exactly have you been doing?"

Averting her gaze, she stared down at the bowl of pretzels as though they held the answer to life's mysteries. "I don't really know. Driving, I guess. Before my car broke down, things are kind of a blur."

Her wheels clearly spinning, she took another pretzel and toyed with it, clicking it on the bar.

He kept quiet, taking another sip of beer. Over the bar, the television was tuned to ESPN. The barflies watched, nursing their drinks of choice, only casting occasional looks of puzzlement in the bride's direction. Mitch glanced over at his bartender, Sam. Ignoring the paperwork sitting in front of him, he watched Maddie with avid interest, raising one brow at Mitch in question.

He shrugged. He had no idea what he was doing, but he wanted to keep talking to her.

Finally, Maddie smoothed down her veil. "Hey, how'd you know I was from Chicago?"

"You're not from here." He scrubbed a hand over his scruff, realizing he'd forgotten to shave today. "I lived there until about three years ago. I guessed."

Slim, perfectly manicured white-tipped nails touched her parted lips before flitting away. Slowly, she craned her neck, surveying the sorry state of the bar, then turned to him once again.

"Why'd you move here?" She asked the question as though Mitch might be touched in the head.

He understood: it wasn't too long ago that he'd have reacted the same way. "Why not?"

Her forehead crinkled as though concentrating very hard. "Do you have family here?"

It was a normal question, the obvious question, but his gut tightened. He never spoke of his past, let alone invited questions he didn't want to answer. "I have ties, but no family."

"What's that mean?"

A muscle jumped in his jaw. "My grandmother grew up here, but my family lives in Chicago."

"Why did you move here?"

"I spent summers here when I was a kid. I know people, and it seemed as good of a place as any."

She popped a pretzel in her mouth, chewing slowly. "Did you own a bar in Chicago, too?"

"No." The word flat. Why had he mentioned Chicago? A tactical error on his part, forgetting she wasn't in a hurry to discuss her life any more than he was.

She picked up a sparkly piece of fabric and toyed with the beads. "What'd you do?"

He shrugged. If he started evading now, she'd only make a bigger deal of it, and besides, it didn't matter. It wasn't a secret. He just didn't talk about it. "I was a lawyer."

Surprise flickered over her face. "Really?"

"Really."

"But . . ." She pointed to his arm. "You have a tattoo."

Laughing, his muscles eased. "Princess, haven't you heard? Lawyers are deviants."

"Maybe." Her lips curved, her gaze resting on the black scrolls over his biceps. "But I'm pretty sure none of the lawyers I deal with are hiding tats under their suits."

Happy to change the subject, he leaned over the bar, close enough to breathe in her honey-and-almond scent. An urge to lick her came over him. What would that smooth, pale flesh taste like on his tongue?

"And what kind of lawyers have you known, Maddie Donovan?" His voice sounded low, with a hint of seduction threaded through it. He really should be ashamed of himself—after all, she *was* in a wedding dress. But he'd stopped caring about that detail as soon as she'd started arguing with him about pretzels.

Wide eyes met his. Blinking, she cleared her throat, then squared her shoulders. "Um, is something going on here?"

The smile twitched on his lips, and he let it spread. "Maybe."

She placed a hand on her stomach, her waist appearing impossibly small in the tight, corseted top. "This is making me nervous."

"Good nervous or bad nervous?" he asked, leaving the past where it belonged to enjoy the unexpected surprise of her wandering into this shithole bar.

"I'm not sure yet. It's been a while." She propped her chin on her palm, auburn curls falling over one shoulder. Even in the dim, yellow-tinted light, her hair shimmered with a hundred different strands of red. She wasn't drop-dead gorgeous, but there was something absolutely breathtaking about her.

He wanted closer. The question was, would he work on those nerves or take it easy on her? Maybe a little nudge. "I do like to make pretty girls nervous."

She gave him a delicate little snort. "I bet that line works all the time, doesn't it?"

Laughter shook his chest, drawing several surprised glances from his patrons. He always liked a woman who cut him no slack. A rarity. A challenge. It had been far too long since he'd felt the surge of challenge. Hell, it had been a long time since he'd felt the surge of anything. "Hey, I thought it was better than"—he lowered his voice to sleazy—"'Baby, are you tired? Because you've been running through my mind all night.'"

With a groan, she buried her face in her hands. "Oh my God, it's awful. Is that what I've been missing?"

"I'm just getting started."

Lashes lifted to the ceiling. "Deliver me from hell."

"Damn, you're hard on a man's ego, Princess."

"Somehow I doubt that, Slick."

Amused, he grimaced. "Slick, huh? I'm thinking that's not a compliment."

"You don't need compliments." She waved a hand over him. "Look at you, all gorgeous. I bet you don't even have to try."

With a grin, he pushed the brown bowl closer. "Have another pretzel."

Auburn brows drawing together, she flashed him a flirtatious scowl. "You don't even have the decency to deny it."

The more they talked, the harder it was to keep the smile off his face. The long-dormant muscles started to ache. "Now, why would I go and do that?"

"Because that's what you do." She grabbed another pretzel and popped it in her mouth. "That's the rule: when someone gives you a compliment, you deny."

"No, that's what women do." He placed his palms on the bar. "If I denied it, you'd accuse me of fishing."

"True. You're smart and insightful, too? That hardly seems fair." She pointed to the ceiling. "Somebody up there likes you."

That was definitely a matter of opinion, but he teased her right back. "At least you know I didn't earn my degree on my back."

"Where'd you go to law school?" She gave him a crooked half-grin. "Some obscure school in the Caribbean?"

"Nope. Not even close."

She scrutinized him, looking him up and down with

exaggerated care. "One of those infomercial Internet deals?" She straightened on the stool and cleared her throat. "You too can chase ambulances in thirty amazing days."

Goddamn, she was cute. He wanted to eat her up in only the very best way. Any last remnants of conscience about her sitting in her wedding dress evaporated. He chuckled, shaking his head. "You don't think very highly of me, do you?"

"That's the problem, I do. Now I've got to find your tragic flaw."

"I have plenty of flaws." A list too long to count, actually. Flaws a good girl like her might not be able to overlook. "But my law degree doesn't happen to be one of them."

"I know." Her tone excited, she guessed, "You were a Navy SEAL who earned your law degree at night after a long day of special ops?"

Damn, his polish must be long gone. "Where in the hell did that come from?"

"Romance novels," she said, the *duh* clearer than if she'd spoken it out loud.

"Not even close."

She blew out a breath and threw up her hands. "Fine, I give up."

He grinned. "I went to Harvard."

The loud burst of laughter had the barflies startling in her direction. "You're kidding."

"'Fraid not." That she found the idea preposterous both amused and irked him. There'd been a time when anything less would have been a surprise. "I guess now's not the time to tell you I graduated in the top five percent of my class." Shit. What was wrong with him? How was she getting him to talk about things he'd refused to even think about?

"Let me get this straight." She tapped her manicured index finger on the bar. "You graduated from Harvard at the top of your class?"

"Yep."

"Did you have a job in Chicago?"

"I did."

"As a lawyer?"

He nodded, refusing to say more.

Confusion was etched in the corners of her mouth. "But you left that behind, for this?"

"That about sums it up." He tried to make the words light, casual. Some of his enjoyment dimmed as he remembered those days when the whole world had stretched before him, ripe with possibilities. It reminded him why he'd chosen to stay numb instead of joining the land of the living.

"Why?"

"Why not?"

She studied him for fifteen long seconds. Head tilted to one side, lips pursed in concentration. Suddenly, her face brightened and she waved a hand through the air. "Never mind, you don't have to answer. After all, who am I to question crazy decisions?" She pulled at the skirt of her wedding dress, the pristine white ruined by smudges of dirt and a long ragged tear. "I climbed out of a church window and in less than twelve hours I'm shamelessly flirting with the first guy I happen across."

"Life's got an interesting sense of humor." He was relaxing now that she'd decided to drop the subject.

A long, put-upon sigh. "Isn't that the truth? Clearly, I'm being tested."

Curious, he asked, "And are you passing?"

Another adorable pout. "I don't think so."

That mouth looked like she'd just eaten a bowl of strawberries and the juices had stained her lips. He wanted to bite her. Lick her to see if she tasted as sweet as she looked.

She got all squinty, another pretzel firmly in hand. "I'm drunk."

Unfortunately. "I don't doubt that."

Her gaze caught his. Darted away. Her pink tongue flitted out to wet her full lower lip. It glistened like an invitation. "I'd leave, but I can't walk. My feet hurt."

"I wouldn't let you go, anyway." He was a little taken aback to find the words true. It had been a long time since he'd wanted anything, but he still recognized the spark of desire. He wanted her, and wasn't ready for her to walk off into the sunset yet. The right or wrong of the situation didn't much matter.

She swirled a finger over the edge of her ice water. "Do you think you could stop me?

He cocked a brow and gave her a once-over. "Considering the way you hobbled in here, I think I can take you."

Dark lashes almost obscured the green of her irises as she squinted. "I'm supposed to be getting independent now."

"I see," he said, considering the guy she'd ditched at the altar for the first time. It took a lot to drive a woman out a church window with nothing but the clothes on her back. "Everyone needs a little rescue sometime."

"You're not one of those knight-in-shining-armor guys, are you?" She said the words as if they were foul.

"Not normally, but I'm making an exception for you." He was surprised to find he wanted the role, despite her distain.

"I don't want an exception." Her tone had taken on a decided wail.

"Too bad." Yep, he wasn't budging on this one. She wanted to stand on her own two feet. He understood, but it only made him more determined.

"Why me?"

"Because I want to." It was that simple. Besides, she'd probably take off in the morning and he'd never see her again. One night to break the monotony wouldn't hurt. Before she could respond, he turned and walked the length of the bar. Flipping open the counter, he rounded the corner, striding to stand in front of her. "It's been a long time since I've done anything chivalrous. Won't you let me?"

Even white teeth nibbled on her bottom lip and he curled

his hand into a fist to keep from stroking his thumb over the abused, moist flesh. Glassy, pensive eyes blinked up at him.

He stepped close enough to feel the warmth of her skin. "What kind of a man would I be if I left you stranded?"

"I'm sure I'll be fine." But her voice quivered, giving away her doubts.

The last thing he should do was touch her, but he did anyway, trailing a finger along the line of her jaw. "Come to my office. You can lie down on the couch and get off your feet. Give yourself some time to think about your options."

She sucked in a shaky breath. "Are you going to take advantage of me?"

"Maybe later, after the whiskey has worn off." He brushed the veil away from her face, pushing the tulle from her shoulders. He wanted to rescue her, but had no intention of deluding her into thinking he was a saint.

"Now's the time I'm supposed to say something proper, right? Like, 'I'm sorry but I'm off to join the convent'?"

"That would be a waste." He stroked over the curve of her shoulder.

She shivered under the tips of his fingers. "I was getting married today."

And he really should care, but he didn't. Not even a little bit. He leaned down so his mouth hovered next to her ear. "The dress gave you away."

She pulled in a great lungful of air. "Are you trying to seduce me?"

"Nope." He straightened and looked into those big, wide eyes. "Just making sure you're clear my intentions aren't one-hundred-percent honorable. Are you going to come with me?"

She scrutinized him for a full thirty seconds, then nodded so slightly that he couldn't be sure he hadn't imagined it until she hopped off the stool.

The second her feet hit the ground, her face contorted into a grimace. "Ouch!" She threw out her hands, using his body to catch herself as she swayed, giggling. The alcohol she'd consumed was surely rushing to her head. "I guess you were right about those shots."

He slid his arms around her waist, wishing for skin instead of the scratchy beads. "I usually am."

"Aren't you modest?" Cheek resting against his chest, she sighed.

The sound was so content that it warmed some of the ice inside him. It had been a long time since a woman had rested against him, and Maddie Donovan felt particularly good.

Over her head, Sam caught his gaze, mouth quirked in a sardonic smirk.

Mitch ignored the smug bastard as she cuddled into his arms like a newborn kitten. Next to Mitch's six-three height, she was tiny and delicate in his arms. The smell of honey and almonds wafting from her hair enveloped him. Absolutely delicious.

Nails tickled his back through the cotton of his T-shirt as she wound herself around him. "You feel awesome." She must have put her earlier misgivings to rest.

Damn, he'd always been good at crafting a compelling argument. He smiled. "Do I need to carry you?"

"You have no idea how much I want to say yes." She pulled away, standing straight. Mitch wanted to snatch her back, but resisted when she squared her small shoulders. "But I've already pissed off the Father, Son, and Holy Ghost today. It might be best not to push my luck."

A deep rumble of laughter shook his chest. With one finger, he tilted her chin. "Let me guess, you're Catholic?"

Her expression went wide. "Hey, how'd you know?"

She had no clue how irresistible she was. He tucked a lock of auburn hair behind her ear. "Just a wild stab in the dark, Princess."

Chapter Three

The whiskey and Mitch's intoxicating scent made Maddie's head spin.

She placed a hand on her forehead, closing her eyes for a moment and hoping to get her bearings. What was she doing alone in some decrepit back office with a man she hardly knew? Obviously, her sanity had escaped with her out the church window and run off in another direction.

The right thing would have been to say, "No, absolutely not." The proper thing would have been to call a cab, thank him for his hospitality and excellent flirting, and be on her way. She would have done all those things, too, except his big, capable hands had stroked over her skin and she'd forgotten about anything other than how strong and safe he felt. When those burnished-gold eyes peered into hers, warming her, hell had simply seemed worth it.

She shifted, trying to find a comfortable spot on the lumpy tan couch. The office décor was a messy mishmash of thrown-together thrift-store rejects, and the uncomfortable sofa fit right in. She squirmed, settling when she finally found a spot without a spring gouging her backside. She folded her hands in her lap.

Was she really doing anything wrong? She was resting. That was all.

It wasn't like she'd agreed to hot, dirty sex.

Mitch moved, drawing her attention. In the yellow glow of a lamp that looked as though it had been taken from a Dumpster, she watched him as he arranged heaps of the wedding dress, which was overflowing into every inch of available space.

When he'd first confessed his former profession and Ivy League education, she'd been shocked. After all, how could she have guessed when he looked like some rogue golden god crossed with a Hell's Angel? But now, watching him unobserved, she saw hints of his past in his strong features, caught a glimpse in the hard set of his jaw.

Since investigating the mystery of Mitch was far more intriguing than delving into the motives that had made her climb out a church window, she asked, "What kind of lawyer were you?"

His expression flickered, and Maddie didn't miss the whitening of knuckles on the fistful of satin he held. The lines around his mouth tightened before his lips curled into a smile that didn't quite reach his eyes. "I was a criminal defense lawyer."

Yes, she had no problem picturing him in front of a jury. He had the powerful presence, intensity, and charm to command a courtroom. Treading lightly, she said in an easy tone, "That must have been exciting."

With the skirts of her dress still clutched in his grip, he shrugged. "I defended rich, powerful assholes and sent them back into society. There wasn't anything exciting about it."

Rich, powerful clients tended to produce rich, powerful attorneys, and a million questions sprang to mind. As curious as she was, his past was plainly a bitter subject, and Maddie decided to drop it. It wasn't any of her business. Besides, if she pressed, he might press back, and the last thing she wanted was to explain what she didn't herself understand. She nodded at the dress. "It's awful, isn't it?"

"Yes," he said, almost absently. Then his gaze flicked to her. "Sorry."

"Don't be, I hate it. If I had anything else to wear, I'd burn it."

Confusion replaced the tension in his features as the white fabric fell from his now relaxed grip. "If you hate it, then why did you pick it?"

The day in the bridal shop came back to her with a fresh stab of resentment that surprised her. She'd stood on a round platform, head over heels in love with a white satin slip dress that slid deliciously over her body. Her best friends, Penelope and Sophie, had gushed excitedly behind her. It had been "the one." Captivated by her image, she'd been sold. Then she'd glanced in the mirror. There'd been disapproval on the faces of her mom and Steve, and all her excitement deflated. She'd stepped off the platform and quietly gone back to the dressing room, resigned to pick their favorite. In the end, there'd been no other choice. She'd owed them too much to disappoint them.

Throat clogging, she shook away the memory. She was in the dangerous limbo phase of her buzz, where emotions threatened to rise and take over. She wouldn't think about that anymore. Besides, it didn't matter now.

She plastered a smile on her face and waved a hand at Mitch. "Haven't you heard? Brides are crazy."

His eyes narrowed, and the set of his jaw made it clear he didn't buy her dismissal. "Want to talk about it?"

"Nope." She looked over his shoulder, away from him. It was odd. She'd been praying for someone to notice her distress, to *see* her, but as Mitch Riley watched her with those intense, knowing eyes, she wished she could curl into a ball and disappear.

If only she could strip off this stupid dress, stand under a hot shower, and scrub this day away. She blew out an exasperated breath. "God, you have no idea how much I want out of this torture device. You don't happen to have a spare set of women's clothes lying around, do you?"

"Sorry, Princess, you're out of luck." He pushed aside a heap of fabric and helped himself to a seat on the couch next to her knees.

She pressed her legs against the cushions and tried not to think about how good those hard muscles felt against hers. Wanting to recapture the light flirtation in the bar and to forget about the past weighing her down, she said, "I thought guys like you stripped enough women out of their clothes that they would have left a few stragglers behind."

His expression transformed from thoughtful to heated as he ran his fingers over the back of her hand. "I don't bring women in here. And I don't bring them home. But I'm making another exception for you."

Throat drying up like a desert, she swallowed hard. For the past hour, she'd reminded herself—almost pathologically—that she had been supposed to get married today. But the normal strategies she employed to stay responsible and good kept short-circuiting in her brain. Fizzling out before she could muster any real moral fiber.

She wished she could blame the shots. Or that he was irresistibly gorgeous, with a body designed for sin. Or even something noble, like his quick wit and intelligence.

But she couldn't blame any of those things.

It was the way he looked at her, like he really saw *her*.

She drew her hand back before his touch hypnotized her. "I should go to a hotel."

His gaze dropped to her lips for a moment. Darkened. "Do you have any money?"

Only the change from the fifty tucked in her purse: not nearly enough. Too bad she was drunk enough to be dumb, but not enough to be stupid. She shook her head.

"Where do you plan on sleeping?" His voice had deepened to match the sudden heat in the small room, and thickness coated the air.

Powerful thighs pressed close enough for her to feel his hard muscles beneath the jeans he wore. Her breath did a little stutter. Was this seduction? The better question was, did she want to find out?

She clasped her hands and attempted to concentrate through her alcoholic haze. She had no money, no clothes, and no car. What options did she have?

The smart, safe, and obvious choice was to call her oldest brother. Once Shane found out where she was, she'd be rescued by the time she hung up the phone. One call and she'd be tucked into her childhood bed before the break of dawn. The thought made her want to heave up her shots.

No. Not an option.

The dangerous choice sat right next to her, watching her with a focus that made her want to squirm. It would be so easy to take what he offered, but really, wasn't that another rescue?

Was that so bad?

It saved her from crawling back to her family, proving she couldn't even last one night on her own. Rescue, along with getting drunk, had been her only thought as she'd walked through the night, following the red BAR sign like it was the North Star.

So why couldn't she stomach the thought now?

She breathed out a long sigh that felt like it came from the tips of her toes. That left one other option. She raised her chin. "I'll call a cab and go to my car. I'll sleep there for the night and figure out what to do in the light of day."

He'd started shaking his head about halfway through her proclamation and hadn't stopped. "Do you honestly think I'm going to let you sleep in a car abandoned in some ditch on the side of the highway?"

She scowled, hackles rising. "There's no *letting* me. I'm perfectly capable of taking care of myself." *I think. No, screw that. I know.*

"Hey," he said, voice soft. He wrapped his fingers around her wrist and, when she tried to yank away, held tight. "I know you can. You've already proven yourself."

Her frown deepening, she cast a suspicious glance in his direction. She was stuck in the middle of nowhere with no resources. Any idiot could see that. "I've proven nothing other than I can land myself in a huge mess."

One brow rose. "Oh? How long did you walk tonight? By yourself, in the dark?"

"I didn't have a choice, and I don't have a choice now."

"There are always choices, Maddie. Don't forget, you made a hell of a big one today."

"That doesn't count," she said, voice rising. *Temper, temper, Maddie.* She shook the voice away. "I know my options, and I'm going back to my car."

He studied her. Summing her up like the lawyer he used to be. "I don't want to ask, but I'm going to anyway. Why don't you want to call your family?"

"Because I don't want to." The words shot out of her mouth, surprising her with their force.

"What about friends?"

Penelope and Sophie would walk through fire for her, but they weren't an option, at least not tonight. "They're probably at my mom's house, consoling my family."

He scrubbed a hand over his stubbled jaw. "Won't they be worried?"

"I'm sure they are," she said. Her voice had taken on an edge that she hoped would pass for determined, but she feared that it bordered on petulance. "But I'm not calling them. I wrote a note and stole my own car from the parking lot, so it's not like they'll think I've been kidnapped."

"What did you do, hotwire the thing?" Amusement was plain in the deep tone of his voice.

"If you must know, I have three extremely overprotective older brothers, a worrywart mother, and a . . ." She paused, trying out the words in her mind and deciding she wanted to own them. ". . . suffocating *ex*-fiancé. They insisted I have one of those industrial-strength, military-grade, combination-lock hideaway keys. My uncle brought my car to the church because his was in the shop. So really, it's their fault this happened."

That was the moment she'd known she was going to run.

Surrounded by the smell of gardenias that made her want to gag, she'd pushed her bridesmaids out the door, begging for a few minutes of peace and quiet. She'd gone over to the window, desperate for the smell of fresh air, and there sat her little Honda. The cherry red of the car had glowed in the sun like a gift from heaven. A sudden, almost reverent calm descended on her. It had felt like peace: a feeling so foreign to her that it had taken a moment to recognize it.

Mitch laughed, pulling her away from those last minutes in the church and back to the temptation sitting next to her.

"Princess, you really are something," he said, still chuckling. "Okay, back to your current options. Tomorrow, you're going to be in the same situation you are tonight. So how will sleeping in your car help?"

"I don't know yet, but I'm not calling them." Every time she said the words, her conviction became stronger, and that damn knot in her chest loosened.

He shifted on the couch, his grip loosening. "Did something bad happen? I mean, other than climbing out the window?"

"No. What do you mean?" This conversation was making her head hurt and ruining a very fine buzz. She wanted to be back out front, where teasing flirtation ruled the day.

He shrugged, his thumb stroking over the fine bones of

her wrist. "I don't know, I thought maybe you caught the groom with a bridesmaid or something."

"I only wish," she blurted, then froze. What was she saying? She wished Steve had cheated on her? She cleared her throat. "Wait. That didn't sound right. I only meant I don't have a good excuse."

"You had the best excuse, Maddie." Sympathy warmed his eyes, and she wanted the charming, dangerous rogue back. Danger was better than this . . . this . . . concern.

"I don't want to talk about this." Her words snapped through the air like a whip. "I'm not calling."

"All right," he said, gentle tone matching the light brush of fingers against the flesh of her inner wrist. "I only asked to make sure nothing traumatic happened." A slow smile slid over his lips. "Since I don't want anything getting in the way when I make my move."

"Oh," she said, dumbly. "I thought you wanted to rescue me."

He laughed, and some of her agitation drained away. "And why do you think I want to do that? Out of the goodness of my heart?"

"Well, yes." The tension twisting in her belly eased with every passing second.

"No. Not even close." He raised their joined hands. Turning her palm over, he pressed a kiss to the center, his tongue flicking briefly over the sensitive skin. That tiny lick spread everywhere, from the top of her head to the tips of her toes and all the wanton places in between. No other man had touched her like this, and she didn't know if she wanted to run screaming from the room or lunge for him.

With her mind a complete blank, she could only stare at him like a deer caught in headlights.

"I can see you're a woman who appreciates the bottom line, so I'll put this in the clearest terms possible. I won't insult your intelligence by pretending I don't want to take you home and lick you until you scream, because I absolutely do. But I have no intention of taking advantage of you while you've been drinking, so you're safe tonight. I want you conscious, level-headed, and willing when we go down that road."

Maddie licked dry lips, her breath hitching a little as he described such a sexual act in such a blasé manner.

Another swipe of his thumb along the pulse pounding in her wrist. "I want you to come home with me because I find you fascinating and want to understand what's going on in that good-girl, Catholic brain of yours. I want you to come home with me because I've laughed more in the last hour then I have in a long time. And I want you to come home with me because I don't think I can let you out of my sight, which means if you sleep in a car, I'll be sleeping there too. I'm thirty-four, way too old to sleep twisted like a pretzel all night."

He let go of her wrist. She opened her mouth to speak, but he shook his head and the words died on her lips. "The truth is, Maddie, I need *you* to rescue *me*."

Chapter Four

Standing on the threshold of Mitch's living room, Maddie twisted her hands like a nervous old lady. They'd said their good-nights. He'd sent her to bed, and having to go and find him was the last thing she'd wanted.

She rubbed a finger over the slight indent where her engagement ring had been. Why must every stab at independence be met with more tests? She'd tried to take care of things herself but even the basics were challenging her.

Now here she was, once again forced to ask for help.

She cleared her throat, hoping to get his attention, but a car exploded on the large flat-screen TV, drowning her efforts. Of course he had surround sound. In a house dedicated to the 1930s, it was befitting that one of the few concessions to modern life would thwart her.

In the flickering gray light, his attention stayed firmly on the action movie and her glare was lost on the back of his head.

At the bar, when she'd been buzzed on whiskey and his intoxicating flirting, spending the night had been the ultimate temptation. But the second they'd entered his kitchen, all of that ease had evaporated like a desert mirage, replaced by the tension of two strangers forced into close proximity too soon.

After a few minutes of awkward conversation, he'd led her upstairs, handed her a T-shirt, and shoved her in a room straight out of her grandmother's decorating book. In clipped tones, he'd pointed to the telephone, shown her how to lock the door, and offered to call the chief of police, who he apparently knew, to provide a character reference.

She'd said that wouldn't be necessary and he'd said good night.

She'd hoped she wouldn't have to face him until the following morning, but that was no longer an option. She had no other choice. Unable to avoid the inevitable any longer, she said, "Mitch?"

He jumped, whipping around to pin her with a scowl, obvious even in the shadowed room.

A tiny bolt of fear shot through her, and instinct had her two-stepping back.

"Sorry, you scared me." The rigidness of his posture eased as he smiled. His gaze roamed over her wedding dress, which was practically filling the doorway with its overflowing skirts. "I thought I'd sent you to bed."

Out of nowhere, the alcohol betrayed her. Her hand fluttered to her neck, fingers entwined on the crystal choker at her throat as something unforgivable welled inside her. "Um . . . I'm sorry," she babbled, unable to form a coherent sentence. *Please, God, no.*

"Is something wrong?" Concern tightened his expression and he slid one arm over the length of the sofa.

Another step back. She couldn't do this. The pressure in her chest grew. "I, um, it's just . . ."

"Come here, Maddie, and tell me what's wrong." His voice was soft but insistent.

She took one small step forward, but the pressure threatened to crush her and her throat closed over. She stopped and looked down at the floor.

No. No. No. But it was too late.

She picked up a large handful of the dress. In this crazy, unreasonable moment, every problem in her life could be blamed on this stupid, god-awful, horrid princess wedding gown.

The floodgates opened and she burst into tears. Loud, wailing, obnoxious tears.

Her whole body shook as big, fat drops slid down her cheeks. Mortified, she covered her face as though she could hide her wailing.

Strong arms enveloped her and Mitch pulled her close. She gave one thought to protest, and then sank into the warm, solid strength of his chest. He was big and broad, so different from what she was used to. The thought made her cry harder.

She should push him away, but instead she curled closer. Needing him. She was the most wicked kind of woman. There'd be no escaping hell now. All those years of penance washed away by one night of rash behavior.

Mitch kissed her temple, rubbing his hands over her bare skin. That he let her cry, and didn't start lecturing her on emotional outbursts, made her want to crawl into him and never let go.

He swayed them both, murmuring nonsense and tracing slow, soothing circles over her back. "Come on now, Princess. Tell me what's wrong so I can help you."

She hiccupped into his shirt while she clung to him as though he were her life vest on a sinking ship. A great gush of air was followed by a hiccup. She blurted her very pressing and very embarrassing need. "I-I h-have to go to the b-b-bathroom."

The gentle sway stopped. A rumble in his chest was followed by a cough.

He was trying not to laugh. The jerk.

She sobbed harder: great heaping wails straight from the pit of her stomach. Now that she was on a roll, she keened pitifully, "A-and m-m-y f-feet hurt."

"It's okay." His tone was most definitely amused. "Why didn't you go?"

Now came the worst confession. "M-my dress i-is too b-big."

"Well, take it off."

Did he think she was an idiot?

"I c-can't get it off." With a fresh batch of hysterics, her shoulders trembled as she buried her face in his T-shirt, now wet with tears. No one at the store had mentioned she'd need a crew of people to go to the bathroom, and now a stranger had to undress her. She hiccupped. They really should mention these kinds of details at the time of purchase.

He ran his fingers down a million tiny buttons from the blades of her shoulders to the curve of her ass. "It's okay. We can take care of this."

"B-but," she cried. The thought almost unbearable. She was being tested. How was she supposed to be good when she had to disrobe in front of the most gorgeous man alive? "You'll s-see me almost n-naked."

When he said nothing, fresh tears welled in her eyes. He probably thought she was propositioning him. Surely women threw themselves at him all the time.

He rubbed her bare arms. "I'm thirty-four, Princess. I've seen a naked woman before."

"But you haven't seen me." No one had seen her—well, except Steve, but he hardly even counted. "I'm twenty-eight, and only one guy has seen me. And he isn't like you. Why can't you be someone else?"

"Like who?" He trailed a path over her bare skin, creating a rush of tingles up and down her spine.

She burrowed closer, some of her hysterics finally calming as his soothing but intoxicating presence worked its charm. "You're not Mister Rogers, you know."

"You can trust me, Maddie. I won't attack."

Ha! Not a concern. Once he saw her puny body, he'd probably wonder if she was a boy. Who knew what she'd do in her weakened emotional state with no clothes to protect her? She hadn't been on her own since she was fifteen. What if she went crazy? She'd believed she'd been cured of her former wildness, but now she wasn't so sure. Maybe it had only been hidden by years of emotional repression. Unable to stop the constant blurting of confessions, she cried, "But I might attack you."

His hands tightened at her waist as though he wanted to curl his fingers into fists.

Embarrassed, she pressed closer, not wanting to let him go despite the growing urgency of her bladder. If she let go, she might start blubbering all over again.

His grip loosened and he traced a path up her arm to cup her jaw. With an insistent hold, he gently forced her chin up until she met his gaze. Eyes watery from her tears, she blinked him into focus.

He gave her an easy smile. "Princess, I'm six-three, and probably outweigh you by a good eighty pounds. I can fight you off."

"I'm sorry, I'm sure you get this all the time." She sniffed. "With your unfortunate good looks."

"Now that's one I've never heard before," he teased.

Her eyes welled up again. "I'm trying so hard to be good, but things aren't going my way."

"I'm sure the Pope will understand," he said, laughter threading his voice.

A few more tears slid down her cheeks. No one would ever understand. "I'm going to hell."

"No way. You're far too sweet." He stroked over her cheek, and she buried her face in his chest. He started that slow sway again as she took deep, calming breaths.

"How about this?" he continued. "Let's get you out of this dress and then we can talk."

She nodded, her cheek rubbing along his T-shirt. "I tried to squirm out of it myself, but it's too tight."

"Turn around, and I'll get you out of this thing."

"Are you sure?" She burrowed deeper, even though the pressure on her bladder was increasingly uncomfortable.

"I'm positive. No big deal. I promise." He sounded casual enough, and as he'd pointed out, he'd seen plenty of naked women. Besides, now that she was thinking clearly in the aftermath of her outburst, she realized that after he unbuttoned the dress, she could hold it up until she reached safety.

See? She could do this. It'd be easy. The dress might weigh fifty pounds, but she had the strength to hold it. Under her brother James's tutelage, she'd been working on her biceps for months in the gym.

She stopped clutching his waist and bravely stepped away. "I'll be good."

A wide, devilish grin flashed over his lips, and he looped an arm around her and pulled her back. For a split second, he lost the hard set of his jaw and looked downright carefree. "Or I can make you come three or four times until you're too exhausted to pounce."

Shocked, she widened her eyes, and heat seared her cheeks. "That's not being good!"

"It is if you do it right."

"Um . . . I . . . ," she gasped, stepping back. "Um . . . ," she sputtered, not knowing what to say. Was that even possible? She darted a glance at Mitch and bit her bottom lip. With him, it might be, assuming she could get out of her own head. She frowned. Why was she thinking about this? She was *not* considering this. She wasn't. This was something the old Maddie would have considered, back when she was young and reckless. Rash.

She wasn't that kind of woman anymore. Or was she?

Concern flattened the smile that had graced Mitch's lips moments ago. He held up his hands, as though she were a frightened animal and he had to demonstrate how harmless he was. "Shit, I'm sorry. I forgot myself for a second, and you're fun to tease."

Oh, so he'd been joking. She steeled her spine. Such a relief. She didn't want to find out anyway.

Because that would be very, very wrong.

Now why the hell had he gone and said that?

He'd finally calmed her down, and now he had to fuck it up. He raked a hand through his hair and tried not to get distracted when her pink tongue darted over her strawberry-stained mouth.

Since she still hadn't said anything, he continued to work on digging himself out of the hole he'd dug. "Can you forgive me? Men are complete idiots when a woman cries." He gave her the smile he'd reserved for old ladies in the jury box.

She nibbled on her lower lip, looking pensive and wary.

The bluebird in his grandma's cuckoo clock sprang from its door and chirped, breaking the silence. Maddie jumped, pressing her hand to her chest as though trying to keep her heart from jumping out.

As the clock struck, he cursed himself for making her uncomfortable. How could he have made such a tactical error? From what he'd discerned, she might as well be a virgin.

He'd simply forgotten himself. Lost in her charm and

good-girl complex, he'd said the first teasing thing that sprang to mind.

And since he was a guy, it had been sexual.

He took two cautious steps toward her, hoping she wouldn't bolt upstairs. "That wasn't the best thing to say when I'm trying to get you out of your clothes."

Auburn brows drew together in what he could only suspect was disapproval.

He shook his head. What the hell was wrong with him? This wasn't the time to mention seeing her naked. Shit, it was like he had no experience with women.

She still said nothing, just stared at him with those uncanny green eyes. And damn if it wasn't making him a bit unsettled. It had been so long since he'd been anything but cool and detached, even before his troubles in Chicago. The knowledge caused a stirring of unease.

"I swear, I didn't mean it." He was starting to sound like a sixteen-year-old apologizing for trying to get to second base.

Quietly, she toyed with the fabric of her dress, picking at one of the sparkly beads.

At a loss for how to make the situation right, he offered the one thing he wanted to avoid, but was guaranteed to put her at ease. "Do you want me to call my neighbor, Gracie, to come help you out of your dress? She eats shit like this up, so you'll make her day."

Maddie shifted on the balls of her feet.

He narrowed his eyes. No matter how hard he peered at her, she remained a mystery. He sweetened the offer. "She's a baker, so I bet she even has some cupcakes or cookies lying around."

Maddie placed her hand on her stomach.

Why wouldn't she speak? He raked a hand through his hair. "Princess, take pity on me here. I can't begin to guess what you're thinking. Did I scare you away forever?"

She blinked, her face clearing as though she'd suddenly come out of a trance. "I'm sorry. Other than being an emotional basket case, I'm fine."

This was why he needed to refrain from any more cute remarks. "Let me call Gracie."

"No," she said, shaking her head. "I'm not up to meeting anyone."

"Are you sure?"

"I'm sure," she said, taking a deep breath. Hand still resting on her stomach, she took a step, closing the distance between them.

God help him.

Determined to remain a perfect gentleman, he encircled her wrist and said in a light tone, "Let me get you out of this dress."

"Thank you." That defiant little chin of hers tilted as though to gather her courage.

He twirled her under the curve of his arm until she faced away. "Once you're free, go run right upstairs. I want you to feel safe, so use the lock if it makes you feel better. Okay?"

She craned her neck to peer at him. Even red-rimmed and puffy, her eyes were luminous. The line of her neck curved into the hollow of her shoulder, creating a stunning silhouette that about knocked him to his knees along with her next words. "I trust you, Mitch."

His chest squeezed tight. Everything about her tempted him. He released his hold, running a hand up her bare arm. "Don't."

He'd given in to this kind of desire once and his whole life had gone up in flames, leaving him with no other option but to start over. And he had. He'd created a nice, comfortable life for himself here in Revival. He'd believed he was content. But now he knew it was a lie—he'd been complacent, bored.

Maddie made him remember why he'd loved the chase. Why he used to hunt down a challenge like a bloodhound. After he'd left Chicago, he'd sworn he'd never make the same mistakes.

He was older now, and wiser. This time, he'd do the smart thing.

He trailed a path down between her shoulder blades, catching on the band of fabric. Damn, she had beautiful skin: ivory pale and smooth as silk.

She sucked in a breath, holding it.

Would this be his only chance to touch her? He toyed with the first button. Dallying. For all he knew, he could wake up in the morning and find her gone.

"Um." She shifted and cleared her throat. The sway of heavy satin rustled in the thick silence. "Aren't you going to get on with it?"

That was the last thing he wanted, but he let the first satin-covered button slip free. The pad of his finger brushed exposed skin. So fucking soft.

Her dress began to slip. "I can't have sex with you."

He undid another button, ignoring how hard he'd been for her all damn night. "That's why you're going straight to bed after I get you out of this thing."

She clutched the thick band of fabric to her chest as her head dipped low. "Can you really do that?"

Distracted by the slow, excruciating exposing of skin, he absently asked, "Do what?"

Another button opened, and she made a little squeak. "You know . . . *that*." Her voice was a whisper as she hiked the dress up to keep it from falling to the floor.

Two more buttons undone revealed the first hint of the white silk she wore under the satin. Unable to resist the lure of her, he leaned down and sucked in her sweet, feminine scent.

He needed to get this conversation onto safe ground, but he was unable to push back the words. "Make you come?"

"Yes," she said, with a soft intake of breath. "Like you said."

Shit, he was in trouble here. His fingers played down the curve of her spine. Male satisfaction settled deep in his bones when goose bumps rose on her skin. "Yes, Maddie. I'd love nothing better than to make you come." With another stroke along her flesh, he ignored the remaining buttons. "With my hands. My mouth." He pressed his lips close to her neck but didn't dare touch. "You wouldn't have to do any work at all."

"I see." A little squeak.

A muscle jumped in his jaw. He had to stop this. With gritted teeth, he made quick work of the last remaining buttons, and then, even though it killed him, he stepped away and let her go. "You're free."

She turned around slowly, still clutching the heavy fabric to her chest. Her arms shook a little. "What about you?"

Was she trying to kill him? Test him to see if he was a candidate for sainthood? He assessed her, studying her closely. He didn't see any coyness lurking. No artificial flirtation or feigned innocence. If anything, she looked—he cocked his head, taking in the line of her jaw, the tilt of her chin—curious. He made an impulsive decision and opted for bluntness. "There are a million things I can do to you that don't include my cock, Maddie."

"Oh." A gasp. She took an involuntary step backward, then froze in her tracks. The bodice of her dress slipped a little. "But I don't understand."

"What are you confused about?" There was a razor-sharp edge in his tone. He swallowed to remove the tension choking him.

She nibbled her bottom lip, her auburn brows drawing together. "What do you get out of it?"

"I get to put my hands and mouth all over you. That's what I get out of it."

Her expression went blank. Her lips parted, only to snap shut again.

Her reasons for climbing out a church window were becoming clearer by the second. He should keep his mouth shut and let her work through her own thoughts, but screw it. "Not all men are selfish pricks in bed."

She stepped back, and the dress faltered, threatening to slip from her grasp. "This conversation is inappropriate, isn't it?"

"No," he said, watching her precarious hold on the heaps of fabric. He wasn't sure if he was praying for it to fall or stay up. He cleared his throat. "But it's still time for you to go to bed."

With a sharp nod, she backed out of the room. "Thanks for helping me."

"Anytime, Princess." She'd better get out of here fast, or he'd be coming after her. She turned and started to climb the stairs, and he called innocuously, "Sleep well."

"You too," she said, moving more quickly, until she disappeared with a final swish of white. Fifteen seconds later, he heard the slam of a door.

He blew out a deep breath and ran a hand over his day's worth of stubble. This was going to be a long fucking night.

Chapter Five

Maddie pressed two fingers to her throbbing temple and blinked against the morning light straining her eyes. Food and coffee, both of which would do wonders for her hangover, waited downstairs, but she wasn't quite ready to face Mitch Riley yet.

Instead, her life tugged at her. An incessant pull of guilt had her gaze drifting time and again to the old-fashioned telephone sitting on a secretary's desk. It was a beautiful piece of furniture, even with the painted flower detail work chipped away.

She turned to stare out the window at the yard below, mentally landscaping the unkempt grounds beneath. With a little work, it would be gorgeous. Even now, weeping willows and wild flowers swayed in the gentle summer breeze, creating an idyllic view. Oak and maple trees well over a hundred years old lined the grass. Peeking through the leaves was a river, lazily moving downstream. It was so picture perfect that an urge to draw the scene stole through her, surprising her. She hadn't drawn or painted anything since her dad died when she was fifteen.

At the thought of her father, her gaze jerked to the phone. It worked. She'd checked last night and even considered using it, but she hadn't. She needed to call her family and let them know she was alive and safe. But every time she thought about calling, her stomach rolled.

She loved them and wanted to do the right thing, but if she called now, they'd convince her to come home. Her mom would cry, and Steve would tell her how irrational she was being, and Shane would take over. By the time she hung up, her shoulders would be tense. Her belly would be coiled tight with guilt. She'd fall all over herself trying to make them happy, and somehow, what she wanted would end up sounding ridiculous and silly.

That wasn't an option. She refused to have her freedom snatched away before she'd even had a chance to experience it. After one short night, the knot of tension she'd been carrying around for as long as she could remember had eased—not a lot, but enough for her to recognize the difference. Enough for her to know she wasn't ready to leave.

The simple solution was to call her best friends. Penelope and Sophie wouldn't judge her. Maddie could kill two birds with one stone—inform her family she was safe and allevi-ate some of her guilt.

She'd try Penelope first. Penelope Watkins was all cool efficiency and grace under pressure. Her brother called her the "Iron Fist." Unlike Maddie, who had a faux, sister-to-the-boss job, Penelope was integral to Shane's business. If someone wanted access to Shane, they had to get through Penelope first. Naturally, she was the logical choice to keep the family at bay for a while longer.

Maddie walked to the bed and sat down. On impulse, she blocked the number before dialing her oldest girlfriend's cell. After half a ring, Penelope came on the line with a clipped, "Hello."

Maddie twisted the cord around her finger and whispered, "Are you alone?"

"Maddie, thank God," Penelope said, although her tone held no harried urgency. "Where are you?"

Maddie darted a nervous glance around the room, irrationally worried that her brothers would jump out from behind the lace curtains. "I'm fine. Are you alone?"

"Sophie's here," Penelope said. "Are you sure you're okay? Everyone has been crazy with worry. Your mom is in hysterics, Shane's popping antacid like it's candy, and the rest of the clan is pacing the floors like caged lions."

Maddie heard Sophie Kincaid's urgent "Where is she, where is she?" in the background.

Penelope's voice grew distant. "Geez, give me five seconds to find out."

Maddie's chest tightened, and she wished she hadn't called. She didn't want to think about home and reality.

"Where are you?" Penelope asked again. "We're worried. Do you need help?"

"I'm okay," Maddie said. "Can you let them know?"

Silence. Maddie could picture Penelope standing there, completely put together, not a hair out of place. She'd always been like that even when they'd been in kindergarten, with her pressed Catholic uniform and black patent leather shoes so shiny that Maddie had been able to see her reflection.

"You're not going to call?" Her friend's quiet question pulled Maddie out of her thoughts.

"Please, I don't want to talk to them. I can't."

"Hey," Penelope said, her voice softening. "It's okay—I'll take care of it. Tell us what you want us to do."

"Tell them I'm okay." Maddie wrapped the telephone cord around her fingers until they pulsed from lack of blood. "Tell them I'm sorry, and I'm safe."

In the background, Sophie said, "Let me talk to her."

"In a minute," Penelope said, with her tone calm and soothing. "Are you sure you're okay? I can't believe you ran away and didn't tell us."

"I left a note," Maddie said, lamely.

"Did something happen with Steve?"

Maddie shook her head even though Penelope couldn't see her. "No, nothing happened. I don't know. I was sitting there by myself, feeling like I wanted to throw up. And I knew. Knew it wasn't supposed to be this way. Pen, I don't feel the way I should." Maddie's voice cracked as her eyes filled with tears. "Does everyone hate me?"

"How can you even think that?" Penelope said sharply. "I only wish I'd known how unhappy you were."

"I'm sorry." Maddie brushed away the wet tracks on her cheeks. "Everyone loves Steve. He's perfect."

"No. We love you. We tolerated him."

"But all he's done for me—"

Penelope cut her off. "You were fifteen; it's time you stopped doing penance. And just because he was nice and helped you doesn't mean you have to marry him."

"My mom—"

"She'll get over it." Penelope mumbled something under her breath that Maddie couldn't hear. "It's your life."

Maddie pressed a finger to her throbbing temple. She didn't want to think about Steve right now. "Tell them I'm sorry, okay?"

"I will. What about money?" Penelope asked. Forever practical, she was probably already opening a spreadsheet to compile a runaway-bride to-do list. "Do you need any? I could wire some to you."

Yes! Maddie's mind screamed, but then she'd have to say where she was and for some reason, she couldn't. Not even to her best friends. Wire transfers were traceable, and Shane had connections everywhere. "I'll get by."

"You sure?"

"Yes."

"At least tell me where I can reach you." There was

rustling in the background, as Penelope probably got out her trusty notebook.

"I don't think that's a good idea."

The background noise stopped, and quiet fell over the line. Several beats passed before Penelope said, "You know I'll never tell anyone."

"Yeah, I do," Maddie said. Her friends had always had her back and always would. "But you know how my brothers are."

Penelope let out a huff. "Point taken."

A laugh bubbled up, surprising Maddie.

"Okay," Penelope said, her manner taking on a businesslike tone that always made everyone sit up and take notice. "On one condition: you have to call either Sophie or me every day and check in. Deal?"

Maddie smiled. "Deal."

"Good," Penelope said. "Call tomorrow or I swear to God I'll sic Shane on you. Don't make me play dirty."

"I won't. I promise." Maddie watched the dial on the clock click over. "Put Sophie on."

"If you need anything at all, you let me know, right?"

"I will," Maddie swore. "Until tomorrow."

"Good. Here's Sophie."

A few seconds later, Sophie came on the line.

"I didn't know you still had it in you!" Sophie's excited voice instantly made Maddie feel better. They'd met in junior high and developed an instant bond over teenage rebellion. "Are you okay?"

"Yeah, I think I am," Maddie said, and actually, she thought it might be true.

"I'm so proud of you."

A grin tugged at the corners of Maddie's mouth. "I'm glad you approve."

"It's about time. I've missed the old Maddie," Sophie said.

"I knew he wasn't right for you. Sure, he seems like the perfect guy, but I couldn't stand how he always corrected you."

Maddie frowned. "You never said anything."

Sophie huffed. "I wasn't about to badmouth your boyfriend, and you always talked about how much he did for you. It's not like he was doing anything outright nasty or mean that I could point my finger at. I'm happy you finally got fed up and bailed."

"Thank you." It was the only thing Maddie could think of to say.

"I only wish I was with you so we could go on a *Thelma and Louise* road trip."

Maddie laughed, remembering all the times they'd watched the movie, drooling over a young Brad Pitt. "I think I need to go on my own road trip and figure out who the hell I am."

"I understand, but promise me one thing."

"What?"

"If you meet a hot guy along the way, you have to tell me every last detail."

"Sophie!" Maddie's cheeks heated as she instantly thought of Mitch, the hot guy right downstairs. She pressed her lips together, fighting the sudden urge to confess. Sophie had always had that effect on her, never letting Maddie forget the girl she used to be before she'd gone down the virtuous path.

Maddie heard Penelope's voice in the background and Sophie snorted. "I'm getting the reprimand."

The clock on the nightstand clicked through another minute. "Soph, I need to go. But I'll call you guys tomorrow."

"Promise?"

"Promise." Maddie gently hung up the phone and hugged herself. The T-shirt Mitch had given her to sleep in smelled of him: that curious mix of soap and man, with a hint of danger.

Last night, on what was supposed to have been her wedding night, she hadn't been thinking of her abandoned groom. She hadn't been thinking of God, or hell, or how horrible she was, like a decent person would. No, she'd spent a good hour staring at the cracks in the ceiling, having wayward, illicit thoughts about Mitch Riley. Thinking about what would have happened if their conversation had continued. Or even if she'd let the dress fall to the ground.

This stranger who'd invaded her thoughts and preoccupied her body had made her forget all about the good thing and remember what it was like to be bad.

And now she had to face him.

Halfway down the stairs, she heard the murmur of voices. Unable to make out what they were saying, Maddie could hear enough to know that one of them was female.

She faltered and stumbled. Screeching, she caught herself on the banister and clutched it like a long-lost lover. Pulse slowing to a reasonable rate, she regained her footing and cast a prayer of thanks at the ceiling that she hadn't tumbled the rest of the way down. The last thing she needed was another grand entrance. Feet firmly planted on the ground, she let go of the railing and brushed a tangled lock of hair from one eye.

"Maddie." Mitch's voice right underneath her sent her pulse racing all over again.

She let out another yelp, hand flying to her chest. If she stayed in this house much longer she'd drop dead from a heart attack.

"What?" she snapped.

One glance at him and the pounding in her head grew. Curse him. It was completely unfair that she looked like something pulled from a pile of trash, while he looked like *that*.

Pure sin standing in the golden light of the sun.

Yesterday he'd been gorgeous, but this morning he was downright devastating in a black T-shirt and faded jeans. Shaved clean of yesterday's stubble, his chiseled features were highlighted to perfection.

Not in the mood to be reasonable, she glared at him. Some part of her had harbored a tiny shred of hope that she could blame her attraction, and subsequent behavior, on the whiskey.

But, no, he had to go blow that theory straight to hell.

He smirked. "Does someone have a hangover?"

"No," she said in a loud whisper, shaking her head with vehemence and setting jackhammers off against her temples. "I'm not dressed for company."

"I heard you scream. What happened?"

For the love of god, must she be tested at every turn? She tilted her chin and said in her most haughty tone, "If you must know, I almost fell down the stairs."

Faster than a man his size should move, he rounded the stairs and bounded up the steps two at a time, stopping when he stood one below her. Of course, she still had to peer up at him, irritating her further.

"Are you okay?" he asked, those golden eyes warm with concern.

"I'm fine." She straightened to her full five-three, but still felt small and dowdy next to him.

"You're not hurt?"

"For God's sake, I'm fine. It was just a little stumble."

He chuckled, the deep, rich timbre sending tingles down her spine. "And here I thought you wouldn't be any fun sober."

Her mouth fell open, indignation bubbling in her throat, but before she could speak, he held out a plastic grocery bag that she hadn't seen because she'd been too busy staring at his face. "My neighbor brought you some things she thought you might need."

Forgetting her momentary agitation and the pounding in her head, she took the bag. "That was very thoughtful."

Mitch grinned. "Don't let Gracie fool you—she's here for gossip."

Curious, Maddie opened the bag and sighed with pure pleasure. Inside were a variety of female essentials and—Maddie closed her eyes in thanks—clothes. She had clothes! She rummaged around, spotting a toothbrush, toothpaste, a trial-size moisturizer, and face wash. She shifted the contents around, unearthing shampoo and conditioner, and even a miniature bottle of hairspray.

And then, in the bottom of the bag was the best present of all—a pair of flip-flops.

She'd never be stuck in those torturous shoes ever again. Should she set them on fire? Maybe hack them up with a saw? Maybe she'd do both. Or was that overkill?

Maddie clutched the bag to her chest and said, reverently, "I don't care what she's here for, I will owe her forever."

"Yeah, she has that kind of effect on people." Mitch's wry tone was tinged with amusement. "Why don't you run upstairs and get yourself dressed, then you can meet her. She's chomping at the bit, and no matter how hard I try, I can't get rid of her. Short of me picking her up and throwing her out on her ass, she's not leaving."

Maddie was so happy, so thankful, that she had an impulse to kiss Mitch full on the lips. Since that would be a terrible idea, she pressed the bag of treasures tighter to her chest. "Thank you."

Mitch grinned and tugged a lock of her hair. "Don't thank me, Princess. I had nothing to do with it." He leaned down, his breath warm against the shell of her ear. "If I had my way, I'd have kept you naked for as long as possible."

A hot flush crawled up her neck and she jerked back. "Oh!"

He chuckled. "Go get dressed, Maddie."

Fifteen minutes later, she bounded downstairs with a new lease on life. The bag of goodies had set off something inside her and renewed her sense of purpose. Yesterday, she'd had no plan. She'd been in panic mode, pure and simple. But being stranded without money, clothes, and modern conveniences had forced her to realize the truth. She hadn't been running away; she'd been running toward freedom. This disaster had pushed her from the nest—she'd either fight for it and fly, or fall to the ground with a splat.

But the choice was hers.

Wearing clothes two sizes too big, her hair in a ponytail and her face scrubbed free of makeup, she'd never felt better or more alive. Upstairs, pulling on the pair of jean shorts and powder-blue tee, she'd decided to tackle one problem at a time and not worry about the big picture.

First order of business: food and coffee.

Since she smelled a fresh pot, this should be easy to check off the list. She pushed into the kitchen, sucking in the scent of caffeine goodness, and froze.

The swinging door whipped back and forth on its hinges, hitting her once in the butt before settling into place.

Maddie blinked, stunned speechless. Talk about false advertising.

Maddie had assumed his neighbor was an elderly, meddling busybody with a heart of gold. The woman propped against the blue-and-white-checked tiled counter was a freakin' sex goddess.

"Maddie Donovan," Mitch said from somewhere off to her left. "Meet my neighbor, Gracie Roberts."

Maddie blinked again, staring at the woman with curves

so lush they should be illegal. *This* was his neighbor? She tried to reconcile perception with reality, but it was too difficult.

Finally, she realized she was standing there openmouthed like a complete idiot, and remembered her manners. "Thank you for your generosity. You have no idea how grateful I am."

"Oh, believe me, honey, it's my pleasure." Cornflower-blue eyes twinkling, Gracie put the coffee cup she'd held onto the counter. With a careless swipe of her hand, she pushed a wayward sunshine-blonde curl back from her forehead and tucked it behind her ear. "I've been dying to meet you ever since my brother, Sam, told me about your ordeal last night."

Completely confused, Maddie darted a questioning glance over at Mitch.

Casual as could be, he hooked one ankle over the other, drawing her attention to his bare feet. "Sam's my bartender. He was sitting in the corner booth last night."

Maddie nodded, remembering the good-looking blond surfer type who had been watching them.

Gracie grinned from ear to ear, her full mouth a pale, glossy pink. "Well, my brother said Mitch pounced on you like a prisoner granted his first conjugal visit. So I had to see what all the fuss was about."

Maddie had no idea what to say, but she was pretty sure the heat infusing her face made her look guilty, which was ridiculous. She willed her cheeks to cool. She had nothing to be ashamed of. Last night had been perfectly innocent. Sure, she'd had a few impure thoughts, but geez, everyone had those.

"Would you shut the hell up?" Mitch's words held no heat, just good-natured exasperation. He shook his head at Maddie. "Don't mind her, Princess. She has no control over her mouth."

"Look at him, all protective." Gracie gave Mitch a slow once-over. "That's new."

That earned her a menacing look from Mitch. "You can go home now."

Gracie laughed, a full-bodied, throaty sound. "Not on your life."

"I've thrown you out before," Mitch said, putting his own coffee mug down on the counter as if preparing to do just that. "I'll do it again."

Maddie kept quiet, observing the interaction between them. There couldn't be anything romantic between them, since even the most enlightened woman wouldn't be this cool about a boyfriend bringing a strange woman home. That left friends, which, in some ways, was harder to believe.

How could any man have platonic thoughts about Gracie Roberts?

She wasn't exactly Hollywood beautiful. More, she was jaw-droppingly cute mixed with downright sexy. Like Mary Ann and Ginger rolled into one drool-worthy package.

Gracie vaulted off the counter and planted her hands on full hips encased in a pair of jeans so low and tight that Maddie couldn't figure how they stayed up. "Is that the thanks I get for coming to your rescue?"

"I didn't need a rescue," Mitch said, tossing a sly glance at Maddie. "I was doing fine without you."

Maddie cleared her throat. "Well, I do appreciate the clothes."

"Of course you do," Gracie huffed. "He'd have kept you naked like a complete Neanderthal."

"I was taking care of her. Wasn't I, Maddie?"

Both of them looked at her. Having grown up in a household where these types of arguments had been a daily occurrence, Maddie wanted to protest the "taking care" comment, but decided that this wasn't the time. Instead, she smiled calmly.

"Yes, if it wasn't for you I'd probably still be stranded in my car. And you were very . . . um, kind last night." Before she could think too much about the orgasms they'd been discussing, she turned her smile toward Gracie. "But I can't deny the essentials you gave me are a godsend."

"See, I told you she needed those things." Gracie's expression held pure victory.

Mitch scrubbed a hand over his newly smooth jaw. "Yeah, you did."

A smug, sly expression crossed Gracie's features. "And I brought homemade treats."

At the mere mention of food, Maddie's stomach growled. She shrugged at Mitch. "She wins."

"She usually does." He sighed, shaking his head, but Maddie didn't miss the amusement gleaming in his eyes. The amusement changed to heat as his gaze caught hers, pinning her to the spot. A reminder, without words, that he hadn't forgotten last night. A warning not to forget he wasn't harmless. His attention dropped to her mouth, lingered, and then rose again to meet her unblinking stare. "I'll get the plates."

He pushed off the counter and the spell broke. Flustered, she wiped her palms on her shorts, then smoothed her ponytail and turned to find Gracie watching her with avid curiosity. Maddie willed herself not to blush, and said, "Thanks again for the clothes."

"Honestly, it was nothing." Gracie surveyed Maddie and snorted, waving her hand up and down, making her *Playboy*-worthy breasts jiggle in a red tee with the words MIDWEST FARM GIRL sprawled across it. "Sam said you were tiny, so I scrounged in my closet looking for the smallest clothes I had. Those shorts you're swimming in haven't made it past my hips since practically the sixth grade," Gracie said, her lower lip puffing out. "It's so unfair."

Before Maddie could stop herself, she blurted, "You're not expecting me to feel sorry for you, are you?"

Horrified, Maddie covered her mouth.

Three mismatched plates in hand, Mitch roared with laughter, drawing a surprised glance from Gracie before she joined in.

"I'm sorry," Maddie said, talking over the two of them laughing like a couple of hyenas.

"Don't be. She deserves it," Mitch said, the laughter dying to a chuckle.

"My only excuse is I haven't had any coffee yet, and you're . . ." Maddie waved a hand. "Not what I expected."

Gracie eyed Mitch with a sniff. "Mitch always makes me sound like a pain in the ass."

"You are a pain in the ass," Mitch said, putting down the plates in the center of a worn kitchen table. "Do you want coffee, Maddie?"

"That'd be great," Maddie said. "Point me in the right direction."

"You sit." Mitch's tone was laced with the "obey me" command that both raised her hackles and sent a peculiar jolt of heat through her lower belly.

"I got it," Gracie said, pointing to an empty seat and gesturing for Maddie to sit. "How do you take it?"

Maddie nibbled on her bottom lip and contemplated kicking up a fuss at their bossiness, but decided against it. It wasn't worth the hassle. She needed to sit anyhow, because her abused feet certainly couldn't handle standing to make a silly point. So, like a good little girl, she pulled out the chair and sat. "I take it black, thank you."

A moment later, a steaming cup of coffee sat in front of her. She wrapped her hands around the mug and sucked in the strong scent. She'd never smelled anything so delicious in her life. She took a sip, savoring the rich flavor.

A pink bakery box with the words DESSERTS DIVINE in

black scroll writing slid into her line of vision and her stomach gave another growl. Mouth watering, she envisioned what treat might be waiting for her. Maybe God didn't hate her after all. If he did, wouldn't he design a better punishment than homemade baked goods?

She smiled at Gracie, who slid into the chair next to her. "I hope you didn't go to any trouble on my account."

"Not at all," Gracie said, running her finger through the seam of the box and flipping open the lid. "In fact, you're doing me a favor. This is a new experiment, and I always need taste testers."

Mitch sat down across from her with a wide smile on his face. "How are you feeling this morning, Princess?"

Maddie nibbled on her bottom lip. "I'm fine, thank you."

"Not too hungover?" He stretched his long legs under the table and leaned back in his chair. Maddie did her best to ignore the way his black T-shirt pulled tight over his flat abdomen.

"Nothing coffee and food won't cure," Maddie said, taking another sip as though to prove her point.

"Well, we've got that covered." Gracie slid a golden concoction sprinkled with powdered sugar from the bakery box. "It's Swedish flop. But I infused some raspberry into the cream."

Out of nowhere, Maddie's throat closed over and she had to blink back sudden, unexpected tears. Teeth clenched, she stared at the flaky pastry, which was overflowing with pink-tinged buttercream.

She hadn't had Swedish flop in thirteen years. It had been a Sunday-morning tradition that ended when her dad died.

She remembered every detail of their last Sunday together. The sound of her dad's voice as it echoed through the house. The whole family around the table. The laughter. Her brothers, happy and carefree. Her mom singing "Leader of the Pack" along with the oldies station.

A totally different life, belonging to a girl she'd almost forgotten.

"Maddie?" Mitch's voice, filled with concern, pulled her to the present. "Are you okay?"

The unexpected memory triggered the grief. The guilt. Throat tight, she gripped her mug and looked away from the cake. She needed a moment to pull herself together and then she'd be fine. She managed to grit out, "Great. Bathroom?"

Silence.

Maddie pressed her lips together and stared into the brown liquid swirling in her mug, praying he wouldn't press. Unshed tears pricked at the corner of her eyes. All she needed was one minute alone to compose herself. Just one minute.

"Down the hall on the right," he said, each word slow and deliberate.

Maddie nodded, pushed back her chair, and escaped.

Mitch stared after his runaway bride, wishing he could peer inside her brain and figure out what the hell had happened, but she remained as much a mystery to him as she had last night. Dragging a hand through his hair, he frowned at Gracie.

She pressed her lips together. "What set her off?"

"I have no idea," Mitch said, turning his attention to the pastry Gracie had brought. Maddie had looked at it as though she'd seen a ghost.

"I like her," Gracie said, the questions as clear as if she'd spoken them.

Mitch gave the woman he'd come to think of as a sister a level-eyed stare, keeping his mouth shut.

Gracie tilted her head to the side, sending her mop of blond curls flying. "How are you going to keep her?"

"She lives in Chicago. I'm not keeping her." He was

temporarily borrowing her until she decided to hightail it to her real life.

She gave a smug smile. "I meant keep her *for now*."

Mitch scrubbed a hand over his jaw, contemplating. "I'm not sure she has any other options."

"Don't tell me you're banking on that?" Gracie looked up to the ceiling as if exasperated by his complete stupidity. "A woman always has options, and she'll think of plenty if you're stupid enough to point out that she has to choose you by default."

Of course, Gracie was right.

But he'd talked her into staying once; he could do it again. The question was, how? Mitch sat forward, placing his elbows on the table, his brain starting a slow, methodical spin. He took a sip of coffee and looked at Gracie. She practically danced in her chair.

He rolled his eyes. "What's on your mind?"

"The way I see it," Gracie said, not letting grass grow under her feet with any long dramatic silences, "her car's broken down, and Tommy's is closed today. That buys you a couple of days."

Immediately finding fault with her logic, Mitch shook his head. "Not necessarily. She has family. She could come to her senses and call them, and be gone by noon." Just because she'd been adamant last night about not contacting them didn't mean her justifications would hold true in the light of day.

"I don't think so." Gracie peered behind him, looking thoughtful.

"She told me she has no money." Mitch pressed the bridge of his nose with his thumb and forefinger. The more he thought about it, the more he saw it as the most likely outcome. He'd only been able to convince her to come back to his house last night because she'd been tired, scared, and drunk. "There's no way she'll take any from me. What other option is there?"

"One little hitch and you're giving up?" Gracie's gaze raked over him, her lip curled in disgust. She started to speak, but her expression cleared as he heard the door swing open behind him. "Hey, we were talking about your car."

Maddie slid onto her chair, all her focus on the bakery box. "I'm not sure I'm ready to tackle that problem on an empty stomach." Her tone was light, even breezy, but Mitch thought he detected the sounds of strain underneath.

"Let me get you a piece." Gracie jumped from the table and moved to the drawer of kitchen knives.

Mitch studied Maddie, who fidgeted in her chair but refused to look at him. What was going on in that brain of hers? With Gracie here, making her presence known, he was unable to reestablish the connection they'd had last night. With every second, Maddie felt farther out of his grasp. He didn't like it.

It surprised him to realize he gave a shit.

He didn't know how, but in less than twelve hours Maddie had slipped past his defenses. He continued to watch her as Gracie moved around the kitchen doing God knew what.

Even if he managed to talk her into staying, then what? Her life was a mess. She was a mess. And what did he hope to gain?

Maybe it was best to let her go. It wasn't giving up. It was being smart.

Maddie darted a nervous glance in his direction. Her green eyes were bright. Too bright. He frowned. She'd been crying. He leaned closer to her, reaching across the table to close the gap between them. His thumb stroking her hand, he asked, "Are you all right, Maddie?"

The muscles in her neck worked as she swallowed. "Sure, I'm great."

Before he could press, Gracie butted in and plopped a

plate down in front of Maddie with about half of the cake. She pulled her hand away from him and her fingers traced the faded, blue flowered porcelain edge. "Thank you, this looks delicious."

Mitch glowered at Gracie, mentally listing the different ways he could wring her neck.

Maddie looked around the table, auburn brows drawing together. "Where can I find a fork?"

Gracie gasped, placing a hand dramatically over her ample chest. "You don't eat Swedish flop with a fork. Silverware ruins the texture."

"I see." Amusement replaced the shadows in Maddie's eyes, and as the smile tugged those strawberry-stained lips, Mitch's irritation with Gracie evaporated. "Well, then, I guess I'll eat it with my hands."

Her small, delicate finger swiped at the pink-tinged cream spilling from the flaky crust. She raised it to her mouth. Licked.

Jesus. He raked a hand through his hair and tried to think about baseball as Maddie picked up the pastry and flicked her tongue over the frosting spilling from the sides.

He gritted his teeth, his cock hardening as though he were fucking sixteen.

Oblivious to his predicament, Maddie took a bite, moaning in pure pleasure. When she'd finished chewing, she looked adoringly at Gracie. "This is the best thing I've ever tasted."

Gracie beamed. "I knew I was going to like you."

Mitch dragged his mind from the gutter and said the first thing that popped into his brain. "I had your car towed this morning."

The slice of Swedish flop stalled halfway to Maddie's mouth. She slowly lowered it to the plate. "Did you pay for it?"

He shook his head and lied through his teeth. "No. The

guy who owns the garage is a friend—he owed me a favor. It was nothing."

The corners of Maddie's mouth tightened. Eyes narrowed, she met his gaze in a good old-fashioned stare-down. Leaning back in his chair, he gave her his best lazy grin. He'd played this game his whole life: she could scrutinize him all day and he'd never break.

"What kind of favor?" Maddie asked. Her tone was filled with doubt.

"I drew up a will for him and his wife," Mitch said, coolly.

"I thought you were a bartender now?"

Mitch shrugged. "What's a little legal work among friends?"

None of the distrust cleared from Maddie's face. She opened her mouth, presumably to grill him some more, but before she could speak, Gracie cleared her throat. "I can vouch for him, I was the witness."

It didn't surprise him that Gracie had picked up his lie and run with it: that was how she was. He might not understand why she was invested in having Maddie stay, but he was grateful.

"So you didn't pay for the tow?" Maddie asked.

"No." He didn't have the slightest compunction about lying. He'd learned enough about her last night to know that being taken care of rubbed her the wrong way, and paying the tow fee didn't help his case. If she was determined to leave, he couldn't stop her, but he sure as hell didn't want her decision made because of money.

Maddie's head tilted to the side, sending her long ponytail waving. With her hair pulled back and her face free of makeup, she looked about eighteen.

"How much did you charge an hour?" Maddie asked. "I'll pay you back."

"You will not," he said, his tone taking on a decided edge.

"I had no out-of-pocket expenses and you do not owe me one cent."

"But your time—I insist." Maddie's expression took on a decidedly stubborn edge he'd already learned to recognize.

"No." As if he had a right to the final say.

She strummed her manicured nails on the table, her wheels spinning as she stared off to a spot over his left shoulder.

Gracie nudged him under the table, then jutted her chin toward Maddie.

He shook his head.

She scowled and kicked him.

Ignoring her, he moved his calf out of the line of fire. Instinct told him that it was better to let Maddie think it through than talk her into his way.

Fifteen seconds passed before Maddie straightened in her chair and shifted her attention to him. "As you know," she said, her tone taking on a professional quality as though she were about to give a presentation, "my funds are rather . . . limited at the moment."

Mitch nodded seriously, pressing his lips together to repress his smile. Damn, she was cute.

"However," Maddie continued, her chin tilting even higher, "I will write you a check for your time and trouble when I return home. How much did you charge an hour?"

Mitch scrubbed his jaw with his hand, contemplating. While he wanted to argue, he decided that letting her win this round helped his overall strategy. He'd never cash the check anyway, so there was no point in the debate. His lips quirked. "I charged four hundred dollars an hour."

She blanched, her skin turning a shade whiter. "Oh, well, I can see why you'd leave that behind. It must have been horrible to make that kind of money."

He laughed. If she only knew. Out of the corner of his

eye, he saw Gracie looking at him with avid speculation. "You asked, Princess."

"Yes, I did." Maddie blew out a breath. "Let's back up—how much does your friend charge to tow a car?"

"Only about a hundred bucks," Gracie chirped helpfully.

One-fifty was more like it, but Mitch wasn't about to volunteer the information.

Maddie's gaze narrowed. "Okay, so that's a hundred for the tow, and I'll call and find out the going rate at the motel. There's food." She turned to Gracie. "Then there's the stuff you gave me. I'd better get a pen and paper and start a tab."

"You are not," Mitch said with a low threat in his voice, "starting a fucking tab."

Gracie sputtered. "I have to agree with Mitch here. I tossed in a bunch of stuff I had lying around my house. It was nothing."

Her defiant little chin raised another notch. "I don't know how yet, but I'm paying my own way and there's nothing you can do to stop me."

Chapter Six

"What's next, Princess?" Mitch asked, as silence descended over the kitchen.

Tension coiled in Maddie's belly. With Gracie gone, she didn't have anything to distract her from the current situation.

She picked up a napkin and dropped it primly in her lap. The list of problems waiting to be tackled grew in her mind, threatening to overtake her. She twisted the thin white paper around her finger. She didn't know "what's next."

What if she failed? Fell flat on her face? It would prove to everyone how incapable she was of taking care of herself.

No. Stop.

She would not give up. She straightened her shoulders. "I don't know, but I'm going to figure it out."

Amber eyes darkened. "Let me guess, you don't want any of my help."

The "No" hovered on her lips, but she pushed it back. She peered over his broad shoulder to study the blue and rose flower-patterned wallpaper and white cabinets, so distressed from age that they were once again in style. "You've already helped me. More than I can ever repay."

"Maddie," he said, his tone taking on the decided cadence

of an exasperated male. "I gave you a place to sleep. It was nothing."

"Easy for you to say when you're the one with food and shelter."

"True," he said, scrubbing his hand over his jaw. "But if the situation was reversed, wouldn't you have done the same?"

She looked away from the cabinets at the man causing her distress on an entirely different level from her base survival. The black T-shirt stretched over his broad chest and muscled biceps. That tribal tattoo scrolled, curling down his arm like the snake in the Garden of Eden, tempting her with lust and danger. The image of him sitting around the kitchen table in the brick bungalow she shared with her mother was so preposterous that she laughed. "God no, I live with my mom."

A slow grin slid over his lips and some of the tension filling the room eased. "Really, now?"

Most twenty-eight-year-olds in this day and age lived in their own condos in Chicago's trendy neighborhoods. She would have, too—she'd saved every cent of the money she'd made as her brother's office manager to do just that. She'd even found the perfect place, but then Steve proposed.

Desperate to live on her own, she'd insisted on still getting the place, but everyone kept telling her how impractical it was to buy. How much more sense it made to save for another year and buy a house when they were married. She'd listened to lectures on the state of Chicago real estate, mortgage rates, and how the condo was too small and the plumbing was subpar. Finally, sick of the whole ordeal, she'd ripped up the check for five percent of the down payment.

Why did she *always* give in? Her hand trembled and she clutched the napkin tighter. She knew why. Guilt, pure and simple.

She'd been living with it for so long that she didn't know how to live without it. It sat like a lump of coal in her belly, making her shoulders ache and knotting the muscles in her back.

Realizing Mitch was watching her, she shrugged. "It's not *that* uncommon in my neighborhood."

"And where's your neighborhood?" A small smile softened the hard line of his jaw. He held up a hand. "Wait. Let me guess. . . . You're a South Sider, aren't you?"

The dispute between Chicago's working-class South Side and the more affluent North Side was notorious and passion-filled among locals. And Mitch Riley—tattoo and ramshackle dive bar excluded—had "North Sider" written all over him. She wrinkled her nose. "And you're probably some frat-boy, white-bread, North Sider?"

A flash of that sinful, got-to-love-me grin. "Guilty."

She rolled her eyes. "You probably grew up someplace really ostentatious and obnoxious."

"Winnetka, if you must know," he said, naming one of Chicago's wealthiest suburbs.

"Ha!" She jabbed a finger at him, her stomach easing again. "I was right."

His gaze glimmered with warmth and something else. Something that made her nervous. Excited. His attention shifted to her lips, and the mood shifted right along with it. Heat infused her cheeks as he studied her mouth as though he had wicked plans.

Plans that might include things a good Catholic girl wasn't supposed to think about.

"Back to the situation at hand, South Side girl." His low voice, laced with the rumble of seduction, raised the fine hairs along the nape of her neck.

"What's that?" Her tone was breathless, filled with antic-ipation. She snapped straight in her chair. What was wrong with her? Sister Margaret would be so disappointed. She cleared her throat. "Oh right, my current predicament."

"Yeah, that." He stretched in his chair and laced his fingers over his stomach, the picture of a man who thought he had a woman right where he wanted her. "I think you want my help, and I want to help you. Why deny us? Let me." The gleam in his eyes bordered on smug.

He thought he was slick, didn't he? She sat back in her own chair, mirroring his oh-so-relaxed posture.

It was true. If she didn't want to crawl home with her tail between her legs, she needed his help. There'd be no way around that.

She weighed her options and pictured calling her oldest brother. Once Shane was involved, he'd take care of everything. As honorary head of household, he considered it his duty. She wouldn't have to lift a finger. Her car would be towed, he'd pay for the repairs, and she'd be sitting in the kitchen surrounded by her family, trying to explain her actions, by dinnertime. Steve would probably be there, too. Her temples started to pound again as she thought of them talking her to death. It would be her engagement all over again.

Steve had known she wasn't ready to get married. She'd told him. In fact, it had been one of the few discussions in which he hadn't been able to bend her with logical arguments that made her feel like an idiot. In her mind, she'd had the best reason. She hadn't been ready.

But that hadn't mattered. He'd made sure she couldn't say no.

He'd proposed in front of her entire family at her great aunt and uncle's sixtieth wedding anniversary. In all of the chaos and congratulations, no one had noticed she hadn't said yes. Then her mom had looked at her, tears of joy shining in her blue eyes, and Maddie hadn't been able to break her heart. Not again.

She pulled her thoughts away from the past to find Mitch Riley watching her with an intense look of concentration at odds with the easy posture. She had no doubt that he was a man used to getting his way, especially where women were concerned. And for whatever reason, right now, he wanted her.

She tilted her head, and her ponytail swung, the heavy weight pulling at the last remnants of her hangover. "Why?" She didn't elaborate, because she wasn't really quite sure what she was asking.

Amber eyes flashed, but didn't waver. "I don't know why. All I know is when I look at you I don't want you to go."

It was the best answer, the safe answer.

What woman wouldn't want to hear those words from a man like him? Two days ago, it would have satisfied her. But two days ago, she hadn't climbed out the church window. "As soon as my car's fixed, I'm going back to Chicago." It was a statement. A promise.

The laziness slid off him as he sat forward and placed his elbows on the table, nodding slowly.

"It makes sense to leave now," she said. Another statement of the obvious.

A razor-sharp cut of a glance. "Sometimes you just have to fuck common sense and go with your gut."

Her heartbeat kicking up a notch, she shifted in her chair. "I shouldn't."

"No, you shouldn't." The low, heated rumble of his voice made her breathless. "But you're going to anyway."

The words were delivered as fact without even a hint of entreaty. So why didn't she feel coerced? Spine straight, she stuck out her chin. "If I stay, I insist on doing things my way."

He scrubbed a hand over his jaw, studying her with a pensive look. Probably wondering what he could get away with. "I have some conditions."

"You're not in a place to negotiate," she said, her tone taking on a slightly haughty edge that held no real ice.

"Neither are you, Princess," he said, his voice laced with the first traces of genuine amusement.

The tension, coiled tight between them since Gracie had left, loosened, lightening both the air and their mood.

A hint of a smile teased her lips. "I have something you want." As soon as the words were out, she caught the underlying implication. Cheeks heating, she pressed her lips together, refusing to snatch them back.

He laughed. The sinful, decadent sound had goose bumps breaking out along her skin. "And I've got something you need."

Out of her depth with the game she was playing, she said lightly, "I guess we're at each other's mercy."

"I guess so." His attention once again drifted to her mouth. "What do you want to do first?"

The triumphant gleam in his golden gaze made nerves dance in her belly. What was she getting into? Something dangerous. Something exciting. Something that had been missing for a long time: mischief. He reminded her of the wild, reckless girl she use to be, and it was addictive.

He watched her expectantly, and she realized he was waiting for her to speak.

"I called my girlfriends," she said mildly, watching his reaction closely. "I'll owe you for long distance."

His expression flickered, then shuttered closed. "Long distance is included in my package. What did they say?"

She shrugged one shoulder. "They offered to wire me money."

"And?" The word held no inflection.

"I said no."

His shoulders dropped a fraction of an inch. "Why?"

She bit the inside of her cheek, thinking carefully about her response and then opting for honesty. "I don't want anyone to know where I am. And I'm tired of taking the easy way out."

"Good." That one single word was filled with a thousand currents of electricity. "What's next?"

Her path finally becoming clear, she straightened. "You can start by taking me to my car."

"Here's another one!"

Mitch shook his head, grinning like a fool as Maddie held up another quarter from between the seats of her little red Honda.

Someone would think she'd found buried treasure with every discovery of spare change. He took the coin and dropped it into the plastic bag she'd brought along. So far, she'd unearthed a couple of dollars, some spare change, her favorite lip gloss, and a stainless-steel travel coffee mug as she rifled through the automobile with impressive thoroughness.

With her ass swaying high in the air, she climbed onto the driver's seat and dove down to scour under the passenger's side with a flashlight. He groaned as she wiggled, her heart-shaped rear taunting him. He'd been hard more in the past fifteen hours than he'd been in the past month, and she was driving him crazy.

With her innocence, those hints of sass, her flaming hair, and her flashing eyes, she was irresistible. The longer he stood in the parking lot of Tommy's closed garage with the hot midmorning sun beating on his back and watched her contort her tiny body into all sorts of interesting positions, the more he wanted her. He had to force himself to not grab her, strip her naked, and have his way with her.

The thing that really killed him was that he could. It didn't matter that he hadn't touched her. Some things a man just knew. Attraction burned a hot, almost a palpable thing between them.

Time was limited, but still, he ignored temptation.

He wiped a bead of sweat from his temple, wondering if the change in his previous MO where women were concerned should worry him.

One smooth leg flexed as she stretched another inch and whooped excitedly. "I found a sawbuck!"

Fuck it. How much damage could a couple of days cause?

She whipped around, sending her ponytail flying as she waved the ten-dollar bill. Cheeks flushed with the thrill of discovery, eyes gleaming like sparkling emeralds, she giggled. "My dad used to call it that."

One brow rising, he stared at the bill. A trickle of unease dimmed some of his enjoyment over watching her squirm. He mentally tallied her available funds before breathing a sigh of relief. Still not enough for even the cheapest, seediest hotel.

He peered in the car. It looked as though a tornado had blown through it. How much more money could she find? She'd already combed through the backseat, so he should be safe.

He had no idea why her staying under his roof had become vitally important, but it had. He wasn't going to think about how much she made him sweat. He'd just enjoy how she made him laugh and how his pulse kicked up when he looked at her, and remember what it felt like to be alive instead of numb.

He plucked the bill from her fingers and dropped it into the bag. "Oh, what did your dad say looking at this mess of a car?"

Her expression clouded over with the suddenness of a summer storm. She blinked, hands clasping in her lap. "Nothing. He died."

Ah, fuck. He took a step closer and kneeled down. He brushed a finger over her cheek. "I'm sorry, Maddie."

More rapid blinking, as if she was suppressing unshed tears. "It's okay. It was a long time ago." She shrugged one small shoulder, her lower lip quivering the tiniest bit. "I keep thinking about him. This morning . . ." She paused, and the delicate muscles in her neck worked as she swallowed. "The

Swedish flop reminded me of him. He used to get one every Sunday morning."

That explained the trip to the bathroom. He stroked a thumb over her jaw, aching to kiss away her grief. "I'm sorry."

Bright eyes, an impossible shade of green, met his. "It was an accident."

At a loss for what to say, he curved his hand around her neck, working his fingers gently over the tight muscles there. "That must have been terrible for you."

She nodded. Her attention shifted, dropping to his mouth. Her pink tongue snuck out and licked at her bottom lip before retreating.

He bit back a groan at the illicit images assaulting him.

Jesus. Here she was talking about her dead father and all he could think about was defiling her. He pushed the impure thoughts away. "Is there anything I can do for you?"

She shook her head. "I should get back to work."

He dropped his hand from her neck, refusing to think about how much he liked the feel of her skin under his palm. "Are you sure I can't help you look?"

"I want to do it myself," she said, her voice still thick with emotion.

"All right, Princess." He straightened and crossed his arms. He wanted her to forget: forget about her family and what she'd left behind. He wanted her sass, not her sorrow.

And he wasn't above baiting her to get it.

He fixed a stern expression on his face and jutted a chin at the car. "Get busy, little girl. As much as I'd love to clean out this garbage pit of a car, I don't have a Dumpster available. Trash bags alone won't get the job done."

She shot up, planting her hands on her hips. "What did you say?"

Yes, there it was: the fire she hid under those layers of Catholic guilt. He cocked a brow. "What's your objection? That I called you little girl, or messy?"

She threw her shoulders back, thrusting out breasts that were almost lost in Gracie's too-big T-shirt. "Both!"

"I call it like I see it." He shrugged a shoulder. "What are you going to do about it?"

Her mouth fell open, and her eyes flashed all sorts of interesting variations of green. She stepped forward and poked him in the center of his chest. "You . . . you . . . ," she sputtered.

He leaned in close, sucking in the scent of lavender, breathing in her hint of wildness. Jesus, he wanted her. He needed every ounce of control to not take her mouth in a hard, brutal fuck-you-where-you-stand kiss. Instead he whispered, "You what?"

With another hard jab of her sharp, white-tipped nail, she stomped a foot, temper riled. "You, you jerk!"

"Come on, you can do better than that, can't you?" He paused, waiting one delicious beat that made her lean in closer. "Little girl?"

"You arrogant, egotistical . . ." With a strangled scream, she hauled back and punched him in the chest, hard enough that some of the air in his lungs whooshed out.

Before she could strike again, he snagged her wrist, caught her around the waist with his free hand, and pulled her close. Her cheeks were flushed a pretty pink. Body rigid, she met his gaze with fiery defiance.

He searched her face and found what he was looking for under her righteous, indignant temper: excitement. Hunger.

He tightened his hold, pressing along her spine to force her the last couple of inches she needed to be flush against him. He needed one taste of that mouth.

But before he could give in to the impulse that was riding him hard, a police cruiser pulled into the parking lot and flashed its lights.

"Ah, fuck." He dropped his hold. Impeccable timing. He'd kill the bastard.

"Are we not supposed to be here?" Maddie asked, her tone a bit breathless.

The black-and-white pulled to a stop and the door swung open. Next to him, Maddie cleared her throat and smoothed down her rumpled clothes.

"It's fine. He's just an asshole," Mitch said wryly.

Charlie Radcliff stepped from his vehicle, looking the cliché of a small-town cop, complete with mirrored sunglasses.

"He looks . . ." Maddie shifted closer to Mitch's side. "Imposing."

He supposed that was one way to say it. Decked out in a tan uniform, Charlie strolled toward them, flashing a cocky-ass grin when he stopped in front of them.

"I just happened by," he said, in the slow drawl of his that hinted at Southern roots. "Is there a problem, ma'am?"

Mitch slanted a glance in her direction. She stood military straight, vehemently shaking her head. "Everything's fine, Officer."

"Sheriff. You sure about that?" Charlie said, sounding like a complete hard-ass. "Looked to me like you were being accosted."

"N-no—"

Mitch cut her off. "Would you get the hell out of here?"

"Mitch," Maddie said, with a low hiss.

Evidently in a devious mood, Charlie stalked forward, placing a hand menacingly over his baton. "What did you say?"

"Fuck. Off." Mitch fired each word like a bullet.

"Mitch, please," Maddie said, tone pleading.

"Do I have to take you in?" Charlie's attention shifted in Maddie's direction and his mouth twisted into a smile that Mitch had seen him use on hundreds of women during their fifteen-year friendship. "I'll be happy to look after her for you, Mitch."

A stab of something suspiciously close to possessiveness

jabbed at his rib cage. Mitch shot Charlie a droll glare. "Over my dead body."

One black brow rose over his sunglasses. "That can be arranged."

"Please, don't take him to jail," Maddie said, sounding alarmed.

Both Charlie's and Mitch's attention snapped to her.

"Now, why would you be thinking that?" Charlie asked, in an amused voice.

Maddie's gaze darted back and forth. "He threatened you."

Mitch laughed and Charlie scoffed. "Honey, he's nothing but a pesky little fly I'd have to bat away."

Comprehension dawned and her worried expression cleared. "Oh, I see. You know, you should tell someone this is some macho-guy act before you get rolling."

"And what fun would that be?" Charlie rocked back on his heels. Even with his eyes hidden behind the mirrored frames, it was damn clear he was scoping Maddie out from head to toe. Under his scrutiny, she started to fidget. She pressed closer to Mitch, almost as if by instinct, pleasing him immensely.

"Don't mind him, Princess." He slid his arm around her waist, pulling her tighter against him. "He likes to abuse his power over unsuspecting women."

"Um," Maddie said, fitting under the crook his arm as though she were made for him, which was odd considering he towered over her by a foot. "I bet it's quite effective."

Charlie laughed. "Maddie Donovan, you're everything I've heard and then some."

Maddie stiffened, pulling out of Mitch's embrace and cocking her head to the side. "How do you know my name?"

"Honey," Charlie drawled, the endearment scraping a dull blade over Mitch's nerves. "This is a small town. People don't have anything else to do but talk. Give me time and I'll know your whole life story."

That strawberry-stained mouth pulled into a frown, and two little lines formed between auburn brows. She studied the cracked concrete at her feet. Suddenly, she looked up, her cheeks flushing when she realized they were watching her. She smiled brightly. "Oh well, I guess this is what I get for making an entrance."

Charlie chuckled, shifting his attention to Mitch. "I like her. Are you bringing her tonight?"

Mitch nodded. "That was the idea."

Maddie glanced at him, shielding her eyes against the sun. "Tonight?"

"Sunday night is one of the few times none of us work," Mitch explained. "Sam, Gracie, Charlie, and I usually get together and have dinner. I'd planned on mentioning it at some point."

"That sounds fun." She gestured at her car. "I should keep looking."

Charlie bent and peered into her car, smiling. "I can see you're one of those tidy women who likes everything in its place."

Maddie's chin tilted with that defiant little lift. "If you must know, I actually am. My car is one of the few places I throw caution to the wind."

Mitch studied her. Somehow, he didn't quite believe that. He thought that the real Maddie was represented in that mess of a car. Hell, he should know: she'd managed to blow through his life like a tornado in less than twenty-four hours. But unlike her, he welcomed the chaos. After three years of mind-numbing monotony, it felt good to use his brain again and even better to feel the kick of excitement, the rush of challenge she presented.

"I see," Charlie said, resting his elbow on the top of her car. "Is there anything I can help you with?"

Maddie shook her head. "Nope, just looking for money."

Charlie stepped back and walked up to Mitch while

Maddie climbed into the driver's seat on her hands and knees, oblivious to the taunting view her ass presented.

Mitch said, in a dry tone, "Thanks a lot, asshole. I'd almost had her relaxed before you showed up."

"Is that what you were doing?" Charlie asked in a slow, amused drawl. "Relaxing her?"

"I was working on it."

"That's not all you were working on," Charlie said. "What's the plan?"

"At this point, I'm winging it."

Maddie's calf flexed as she contorted herself in an impossible position and she disappeared into the well of the passenger's seat.

"And to think," Charlie said, "if she'd have stayed in her car, I would have been the one coming to her rescue."

"Fuck off," Mitch said in his mildest voice, ignoring the kick of possession thumping insistently against his chest. He'd known Charlie since they were teenagers. Charlie knew all the right buttons to push and was looking for a reaction.

Mitch wouldn't be giving him one.

Besides, even if Charlie had found Maddie first, it wouldn't have mattered. Charlie had been sleeping with Gracie for over a year, and while they were more friends with benefits than lovers, it had been a while since either one of them had gone looking elsewhere.

Maddie's body twisted and she emerged from the car. A beam of sun caught the thick tumble of waves in her ponytail, highlighting a million different strands of red. Hair that beautiful could only have been a blessing from God. Her lips tugged down. "I couldn't find anything else."

"I'm sorry," Mitch said, not sorry at all. The certainty that she needed to stay had only grown since last night, and the less money she had, the better. The trick was to make sure she had enough that she didn't worry about taking advantage, but not so much that she could go any-where. Like a motel.

"Did you look in your trunk?" Charlie asked, ever so fucking helpful.

Mitch shot him a glare, but the bastard just gave him a smug smile.

"Duh," Maddie said, banging the heel of her palm on the side of her head. "Most of the mess is in the car, so I didn't even think to look." She reached inside the car and pressed a button. The trunk popped open. She trotted over and flung it the rest of the way.

With a loud gasp, Maddie's hand flew to her chest.

Mitch's gut tightened. Why did he have a bad feeling?

She pulled out a gym bag and jumped up and down in the excited way women had. "I'd forgotten I'd left it in there. I remember now: my hands were full and I couldn't carry it."

Mitch crossed his arms over his chest, his eyes narrowed on the gym bag.

"It won't be much, but at least I'll have some clothes!" She dropped it to the ground and crouched next to it. The zipper seemed to echo in his head as she opened the damned thing and started to rifle through the contents.

The duffel contained workout clothes, a towel, running shoes, and a variety of other female items. She clutched a bottle to her chest and hugged it tight, beaming at him with a smile so bright his breath caught. "My shampoo." Another bottle clutched tight. "My perfume."

The contents should have eased his mind, but didn't.

"Oh my God, makeup." She held a bag and raised her gaze to the heavens. The sunlight caught her ivory skin so she fairly glowed. "Thank you! Thank you! Thank you!"

Charlie chuckled. "She is a cute little thing, isn't she?"

The knot in Mitch's stomach grew, and he realized he had ground his teeth so tight that his jaw was starting to ache.

With considerable effort, he forced his muscles to relax. He was safe. She hadn't found anything that would send her away.

She opened a side pocket and squealed with delight as she unearthed toothpaste and a toothbrush. In a split instant, all of her frantic motion stopped as she froze. Her eyes widened, and a huge smile split her face. "I can't believe it. Going to the gym to work out my frustration finally paid off."

She slipped her hand into the side pocket and pulled out a shiny silver credit card.

Ah, fuck.

Chapter Seven

Sitting in the parking lot of Revival's only motel, Maddie clutched the credit card tightly enough for the hard plastic edges to bite into her skin. In the hoopla of the week before the wedding, she'd forgotten about tucking the card into her gym bag to renew her membership.

At first, the discovery had seemed like a gift from God. But like most gifts from the heavens, this one had come with strings and unforeseen tests.

Mitch sat next to her. The hard and impenetrable quiet between them was a stony, almost tangible thing.

Outside, the sun blared too brightly against the asphalt parking lot as the temperature climbed steadily over the afternoon. Even with the air-conditioning blasting, her bare thighs stuck to the black leather seats of his BMW.

Another minute ticked by on the electronic display.

At a loss for how to tackle the elephant in the room, she trailed a path over the sophisticated electronic console. "Is this car a holdover from your lawyering days?"

The corners of his mouth turned down. "Something like that."

They'd managed to keep up an affable front after the sinfully good-looking sheriff had driven away in his cruiser, and Mitch had driven her to the "local" Target, twenty miles away. As they'd roamed the various aisles, he'd broken the ice with his wicked charm and teasing attempt to seduce her back to his house. She'd lapped it up, enjoying every second, because she'd known it would come to an end soon enough.

Even lunch had been heartbreakingly fun as he'd presented numerous closing arguments to sway her. But the bad mood lurking under the surface had reared its ugly head when she'd offered him gas money.

She scowled. What was the big deal?

He'd driven her around practically half the day and taken his time, effort, and resources to help her. It wasn't a cardinal sin to pay her own way, although he clearly didn't agree.

On the ride to the motel, the tension grew as discontent stirred like a boiling pot waiting to spill over.

Why wasn't she happy?

With the backseat loaded with Target bags, and five hundred dollars in her pocket from the cash advance she'd taken from the ATM on her way out the door, she'd accomplished exactly what she'd wanted. Except what had she really proved? That given a credit card with a healthy limit, she could take care of herself?

She stared out the window at the motel that would be her home until her car was fixed. Rundown and decrepit, the sign advertised color TVs and vacancies, with the v blinking at intermittent intervals. The parking lot was littered with the usual cars and pickup trucks pulled into neat little rows outside their accompanying doors. A carport decorated with multicolored tinsel housed a pack of Harleys. Maddie didn't know if the odd touch made the place more ominous, or less. She pointed at the strange sight. "Isn't it a little early for Christmas decorations?"

The air conditioner blasted from the vents, rustling the plastic from the backseat.

"Please reconsider." Mitch's words were soft, yet firm, as

if he was fighting back a demand he couldn't quite leash. "I don't want you staying here."

She fixed her attention on the lobby door. The vacancy sign winked mockingly. She clutched the credit card more tightly. "I can't."

He turned, shifting in his seat, his long legs hitting the console. "Why?"

She bit the inside of her cheek. Why was this so hard? It should be easy to walk away. For all intents and purposes, he was a stranger: leaving should be simple. Her gaze dipped down to the door handle. The hard lump of guilt sat like a rock in her stomach.

What kind of a person was she that she'd had an easier time walking away from her wedding than getting out of this car?

Next to her, Mitch waited; the air was tense with everything unsaid.

He was different from Steve in that way. If she'd had this conversation with Steve, he would have answered his own question already. She traced her index finger along the cool metal door handle.

If he bothered to even ask the question in the first place.

She took a deep breath and expelled it slowly. "People have been taking care of me for so long, I can't remember what it's like to make my own decisions." The confession surprised her. She hadn't planned it.

"Go on," Mitch prompted. That soft, low voice sent a shiver down her spine.

She craned her neck to look at him. The sun caught the dark gold of his hair, highlighting his warm skin and eyes. He was a beautiful man. He was rugged and powerful, a walking fantasy come to life, and he wanted her. Even more startling, she wanted him back, almost fiercely.

Maybe this was God's idea of a practical joke. Or maybe it was just another test.

She swallowed past the tightness in her throat. She didn't

know what it was, other than not meant to be. "I need to take care of myself right now. To prove to my family and myself I can do it."

"And you can't prove yourself and stay with me?" Resignation slid into his expression.

The desire to change her mind rose swiftly, filling her chest. She bit her bottom lip hard enough to feel the sting of pain until she composed herself. "I'm sorry."

"Why?" The word rasped across her skin like the blade of a dull knife.

Her throat closing over, she shrugged. "I don't know why."

For several long-drawn-out moments, he studied her. His eyes narrowed as though he was looking for something; then finally he gave a sharp nod. "Okay. I don't like it, but I understand."

A confusing mixture of unhappiness and regret washed through her. How she longed to be convinced. Ironic, considering her main gripe about Steve was that he'd never take no for an answer.

She lowered her lashes. "I guess there's nothing else to say."

"Oh, I don't know about that," he said, crooking a finger. "Come here."

Her throat went dry, and her heart gave a thud. On instinct, she shook her head.

His expression turned ruthlessly intent. "Maddie, I've been thinking about that mouth of yours for almost twenty-four hours straight. You don't think I'm going to let you go without touching you, do you?"

Had it only been one day? How was that even possible? It seemed as though a lifetime had passed since she'd run out on her wedding. "Um . . ." She swallowed hard and squeaked out, "Yes?"

A long pause filled with sexual awareness so thick it practically coated the air.

How did he do it, flip the mood? Only moments ago,

she'd felt bereft, but with one wicked glance she'd forgotten everything dogging her.

"I'll tell you what." He smiled, and it was so filled with cunning that the fine hairs on her neck rose in anticipation. "Tell me you won't regret it and we can end things right here with a friendly pat on the back."

"I-I d-don't know what you mean," she lied, loving and hating the direction the conversation had taken.

"Do I need to spell it out?"

"No?" The word was a question instead of the statement she'd intended.

"You want to take care of yourself, right?"

She nodded, sensing a trap but unable to stop playing into his hands.

He leaned close, placing his elbow on the console, taking up every spare inch of breathing room. "You're ready to ditch the good Catholic girl and start doing what you want?"

The strange mixture of lust and irritation he evoked pulled in her stomach. "Well, when you put it that way."

The curve of his lips held a distinct sexual tilt. "If you get out of this car untouched, tell me you won't lie in bed late at night and regret it. Tell me you won't wonder and wish you'd done things differently."

Her pulse hammered and her throat dried up, leaving her unable to breathe, let alone speak.

He stroked a path over the line of her jaw, and Maddie forced her eyes to stay open instead of fluttering closed from sheer desire.

Why did it feel like an eternity since he'd touched her? Even more troubling, why did his hands feel so right? The slightly rough pads of his fingers trailed down the curve of her neck, leaving an explosion of tingles coursing through her.

"And remember, Princess," he said, in a deep rumble of a voice that vibrated through her as though he were her own personal tuning fork. "Lying is a sin."

She gasped, sucking in the last available bit of air left in the car. "That's a low blow."

He gave a seductive laugh, filled with heat and promise and the kind of raw passion she'd always dreamed about. "I'm not above playing dirty." A sly smirk as he rubbed a lazy circle over skin she hadn't known was sensitive. "In fact, I think you prefer it that way."

"I do not!" Her heart beating far too fast, she clutched at the credit card hard enough to snap it in two.

"Liar." He slipped under the collar of her T-shirt to wrap a possessive hand around the nape of her neck. "I'm waiting."

She gritted her teeth to keep from moaning. How did one man feel so good? Hot and sinful. Irresistible. She whispered, "For what?"

"My answer," he said, inching closer. Their mouths mere inches away.

She swallowed hard. The truth sat on the tip of her tongue, and for once in her life, she decided to speak it instead of stuffing it back down. "I'd regret it."

"Exactly," he said, the word a soft breath against her skin. The pad of his thumb brushed over her bottom lip, sliding over the dampness until it felt swollen. Needy. "I can't live with myself unless I've tasted this mouth."

This was one regret she wouldn't have to live with. Her anticipation was a hot rush, and everything stilled inside her.

Another brush over her lip. The roughness of his fingers was an erotic slide over the smoothness. Sensual.

He leaned in.

She waited.

His tongue flicked over her moist, ready flesh. Her nails dug into the palm of her hand, and she let out a frustrated squeak. She'd never wanted to be kissed more.

A hard nip of his teeth.

"Oh!" Surprise and lust mixed together. It heated her

blood, making her pulse beat wildly in her throat, jolting through her nerves and sending them into rapid fire.

She'd never experienced this before, this kind of desire.

She wanted more. So much more. Wanted to force the raw, uncontained passion she'd read about but never experienced, to force his mouth to hers and wrap her body around him to feel the hard press of muscle and bone.

But she was too afraid.

So she balled her hands into fists to keep from reaching for him. The plastic cutting her skin was a harsh reminder of where this interlude would end.

His lips brushed hers. Nothing but a tease.

Her breath stuttered in her lungs. *Do it. Please do it.*

His gaze met hers, a blaze of heat. "I might never get to have you, but I'm going to make damn sure you never forget this kiss."

"Yes," she said, the plea in her voice making her cringe.

And then his mouth covered hers. So possessively arrogant that her head spun.

It was every fantasy she'd ever had and then some.

A fierce claiming. Carnal passion. Mad, crazy lust. Her mind went blank. She forgot everything and everyone but this man and the sensations rioting through her.

His tongue swept past her lips to tangle with hers. She moaned deep in her throat, a low primal sound.

He pressed closer, slanting his lips, angling deeper. Pushing her harder. He twisted her ponytail, coiling the thick strands around his hand.

He tugged hard enough that she jerked against him. The sting mixed with desire in her veins, sending her blood racing.

She forgot about propriety. Forgot about right or wrong. Forgot everything but wanting—no, *needing* more.

Her fingers uncurled, and the credit card slid from her

grasp, falling to her lap. For the first time in as long as she could remember, she reached to grab what she wanted. Him.

Shifting in her seat, she pressed against his solid chest. Greedy, she snaked a hand around his neck and pulled him close. Not caring that it wasn't like her, she took.

Harsh breathing filled the car as he yanked her closer.

The kiss grew wetter. Hotter. More demanding.

A low growl vibrated against her lips. He twisted her hair tighter, pulling until a sharp tug at the base of her neck sent a shiver of pleasure down her spine. She ached. Needing to relieve the pressure, she rubbed her breasts against his chest like a cat in heat.

He slipped a hand between their bodies and cupped one full, swollen mound. His thumb swiped over her nipple. She cried out, the sound captured by his mouth.

God help her.

He rolled the bud.

Her hips jerked, longing for friction. Aching for it.

He pinched the stiff peak. The pressure was hard enough to send stars flashing on her eyelids and searing desire low in her belly. *Oh, yes, again. Please again.*

He wrenched away.

God, no. Not yet. Mindless, she chased his heat, wanting him back, needing his mouth on hers, but he held her away.

"No!" The urgent plea so instinctual she couldn't have stopped it if her life depended on it.

He grasped her shoulders. "It's enough, Maddie."

The words were more effective than a bucket of ice water. She ceased her struggle, and reality and sanity returned in a cruel rush. The hot sting of humiliation replaced the burn of passion.

His harsh expression softened. "Come on now, Princess. Don't look at me like that."

She bit her lip, her throat tight with embarrassment. What

was wrong with her? She'd been shameless. "I'm sorry." Her apology was automatic.

"No. Stop." He let go of her shoulder and grasped her chin in his big hand. "You have nothing to be sorry about."

She nodded, wanting to die of mortification.

He gentled his hold. "Believe me, you're perfect. Too perfect."

Then why? She pressed her lips together.

He stroked over her bottom lip, still swollen and wet from his kiss. She wanted more. The lust, low in her belly, demanded it. But she wasn't going to be appeased. Nope, she needed to rein it in. Stuff it back down.

Needing distance, she straightened, pulling from his grasp.

He dragged a hand through his hair. "I'm sorry, I shouldn't have been so abrupt. You took me by surprise."

"Sure," she said, speaking past the lump in her throat. "I should go get the room."

She grabbed the door handle, but before she could pull it open, he grabbed her wrist and yanked her back into the seat.

Why wouldn't he let things be? She whipped around. "What?" Her tone was the snap of a whip in the quiet car as embarrassment turned to anger. "It's time for me to go, Mitch."

A muscle ticked in his jaw and his eyes flashed fire. "I stopped," he said through gritted teeth, "because I didn't think your inner good girl would appreciate being fucked in a seedy motel parking lot in front of God and everyone."

She froze at his blunt words. The confession should have satisfied her, but it didn't. She wrenched her wrist free. "Do me a favor. Take care of your own demons. I can manage my inner good girl just fine!"

Not waiting for a response, she flung open the car door and jumped out.

* * *

What in the hell had happened?

Mitch stared after Maddie as she stomped across the sidewalk toward the lobby, her ponytail swaying in rhythm to the defiant swing of her hips. He had no idea what had set her redheaded temper flaring.

Didn't she understand? For once in his sorry life, he was being a nice guy. He was *protecting* her.

It had taken a fucking Herculean effort not rip off those too-big shorts, yank her on top of him, and impale her. And, Jesus, that mouth. Did she have any idea how hard it was to resist that needy, swollen, wet, intoxicating mouth? He'd never kissed a woman and questioned whether he could stop. Ever.

But in less than five minutes, Maddie had blown his control straight to hell. He'd had to stop, because if he hadn't, he'd have taken her hot, eager little body with a ruthless, demanding lust and scared her to death. With his last remnants of sanity, he'd remembered she was practically innocent and pulled back. For her.

And now she was pissed about it? He shook his head. Women. Who understood them?

Sure, he appreciated her quest for independence, but he hadn't meant it like that. He was only . . . He trailed off, watching her through the dirty window. He caught the movement of Maddie's shadow as she talked to the lobby attendant. Her hand flew as she gestured, obviously responding to something he'd said.

Well, in retrospect, maybe he could have phrased it differently. But, hell, she had to cut him some slack—he hadn't had an ounce of blood left in his brain.

Her ponytail bobbed as she planted her hands on her hips. Goddamn, he wanted her. After that kiss—that mind-blowing, cock-wrenching kiss—was he honestly going to give up and let her stomp off into the sunset?

No way. He was keeping her.

The unexpected thought sent ice through his veins. What exactly was he doing? Keeping her? For what? Nothing good could come from this situation. Maddie was a disaster waiting to happen, and he'd given up complicated women.

Gut instinct had once made him a shark of a lawyer, and even though it had been a while, it told him everything he needed to know: walk away. It had been twenty-four hours, not nearly enough time to do any permanent damage. In a couple of days, she'd be gone and things would return to normal. He'd forget about this momentary diversion and return to his numb, day-to-day life.

It was the smart move. The safe move.

He'd ignored his gut once and paid the price.

Maddie flew through the lobby door, her hands clenched into fists, her beautiful face scrunched in anger.

His chest squeezed.

She marched to the car, threw open the door, and plopped onto the seat.

Before he could speak, she banged her fists on the dashboard and let out a high-pitched scream, startling him.

"Jesus, Maddie, what the hell is wrong?"

"You want to know what's wrong?" she yelled, pointing at the lobby door. "My stupid credit card has been reported stolen. They took it and now the jerk inside won't give it back!"

Relief, strong and powerful, swept through him in a dizzying rush.

Screw safe.

Chapter Eight

"I'm warning you," Mitch said to Gracie in a low, menacing tone. "Don't even think about being helpful." Maddie had pleaded a headache and excused herself to lie down the second they walked into his house, and he'd been acting like a lunatic ever since.

He'd left things to chance today and fate had dealt him the winning hand. He wasn't going to let anything fuck it up, and that included making sure his do-gooder neighbor didn't offer Maddie any alternatives.

She stayed here with him. Period.

Gracie fluttered those long, full lashes that got her whatever she wanted. "What do you mean?"

Mitch shot a sidelong glance to the closed kitchen door, cocking an ear to listen for any sound above. Satisfied when he heard nothing, he lowered his voice. "I know you. When the subject of Maddie's sleeping arrangements come up, don't even think about offering her a place to stay."

Gracie nibbled her bottom lip and snaked another inch closer to Charlie, who rubbed her back while taking a sip of beer. "You've got a real hard-on for this girl," he said.

Mitch ignored the comment, remaining focused on Gracie. "Understood?"

"But—" she started.

"No buts," Mitch cut her off. "And whatever you do, don't mention the empty apartment you have over the garage."

Sam stretched his legs under the kitchen table and slipped his hands into the pockets of his jeans. "She may not have a choice."

A slice of panic, completely disproportionate to the situation at hand, cut through Mitch. He whipped around, eyeing Sam. "What do you mean?"

Relaxed, like he didn't have a care in the world, he scrubbed a hand over his chin. "Well, what would you rather it be? Our house? Or Chicago?"

Mitch wasn't in the goddamn mood to deal with any of Sam's crap. "If you're having some sort of premonition, then spit it the fuck out."

Sam shrugged and slouched lower in this chair. "Just making conversation."

Yeah, right. Sam never just made conversation. Mitch raised his eyes to the ceiling. God help him, he missed the days of dealing with sane, rational people. The sad thing was that three years in this town had turned him as crazy as the rest of them. "She's staying here."

"All right," Gracie chirped. Her white T-shirt, with a cupcake made from pink rhinestones on it, twinkled as though mocking him. "Don't get your panties in a bunch. Mum's the word."

"Thank you," Mitch said, shaking his head. "Was that so hard?"

Charlie, still rubbing slow circles over Gracie's back, pinned him with his cop's gaze. "What exactly do you think you're doing?"

Hell if he knew. Mitch was in pure reaction mode—the words "keep her" pounded in his brain like a mantra, refusing to be ignored. He dragged a hand through his hair before propping a hip against the counter, trying to shake off the adrenaline rioting in his veins. "I'm helping her."

Three faces, filled with varying amounts of disbelief, stared back at him.

Mitch took a slug off his beer to keep the justifications at bay. Fuck 'em, he didn't have to explain himself.

One dark brow rose up Charlie's forehead. "Just remember what happened the last time you went after an unavailable woman."

As if Mitch could forget. He spoke through gritted teeth. "It's not like that."

Charlie shrugged. "It's close enough to be cousins."

A hot poker of anger jabbed in his stomach. "It's not remotely the same."

"You have a thing for unavailable women," Charlie said, his expression as flat as his tone. "And Maddie, as cute as she is, fits the bill."

"I don't have a thing for unavailable women," Mitch insisted.

Charlie's mouth firmed into a hard line. "Do I need to give you a list?"

A completely irrational, stubborn defiance had Mitch clenching his beer bottle hard enough to shatter. "I know who I've slept with, and this isn't the same. Maddie's not married."

"A technicality," Charlie said.

"I know what I'm doing." What a joke. He didn't have a clue.

Charlie put his own bottle down and rested his hand on the counter. "The last time you knew what you were doing, you went down in a blaze."

The reminder was like an uppercut to the jaw. This wasn't the same. Besides, he had nothing left to lose. He leveled

Charlie with a hard-eyed stare. "Do you really want to start comparing fuck-ups?"

Their mutual history covered a lot of sordid ground.

"Hey," Gracie said sharply before Charlie could answer. "Let's not start rehashing the past. We like Maddie. We just don't want to you to get hurt."

"Don't be dramatic. It's a couple days." How much damage could she do? It wasn't like he was getting attached. He just wanted to keep her for a little while. Was that so wrong?

Sam sat forward, resting his elbows on the worn table. "Save your breath, he's a goner."

"I am not," Mitch said. "And why is this any of your business?"

Charlie's expression darkened, his mouth firming into a hard line.

Mitch ground out, "Leave it. Alone."

Charlie gave him the look he used to intimidate criminals, and Mitch took a sip of beer with a laziness he didn't even come close to feeling.

"Stop it," Gracie said, poking her friend-with-benefits in the ribs.

"He's being an idiot," Charlie said, and the stubborn set of his jaw made Mitch want to take a swing at him.

He put down the bottle and cracked his knuckles. Actually, violence sounded damned good.

Gracie's cupid-bow mouth pulled into a frown. "I think—"

"You know what you need?" Sam cut her off, using a low, soothing voice that acted like a salve, diffusing the tension. The strain in Mitch's shoulders eased and his jaw relaxed as though the room itself had breathed a sigh of relief. Mitch had no idea how it worked, but he'd seen Sam stop more than one barroom brawl before the first punch had even been thrown.

"What?" Mitch asked, shifting his attention to Sam, lounging at the table.

"A game of pickup," Sam said in his slow, drawling tone.

What. The. Fuck. How was that relevant? He had things to do. "This isn't the time."

Sam jutted his chin toward the door. "Come on, let's go."

"Now?" Mitch's agitation once again started to climb.

"Yeah, now." Sam stood, the chair scraping over the linoleum floor. He pointed at Charlie. "You too."

Charlie shot Mitch an exasperated, "can you believe this guy?" look. Mitch shook his head, and despite his agitation, a grin tugged at his lips.

Sam stretched his arms above his head like a lazy cat. "I'm in the mood to kick your asses."

"Good luck," Charlie said. "Don't cry too hard when we mess up that pretty face of yours."

Mitch glanced once at the door and then to the stairs leading up to the bedroom where Maddie slept, before returning to his friends and following them out to the backyard.

Maddie was grateful and surprised that she'd slept. It had all been too much: bailing on her wedding, running away, the car, the credit card being reported stolen, and Mitch. Unable to process any more drama, her brain had finally shut down. After the deep, dreamless nap, she felt human again and ready to face whatever new challenges lay in front of her.

Plus, things weren't completely dire.

She had clothes to wear. A toothbrush. A bra. She was pretty sure it was the alternator that had blown on her car, so with the cash advance she'd taken from the ATM at Target, she had enough money to cover the repairs. Of course, she didn't have the funds to stay in a hotel, which left three options: stay with Mitch, call her friends for money, or go home.

In the end, the decision had been simple. He wanted her to stay. She wanted to stay. Wrong as it might be, there was something here. Something tugged at her, whispering to throw caution to the wind.

The question was, what? Was it that girl she used to be, long ignored, stirring up trouble, or something real? She wasn't sure, but couldn't deny that she wanted to find out.

On bare feet, she crept down the back stairs and into Mitch's kitchen.

The room was empty. She scrounged through cabinets until she found a glass, then walked over to the kitchen sink and flipped on the faucet.

A picture window overlooked his idyllic backyard. It was so serene and perfect that she wanted to sit under the huge weeping willow tree forever. Her fingers twitched as a sudden desire to paint the scene burst inside her like a firework.

How odd. That was twice in one day.

She'd completed her last work of art a month before her father died. The graffiti mural on the side of a convenience store had earned her a fine and a hundred hours of community service. The owner of the store had pressed charges, but kept the abstract cityscape depicting Bridgeport. She'd complained at the injustice, but her father had told her sternly that she'd broken the law and now she had to pay.

Despite her sullen, teenage front, she used to walk by the mural on the way home from school so she could look at it. Secretly, she'd been proud. Her dad had been proud, too. About a week before he died, she'd found the pictures he'd taken of the mural, stuffed in the back of his desk drawer.

Tears pricked the corners of her eyes at the memory and she brushed them away. Why did she keep thinking of him? Here, in all places?

She looked down. The glass overflowed, the cool water

spilling onto her hand. She flipped off the water and spilled the excess liquid in the sink.

Out the window, movement caught her attention. She shifted and her breath caught at the scene before her.

Three shirtless men, their toned, sweat-slicked muscles gleaming in the early evening summer sun, played basketball in Mitch's driveway.

Her throat dried up. Mitch, the sheriff, and the bartender from last night all clustered under the basket, pushing and shoving each other as they vied for the ball.

Mitch jumped up, tipping the ball away from Charlie and into Sam's outstretched hands.

"They're quite the sight, aren't they?" a female voice asked behind her.

Maddie shrieked, whipping around.

Mitch's blond cupcake of a neighbor stood framed in the open doorway, a crooked smile on her lips. "Sorry about that."

"Gracie," Maddie said, her pulse slowing back down to normal. "You scared me."

"Did you have a good nap?" Gracie closed the back door, moving fully into the kitchen.

"Yeah, I did." Maddie smoothed her mess of hair. She'd removed her ponytail before she'd laid down because her temples had started to ache from the weight, and she'd forgotten to tie it back again.

"Come outside; the view's better." Gracie wrinkled her nose. "Except for my brother. It's not his fault we're related so I try not to hold it against him."

Maddie craned her neck, glancing back out the window. Sam bordered on pretty, with those blond California surfer looks, as she suspected his sister knew full well. Still, Maddie could sympathize. "Oh, I hear you there. You have no idea how many conversations I've had to endure over the years about my brothers. Annoying, isn't it?"

"Immensely." Gracie winked. "Good thing Mitch caught you first so I don't have to worry about any gushing."

Mitch ran down the length of the driveway, his movements graceful and lithe. Even sweat-soaked, with his hair a mess, he was unbelievable.

Maddie didn't know what to say. She tucked a lock of hair behind her ear and shrugged. "He's certainly something to look at. The sheriff isn't bad either." An extreme understatement.

"He rocks between the sheets, too." Gracie grinned as widely as a Cheshire cat.

Maddie burst out laughing. "Ah, you're not a saint after all. I was wondering."

Gracie gestured toward the window with a dismissive sweep. "Yeah, well, Mitch and I have been friends since I was about six and he was eight. He spent a month up here every summer while his grandparents were alive. Mitch and his sister, Cecilia, were summer staples." She propped one jean-clad hip against the counter and placed her palms on the laminate, thrusting out a pair of breasts so magnificent that Maddie couldn't help the stir of envy. On the smaller side of a B-cup, Maddie only dreamed of filling out a T-shirt that well.

Gracie's head cocked to the side and a curl flopped over one eye. "I'll admit, when I was fifteen I developed a mad crush on Mitch for about fifteen minutes. We were hormonal teens and he was different from the boys I'd known since kindergarten, being from the big city and all. We spent a few weeks circling each other, flirting shamelessly, before breaking down and engaging in a hot-and-heavy make-out session. He was an awesome kisser, but after all the tension broke it didn't feel right, so we high-fived and called it friends."

The confession brought back the memory of Maddie's own, frantic, knock-you-on-your-ass kiss with Mitch earlier that afternoon. Except in her case it had felt all too right. Dangerously right. Maddie said, keeping her tone casual, "You're only human. And it looks like you did all right in the end."

Gracie glanced toward a side window that provided a much better view of the men than the one Maddie had been looking out of. "Yeah, I guess. Charlie's great, and we suit each other's needs, but we're not together, together. You know?"

Maddie had no idea, but nodded anyway.

Gracie gave a wry chuckle, shaking her head. "It's complicated."

Not wanting to press, Maddie said, "Isn't it always?"

"Yep." Gracie gave one more passing glance toward the window, an odd expression crossing over her face before returning her attention back to Maddie. "How are you doing, by the way? Mitch told us about your troubles. I hope you don't mind, but he asked Charlie to see if he could find anything out."

"Charlie doesn't have to do that." Shane had friends everywhere and Maddie didn't want to take any chances at Charlie's inquiry tipping her brother off to her whereabouts. "Actually, I'd prefer if he didn't."

Gracie studied her, head tilted to the side. "You'll have to talk to him about that. But how are *you*?"

"I'm fine." She took a sip of the water she'd been holding but forgotten. Even room temperature, the liquid cooled her dry, scratchy throat.

"I know we don't know each other," Gracie said, flashing a genuine smile. "But we're girls. If we don't talk, our heads will explode."

Maddie laughed, and some of the tension in her shoulders eased. "Thanks. I think I'm okay. I have no idea what I'm doing. I don't want to go home, but I worry I'm imposing."

"I hope you're not talking about Mitch."

Maddie shrugged, pushing back the desire to be a teenage girl and grill the woman about what he had said about her.

Gracie cast a sideways glance toward the window as if ensuring herself that the men were still playing. "Trust me, you're not an imposition. Mitch wants you to stay more than I've seen him want anything in the last three years."

Maddie bit her bottom lip, staring at the blue and white checked pattern on the kitchen floor as an unexpected giddy pleasure made her dizzy.

What was wrong with her? She was supposed to find her independence, not her inner slut. All those years of Catholic school had clearly failed her.

"Look, minding my own business isn't really my strong suit," Gracie said.

Almost breathless with interest, Maddie perked her head up.

"I've never seen Mitch like this and I love him like a brother. You're the only thing he's shown even a spark of interest in since he's come to live here. Around you, he acts like the boy I remember growing up. I love seeing him happy, and breaking out of the rut he's been in, but he's been hurt enough."

"Hurt?" The question slipped from Maddie's lips. Of course, she'd already figured something had made him leave Chicago, but she didn't have a clue about what.

"No. Shoot. Forget I said that. It's not my story to tell." Gracie dragged her fingers through her curls, her lips pressed together. "Just please, try not to hurt him."

"Me? I'm harmless."

Gracie shook her head. "Actually, I don't think you are."

Maddie frowned, all her upheaval and unease from earlier rushing back. She put down the glass of water and hugged herself.

How many more signs did she need?

She'd taken a stab at freedom, but it wasn't working out.

She nodded. "I understand, and you're right. Mitch has been great. I don't want to cause any harm. It's best anyway."

She didn't want to cause Mitch trouble. As much as she longed for another outcome, she forced out the words she'd known all along she'd have to say. "I understand. I'll call my brother and he'll come get me."

Gracie's hand flew up and her eyes went wide. "Wait, what?"

"I don't want to hurt anyone." After thirteen years, she was used to giving up her desires to do the right thing; she only wished it wasn't so hard. "You're right, it's best if I go home."

"No!" Gracie shouted. She straightened and stepped closer to Maddie. "No! That's not what I meant. I was only trying to say, 'be careful.'"

The men chose that moment to burst in the door like a bunch of rambunctious puppies, filling the room with chaos and testosterone.

Gracie placed her hand over her forehead. "Oh, shit, he's going to kill me."

Mitch stopped on a dime, his attention going first to Maddie and then to Gracie. A muscle in his jaw jumped. "What did you do?"

All three men turned to Gracie. They advanced on her, gleaming with sweat.

Alarm stirred. Maddie didn't need to see their faces. The aggression was clear in their stance.

The sheriff crossed his arms over his broad chest, and the muscles in his back rippled with the movement. Like Mitch, he also had a tribal-looking tattoo, although it was on his left shoulder instead of wrapping around his bicep. "You couldn't keep your mouth shut, huh?"

Gracie seemed to regain some of her composure, and her chin tilted. "I was only . . ." She cleared her throat. "Being friendly. And helpful."

Sam pinched the bridge of his nose with his thumb and forefinger. "Didn't I tell you to leave it alone?"

"Yes, but . . ." Gracie glanced at Maddie. "I was worried, and—"

Mitch sliced a hand through the air. "What happened?"

The men reminded Maddie so much of her brothers and their tactics lit her temper. "That's enough!"

They all swung around. The men's eyes were sharp, hard with leftover adrenaline. It gave her a moment of pause, before she brushed their daunting presence aside and vaulted off her position by the sink. They tracked her as she stomped around them to stand in front of Gracie. "Stop intimidating her."

Charlie laughed, a wry, amused sound. "Honey, we couldn't intimidate her if we tried." His gaze slid over Gracie in a familiar, intimate way. "Although I do think she's angling for a spanking."

"Ha! You wish." Gracie placed a hand on Maddie's shoulder. "Thanks for trying to rescue me. You're a doll." She sniffed. "It's nice to have another female here. I never have anyone on my side."

Sam shook his head. "What did I tell you?"

Maddie planted her hands on her hips. "She didn't do anything, so stop it."

Mitch's eyes narrowed. "What did she say, Maddie?"

"I was just—" Gracie said.

"Nothing." Maddie cut her off as a sudden loyalty toward the woman behind her swelled in her chest. "It has nothing to do with any of you. Now back off."

Charlie's lips curled into a smile. "Aren't you a feisty little thing?"

"I might be little," Maddie said, in a righteous tone. "But I'm used to dealing with my brothers, who are all bigger and scarier than you."

Charlie laughed and elbowed Mitch in the ribs. "That sounds like a challenge."

Maddie risked a glance at Mitch to find his expression still hard, not amused at all. He crossed his arms. "I want to talk to Maddie. Alone."

Sam jutted his chin toward the door. "Let's go."

Gracie squeezed Maddie's shoulders. "Thanks for sticking up for me. And remember, I'm right next door if you need anything."

"She won't," Mitch said, his tone matching the dark expression he wore.

Strangely, it didn't scare her. It should—as should being alone with a strong, disgruntled man—but with Mitch, she stirred with excitement. Anticipation.

Gracie's hand fell away and they all filed out the back door.

The resounding click of the door made Maddie's heart rate kick into high gear.

Mitch stalked toward her, everything about him predatory, dominant, and aggressive.

Her pulse pounded. What was wrong with her? She backed up, hitting the cabinets with a thud. She gripped the sides of the counter to steady herself. Her belly dipped as he closed in on her.

He invaded her space, filling her senses. He was all taut muscles and golden skin that she itched to touch but didn't dare.

He gripped her chin, and the air stalled in her lungs as he peered down, searching her face. "Are you going to tell me what she said?"

A small shake of her head.

His fingers tightened fractionally, reminding her of his strength, though they didn't hurt her. "I'd be wasting my breath trying to get it out of you, wouldn't I?"

"Yes," she said, her voice just above a whisper.

He pressed an inch closer, still not touching anywhere but her chin, but close enough for her to feel his heat everywhere. "You're not leaving and that's final. Got it?"

Any protest died as everything inside her melted. Reaching

into some hidden reserve, she pulled away. "What are you going to do if I don't 'got it'?"

The gold in his eyes darkened as his head tipped forward. "Why don't you test me and find out, Maddie?"

She swallowed, out of her depth in this mysterious game they were playing.

His gaze dropped to her lips and she held her breath, waiting for the hard press of his mouth on hers. Wanting it. Needing it.

"I'm going to take a shower." With that, he stepped back, taking all his heat with him. He turned and walked toward the back stairs. He stopped at the bottom and looked back over his shoulder. "You'll be here when I'm through."

It wasn't a question, and without thinking, she nodded, giving him the only answer she could. The only answer she wanted to give. "Yes, Mitch."

He nodded and bounded up the stairs.

It was settled. She was staying. To her surprise, she re-laxed for the first time in as long as she could remember.

Chapter Nine

She couldn't sleep.

Moonlight streamed through the white eyelet curtains, casting a dim glow on a crack in the ceiling. Maybe tomorrow she'd go to the hardware store and buy some plaster.

Or maybe not.

It was odd, not having her days endlessly scheduled. No more wedding plans, no last-minute details to catch up on, no work to go to, or tasks to accomplish.

Sure, her life was a disaster, but that was different from having something to do.

At least she'd given up pretending she was going home. It was a couple of days. For once, she was going to do what she wanted. And what she wanted was Mitch and more nights like tonight.

She'd had more fun that night than she'd had in the past year. They'd spent the evening at Gracie and Sam's house, drinking margaritas and eating fajitas while the four long-term friends filled her head with crazy stories. Maddie had laughed until her sides hurt. They were crass, inappropriate, and not at all polite—so familiar and comfortable together, it caused an unexpected stirring of jealousy.

Her family used to be like that. She missed them, missed the way they used to be.

She tossed about on the bed, throwing the mint-green sheets and quilt to the floor so she didn't suffocate in the late-summer heat. She didn't want to think about them now. Thinking about her family brought back her anxiety.

She wanted to think about the way Mitch had kissed her in the car that afternoon, about how he'd touched her through the night. Light, casual touches—a brush over her arm, the slide of his fingers in her hair, the press of his thigh against hers under the table.

But that was impossible while her mind raced with never-ending thoughts of guilt and a life she'd lost when her father died.

She glanced at the closed bedroom door, then back at the clock sitting on the nightstand.

It was one in the morning, and sleep was farther away than ever.

Unable to stand it for one more second, she rolled off the bed. Normally, when her mind wouldn't stop racing, television was her drug of choice. She walked across the soft, faded Oriental rug, opened the door and peered into the hallway.

All was quiet.

She padded down the narrow hall toward the front stairs that would lead to the living room. When she got to Mitch's door, she stopped, pondering it as though it were a mathematical equation.

What was she doing? *Go downstairs.*

She stared at the dark wood, six-paneled door. It was nice quality. It looked sturdy and strong. Old construction, like the rest of the farmhouse.

She nibbled on her bottom lip, scowled. Her heart was beating so loud, she could hear it in her ears. *Go downstairs, Maddie.*

It was ironic that after months of desperately wanting to be alone, she couldn't stand the solitude.

But that wasn't Mitch's problem. She couldn't pound on his door in the middle of the night and demand he entertain her. Besides, he'd get the wrong idea.

She scowled at the closed door and her fingers twitched. *Walk away.*

But then some demon possessed her and she knocked.

Complete silence.

Relief stole through her. Had she gone insane? She turned away.

It was better this way. She'd go downstairs and watch HGTV until she fell asleep. She took one step, stopped, and swung back around. She knocked again, much louder this time.

What was she doing?

"Come in," he called, his tone muffled.

Go away. Leave, before it's too late.

She pushed open the door. Reason had deserted her when she'd climbed out the church window, and apparently it hadn't returned. She was as crazy now as she'd been yesterday.

Mitch looked at her. He was stretched out on a king-sized bed with a mammoth, dark mahogany headboard. His chest was bare and the stark white sheet rode low. One brow raised, he peered over a thick book perched on his stomach.

Too late, she realized she hadn't changed.

Why would she? She'd been going to watch TV. Clad in only a tank top and cotton sweat shorts, she rocked on the balls of her feet, wondering what he must think.

"What's the matter?" he asked, laying the book on the nightstand.

"I couldn't sleep," she said lamely.

She couldn't be sure, but she thought she detected the hint

of a smile tugging at his lips. "Do you want me to make you some warm milk?"

"No," she said. Her gaze shifted to the bed and she swallowed, then jerked her attention back to Mitch. What was she doing invading his room in the dead of night?

They stared at each other.

A clock, somewhere in the room, ticked as each second passed.

"Come here, Maddie," he said, finally.

She waited for sanity to prevail.

It didn't.

She was inviting herself into his bedroom; he was bound to get the wrong idea. She twisted her hands and shifted in the doorway.

His lips quirked. "I promise not to bite."

"I'm not here for—" Her voice came out like a croak, and she cleared her throat. "You know . . . sex."

The smile grew. "Understood. Now come here and tell me why you can't sleep."

The muscles in her shoulders relaxed. How did a man so sexually dangerous make her feel so safe?

She didn't understand it, but that didn't make it any less true.

She walked over to the bed and climbed up next to him. The mattress bounced as she settled. She focused on the intricate headboard instead of the man in front of her and asked, "Is this an antique?"

He nodded. "It was a wedding present from my grandfather to my grandma."

She traced the pattern with her fingers. "It's beautiful."

"Yeah, it is," he said, in a thoughtful tone. "They were honeymooning in France and she fell in love with it. When they got home, it was waiting for her."

"How romantic," Maddie said, studying the rich detail work. Even back then, it must have cost a fortune.

"My grandpa was desperately in love with her. If she wanted something, he moved heaven and earth to get it for her."

What would that be like? To be loved like that.

Steve always acted like he'd do anything for her, but if he'd loved her unconditionally, wouldn't he have *liked* her more?

She looked back at Mitch. "How'd they meet?"

He chuckled, a soft, low sound. "You're not going to believe this."

She crossed her legs. "Try me."

He flashed a grin. "I swear to God, this is not a line."

"Oh, this is going to be good." She shifted around, finding a dip in the mattress she could get comfortable in.

He stretched his arm, drawing Maddie's gaze to the contrast of his golden skin against the crisp white sheets. "My grandfather was old Chicago money. He went to Kentucky on family business and on the way home, his car broke down."

Startled, Maddie blinked. "You're kidding me."

He shook his head, assessing her. "Nope. He broke down at the end of the driveway and came to ask for help. My grandmother opened the door, and he took one look at her and fell." He pointed to a picture frame on the dresser. "She was quite beautiful."

Unable to resist, Maddie slid off the bed and walked over, picking up the frame, which was genuine pewter. She traced her fingers over the glass. It was an old-fashioned black-and-white wedding picture of a handsome, austere, dark-haired man and a breathtakingly gorgeous girl with pale blond hair in a white satin gown.

"He asked her to marry him after a week," Mitch said. "It caused a huge uproar and his family threatened to disinherit him. She was a farm girl, and he'd already been slated to marry a rich debutante who made good business sense."

Maddie carefully put the frame back and crawled back

onto the bed, anxious for the rest of the story. "Looks like they got married despite the protests."

Mitch's gaze slid over her body, lingering a fraction too long on her breasts before looking back into her eyes. "He said he could make more money, but there was only one of her. In the end, his family relented, and he whisked her into Chicago high society."

"It sounds like a fairy tale."

"It was," Mitch said, his tone low and private. The story and his voice wrapped her in a safe cocoon where the world outside this room didn't exist. "In the sixty years they were together, they never spent more than a week a part. He died of a heart attack and she followed two months later."

She studied the bedspread, picking at a piece of lint. "I guess if you're going to get married, that's the way to do it."

"Any other way sounds pointless." The sheets rustled as he took a pillow and propped it up against the headboard.

"Do your parents have a marriage like your grandparents?" Maddie asked.

He made a cold, scornful sound, and Maddie peered up at him. A hard, remote look chilled his eyes. "No." He delivered the word in a flat monotone.

Willing to let the subject drop, she cleared her throat. "It's not very proper of me to barge into your bedroom in the dead of night."

Expression easing, he laughed. "This isn't the Victorian age, Maddie; there's no one to think you improper."

"But still, it doesn't look right."

"I promise, your virtue is safe." He brushed an open palm over her knee. "For now."

The touch was electric. Unable to help herself, she scoped out his broad chest and lingered over the clean lines of his body, wishing she could reach out and touch the valley of his hip and the stretch of muscles across his stomach, and trace the intricate pattern of the tattoo that scrolled over his hard bicep.

God, he was a work of art.

He squeezed her thigh—not hard, just enough to remind her that he watched her.

She blinked, tearing her gaze away. A hot flush crept up her chest. Flustered, she blurted, "I used to paint."

Surprise flashed across his features. "But you don't anymore?"

She frowned. Why had she said that? She hadn't told anyone in years. "No, not anymore. I used to draw too. A little sculpture, but I never was very good at that."

She tried to recall the weight of the charcoal in her hand, the smudge of black on her fingers, the sweep of lines across clean white paper, and found she couldn't. It had been so long, the memory was like a fuzzy dream belonging to another girl in another life.

"Why'd you stop?" he asked.

She stared at the chocolate comforter until her vision blurred, then lied, "It just happened."

"What about marrying a man you don't love? Did that just happen?"

She reared back as though she'd been struck.

He held up his hands in a gesture of surrender. "Hey, I'm sorry. I was out of line."

"I loved him." The indignant words were automatic. She'd been telling herself they were true for so long that she believed them.

He laced his fingers over his stomach in what she assumed was an attempt to be casual. "Did you?"

"Yes." Of course, she had . . . kind of . . . only—she bit the inside of her cheek—not in the way she was supposed to. But that was her fault, not Steve's. Steve was perfect. Except, somehow, she could never find a way to make him perfect for her.

"I don't believe you." Mitch's tone was matter of fact.

A little flicker of temper sparked inside her, but instead of repressing the emotion the way she always did, she let it flame to life. She shrugged. "That's okay. I don't believe you want to own a dive bar in a dinky little town."

His amber eyes flared with warning, and his jaw hardened. "I like the town fine."

"Do you?" she asked, repeating the same question he'd asked her.

"Yes." The word sounded as if he'd been chewing it too long.

They stared at each other, the air rife with tension. This was a crossroads. She was tired: tired of pretending, tired of never saying what she truly thought or felt. She had a choice—stay safe and on the surface, have fun with him until her time in Revival was over, or be real.

She took a deep breath and chose real. "I met Steve when we were fifteen. It was a case of opposites attract. I was a real wild child, and he was on the high school honor roll, the captain of the junior varsity football team, and an all-around good guy." She tucked a curl behind her ear and offered Mitch a tentative smile. "Quite simply, he was a catch."

Once again, Mitch's hand covered her knee, and his strong palm felt so good, so right, that muscles she hadn't known were tense relaxed. "You were a wild child?" His tone was so incredulous, Maddie couldn't help but laugh.

"You have no idea," she said, letting some of the good memories she'd locked away creep back in. "The principal of my very strict all-girls school, Sister Margaret, had my parents on speed dial." She leaned in close, conspiratorially lowering her voice. "I even have a juvenile record."

That crooked grin flashed. "For what?"

She waved an arm in the air. "Oh, you know, the usual: vandalism, some shoplifting, harmless stuff like that."

"Why, Maddie Donovan, aren't you a surprise?" He

chuckled, stroking up her thigh before returning to the safe territory of her knee. "What happened?"

She sobered, the lightness leaving her in an instant. "About four months after I started dating Steve, I was in a bad car accident. My dad died. I was in a coma, and when I came out of it, I needed over six months of rehabilitation."

"Jesus, Maddie," Mitch said, his voice strained. "I'm sorry."

If he only knew the half of it. But she didn't want to talk about that. Couldn't talk about it. It wasn't the point she was making anyway. She only wanted him to understand how she'd ended up almost marrying a man she hadn't loved the way she should. She drew a steadying breath. "Steve never left my side. He helped my mother with whatever she needed while she fell apart with grief. He took care of me because she couldn't. How many teenage boys do you know who would do that?"

"Not many."

Maddie's throat tightened, and tears pricked at the corners of her eyes. She swiped under her lashes before they could fall. "Everyone kept telling me what a saint he was, how perfect he was, how indispensable." A tiny sob caught in her throat. "I just didn't know how to leave."

He rubbed slow circles over her leg, the touch soothing and platonic. "I understand."

For some inexplicable reason, those two little words made her breathe more easily. "So that's how I ended up almost married."

His fingers stilled, squeezed a little. "Do you regret climbing out the window?"

Her teeth clenched. The truth, regardless of how it made her sound: "No, I don't. And you know what's really terrible?"

His slow, methodical stroking started again. "What?"

Real. No more hiding. No more denying to the outside world what she felt on the inside. "I've never been so relieved in my whole life. It was the first time since before my dad died I felt free. Do you know what I mean?"

With his gaze thoughtful, he studied her, the tilt of his head and jut of his jaw highlighting his masculinity. "Yeah, actually, I do."

"I don't know why, but I like being here." She nibbled her bottom lip. "With you. You're helping me remember who I used to be."

"And who did you used to be?"

New tears welled in her eyes. "I don't know. Not really. That girl seems like a dream just out of my grasp, but here, I keep getting hints. I miss her."

"Tell me what you miss about her," Mitch said, those golden eyes boring into her.

"I was, I don't know." She waved an arm. "Wild and impulsive. I'd do anything on a dare, and I wasn't ever afraid."

"Maybe that's why you're here? Why you're not ready to go home?"

She blinked and one tear slid down her cheek. "I don't want to go back because I don't have a choice. I want to go home on my terms, not because my car broke down and I'm helpless to fix it."

"And after? When that's no longer keeping you here?" Mitch's hand still stroked over her skin, but the corners of his mouth tightened.

She wiped the wet track from her cheek. "I don't know, I'll figure that out when the time comes."

"So we'll take it day by day." He squeezed her knee. "But I don't want you to leave. You're helping me, too."

"How?"

"I thought I was content, but since you came along I realized I was just numb. I thought they were the same thing, but they're not."

"Maybe we're not bad for each other after all?"

Another smile, so sinful that her heart stopped. "I don't

know the answer to that, I guess time will tell. In the end, like most things, it will probably be a little bit of both."

She met his gaze. "Do you want to tell me why you're not a lawyer anymore?"

"Not really." That shuttered, closed-off look slid over his features.

More than anything, she wanted to pry, but something stopped her. Just because she'd confessed didn't mean he'd automatically reciprocate. "All right."

He released his hold on her leg and shook his head, almost as though exasperated. "Christ."

"What?"

With another shake of his head, he shifted on the bed, fidgeting more in the last minute than he had the entire time she'd known him. "I'm afraid."

The idea that he'd be afraid shocked her. "Of what?"

He viciously raked his fingers through his hair. "I like the way you look at me. I'm not ready for that to change."

What could have happened three years ago to cause this much distress? She swallowed, her pulse hammering in her throat. "You don't have to tell me."

His chest expanded as he took a breath and slowly exhaled. "I know, but I think I want you to know the truth more."

Maybe it was better not to know. She folded her hands in her lap. "It's up to you."

He stared at a spot over her shoulder. "I was indicted for embezzlement."

Chapter Ten

"Y-you what?" Maddie sputtered, green eyes wide.

"I was indicted for embezzlement," Mitch said, in a remarkably calm voice. He supposed it was better than being
an axe murderer.

She reared back. Her auburn brows drew together. "That
can't be right. You're not a criminal."

He might not have been caught, but he'd committed illegal
acts—criminal acts that he'd be disbarred for if discovered.
"I was never convicted. The case against me was dropped
before I went to trial."

Her face smoothed over, relaxing. "So you were cleared?"

"Not exactly." He sighed, a deep, weary sound. God, he
wanted to avoid this topic. He had avoided it for three years,
but Maddie had made that impossible the second she'd told
him her story and hadn't asked for anything in return. "The
evidence disappeared."

"How?"

After one day, he cared what she thought and it scared the
shit out of him. It'd been twenty-four-fucking-hours and
she'd twisted him up in knots. That he didn't want to destroy
her heroic illusions made him more determined to carry on.
"When I graduated law school, my father landed me a job at

one of the top law practices in Chicago. His lifelong friend was a senior partner there. My dad and Thomas Cromwell both grew up poor, and they clawed their way up out of the trenches. Their shared background bonded them like brothers. I grew up calling him Uncle Thomas, and he was part of the family. He gave me the highest recommendation. He worked in the corporate division of the firm, and I was under his tutelage for two years until it was discovered that I had a knack for criminal law and was moved."

Mitch had avoided thinking about this part of his life for so long, he was surprised to find himself viewing it from a distance, as though it had happened to someone else.

Sitting cross-legged on the bed, Maddie looked pensive but not ready to run screaming from the room.

He gathered his thoughts and continued, "Long story short, Thomas was corrupt, and when I was working under him, he'd named me assisting council for some of the clients he was accused of swindling."

It had been one of the worst days of his life: one of those before-and-after tipping points when the world had tilted off its axis and never quite righted again. "By then, I was high up in the firm. I'd created a lot of press and brought in a ton of billable hours. I'd just won a high-profile case and was up for partnership."

"What happened?" Maddie asked, her voice soft as she twisted her hands.

Mitch wanted to touch her, feel her satin-smooth ivory skin under his hands. It wasn't just sex, although he wanted her like wildfire. Something about her grounded him. He cast one wayward glance at her thighs and laced his fingers over his stomach to resist the urge.

"The senior partners called me into the office and informed me I was being indicted and suspended until further notice." He scoffed, a hard, scornful sound as his chest squeezed. "Of course, I had no idea what was going on. It's strange, parroting the same lines of innocence I'd heard from every client I'd ever represented. Needless to say, they didn't buy my story any more than I'd bought my clients'. Only difference was, I wasn't paying them to defend me, so they didn't bother pretending."

Fiddling with the comforter, she watched him in that careful way of hers, measuring his words. He didn't expect her to believe him—why would she? He'd listened to countless people spit out the same lines of bullshit time and time again. Sure, he'd gotten them cleared of their crimes, but he'd rarely *believed* them. In the world he'd come from, almost everyone was guilty of something.

She cocked her head, tucking behind her ear a lock of that long red hair he wanted to wrap around his fist. "So you didn't do it?"

He'd done plenty of other things, but on this point he was innocent. "Nope, and if I did, I'd never be so fucking stupid about it. I sure as hell wouldn't lay blatant tracks pointing in my direction."

"But why you?" She narrowed her eyes, staring at the intricate woodworking of the headboard, trying to piece the puzzle together. "You said yourself that Thomas was like family, so why? What could he possibly have to gain?"

He shook his head, gritting his teeth. He'd been hoping to avoid this part. No wonder he'd stuck to women with low expectations for the last three years. "I haven't always been a nice guy, Maddie."

"Yeah, yeah." She waved her hand in dismissal. "What's your theory?"

"I don't have to theorize," he said, shrugging. "I know why."

"So?"

"I slept with his wife."

She froze, blinking at him like a deer caught in headlights. "How stupid could you be?"

For the first time in three years, he laughed about it. "Pretty fucking stupid, Princess."

She wrinkled her nose, her gaze darting away as she ran a hand through her hair. "Why would you pick her, out of all women in Chicago?"

How could he explain to a good, Catholic girl who'd only had sex with one guy her whole life that sometimes you're just an idiot? That's how things had been in his world. He'd moved in a circle of entitled, privileged people who took what they wanted, and he'd been one of them. Consequences hadn't even been part of the equation.

"I didn't *pick* her. It was more like she fell into my lap and I didn't say no."

She rolled her eyes. "Give me a break. You weren't eighteen. You'll need to do better than that."

He thought about Charlie's comment earlier about his preference for unavailable women. He blew out a breath. "I worked sixty to seventy hours a week. It didn't leave a lot of time for relationships. Sara was his second wife and not much older than I was. I took her home one night after a benefit we both attended and it just . . . happened."

It sounded like the cop-out it was. They hadn't stopped after the first night or the second. They'd screwed every second they could, the riskier the circumstances the better. Two bored people, desperate to break up the monotony of being handed everything they'd ever even thought to desire on a silver platter.

The mistake had blown up in his face and cost him everything.

If he'd left Sara alone, he'd have made full partner by now and would still be dressing in custom-made suits and dating women so glossy that it was hard to remember them as real.

Those strawberry-stained lips of Maddie's pursed, and her eyes narrowed. "Still, Thomas was a family friend and mentor."

He ran a hand through his hair. "I grew up with powerful

people. That kind of life, it's a different world than you're used to: everyone fucked everyone over. No one expected loyalty and trust." The statement made his old life back in Chicago sound ugly and made him wonder what the hell he'd been pining for.

"Ah, I see," she said, her tone unreadable. "I guess he got the last laugh."

"Not really. He died in a plane crash." The small Cessna had gone down in the Pacific. Nothing but the black box had survived.

"And then what happened?"

"The charges were dropped. Thomas had taken his records with him. There wasn't enough evidence to convict me. There wasn't enough evidence to clear me, either, so in the end, my name was still mud."

Maddie met his gaze. "What happened to Sara?"

"She died with him," Mitch said, his voice flat.

Maddie was quiet for several minutes, staring down at the comforter as though it held the answers to all of her unanswered questions. Finally, she raised her head. "I'm sorry."

"Yeah, me too," he said, because he didn't know what else to say. "But it was my fault. I was stupid and arrogant, and I paid."

A heavy silence filled the bedroom. She picked up a corner of the comforter and started playing with it. "Was Sara beautiful?"

He tensed on instinct as she uttered the question every male in the universe hated. He wanted to lie, but couldn't. "Yes, Maddie, she was very beautiful."

"What did she look like?" She tilted her head.

Seductive and glamorous. The killer red dress she'd worn to the benefit the first night they'd been together was burned in his brain. It was almost always how he remembered her. In a sea of black, he'd spotted her from across the dance floor. Most of the other women had worn their hair up in

some complicated arrangement like they were flowers instead
of women, but not Sara: she'd worn her straight, midnight
glossy hair down.

He'd smiled at her and she raised her glass in a toast.
Their eyes had locked, and he'd known right then that she'd
be under him.

Mitch sat straighter and looked at Maddie, cross-legged
on the bed and decked out in her cotton tank top and shorts,
red hair a tumbled mess around her cheeks. She managed to
look cute and sexy in a way Sara would never have been able
to pull off.

He cleared his throat. "She was tall, with long black hair
and really blue eyes."

"What was she like?"

"She was . . ." He paused, hating the conversation, but for
some reason, Maddie wanted to hear this and he couldn't
deny her. Not after her painful story about her father's death.
It made his ordeal sound shallow. Insignificant. He sighed,
continuing, "She was vivacious and charming. She had that
'it' factor and could pretty much have anyone eating out of
the palm of her hand."

"Did she have a job? Or was she a socialite?"

"She was a corporate attorney."

"So she was smart and beautiful?"

Her cunning wit had been part of the attraction. "Yes."

"Did you love her?"

He braced himself and told her the truth. "Yes, I did."

Maddie wasn't surprised. She'd known by the tone of his
voice, by the shadows that crossed over his expression while
he spoke, that he had.

Of course she'd been beautiful. He was beautiful. Even
though Maddie had never seen Mitch in anything other than

jeans and T-shirts, she had no trouble picturing him moving with Chicago's elite.

Propped against the headboard, the white sheet a stark contrast to his golden skin, he watched her. The qualifiers gleamed in his eyes, but he was too smart to add them.

Talking about her father's death had left her vulnerable. As much as she didn't want to hear about the married woman Mitch had had an affair with, she trudged on. That time in his life was obviously painful. He'd lost everything, just like she had.

"Do you still love her?" Maddie forced her expression to neutral, surprised and worried that his answer mattered. How ironic. She'd been professing her love for Steve since she'd met Mitch, so she shouldn't be bothered if he said yes. But that was different.

Both of them knew she didn't love Steve the way she should.

His brow furrowed as his mouth turned down. "No. I haven't thought about her in a long time."

She kept quiet and waited, not allowing him the easy answer.

He ran his hand over his jaw, then sighed. "She's all mixed up with my past. I think we were infatuated. Addicted to each other so we thought we were in love. But looking back, I doubt any of it was real, and even if it was, we'd never have lasted."

"Why not?"

He shrugged. "She would have hated Revival, and I had to leave Chicago."

"Do you hate Revival?" She'd wondered. He hadn't kept up this gorgeous house and didn't seem to care about the bar, but tonight, with his friends, he'd seemed right at home.

"No." He shook his head as though the words weren't convincing enough. "Not anymore. I thought I'd go crazy when I first got here, but after a while I adjusted."

"And are you happy now?"

A small smirk curved over his lips. "I'm about as happy as you are."

She nodded. The subject of happiness seemed too big to tackle right now.

Silence fell like a heavy blanket as they were once again caught in the awkward place between strangers and intimacy. She glanced around the room, her attention settling on the door. "I should go back to bed."

"Stay." His hand tightened on her leg. "Please."

She pressed her lips together, propriety and desire warring inside her.

"To sleep," he added quickly, as he ran his hand up her thigh. "I like the way you feel next to me."

A shiver ran through her. The bed had plush, down pillows, a rich, velvety comforter, and Mitch. He'd be strong and warm. Wrong and right collided and merged into one insurmountable temptation.

Their eyes met and that delicious hint of sexual tension spiked between them.

She gave up the virtuous fight. "All right."

He swung back the covers and she climbed in. The tribal tattoo rippled as he leaned over to flick off the Tiffany light on the bedside table. He scooted down, his solid body sliding against hers. He turned toward her, smiling in the pale moonlight cast through the window. "Maybe you'd better face away or I'll risk getting carried away."

She rushed to turn over, the ache he evoked warming her belly.

His arm slid over her waist, and he pulled her close. Out of nowhere, the urge to weep swept over her. In the darkness, emotion swelled to the surface, and she blinked back fresh tears.

Behind her, his breath was slow and steady. She placed her arm on top of his and automatically their fingers tangled.

His leg slid against hers. The tickle of his hair against the smoothness of her skin was delicious. He kissed her temple, and the covers rustled as he put his head on a pillow.

She was in bed with another man, and it didn't feel wrong the way it should. It felt all too right.

She stared at the bedside clock as its red numbers blurred, then came back to focus when the tears subsided.

"So you understand about Steve?" she blurted into the darkness, unable to stop her confessions to this man she didn't really know but somehow felt was integral to her life. "I wasn't nice when I woke up from the coma: I cried uncontrollably. Raged. Had hysterical fits of temper. He didn't even blink when I'd lashed out or yelled at him to go away. He just stayed right by my side. My whole world was in upheaval, my family in chaos, and he was like an unmovable rock."

Mitch's fingers squeezed hers, but he said nothing, so she went on. "It endeared him to my family in a way nothing else could have. My mom, in particular, treated him like a son. Steve grew up in a very bad home. All he ever wanted was a normal family, so mine adopted him. I didn't want to make them unhappy, not after . . ." She swallowed, unable to think about the rest. The real reason she was going straight to hell with no chance at redemption.

Mitch pulled her closer.

"So, can you see? Do you understand why I couldn't leave him?"

"I understand, Maddie." His voice was a soft, sure whisper in the darkness.

"Why couldn't I love him the way I should?" It was the same question she'd asked herself millions of times. No matter how hard she'd tried, she'd been unable to talk herself into it.

"Because life's not that neat."

No, it wasn't, which made her wonder what kind of disaster lurked around the corner.

Chapter Eleven

The next morning, while Maddie slept curled in his bed, Mitch called the garage.

"Tommy's," Mary Beth Crowley said, her voice hinting at the last bit of drawl left over from her Carolina days.

"How's my favorite girl this morning?" Mitch asked, teasing her like he always did.

Mary Beth was a thirty-five-year-old, five-foot, blond-haired firecracker who ruled Tommy and half the town with an iron fist. Head of the Junior League and on every committee known to man, she was not the kind of woman you wanted on your bad side.

"Don't you give me your smooth talk, Mitch Riley. You should be ashamed of yourself, taking advantage of a poor runaway bride on her wedding day." The sound of the Juicy Fruit gum Mary Beth always chewed snapped in his ear.

"Yeah, well—"

Mary Beth cut him off, talking right over him. "And in her wedding dress! Have you no shame?"

Apparently, when it came to Maddie, he didn't.

"You know the whole town is talking about this," Mary Beth continued, and Mitch kept quiet, picking up his coffee mug and leaning against the counter while she lectured.

When she finally wore herself out, he said, "You're absolutely right, Mary Beth. Is Tommy around?"

More gum snapping, followed by what Mitch was pretty sure was a bubble. With the sigh of the truly resigned, she said, "Hang on, sugar."

A minute later, Tommy got on the line. "Hey, good news. She's lucky and it's only a busted alternator. I called over to Shreveport and they have the part. I can send Luke to get it and have this baby fixed by the end of the day."

The "good news" felt more like a kick in the gut, and Mitch put his mug down as a cold sweat broke along his forehead, chilling him inside and out. What would Maddie do without the excuse of her car to keep her here?

"You still there?" Tommy asked.

Mitch shook his head, trying to clear the rush of panic from his brain. "Yeah, one sec."

"'Kay." The rustling of Tommy's papers in the background was like nails on a chalkboard to Mitch's ear.

Would she leave? Sure, they'd agreed to day-by-day last night, but without her broken-down car she had no reason to stay. She could just as easily go find herself in the next town over.

Shit. What was happening here? He'd known her for less than two days, so why in the hell was he having this reaction?

It was too fast, too quick.

Whether it was today, tomorrow, or next week, Maddie was leaving. If her leaving was already an uppercut to the jaw, another week together would only make it a hell of a lot worse.

He cleared this throat. "Sorry about that. So, how much is this going to cost?"

"About three to four hundred."

Mitch's chest tightened, and he rubbed at it while he stared blankly at his kitchen table, worn and scratched by time and use. He'd spent hours playing gin rummy there and drinking his grandma's homemade lemonade—simple, warm times, completely unlike the cold, sterile nights around the dinner table in the six-thousand-square-foot house he'd lived in with his parents.

When he'd hug his grandma, she wouldn't let go until he did, and his grandpa would take him fishing until Mitch was tired, sunburned, and happy. Even his sister had been different here. As the long days passed, Cecilia's hair would become a little messier and her dress a little more rumpled. Before long, she'd be swinging from the rope attached to the tree and screaming like a banshee as she splashed into the river.

Revival, this house, the river out back, they were good places to remember. To find some peace.

"Mitch?" Tommy's voice pushed away the memories and brought him back to the matter at hand.

Maddie had the cash. She had more than enough.

"I'll pay you two thousand dollars if you stall." Mitch blinked, surprised to hear the words that had just come out of his mouth.

"What?" Tommy asked, his own surprise clear in his tone.

"I will pay you two grand to stall the repair," he repeated, ignoring the little voice in his head telling him this was wrong. If there was another way, he'd take it, but every other option had variables. And he couldn't risk variables.

"And how long am I supposed to do that?"

Mitch calculated how much time he could get away with while not raising Maddie's suspicions. The small-town thing would only get him so far before it became unbelievable. "Can you make it the end of the week?"

If he pushed it until Friday, maybe he could convince her to stay through the weekend instead of making her way back home. That gave him about a week.

One week, then he'd let the chips fall where they may.

"So let me get this straight, you're going to pay me two thousand dollars to let the car sit in my garage for a week?"

"Plus the cost of the repair," Mitch added, knowing Maddie would insist on paying for the car herself. "I'll bring her in this morning, and you tell her the repair will be three to four hundred but will take until Friday to fix. I'll pay you two thousand dollars on the side."

"You've got a real hard-on for this girl." Tommy laughed, repeating Charlie's sentiment from last night.

"Never mind that. And for fuck's sake, don't tell your wife." It was only right to point out that Tommy was the pussy-whipped one, not him.

"Now, that's going to cost you a little more," Tommy said in a thoughtful tone.

Mitch narrowed his eyes. "You're telling me two grand isn't enough?"

"It's plenty for me, but Mary Beth's silence will cost you something extra."

Ah, hell. He was about to get hustled and there wasn't a damn thing he could do about it. "Don't tell her and we won't have a problem."

Tommy made disapproving sounds, and Mitch could practically see the big, blond ex-captain of the football team rocking back and forth on his chair. "Now, you know I can't. A good marriage is built on honesty."

Mitch's grip tightened on his mug, and he silently cursed. "You don't give a shit that your wife carries your balls in her purse, do you?"

Tommy's chuckle was pure evil. "It's a small price to pay for matrimonial bliss."

Mitch tried to think of a way out, but for the life of him he couldn't see one. Between lack of sleep and deprived blood flow, his normally agile mind failed. "And this is nonnegotiable?"

"Well, I'm reasonable." Tommy's voice took on the tone

of a resigned man. "But, you know Mary Beth, and she does like her gossip."

Everyone in town would know about the plot by noon, and as much as Mitch wanted to delude himself, he didn't think Maddie would stay locked in the house for a week.

"Fine." Mitch ground out through clenched teeth. "I'll look at your nephew's case. But I'm not making any promises."

Mary Beth's teenage nephew, Luke, had gotten in with the wrong crowd and landed in some trouble with the law. Tommy and Mary Beth had asked Mitch to defend the boy, but Mitch had refused, despite their repeated requests. Mitch couldn't bring himself to play at something he could no longer be a part of.

Tommy and Mary Beth knew the whole story. The whole town did, although no one spoke of it. Mitch couldn't figure out why in the hell they wanted him, but they'd been damn insistent.

"I cannot wait to meet this girl," Tommy said, and Mitch could practically hear the grin.

"Just play your part when I get there or the deal's off."

"Sure thing, boss. Oh, and Mitch, I'll have Luke's files sent over today."

"Fuck you, Tommy."

"Pleasure doing business with you." Tommy laughed and hung up.

Smug bastard.

Maddie stared at the blond mechanic, who had shoulders so wide they almost filled the doorway of the garage office. "What do you mean it's going to take until Friday?"

Tommy scratched his head as though her question confused him. "I need to order the part."

"It's an alternator," Maddie said, crossing her arms. "I

can order the part over the Internet and have it delivered to your shop tomorrow."

She didn't know why she was fighting about this. She wasn't in any hurry to get home, but she couldn't get over this feeling she was being swindled.

Tommy cocked a brow at Mitch. Maddie turned a questioning glare in his direction, but all he did was give her back a little rub and nod at Tommy.

Irritated at them both, she shrugged Mitch's hand away. Tommy grinned.

Despite the confessions and a good night's sleep, she was in a foul mood. Her bad temper had started during breakfast and would not quit. She couldn't put her finger on it, and would be hard-pressed to name her problem, but something about Mitch was different.

He was acting odd and treating her suspiciously like a kid sister. All the sexual heat between them had fizzled into nothing. Yesterday, he'd taken every opportunity to touch her. His gaze had lingered on her lips as though he meant to kiss her, he'd played with her hair, stroked a finger down her arm.

But today—nada. Over breakfast, he'd been a total gentleman, almost as if she were a stranger and hadn't confessed her secrets to him.

Had talking about Sara reminded him that Maddie wasn't even close to being in the same league? Or maybe she'd told him too much, and now he felt sorry for Steve after the horrible way she'd treated him.

She put her hands on her hips, her denim capris slightly rough with newness, and stared Tommy down while she silently fumed.

She'd slept in Mitch's bed and it had been totally innocent and pure. It was what she'd wanted, but still, it bugged her. Sometimes a girl wanted to be a temptation, or at least cause a tiny struggle. It had been okay last night when she'd thought he was being nice, but in the light of morning, things continued.

She missed the sexual threat in his eyes, missed the hints of promise as he looked at her. Like he wanted her. Like he couldn't wait to have her. She'd never had that before. Sure, Steve had been overprotective, but that hadn't had anything to do with sex.

The mechanic scratched his temple again and shrugged one big shoulder. "You won't get quality parts on the Internet."

Maddie frowned. "It's a Honda, not an Alfa Romeo."

Next to her, Mitch tensed. "Tommy's got a great reputation."

What was going on here? Something wasn't right. "I'm not saying he doesn't, but five days for a simple alternator is a long time. I could probably get instructions and do it myself in an afternoon, so why would it take him until Friday?" Maddie crossed her arms. She didn't know with whom they thought they were dealing, but she knew lots of "boy" things.

Mitch cleared his throat. "This isn't Chicago, Maddie. Things move a lot slower down here."

"Yeah," Tommy said.

Maddie expected him to continue, but he just stood there, looking like a big dumb jock.

Maddie tapped her flip-flops on the concrete of the garage. "I understand, but it's not exactly the middle of nowhere either."

Again, Tommy shot Mitch a look Maddie couldn't decipher, but before he could say anything, a cute blond woman who made Maddie look like a giant bustled over to them.

She shoved her hand out. "Hi, I'm Mary Beth Crowley, Tommy's wife." Her voice held a Southern drawl.

Maddie took the offered hand, only to have hers locked in a death grip. She tried not to wince as she said, "Maddie Donovan. It's a pleasure to meet you."

Mary Beth released her and the blood rushed back into her

fingers. The tiny woman slipped her arm through Maddie's elbow and beamed a megawatt smile. "Why don't you and I go have a little talk? You know boys. They've cooked up a little scheme, and they're too dumb to carry it off."

Ha! She knew it! She whirled on Mitch and shot him a menacing glare, but he didn't notice because he was too busy scowling darkly at Mary Beth.

"Honey," Tommy said, his tone placating.

"Well, I'm sorry, but you two are making a big mess of everything and I'm not going to stand for it." She patted Maddie's arm. "I'm not going to let you con Maddie. She's been through enough."

Maddie's fingers curled into fists as Mary Beth pulled her toward a glass-enclosed room.

"Mary Beth," Mitch said, stepping in front of them and blocking their way from the privacy of the office. "You—"

She held up her hand. "No, I'm telling her the truth. Now step away."

A low, frustrated sound emanated from Mitch's broad chest. "You remember our deal."

What *deal*?

Mary Beth straightened, and while she probably only kissed five feet, she looked more formidable than God. "Don't you take that tone with me, Mitch Riley, I remember it perfectly. Now move out of my way before I get nasty."

Mitch raked his hands through his hair in obvious irritation before moving away.

Mary Beth dragged Maddie into the office and shut the door.

When they were enclosed in the room, which was littered with papers and an old metal desk that looked like a prop from an old police television serial, Maddie raised a brow. "What exactly is going on?"

Resignation clouded Mary Beth's cute face. "You know men, always looking out for us."

Anger lit like a match inside Maddie as she turned narrowed eyes on Mitch through the windows. She didn't know what was going on, but she was in the mood for a fight, and this was the perfect excuse to have one.

He gave her a sheepish look, and Maddie wanted to throttle him. She turned away. Her veins practically raced with adrenaline. She'd been tamping down her temper so long she'd forgotten how intoxicating it was to let it rise to the surface.

How much effort did she spend repressing her emotions? The better question was, why did she continue? She stiffened her spine. Not anymore. Through gritted teeth she said, "Yes, I know."

Mary Beth's expression turned consoling and she made some motherly "tsk" noises, even though she couldn't be much older than Maddie. "They can't help themselves. It's in their nature, but obviously execution is not their strong suit."

Maddie turned her attention to the woman. She'd deal with Mitch Riley later.

"What in the hell is going on in there?" Mitch cursed. This was the worst thought-out plan in the world. Why did he leave the details up to Tommy? He knew better. He scowled at the mechanic. "You can't lie for shit."

Tommy shot him a droll look. "What about you? You could have jumped in any time, but no, you just stood there like an idiot."

"I hired you to lie to her so I wouldn't have to, dumbass." With his jaw clenched, the words came out like a growl.

Tommy jabbed a finger in his direction. "Ha! I knew you were pussy-whipped."

"I'm not pussy-whipped." One had to have sex to be

pussy-whipped. Not that Mitch was about to volunteer that information. "I just don't want to lie to her."

"Same difference, dickhead."

Irrational anger flared hot in his blood. God, he wanted to take someone out. He was so fucked. "If you'd thought of a halfway decent story, this wouldn't be happening."

"How in the hell was I supposed to know she'd know anything about cars?"

"She has brothers."

"Yeah, well, you could have mentioned that."

Through the glass window, Maddie shot him a death glare.

Yep, totally fucked.

He shouldn't have told her about his past; it was another strike against him, one he knew from experience couldn't be overlooked. Between tarnishing his knight-in-shining-armor image and the subterfuge, somehow he didn't think he'd be granted a third strike.

They watched the women. Mitch tried to decipher the expressions playing across Maddie's features and finally gave up, resigned to his fate.

Ten excruciating minutes later, the door opened, and Mitch steeled himself for the fight that was sure to come. He didn't care how he managed it, but she wasn't leaving. Maddie walked across the dark gray, grease-stained floor, and unable to stand it any longer, he said, "Now, Maddie, I can explain."

"There's no need." Her voice held no trace of emotion.

Not good.

"But—" he started, but before he could say any more, Maddie flung herself into his arms. Shocked, he caught her and held tight. He raised a questioning eyebrow at Mary Beth, and a satisfied smirk curled over her lips.

"I told Maddie how her transmission blew," Mary Beth said in a pleased tone. "And how it cost twenty-five hundred dollars, but Tommy knows this guy over in Shelby who can trade him for a sixty-five Corvette carburetor so it would only cost her around four hundred. Unfortunately, I had to explain how Tommy was doing you a huge, gigantic favor so you agreed to represent Luke in his legal troubles."

While Maddie's honey-and-almond shampoo enveloped Mitch, he glowered at Mary Beth. He hadn't agreed to that, and she knew it. All he'd said was that he'd look at Luke's file.

Damn Mary Beth. The sneaky woman had managed to ensure that Mitch couldn't back out of helping her nephew without looking like a total ass.

Maddie pulled away and stared up at him, her green eyes shining with appreciation. "I can't believe you did that for me. I feel terrible with everyone going through all this trouble."

"It's no big deal." But it was a big deal. With his reputation, how could he hold a young boy's future in his hands?

She wrapped her arms around his neck, went onto her tiptoes, and pulled him down. Her warm breath brushed his ear. "Don't try and fool me. I know exactly how big of a deal this is."

He squeezed her tight.

"I'm going to repay you, every cent." Her small frame pressed against his, and he instantly drew taut with desire.

"You will not." His voice strained with the lust that threatened to boil to the surface any time she came within arm's reach. Last night, as she'd lain cuddled up in his arms, sleeping peacefully, he'd promised himself he'd slow down and give her space to decide if she wanted to continue down the path they were on.

Mitch refused to be a regret. He wanted her to be sure. Free will and desire, not dazed seduction, had to be the tipping point.

But this damn attraction made her impossible to resist,

especially with her pressed against him, her silky waves brushing over his skin as she wiggled closer.

He looked over her head to find Mary Beth and Tommy watching them with rampant curiosity and twin grins plastered on their faces.

"I will." Her lips brushed the lobe of his ear and he bit back a groan.

"No. There's nothing to repay." He lightly traced the bumps of her spine. "My reasons are entirely selfish."

She dropped her head to his shoulder and her auburn hair fell to the side, revealing the pale skin of her neck like an offering. All he wanted was to lick and bite his way down the delicate cord until she shivered. His cock hardened to the point of pain.

"Mitch." Her voice was like the brush of a feather over his skin.

"Yes, Princess."

She lifted her head and those brilliant green eyes met his, her chin tilting up. "Thank you."

Jesus Christ. He squeezed her tight, determined to be as much of a saint as she deserved while she worked things out. "Anything you need, Maddie."

"See? Pussy-whipped," Tommy chirped helpfully.

Maddie's head jerked in the couple's direction in time to see Mary Beth elbow the mechanic in the ribs.

"Don't mind him. He's mentally challenged." Mitch pulled Maddie close, then gave Tommy the finger behind Maddie's back.

Tommy just grinned. "Welcome to the club, buddy."

Chapter Twelve

After assuring Mitch that she'd be all right on her own, he'd left for the bar, leaving Maddie to wander the farmhouse. Still needing a distraction from her thoughts, she'd jumped at the chance when Gracie had come to keep her company.

Now several hours later and once again on her own, she sat in Mitch's library, which looked like the set for *Masterpiece Theatre*, and dialed Penelope's number. She narrowed her gaze on the row of books lining the bottom shelf of the floor-to-ceiling shelves.

Law books. Why wasn't she surprised?

"It's me," Maddie said as soon as Penelope picked up.

"It's about time. I was getting worried."

Maddie glanced at the clock on the large, executive desk. "It's only eight."

Penelope huffed, sounding disgruntled. "Eight's an eternity when the phone rings every half-hour with demands to know if you've called today."

Guilt, the ever-present thorn in her side, jabbed her in the ribs. "I'm sorry, I didn't think."

A memory rose, of her mom standing in the kitchen as Maddie sat at the table. Her father had been visiting Sister

Margaret again because Maddie had set off the school fire alarm on a dare. *You never think, Maddie. You only act and expect everyone to clean up your mess.*

Was that what she was doing now? Expecting Penelope to clean up her mess? She swallowed hard and cleared her throat. "I'll call them, Pen, right after I get off the phone with you."

"I promised I'd take care of it, and I will."

Her efficient friend was more than capable of taking care of everything. It was one of the reasons Maddie looked up to her. But if she left the mess she made in Chicago to Penelope, where was the change? She was still sitting back, letting someone else manage her life.

She could make the argument that she was letting Mitch take care of her, but deep down she didn't believe that. There was something here, something vital she'd been missing. She didn't feel like she was running away; instead, she felt like she was running toward something.

"No, you shouldn't have to. I'll call Shane."

A long pause, followed by Penelope's sigh. "Okay, but Shane's not really the problem. Oh, sure, he's being his normal, intimidating self, but it's Steve. He's called me fifteen times today, insisting I tell him exactly where you are so he can come rescue you."

"Oh," Maddie said lamely. "Is he upset?"

"That's just it," Penelope said. "He's acting weird, like nothing happened. No anger, no hint of emotion. He keeps saying if he could just talk to you, you'd see reason."

A cold, clammy sweat broke out on Maddie's temples. This was it. As much as she wanted to avoid all things home, she had to take responsibility. "Don't worry. I'll take care of it."

"You don't have to. I can put him off," Penelope said.

"No," Maddie said, sure despite the knot in her stomach. "It's the right thing to do."

There was a shuffle of noise in the background. "Maybe if he hears it from you, he'll listen."

Maddie scoffed, shaking her head. She was the last person Steve would listen to. "Not likely, but at least he'll stop calling."

"I hope so," Penelope said, her voice soft. "More importantly, how are you?"

"I'm good." To Maddie's surprise, she realized it was true.

"Hmmm," Penelope said. "You're still not going to tell me where you're staying, though, right?"

Maddie pressed her lips together. There was no way to spin the story of Mitch Riley without causing major concern over her safety. Penelope was cautious by nature, and unlike Maddie, she walked the straight and narrow because that was who she was. Penelope looked at the facts and played the odds, and going home with a stranger because he made your head spin with illicit thoughts was never the safe bet.

"I think it's best this way. You can't spill what you don't know."

"Ha! I never break."

"I know."

Another long, put-upon sigh. "So tomorrow then?"

Maddie traced the detailed etching on the desk. "Tomorrow."

Maddie took a deep breath, her heart pounding against her ribs as she disconnected the call. She had to bite the bullet and get it done. She picked up the receiver, blocked the number, and dialed as fast as she could before she lost her nerve. Steve's cell phone rang three times before he said hello.

She experienced a moment of unbridled panic before composing herself. "Steve, it's Maddie."

"Thank goodness. How are you?" He sounded completely normal, like she had called him to check in after work.

"I'm fine," she said, as cold sweat broke out on her temples.

"Where are you? I'll come get you," Steve said calmly.

"No!" she shouted; then she lowered her shrill tone. "Look, I'm . . . I'm sorry for leaving the way I did."

He clucked his tongue, and the sound vibrated through her, making her stomach twist. "I'd thought we'd gotten this impetuousness under control a long time ago, Madeline."

The condescension lacing his words was like nails on a chalkboard, and she stiffened, tensing all of her muscles. This was where she failed: he knew her weakness—her guilt. Even worse, he understood where it came from. But she couldn't buy into it, not anymore. Not if she wanted to make changes in her life. She ignored the dig. "Please leave Penelope and Sophie alone. I didn't tell them where I was, and I'm not going to. In fact, I'm not telling anyone because I don't want to be found."

A long, tension-filled silence. "And how are you going to survive without any money?"

Maddie sucked in a breath. Had Steve had something to do with her credit card being reported stolen?

The idea had never crossed her mind. She'd chalked up the declined card to a mix-up at the bank and hadn't given the incident another thought.

No, he wouldn't. She was looking for a reason to assign blame. Steve wouldn't do something so underhanded.

But the notion wouldn't break hold; instead, it burrowed deeper until she was compelled to ask, "How do you know I don't have any money?"

A pause. "It's logical. Your wallet and purse were with the rest of our luggage."

"How do you know I don't have a credit card with me?"

Another too-long beat. "I'd told you I didn't want you to worry about anything on your wedding day so I'd take care of paying all the vendors."

The logic was perfect. The argument was sound, without a hole in sight.

She didn't buy it. "I gave you my records a couple weeks ago because you wanted to go through them to get a handle on finances. You have my information."

"How is this the point, Madeline?" Steve's voice was totally reasonable and totally wrong for a man who'd been ditched at the altar. "We have bigger problems to worry about. Don't you agree?"

He was right. This was about the time in their normal disagreements that she let it go. "Steve, did you report my credit cards as stolen?"

A long sigh. "For heaven's sake. You're being silly."

In a quiet voice, she said, "You didn't answer the question."

"I'm not going to dignify such a ridiculous question with a response. We're wasting time. Tell me where you are so I can come get you."

Right then, she knew he'd reported the card stolen. She didn't need any more confirmation. She asked softly, "Don't you even want to know why?"

"What are you talking about?" His tone was finally tinged with the first hint of aggravation.

A laugh slipped from her lips from out of nowhere, and she shook her head. "You really don't, do you?"

"I'm getting tired of this, Maddie. Stop with these childish games and tell me where you are."

A week ago, the manipulation would have worked, but today, nothing. She wasn't going to budge. She straightened, more composed and centered than she'd felt in a long time. "No, Steve. And stop calling Penelope and Sophie."

"Madeline," Steve said, tone gentling. "Let's talk about this and work things out."

"I don't want to talk."

"You're being very selfish."

The jab hit her right in the solar plexus, but she refused to give in to the pattern. She swallowed past a dry throat. "Yeah, you're right. Consider yourself lucky to be rid of me."

"Mad—"

She cut him off. "Good-bye, Steve."

She hung up. Yes, Steve was right: she was being selfish. But so what? The heavens hadn't opened and poured vengeance upon her. She hadn't been struck by plague or lightning. In fact, she felt . . . good. Better than good: awesome.

Maybe she was on the path to hell, but she was going to enjoy the ride before she started on the path to redemption.

Mitch scrubbed a wet cloth over the old bar's chipped, faded surface, hating the place more with each passing swipe. Sure, he could make improvements to drive in business. Big Red's in the next town was always crowded, so it wasn't like the people in the area didn't drink. But every time he gave it any serious consideration, he found something else to do. He didn't want changes, didn't want to invest. If he did, it'd be admitting that this was what he did.

That owning a dive bar was who he was.

He scrubbed harder, refusing to think about the small box sitting on his desk that was filled with the details of Luke's case. All night he'd been eyeing it like a gunslinger, each time turning away and closing the office door behind him.

It was wrong. Instead of the surge of rightness he'd been half expecting, it felt like pretending. Acting at something he didn't have a right to any longer. Reminding him how his golden fucking life had gone to shit and how he'd never even fought for it.

That was the problem with growing up privileged. No survival skills.

The bar door swung open and Charlie walked in, bringing

in a gust of warm, humid air. Thankful for the distraction, Mitch nodded. "How's things?"

Dressed in a pair of jeans and a black T-shirt, Charlie slid onto a stool. "I just got off and thought I'd swing by."

Mitch opened the cooler and pulled out a bottle of Bud, twisting off the cap before pushing it toward Charlie. "How was your shift?"

"Boring as hell." Charlie scrubbed his hand over the dark stubble lining his jaw. He didn't have to say anything else. Boring as hell was okay for some guys, but Charlie wasn't one of them. Once upon a time, Charlie had tracked down serial killers for the FBI. Small-town police work was something he could do in his sleep.

Tossing the towel onto the cooler, Mitch said, "Yeah, well, what can you do?"

Charlie took a long swallow of beer. "If the boys could see us now, huh?"

Mitch made a grim sound of disgust. "They'd be laughing their asses off."

Charlie shook his head as though trying to shake loose the bad mood. He took another sip before shifting on the stool. "So, about you and the bride."

Not wanting to discuss this again, Mitch shrugged. "I told you already, I'm giving her a place to crash, no big deal."

"For the low price of two grand."

"Goddamn it," Mitch shouted before lowering his voice.

Charlie grinned. "No worries, I think Tommy only told me, Gracie, Sam, and maybe a few other people."

Mitch gritted his teeth. "So basically the whole fucking town."

Charlie picked up the bottle of beer and took a sip. "They won't tell Maddie. She's an outsider and everyone loves a secret."

Agitation pricked along Mitch's skin.

"He also mentioned you were taking Luke's case," Charlie said, too casually.

"I was blackmailed." Mitch crossed his arms over his chest and clenched his hands into fists.

"Yeah, he mentioned that." Charlie nodded. "Don't get too tangled. She's leaving."

"No shit." Mitch kept his tone light despite the tightness in his chest.

Charlie pinned Mitch with an assessing look. "After Sara, I'd thought you'd given up the taken ones."

"Maddie is *not* unavailable." Mitch fired the words like bullets. Yes, she'd been supposed to get married a couple of days ago, but she was available. To him. "What's your problem, anyway?"

"No problem." Charlie's black eyes watched him in that hawklike way he had: like he was waiting for the smallest fraction of error before he dive-bombed. That look had made him one of the best in the Bureau. He'd had an uncanny ability to spot a crack and let it spiderweb out until the whole story shattered at a suspect's feet. "Just be careful."

Hackles raised, Mitch smoothed his expression into a stoic mask. "It's five fucking days."

One dark brow rose up Charlie's forehead. "You keep telling yourself that."

Mitch scoffed. "Are we done?"

Gaze steady, Charlie studied Mitch for an uncomfortably long time before he shrugged. "There's one more thing."

"What?"

"What exactly has she told you about her brothers?"

"That she has three of them? So what?"

"They'll be looking for her soon, and I'm not sure you want them coming this way."

"Why are you digging into her background? She's harmless." Mitch gritted his teeth and waited for Charlie to continue while foreboding crept over his skin like a rash.

"I didn't dig. You asked me to look her up to see if I could find out any information on her stolen credit card."

Oh, yeah, he'd forgotten. "And?"

Charlie shrugged. "She's not reported missing, and there's no official police report of her stuff being stolen."

"Is that good?"

"It's interesting, considering her brothers. One seems fairly harmless: he's a professor at University of Chicago. Although his name sounded familiar, and I can't quite pinpoint where I heard it before."

"So?" The thin thread of his patience started to fray.

"Like I said, he's not the problem. I'm more worried about the other two. I'm guessing she didn't mention one of her brothers is Evan Donovan?"

"The pro football player?" Donovan wasn't exactly as common as Smith, but it was common enough that he'd never connected the names. Besides, why would he connect the petite, flame-haired Maddie with the six-five athlete?

A hometown boy drafted by the Bears had been big news a few years back. But now, at the height of his career, with a fat contract and too much wildness for his own good, he was a media favorite. He was in the paper as much for his exploits as his wide receiver skills.

"That'd be the one," Charlie said.

"I'd think he'd be too busy chasing his next piece of supermodel ass to come get Maddie." Mitch could only hope, because he couldn't ignore that it was the offseason and training camp didn't start until the end of July.

"Don't know." Charlie scrubbed at his jaw. "Maddie seems awfully close to her brothers, but he's not my main concern."

A local football player prone to creating media frenzies showing up in Revival was about the worst problem Mitch could think up. "Just spit it out for fuck's sake! This isn't a soap opera—you don't need to pause for dramatic effect."

Charlie shot him an amused glance. "Fine, her other brother is Shane Donovan."

Mitch blinked. He couldn't have heard correctly. "You're shitting me."

"'Fraid not."

Mitch placed his palms flat on the bar to steady himself. This was not good. Maddie's brother was one of the most connected and influential people in Chicago.

The pieces from Maddie's past clicked into place, forming a new image of one Shane Donovan. Bits of news articles flashed in Mitch's mind. After the man's father had died in a tragic car accident, leaving his family financially destitute and on the edge of disaster, Shane had built a commercial real estate company from scratch until he held contracts all over the city. He knew everyone: teamsters, union heads, the mayor, CEOs. Everyone who was anyone.

He was not the kind of guy who'd let his sister go missing.

"If even half the stories are true, he'll be coming for his baby sister sooner rather than later," Charlie said, echoing Mitch's own thoughts. "His revenge is legendary, and I doubt he'll take lightly to you corrupting her."

Little did Charlie know that Mitch had been a virtual saint when it came to Maddie, although he doubted that her brother would bother with the particulars.

He raked his hands through his hair. "Fuck."

Charlie smirked. "I think that pretty much sums it up."

Mitch's gripped tightened on the bar until his knuckles turned white. "He's had run-ins with dear old dad."

"Yep," Charlie said, almost sounding cheerful. "And you don't have the best reputation."

A chill settled low in Mitch's gut. This had trouble written all over it. He took a deep breath and loosened his death grip on the counter. "I'll worry about it when the time comes."

Charlie shook his head, giving Mitch the resigned, hardened

look he reserved for lifelong criminals. "You never fucking learn, do you?"

Mitch crossed his arms. All his instincts warned of trouble, but he was damned if he intended to listen. Charlie was right: he hadn't learned a fucking thing.

Chapter Thirteen

Maddie ran down the dark sidewalk, her gym shoes pounding on the pavement as the humid night air hit her face. Restless and unable to sit still after the phone conversation with Steve, she'd paced through the house, her mind tumbling with thoughts about both her past and her future. The mental gymnastics did nothing to wear her out, so she decided that the only cure was a run.

She hadn't exercised in a week, and as soon as she hit her stride she remembered why she'd taken up the habit in the first place. It calmed her mind and soothed away all the jagged edges of her emotions. She sucked in a lungful of air, loving the smell of grass and summer.

Out of nowhere, the sound of her dad's loud, boisterous laugh filled her mind, so crystal clear that it made her want to look over her shoulder to see if he was there. Her chest tightened at the bittersweet remembrance. To her surprise, the familiar loss and ache of grief didn't hit her like a ton of bricks the way it normally did. Instead, a distant, long-forgotten memory pricked at the corners of her mind.

She'd been twelve, caught between being a child and becoming a teenager, filled with all the emotional upheaval of that age. She'd been upset because her mom had signed her up for dance class instead of the cool abstract sculpture class she'd wanted to take. Her mom had insisted Maddie needed to be a "more well-rounded young lady," and wasn't it nice that Penelope was also taking dance? Maddie's temper had flared, and she'd stomped around the kitchen, kicking up a fuss about how her mom probably wished Penelope were her daughter because she was perfect and Maddie wasn't even close.

Patrick Donovan had scolded Maddie for her outburst and upsetting her mother, and then he'd taken her fishing at a nearby lake. She'd hated fishing almost as much as she'd hated ballet, and she'd sat there, a sullen, resentful tween refusing to even hold the pole. Her dad just shrugged and cast his line. They drifted along in the quiet for a good forty-five minutes before he broke the silence.

"You know, I've never told anyone this before, but when Evan was born your mom cried because she'd wanted a girl so bad."

The admission shook Maddie from her sulk. "Really?"

He nodded, solemnly. "Now, I'm trusting you not to run off and tell him. She was disappointed to have lost her girl, but she didn't love him any less than a mother should."

It made her feel like an adult to be trusted with such a big secret, and pride replaced her bad temper. "Cross my heart and hope to die," she said, giving him the sacred vow of a twelve-year-old girl.

He placed his big strong hand on her shoulder and smiled. "I didn't want another child, but your mom wanted a girl and I could never deny her anything, so I promised her one more shot. When you were born, she held you tight in her arms, wrapped in a tiny pink blanket, and talked about the things you'd do together. All the cute dresses and baby dolls she'd buy you." He laughed, that full-bodied sound she loved. "By the time you were two you hated dresses and had to be wrangled into one for Sunday mass. Instead of the baby dolls, you wanted to play in the mud and catch a football with your brothers."

Maddie frowned, resentful over her mom's expectations. "That sounds like her."

Patrick shook his head. "Don't be too hard on her. It's hard to let go of your dreams sometimes."

"So she's disappointed in me," Maddie said, her tone sullen. She'd known it and didn't want to care, but she did.

"Heavens no, girl." Her dad squeezed her tight, kissing her temple. "She's just searching for a way to relate to you. Still looking for a way to connect to the tiny baby she held in her arms."

Maddie's eyes filled with tears as her throat closed up. She wanted that too.

"But here's the important thing to remember, Maddie. She's proud of you, even in her frustration, and I am too. And do you know why?"

Maddie shook her head, unable to speak.

"Because it takes courage to walk your own path. Never lose that."

Ripped from the memory, Maddie came to a crashing halt on the sidewalk. Her breath coming in hard pants and her eyes clouded with tears, she felt the revelation washed over her, breaking apart inside her and forcing a whole new perspective.

She'd lost her path. She'd lost her courage. And her father, regardless of what had happened, would have hated it. The man who had sat there in that boat with his disgruntled daughter would never have wanted her to be suffocated by her family, live a life she hated, or marry a man she cared about but didn't love.

The understanding set her free in a way that years of therapy never had.

Energy buzzed through her, snapping along neurons and shaking her out of her self-imposed apathy. The heaviness always in her chest lifted, and she wiped the tears from her eyes. Filled with renewed vigor, her mind clear and focused, she turned and started running back to Mitch's house. She wasn't going to wait another minute. She was going to start her life, walking her own path with courage and hope, just like her dad would have wanted.

It was only a matter of figuring out who she wanted to become.

Despite the late hour, long run, and hot shower, Maddie was alert and refreshed as she waited for Mitch. She sat curled on the couch watching her second movie of the evening, *Bringing Up Baby*.

Cary Grant once again got up from the dining room table to follow the dog, George, out into the yard where he was searching for his precious bone while Katherine Hepburn chased after him. Katherine didn't care one bit if she made a fool of herself over Cary. She wanted him and she went for it, no matter how clumsy and foolish she looked.

Maddie should take notes, minus all the slapstick falling, of course.

For the first time in thirteen years she was going to go for what she wanted, and she wanted Mitch Riley. He was just going to have to put his morals and sense of decency aside. Maybe it was wrong of her—no, scratch that. She was sure it was wrong, lust being a mortal sin and all, but it didn't matter.

She had five days and didn't intend to waste them on her knees—at least, not praying.

She'd put on tiny cotton shorts and a skimpy tank top: seductive, but not obvious, considering it was eighty-five at one in the morning. She'd worn her hair loose, a wild tangle of waves down her back. Full makeup lacked subtlety, so she settled for light and natural: mascara, some pale pink creamy blush, and the raspberry Lip Smackers of her youth.

She heard tires on gravel as a car came up the driveway. Excitement sparked as her heart started to pound.

She was as ready as she'd ever be.

A minute later, the kitchen door opened and Maddie sat up, leaning against the arm of the couch as she waited. Dressed for bed, she hadn't bothered with either a bra or panties, and now felt naked with her nipples poking the thin pink cotton of the tank. The seam of her shorts pressed along her most intimate spots, making her skin tight and hyper-aware.

Jittery with nerves, she gave one fleeting thought to racing upstairs and locking herself in the room when she heard his heavy footsteps in the hallway.

She refused to give into the fear. Not anymore.

When he reached the living room, he paused, shoving his hands into his jean pockets. "You're still up."

The soft light from the foyer silhouetted his broad shoulders and tall, lean frame. His gray T-shirt and jeans fit him as if he were an advertisement for female fantasy.

Dangerous and lethal. Completely delicious.

"I couldn't sleep," she said. After only a night next to him, she'd already grown used to his warmth on her back. "How was your night?"

In the dim, dull light, she couldn't read his expression. She had no idea what he looked at, but her skin tingled. She licked her lips, tasting the hint of raspberry on her tongue.

"Fine." The word sounded strained, and he cleared his throat. "How about yours? I felt bad leaving you."

She ran her hand through her hair. "Don't, I was fine. Gracie came over and kept me company, and after, I went for a run."

"A run?"

"Yes," she said, smiling. "It was just what I needed."

He shifted against the doorframe, his hands digging deeper into his pockets. "You shouldn't be running at night by yourself."

Maddie blew out a hard breath of exasperation. No! Not now. She didn't want him all protective. "Does Revival have a high crime rate?"

He crossed one ankle over his foot and propped his shoulder against the wood molding. "No, but—"

"Then there's nothing to worry about," she said, cutting him off. "I was fine. I'll be sore tomorrow, but it was worth it."

Several beats of silence followed by a heavy sigh. "Did you talk to your family?"

Her stomach dipped. She didn't want to talk about them. Technically, she hadn't called them. "No, I talked to my friend Penelope. She'll let them know I'm alive. Maybe tomorrow."

He stiffened, and Maddie wished he was in the light so she could read him better. With a wave at the couch, she said, "Aren't you going to come sit down?"

He hesitated, standing in the doorway but not moving.

This wasn't going right at all. He seemed reluctant, as though he didn't want to be around her. Teeth clenched, she desperately searched for a plan. She may not have experience with seduction, but she had plenty of experience with testosterone-laden men. She did the only thing guaranteed to work: she challenged him. "Are you afraid I'll bite?"

Sure enough, he sprang off the wall like he'd been catapulted off it. Gaze falling on the chair, he moved toward it, but she slid farther up the back of the couch and crossed her legs, making it clear she'd made room for him.

A muscled ticked in his jaw, but he sat, eyes glued to the plasma screen. "What are you watching?"

"*Bringing Up Baby.*"

"I've never seen it."

"It's a screwball comedy my dad used to watch."

Stiff as a board, he nodded and shifted closer into the corner of the couch.

She blew out an exasperated breath. Well, now wasn't this one more example of God's twisted sense of humor? Stupidly, she'd believed as long as she showed plenty of skin, he'd pounce, but no, he was farther away than ever.

Damn knight-in-shining-armor complex—she didn't care what he said or what he'd done in the past, he had one. As far as she was concerned, he hadn't really delivered on all his bragging and now the time had come to pay up.

"What's wrong with you?" she snapped, forgetting to sound the least bit seductive.

"Nothing," he said in a flat monotone. He stretched his arms over his head, arching back so that the hem of his T-shirt revealed a tantalizing hint of abs, before the strip of skin disappeared from view when he put his arms back down. "Sorry I'm not very good company, I'm exhausted." With a yawn that Maddie was ninety percent sure was fake, he got up. "I'll see you in the morning."

Red dimmed her vision. He was blowing her off, making it clear he wanted to sleep alone. Before she could process the drastic change in his previous delicious behavior, he did the most despicable thing ever.

He patted her on the head! And left!

Her temper flared hot and bright.

He was not going to get away with this.

Mitch sat on the edge of his bed, practically shaking with lust. Elbows on his knees, his head rested in his palms as he fought to control the voracious desire to go to Maddie and exhaust himself in her body.

Keeping his distance was the safest course of action. He'd been talking himself into this argument all day, and Charlie's visit had sealed the deal. He couldn't afford to be rash. He had to get back in control before he made any moves on her. But fuck, he'd underestimated her ability to look like a walking wet dream in shorts and a tank top.

Eyes closed, he willed a control over his body that he didn't even come close to feeling. Christ, had he ever wanted anyone like this? With this gnawing hunger? Even with Sara, it hadn't been like this. She'd been more like a sneak attack, not this onslaught.

He shook his head.

Despite her life as a teenage hellion, deep down, Maddie was a good girl. And the truth was—

The door flew open, practically flying off the hinges.

Mitch jerked up to find Maddie standing in the doorway, rage shooting off of her in every direction. "What. In. The. Hell. Was. That?!" She hurled the words at him like bombs.

He winced, struggling to keep his own violent emotions at bay. Smoothing his expression over into a banal mask, he said calmly, "I'm tired."

She planted her hands on her hips, which were encased in tiny white cotton shorts he wanted to shred off her. Despite her small stature, she looked like an Amazon warrior princess standing there: legs planted, red hair flaming right along with her temper. "So let me get this straight. You have a headache?"

"I'm tired, Maddie. It's been a long couple of days, and even longer nights. Nothing more, nothing less." Couldn't she see how close to the edge he was? He didn't trust himself with her right now.

Without a trace of fear, she stalked into the room, coming to stand toe to toe with him. Bare feet should have made her look cute and harmless, but there was nothing harmless about her.

Wanting nothing more than to stare down at the floor and

find comfort in those pink-tipped toes, he forced himself to meet her gaze, lacing his fingers tightly.

"Don't you lie to me." She jabbed a finger at his chest. "I swear to God, you'd better not be protecting me."

Calm, he needed to remain calm and get her out of here so he could think for one fucking second. He took a steady breath. "I'm not in the mood to talk, Maddie, and that's the God's honest truth."

Her eyes darkened to moss. "That's it, isn't it? Don't treat me like I'm a stupid fragile flower incapable of making hard decisions. I hate that!"

His own anger bubbled to the surface. Couldn't she understand? He had no patience right now. No capacity for gentle coaxing. "Is that what you think I'm doing?"

"Yes!" she yelled. "I ran away to get away from all that, but now you're doing the same thing as everyone else, and I won't stand for it. Not anymore."

He dragged his hands through his hair, every foul word he could think of pouring through his mind as he struggled for a calmness that was more and more out his grasp. "You don't know what you're talking about, Maddie."

"Ha!" She stomped a foot. "You don't think I can take it, do you? You think I'm too much of a nice girl for whatever wild kinkiness you dreamed up. Well, I've got news for you: I got farther with Jimmy Thompson after sophomore homecoming. I'm pretty sure I can take whatever you dish out."

Something cold snapped deep inside him. He shot off the bed and gripped her arms far too tightly. She winced, but her expression remained defiant. "You need to run, little girl."

If she'd had any common sense, she'd back down, but instead she scoffed. "I think you're all talk and no follow-through."

He brought her close, so they were nose-to-nose. "I'm going to give you to the count of five to get the hell out of here." His voice dropped with menace that most people would have the wisdom to retreat from, but her strawberry-stained lips curved into a smile.

"One, two, three, four, five." The words tumbled out of her mouth as though she couldn't say them fast enough. Ripe satisfaction flashed in her eyes.

Shocked, he blinked. Everything froze for a fraction of a second as all reason fled and his body took over.

His mouth slammed over hers with a hard, brutal demand that had her squirming in his arms. Heedless of her struggle, he hauled her closer, his tongue invading her mouth. He didn't ask permission. Didn't tempt or coax. He took. Demanded. Gave her exactly what she'd been baiting him for and then some. She slithered against him. The heat they generated warmed places inside him that he hadn't even known were numb with cold.

He released his hold on her arms, sliding one hand around her waist while the other moved to fist her hair, holding her still for his onslaught.

Small hands scratched at his forearms. With no idea if she wanted to push him away or pull him closer, he pressed against her, invading her space, wanting to suck up all that heat. A low moan vibrated against his mouth, and then her fingers curled into his flesh, and she yanked him even closer.

A mad, hot rush of desire flooded his system. She wouldn't back down. No matter how aggressive, no matter how much he demanded, she'd just keep coming.

Her mouth stroked his. Tongue licking. Dueling. Competing until he was dizzy.

They fought to get closer, their breath hard and fast.

With a firm grip on her hair, he twisted it around his palm until it had to prick with pain.

The retreat didn't come. All she gave him was an urgent groan before molding to him like a second skin.

He'd planned out his seduction, and this wasn't it. There

was no slow tease. No hot, long kisses. No slow torture until she begged for more. This would only lead one place: raw, uncontained fucking.

He released her hair and gripped the edge of her tank top, breaking the kiss long enough to divest her of the article of clothing. Her bare breasts, soft and yielding, contrasted with the hard plains of his chest. She rubbed against him like a cat, not scared, not timid, or shy.

She was not at all what he'd been prepared for.

Hard nipples scraped along his skin. A hard jolt of electricity shocked his system. He grunted, pulling back to nip at her bottom lip with enough force for her to pull away, but instead she bit back.

On a low growl, he turned them around and tumbled them to the bed. The second she landed on the mattress, he had his hands at her shorts. Her hips lifted so he could slide them down her perfect legs.

He froze, staring at her. Half-naked, she lay sprawled and open. Mouth swollen from his kiss; hair a slash of deep red across his white pillow. Beautiful. *His*.

He blinked. Logic and reason crashed down on him: what was he doing?

Lashes fluttered against her flushed cheeks as her eyes opened and looked at him. Her gaze searched, her expression shifted, seeing something he felt sure he wanted to keep hidden. Out of nowhere, panic washed through him, chilling his blood as a cold sweat broke out on his brow.

He looked past her, away from her, as some unnamed emotion made his stomach knot and twist.

Shit. He reared away, moving to the edge of the bed. Dropping his head into his palms, he fought to find his normal composure. But it was a lost cause. Not when the truth was so clear, he'd need to be blind, deaf, and dumb not to see it.

Soft fingers touched his back as she moved behind him. He clenched his jaw, fighting equally powerful urges to lash out and possess. Instead, he didn't speak, didn't dare move. He was immobile with an unfamiliar torrent of emotions.

He was an idiot.

All this time, he'd been telling himself he was protecting Maddie, taking it easy on her, taking it slow so she wouldn't run.

It was all bullshit.

He wasn't protecting her. He was protecting himself.

He was waiting for the control that was always so damn easy for him to kick in, waiting for the distance he always experienced to make Maddie safe for him. But that was never going to happen, because she wasn't safe, and never would be.

"Mitch." Her soft voice was a whisper against his skin. "Please tell me what's wrong."

What was he supposed to say? That he was too emotional to have sex with her? That he'd thought it'd be fun to show her a good time, but now it wasn't enough? That after three measly days he didn't know if he could handle being her five-day fantasy fuck before she went back to Chicago to start her real life?

He laughed, a harsh sound so bitter that he cringed.

No one could know how fast or hard he'd fallen. No one. Least of all Maddie, who didn't need one more reason to nail herself to the cross.

He needed to get the hell away so he could think without her distracting presence. He took a deep breath before he picked up her hand and pressed it to his lips. "I'm sorry, Maddie."

"Please," she said, her tone threaded with worry. "Talk to me."

He wanted to explain that it wasn't her, it was him, but he

couldn't utter the cliché-ridden words. He stood up and walked to the bedroom door. "I'll be back and I promise we'll talk."

He didn't know what he'd say, but he'd figure that out later. Not waiting for an answer, he walked out of the room and down the stairs, and slammed out of the house like the devil chased him.

Chapter Fourteen

Arms wrapped around her knees, Maddie peered into the dark night. A warm breeze blew over her skin as she sat on the front porch, searching the shadows for any clue to where Mitch might have run off to. The shiny, black BMW sat in the driveway, so he hadn't driven away, but where was he?

Throat tight, she swallowed hard. She didn't understand what had happened. One second, everything had been hot and passionate, exactly the way she wanted it, and the next, it was like she'd had the plague.

A heavy weight sat on her chest as she blinked back tears. Maybe she just wasn't cut out for this? Everything had gone crazy the second she'd climbed out the window, and no matter how hard she tried to take control of her destiny, something always got in the way.

She bit the inside of her cheek. Maybe God really was punishing her.

With her mind racing, she tried to determine her next move. She felt lost. Alone. Sad. All her previous bravado sifted through her fingers like grains of sand.

What did she do now?

She stared up into the night sky until the bright stars

blurred. No answer was forthcoming, and the mysteries of her life continued to elude her.

Headlights turned into the drive next door and a pickup truck slowly pulled up to the side of the Roberts' lemon-colored house. The engine shut off and Sam jumped out of the cab. Lips pressed together, Maddie didn't move, hoping he wouldn't see her as he walked around to the passenger seat and pulled out a big duffel bag.

He shut the door and went still. His head cocked to the side before he slowly swiveled in her direction. The moon hung low and bright in the sky and his blond hair almost glowed as he caught sight of her.

He waved. "Hey, Maddie."

"Hi, Sam," she said, hoping she sounded friendly but not approachable.

He watched her, not making any move to come closer, but not heading in the direction of his house. One hand slid into tight, faded jeans that fit his lean body like a second skin.

Maddie didn't like the way he studied her one bit.

He took a step, and her heart leapt with hope, only instead of heading toward his house, he came toward her.

Ugh! Not now.

"What's-a matter? Can't sleep?" His words were casual, friendly.

She released her hold on her knees and relaxed, putting her hands behind her on the floor of the porch. "Just restless."

He walked over, dropped the bag at the bottom of the steps, and then climbed to sit down next to her. "You're one of those overthinkers, aren't you?"

Maddie stared into the night sky, trying to devise a way to get rid of her uninvited guest. On the surface, he was all harmless charm, open and affable. All lazy, satisfied cat. Yet somehow Maddie didn't quite buy it.

He sat there for a while, staring up at the stars with her, his elbows propped on his knees. Finally, he sighed. "What happened?"

"What makes you think anything happened?" she said, her tone stiff.

He glanced at the door behind them, then gave her a wide, aw-shucks smile. "Lucky guess."

She wanted to curl into a protective ball, but she kept her posture open. "Everything's fine."

He looked at her, one brow raised.

She cleared her throat. "It is."

"All right." His tone was soft, as though he pacified her. "Mitch is down by the river."

She sat up straight. "River?"

He nodded, pointing to the corner of the house. "Through the backyard, past the trees."

"How do you know?"

He shrugged. "His car's here, there's no lights on inside, seems the logical bet."

She reached out and touched his arm, a simple brush of her fingers. "Thank you."

He nodded, then got up and stretched before jogging down the steps. When he reached the bottom, he turned back. "Don't be too hard on him. He's out of his element."

Maddie narrowed her eyes. "What do you mean?"

He picked up his duffel and gave her a little salute, walking away. "Night, Maddie."

She called out after him. "How very cryptic of you."

He laughed and disappeared into the night.

A warm breeze blew against her cheek as she looked in the direction Sam had indicated. The Maddie from a couple of days ago would have retreated, but the new Maddie wanted to face her fate, regardless of consequences. She bounded down the steps, rounded the corner of the house, and walked toward the trees.

The flowing water and millions of stars dotting the sky had done their job, calming Mitch like they had since he was six years old. He sucked in a lungful of humid air, the smell of dank earth and river water reminding him of a time when life wasn't so damn complicated.

Behind him, a twig cracked, disrupting the gurgle of the water as footsteps rustled over the grass and leaves. Quiet as a mouse, Maddie sat down next to him, scooting onto the blanket he'd picked up from the back porch and laid on the grass. He tensed, waiting for the questions, the demand for explanations. Instead, she wrapped her arms around his elbow, and dropped her head to his shoulder.

His heart skipped a beat. The unsettling niggle that had hovered in the back of his mind since the first night he'd brought her home came into vivid, unavoidable focus: if he wanted her, he'd have to fight for her.

This wasn't going to be some fun, easy, week-long distraction.

She'd leave a mark.

When was the last time he'd fought for anything? Had he ever? Before he'd crashed and burned, he'd never even broken a sweat. Every opportunity had either been handed to him or had been easy. Sure, he'd had the brains to take advantage of them, but he'd never fought for it. And when the world had come crashing down around him, he had run. Pure and simple.

He looked down at Maddie. All that red hair shimmered in the moonlight as it brushed against his arm. The soft skin of her cheek rested against his biceps, her breath warm as she sighed.

They sat for a long, long time. The lazy trickle of the

river's current, the rustle of leaves in the summer's breeze, and their breathing were the only sounds. The longer they sat, the calmer he grew, until all his turbulent emotions smoothed over into something peaceful.

Untangling himself from her, he slid an arm around her waist, actively touching her for the first time since she'd shown up. She uttered another of those content sounds that tugged deep inside him.

Human again, he planted a kiss on the top her head. "I'm sorry." The words were rusty on his tongue, and he realized he couldn't remember the last time he'd uttered them.

"Me too," she said, far too quickly.

"You have nothing to be sorry for, Maddie." He squeezed her tightly, hating how she took responsibility for everything. "I'm the one who fucked up, not you."

She shrugged one small shoulder, as though it didn't really matter. "I should have listened when you said you wanted to be alone."

"Yeah, well, I can understand why your temper got riled."

A small laugh bubbled from her. "It was the head pat that pushed me over the edge."

"Not my best move. I'm sorry I took off the way I did."

"Don't be," she said, her voice soft as the summer breeze. "I don't know what came over me, but I shouldn't have invaded your space."

"I want you in my space, Princess." Mitch stroked a trail down her spine, loving the slight tremble against his palm. "Wanna stretch out?"

She nodded, and they lay back on the old comforter, their shoulders touching.

He wanted to reach for her, but didn't.

She laced her fingers over her stomach and looked up at the stars. "It's beautiful here," she said, gazing at the heavens above. "I can't believe all the stars—it's like the sky is closing in around you."

"Yeah, it is," he said, his tone thoughtful as he recalled all the nights he'd spent down by this river when he was younger. "When my sister and I were little, my grandparents used to let us stay up extra late to stargaze." He searched out a cluster of stars and pointed to it. "There's Hercules. My grandpa used to tell us the stories of Greek mythology using the constellations as his backdrop."

He looked down at her, surprised to find her watching him with a curious tilt to her lips. "So that's why you came here after your troubles."

His brows drew together. "What?"

She waved her hand in the air in an encompassing gesture. "After you left Chicago. It makes more sense now. Revival's your home. Your real home."

"No, it's not," he said, the idea so startling, so different from what he believed, he forgot to filter his words. "I came here because this is the only place I could think to escape."

Her expression turned quizzical. "Didn't you say your grandfather was old money?"

"Yeah," he said, failing to see the point.

"And you grew up privileged?"

The muscles in his stomach tightened. "Yeah, so?"

The breeze kicked up, blowing a lock of hair over her cheek, and she brushed it away. "Didn't you make four hundred dollars an hour?"

He turned back to the sky and studied the stars. "Yes."

"Well, using my powers of deductive reasoning, I'm assuming you're not exactly hurting for money."

She was right. Not only had he made a lot of money he'd never had time to spend, his trust fund was embarrassingly substantial. Still, he didn't see the relevance. "I don't see where you're going with this."

"You could have gone anywhere you wanted, Mitch." Her

voice was as warm and gentle as the wind, but it chilled him just the same. "You chose here because it was home."

He shook his head. "I came here because my mom had the house and it was the logical choice."

"You never mention your life back in Chicago. Your home, your family, or your memories."

"That's not true," he said, irritated at the stubborn defensiveness pumping through his veins and ruining the tranquility he'd only just grasped. "We talked about it last night."

"Confession's not the same thing."

He repressed the sudden urge to lash out and instead said flatly, "You're wrong." He didn't look at her, but he could feel her eyes on his, studying him. Analyzing.

"Okay, I'm wrong."

What did it matter if she thought Revival was his home? "You are."

"I'm agreeing."

Was there amusement in her tone?

He harrumphed and searched out Orion. The defensive irritation poking him in the gut irked him and he wrestled through the desire to start lecturing her on her faulty argument. He clenched his jaw, putting his hands behind his head, shifting his attention to first the Big, then the Little Dipper before blurting, "And even if that's true, so what?"

She rolled over and propped her head on her open palm. "So nothing."

"You're clearly going somewhere."

"It was an observation." She spoke in the same tone people used to coax suspicious animals.

He should drop the subject. Logically, he knew his reaction was telling, but he was damned if he had control over that right now. He wasn't attached to Revival, and he called nowhere home. It was that simple. "It doesn't mean anything."

"Okay," she said.

He glowered. Surely there'd been no ulterior motive for picking Revival. He had no connection to his family.

He frowned. That hadn't been the case with his grandparents. The best times of his childhood had been spent in this house.

But why did that matter?

He blew out a deep breath and turned to look at this woman who'd invaded his life and turned everything upside down. With her pale skin almost luminous in the moonlight, she looked so beautiful that she could pass for one of those Greek goddesses his grandpa used to talk about. "You know, before you came along, things were calm."

She flashed him a brilliant smile. "Yeah, well, before you came along, I almost never barged into strange men's rooms." She held up two fingers. "I've done it twice now. You're becoming a bad habit."

The knot of tension in his sternum loosened. He wrapped a hand around her wrist and tugged until she scooted close enough for him to see the clear, bright color of her eyes. He released his hold and stroked over her jaw. "I don't think I've ever seen eyes as green as yours."

"They're a Donovan family trait. All us kids have different hair colors, but we all have our father's eyes. I'm the only one with my mom's red hair. My oldest brother is the spitting image of my dad. My mom says it hurts to look at him." Maddie shook her head, running her fingers through the tangle of her hair.

She looked over his shoulder, staring into the trees. "I hated my mom for that, especially when Shane sacrificed so much for us. She's always looking past him when she says it, so she never sees the expression on his face, but I do. And it breaks my heart."

The little bits and pieces of information he knew about Shane Donovan had indicated he'd come from hard beginnings, but they'd been understated. "I'm sorry."

She shrugged, her expression remote. "I should have said something but I never did. I kept quiet, not wanting to make waves."

From what Mitch could tell, Maddie had been keeping quiet since she'd woken up from that coma. He rolled over to his side and mimicked her posture, propping himself on one elbow. He slid a finger over her jaw and down the tendons of her throat. "I don't want you to keep quiet with me, Maddie."

She blinked rapidly, as though repressing tears. "It's habit now. It's hard." She met his gaze, her eyes filling with warmth. "But it's easier with you. I don't know why."

His thumb brushed the pulse beating in her neck. "Maybe it doesn't matter why."

"Maybe."

"Come closer," he said, his voice deepening.

She bit her lower lip, but slid close enough for him to feel the heat of her body against his. He clasped her neck. He wanted to devour her, but held back, wanting something else even more. Instead of the hard, brutal kiss his body demanded, he brushed his mouth over hers. Nothing more than a fleeting touch. "Upstairs, I left because I was so close to the edge that I would have taken you, regardless of consequences."

"Please don't protect me. I'm so"—she exhaled hard—"sick of that."

He stroked the pad of his thumb over the wet, moist flesh. "I wasn't protecting you. I didn't want our first time to be because I was angry and trying to shut you up."

Lashes fluttering, she looked up at him. "Is there going to be a first time?"

He relaxed his hand. "Yes, Maddie, there is."

Her chest expanded as she sucked in a deep breath. "I know it's wrong, but I can't help it. I want there to be."

"Me too." He lay back down on the blanket, pulling her

along with him. He tucked her into the crook of his arm and bit back a moan when she slid her leg over his thighs. He stroked a path down her back.

"When I was fourteen I stole Bobby Miller's girlfriend." The statement surprised him. His mind had been filled with thoughts of Maddie in his bed, not his misbegotten youth. "Her name was Britney. She was the head cheerleader and had long, blond hair she wore in a ponytail."

Maddie's hand slid over his stomach, and all the muscles there went tight. "She sounds like a head cheerleader."

"Yeah," Mitch said, tracing a path down Maddie's side. "I wanted her, and I knew I could have her. So I took her."

"I see," she said, tensing slightly under his palm.

He wanted to shut the hell up, but couldn't seem to make himself be quiet. "And Sara wasn't the first married woman I'd slept with."

Maddie glanced up at him, gaze questioning. "How many others?"

"A few."

"So you prefer married women?"

"No." He stroked her back, and when she relaxed against him, he relaxed right along with her. "I think I liked the challenge."

She was quiet for a good minute, as though working something through in her mind. Without warning, she sat up, swinging around to kneel on the blanket. "I know. Let's play a game."

"A game?" Out of all the things he'd been expecting her to say or do, this had been the farthest from his mind. What was she up to?

"Yes," she said, flashing another one of her killer smiles in his direction. "The 'I Was So Bad' game. We'll trade stories of how horrible we were until a clear winner can be determined."

All of the tension that had rolled up into a big, black ball in the center of his chest unraveled. "Princess, you're a nice, Catholic girl with a guilt complex. How in the world do you expect to beat me?"

She shrugged, apparently unconcerned. "I don't know if I'll win, but I think I can stay competitive."

Oh, this was going to be good. He scrubbed a hand over his jaw. "Okay, what have you got?"

She tilted her head to the side and tapped her chin with an index finger. "Let's see . . . hmmm . . ."

He laughed. "Why do I have a bad feeling about this?"

"Ssshhh, I'm thinking." She pondered, shifting around on the blanket, leaning her head to one side and then the other, and Mitch just took it all in, adoring her more with every passing second that she pretended she didn't have a story already waiting for him.

She snapped her fingers. "Here's one. When I was fourteen, I went to my very first high school party. Of course, like any good Catholic girl who'd been given her freedom, I grabbed the first bottle of Boone's Farm handed to me."

Mitch shook his head in disgust. "Boone's Farm, huh?"

"Being from Winnetka you probably don't know what that is," she quipped. "Boone's Farm is what us blue-collar people drink because there's no hundred-dollar scotch available."

He reached over and pinched her on the hip. "Little brat. I know perfectly well what Boone's Farm is."

She grinned, so wide and lopsided that it should have looked goofy as hell, but it only made her sexier. "Anyway, drunk off my ass, I decided I needed to experiment with other things, so I started making my way around the boys at the party. I'd made out with three boys before someone called Shane and he ruined all my fun."

Surprised laughter burst from Mitch's chest. "Well, hell, Maddie, I can't say I blame the guy."

She wrinkled her nose and crossed her arms, full of indignation. "Would you have rescued your sister?"

He thought of Cecilia, so cold that ice could have run through her veins instead of blood. Even as a teenager, she'd had utter focus, her direction and plans already mapped out in front of her as she desperately worked to please their father. "I don't think Cecilia's ever even been drunk." Her control was too absolute.

"Well, Shane wasn't so lucky with his little sister." She giggled, tucking a lock of hair behind her ear. "I threw up in his car as payback."

"I'm sure he was thrilled," Mitch said.

She reached over and patted his knee. "Okay, your turn."

He thought back to that other life with something other than scorn for the first time in three years. "When I was fourteen, I lost my virginity to our housekeeper."

Her jaw went slack. "Are you serious?"

He nodded, smiling. Lucy had been his first taste with the forbidden, and he'd been hooked ever since. "It wasn't my fault. She seduced me and I was powerless to stop her."

Maddie eyed him with deep suspicion. "How old was she?"

"Twenty-one."

Maddie slapped his thigh. "Yuck! That's disgusting! You were a child."

"Princess, when I was fourteen I was over six feet and not done growing. Lucy thought I was man enough."

"She took advantage of you."

Mitch chuckled, thinking back on the lovely, talented Lucy. "She did, God bless her. She was from Brazil and very inventive. I couldn't be anything but grateful."

Maddie huffed, shaking her head in exasperation. "You know, that really bugs me. It's just as wrong and perverse as those men who have sex with teenagers. You were a child and she was an adult. She stole your innocence." Maddie violently waved her hand through the air. "It doesn't matter if she was a hot Brazilian."

Mitch crooked a finger, smiling. "Come here."

Maddie shook her head, a pout puffing out her bottom lip. "I don't think so."

He reached out fast, striking with the suddenness of a cobra, to grasp her wrist.

She shrieked and tried to pull away, laughing as she squirmed. He pushed up, grabbing her around the waist and pulling her close. She might weigh next to nothing, but the way she twisted and writhed in her attempt to get free made it hard to get a good hold on her.

Before too long, he had her trapped under him, both her hands manacled as he pinned her to the ground. "Where do you think you're off to?"

Her pupils contracted as her breath came fast. Her legs splayed open and she tilted her hips in an effort to throw him off.

They both sucked in a breath as she pressed against his erection. He leaned in, lips brushing the lobe of her ear. "Lucy taught me lots of things about pleasing a woman. She was very instructive."

"With a fourteen-year-old, she'd have to be." The fine bones in Maddie's wrists flexed against his palm. "I don't think I want to hear about it."

"No?" Mitch asked. He gripped her with one hand, freeing his other to explore her body. He stroked down her bare arm, and she shivered, a soft gasp floating on the night sky. "I could demonstrate."

"No, thank you," her voice husky despite her proper words.

"You're lying," he whispered, as he ran a thumb along the underside of her breast. "Isn't that a sin?"

She made a soft sound, somewhere between a moan and

a gasp. "At this point I'm just trading sins at any given moment."

He laughed, wicked and evil. "Let's go inside. It's time for bed." He didn't trust himself to kiss her for fear he'd lose control and take her right here in the grass. He pressed an open mouth kiss to her neck.

She shuddered, her hips jerking up once again to bump against his straining cock. "With you?"

He gave a fleeting thought to protest. It was too soon, he knew it, but then she wrapped her legs around his thighs and rocked into him and he forgot all about being a knight in shining armor.

"Yes, with me." He flicked his tongue over her pulse. She tasted delicious and he intended to lick every inch of her.

"Mitch," she said, in a soft, hesitant tone.

He lifted his head and looked down into her face. Three days ago he hadn't even known her, and somehow that seemed impossible.

Before Maddie was a lifetime ago.

She blinked up at him, expression unsure. He sighed. Too soon. He let go of her wrists and brushed her hair from her cheek. "To sleep. I don't want to do anything you're not ready for." It might kill him, but he could do it.

"No," she said, shaking her head. She turned her head and looked at the river. "That's not it. I need something from you."

"What? Whatever it is, you've got it."

Her teeth sunk into her bottom lip. "I want you to make me a promise."

"Whatever you need." As long as he could feel her against him.

She swallowed. "Promise you won't take it easy on me."

His heart almost stalled out. "What exactly do you mean?"

"I don't want sweet and gentle. I don't want safe. I don't want you to treat me with kid gloves because I don't have a lot of experience."

He ground his back teeth, fighting raw, depraved images in his head. He swallowed hard and asked, "Do you know what you're asking?"

She tilted her face to look at him, and even in the moonlight he could see the stain of pink on her cheeks. The blush did nothing to detract from the determination in her eyes.

"I want it all." She smiled, and if he'd been standing it would have knocked him to his knees. "I'm committing a mortal sin for you. So you'd better be worth it."

Chapter Fifteen

Mitch's bedroom door clicked shut. The sound echoed in Maddie's head as her pulse lurched. Her nerves, which had been a mere rumble when she'd been outside by the river and trapped under Mitch's hard body, had built to a crescendo on the walk back to the house.

All her inadequacies and worry pushed to the surface, dulling her determination to take what she wanted. She stared at Mitch's big king-sized bed, the massive intricate headboard both beautiful and daunting.

She could do this. She wanted to do this.

Mitch's warm palms covered her bare shoulders, sending a jolt of electricity through her blood and making her jump. His body pressed close to hers, hitching her breath.

"Second thoughts?" he whispered, stirring the fine hairs along the shell of her ear.

Maddie licked her bottom lip, transfixed by the bed before her. "I'm nervous."

He slid his hands down her arms, leaving a trail of goose bumps in his wake. "Princess, we don't have to do anything you don't want to do."

With her heart pounding against her ribs, she squeaked, "It's . . . just . . . I don't know. . . ." The chocolate-colored suede comforter looked as lush and inviting as it had last night, but she couldn't take a step toward it. She was frozen to the spot, suspended by indecision.

"What don't you know?" His low voice snaked through her fear.

"It's not what I pictured," she blurted, once again wringing her hands.

He reached around her waist, taking her nervous, quaking fingers in his and stilling them. "What did you picture?"

She took a deep breath. "I guess I thought I'd be overwhelmed by passion and wouldn't have to think too much about it." God, did that sound terrible? Like she didn't want him?

He chuckled, and the slow sinful sound wound her more tightly until she thought she might break. "Would it have been easier if I took you out on the grass?"

She nodded, unable to speak. Why was she like this? Why couldn't she take control of the situation like a grown woman?

He released her, stepping away and taking all his warmth and strength with him. He walked around until he stood in front of her. He stroked a finger down her jaw and cupped her chin. "Do you trust me?"

She bit the inside of her cheek. "I don't know. I want to."

"Fair enough," he said, a small smile lifting the corner of his lips. "Tell me your worries."

A million scenarios, all of them terrible, filled her head. She couldn't tell him. It would ruin the moment even more than it had been ruined. Anxious, she gazed up at him and, unable to help herself, said, "What if it's a disaster?"

"Then we'll try again."

She frowned, her brows pulling tight. "You're not going to reassure me how fabulous it will be?"

His grip slipped down to her throat. "No."

"Why?"

He smiled. "Because that would be taking it easy on you."

With a quick, surprised laugh, she pushed at his chest. "That's not what I meant!"

His fingers tightened, and she could feel her pulse pounding against his thumb. "Think about it. Do you really want some smooth line about how I'm so good you'll come for me like you never have before?"

She pushed away all her mental noise to concentrate on his question. He was right. It would sound like a line and make her uneasy. He was giving her honesty. He didn't know any more than she did.

She studied his face. Those golden eyes were bright with understanding and steady with certainty, his expression relaxed. "But you're not worried, are you?"

He stroked her neck. "No, I'm not."

"Why?"

He slid over the cords of her neck, and despite her nerves, a shiver ran through her. "That's why."

"Sure, that's now, but what if in the moment, I freeze?"

"Then you freeze and we slow down. There's no rush, Maddie."

The first layer of her nerves calmed. "And if it's a horrible disaster?"

His lips quirked. "Then it's a disaster."

Another knot of tension unfurled. "It could be all awkward and fumbling."

"True." He released his hold on her throat and cupped her shoulders, shifting them both to the left. "Maybe we can come up with some teenage fantasies to accompany the awkwardness."

She repressed the smile at the images that evoked. Good images. Fun. Better, but her mind still whirled. "What if I decide I want to stop?"

Another step around. "Then we'll stop."

"No questions asked?"

"No questions asked." He pressed closer, forcing her to step with him.

The anxious jump in her stomach quelled. "What if I don't like what you're doing?"

"Tell me you don't like it."

"You won't be offended?"

Something dark flashed in his gaze. "No. I won't be offended. In fact, I insist you tell me if you don't like something."

"And you'll stop?"

He shrugged, his face holding none of the turmoil whirling inside her. "That'll depend."

"On what?" She twisted her hands once again.

He leaned in close enough for her to see the spikes of brown in his eyes. "On if you really don't like it, or if it just makes you nervous."

Her hands stilled. "How can you tell the difference?"

"That's easy," he said, his thumb brushing over her bottom lip. "The body rarely lies."

She frowned. Was that true? Her body lied to her all the time.

Or did it?

She caught him watching her intently. "Am I frustrating you?"

"Nope." Simple. Matter-of-fact. True.

"Why not? I'm frustrating me."

"I want you to be sure." He tucked a lock of wayward hair behind her ear. "Besides, it's kind of cute."

She scowled, some of her temper kicking in. "I don't want to be cute!"

"Too bad," he said, brushing a quick kiss along her jaw. "You are."

"If I'm cute, it can't possibly be the way I want it to be."

"And how do you want it to be?" His expression was so keen with interest that a flush warmed her cheeks.

Now she'd done it. She shrugged.

"Tell me."

"You know, all hot and passionate," she mumbled, embarrassed.

"You can't be both?"

His expression was so filled with smug, male amusement that she couldn't help answering with a totally female pout.

"This isn't helping. I'm not feeling very sophisticated right now."

"Maddie," he said, his voice warm and rich like melted chocolate. "I've had enough cool, sophisticated women to last me a lifetime."

Surprised, she blinked and said stupidly, "Oh."

He looped one finger on her shorts and tugged. "And the truth is, I haven't ever wanted anyone as badly as I want you."

Throat dry, she swallowed. "You want me?"

"Since the second you walked into my bar."

She nibbled on the inside of her cheek, still fretting over one concern she couldn't possibly say out loud.

"What?" Another hard tug on her waistband shifted her to the left.

"What if I can't . . ." Heat stained her cheeks and she waved a hand in the air. "You know."

"Come?" A full smile stretched his mouth.

She nodded, the movement sharp and jerky.

"Then I'll have to try harder next time, won't I?" His tone was bemused.

"You won't be upset?"

He laughed, the sound low, wicked, and completely sinful, and her belly leapt in desire instead of fear. "Nope, I'll probably pass out before my ego can get too worked up about it."

Laughter burst from her lips. "You jerk."

He flashed the crooked grin from the night she'd met him,

and her heart melted. "That's what you get for asking a trick question."

She shook her head, raising her gaze to the heavens, drawing her next question only to find her mind blank. The anxious, worried tension vibrating in her body was gone, her internal chatter finally quiet. "Okay, then."

"You sure?"

"Yes." The word was more squeaky than intelligible.

He stepped closer, pushing her shoulders. Her calves hit the back of the bed. She straightened. "Hey! How'd that happen?"

"I'm tricky that way," he said. His tone was amused, but his eyes were hot and hungry.

"How did you know I wasn't going to say no?"

"Princess, if you were going to say no, you'd have said it a long time ago." He lifted her and tossed her on the mattress, where she landed in an unceremonious heap.

She scrambled back and he climbed onto the bed, looking like a predator slinking through the brush.

"You're very mean." She was breathless now with anticipation.

He grabbed her ankles. "And don't you forget it."

Oh God. Her nipples beaded and she tried to squirm away, but he straddled her before she could move, trapping her beneath him. His eyes dipped to her breasts. "See, the body doesn't lie."

The hard buds tightened further, and she gulped.

He gripped her wrists, pulling them above her head and into the pillow. "I think you like it a little mean."

Her breath stalled in her chest. *How could he possibly know?* She shook her head, unable to admit to something so depraved.

"Oh yes," he said, the words ringing with something primitive and untamed.

And then he kissed her, putting all her worries to rest with one single press of his lips.

Maddie's mouth opened under his in an instant, and Mitch took full advantage, taking her in a hard, brutal kiss, holding none of his pent-up desire back.

The muscles in her wrist flexed as she clenched her hands.

His tongue stroked into her mouth, coaxing her into a response, into greedy need.

She twisted under him, driving him half out of his mind as he devoured her with all the possessiveness he'd been repressing for days, pushing them both into the lustful, mindless oblivion she'd been craving.

He clasped her hands together, wrapping his fingers around her small wrists, leaving him free to explore. He stroked down her body, noticing every catch of her breath and strain of her muscles as he brushed over the tendons in her neck.

He tore his mouth away, moving down her throat to find the pounding beat of her pulse with his tongue. He sucked, gently at first, and then harder when she gasped.

He'd known it would be like this. Unlike her, he hadn't had a doubt in his mind.

He bit her neck and she wrenched beneath him. She was sensitive and he took full advantage, feasting on her like a vampire until she squirmed under him, moaning. She pulled at her wrists, trying to get free, but he gripped her more tightly, locking his thighs around hers and immobilizing her.

She arched and struggled.

Her soft whimper tugged at his cock as though she'd touched him.

He stroked down her body, covering her breast with his palm and whispering in her ear, "I'm going to lick you until you scream and then I'm going to fuck you so you'll feel me for days."

She gasped and shook her head. "I . . . I can't . . ."

Just like he'd told her, her body betrayed her. She arched, her nipple tightening under his hand as her breath became more ragged.

"Yes," he said, and covered the mouth that had driven him crazy since she'd sat down at his bar.

Despite her protests, she held nothing back.

The surrender vibrated through her as she shuddered. The heat of her mouth made him dizzy as he peeled down the strap of her tank top to reveal one perfect bare breast. He learned her body, circling the hard peak over and over until she strained to get free. He rolled her nipple between his thumb and forefinger, squeezing and pinching until she cried out, letting him know without words that he'd caught the sweet spot between pleasure and pain.

"Mitch." His name on her lips, a need-soaked whisper.

Jesus Christ. He was so damn hard that his zipper bit into his erection. He'd die to get into her, do anything to sink into the depths of her body and ride her hard and furiously. But he couldn't, not yet: first, he had work to do.

He intended to put every single one of her worries to rest.

What was he doing?

Maddie twisted under Mitch as he wrenched another keening jolt of pleasure from her. It felt so good, so impossibly right, that it made her head spin. With his intoxicating kiss, he delivered all of the overwhelming passion she'd craved. She gasped with surprise as he squeezed her nipple to the point of discomfort. Instead of the pain she would have expected, it sent aching, burning desire to her core.

She needed to do something other than lie here, with nothing to distract her from the hot, consuming sensations racing through her. She yanked at her manacled wrists, and he tightened his hold, refusing to release her.

She wanted to touch him, wrap her legs around his waist, force him to move quicker, get inside faster because, God help her, she was desperate.

As though reading her mind, her hands were suddenly free, but before she could get her bearings, he pulled her up, stripping off her tank top. She flopped down on the mattress.

High above her, Mitch loomed large, impossibly gorgeous. Impossibly dangerous. Excitement raced through her blood.

He ripped his T-shirt from his body with a flash of golden skin and hard muscles that she itched to touch. She reached out, but he grabbed her hands, pressing her wrists into the mattress, covering her. A protest rose to her lips, but his mouth claimed hers and her thoughts fragmented, blocking out everything but the feel of his chest rubbing against her breasts.

She'd worried for nothing. All of her concerns were forgotten as he drove her nearly mad with fevered lust.

He broke the kiss, moving lower and skimming his hot mouth along her jaw. Lower still, he licked the mysterious erogenous zone on her throat, right over her pounding pulse.

She closed her eyes and just about melted into the bed.

He nipped at her collarbone, slid down her chest, nuzzling the slope of her breast before capturing one nipple with his lips.

She arched, her heels digging into the mattress as he sucked the hard, aching bud deep into his mouth. The sensation was so exquisite that she thought she might climb out of her skin for wanting him. She buried her hands into his hair, digging her nails into his scalp to keep him close.

He played with her nipples, masterfully using hands, lips, tongue, and teeth until she wanted to cry for relief. Impossibly, her belly coiled tight. So tight she might break.

Still trapped between the ironclad muscles of his thighs,

she twisted. God, she needed friction. Why wouldn't he let her move?

He bit the aching peak. Pleasure snapped through her nerve endings, so sharp it bordered on pain. Unable to hold back, a moan escaped her.

He gave a deep laugh, so filled with carnal intent that she felt the flush deepen on her already hot skin.

His mouth left her breast, the hard bud wet and needy as he slithered down her body. His hands rested on her hips. "Lift."

Without even a thought to the contrary, she complied.

He shifted, nudging her legs with his knees until her thighs splayed open and vulnerable. He moved between them, resting on his haunches as he looked his fill.

An urge to cover herself snuck over her, dimming some of her desire. Her arm twitched and his gaze snapped to hers. "Don't even think about it."

God, that voice. The low threat. The command.

"You are gorgeous." His smile was wicked as he slid a finger along her wet center. "And this is a surprise."

Her lashes fluttered at the feather-light touch. "What?"

"You're bare." Another soft brush passed over moist flesh, not touching where she needed it most.

Oh, yeah. She'd forgotten. She managed to pant out, "The woman . . . at the salon . . . said it was trendy."

He scooted down, never ceasing his slow, methodical stroking of her slick folds.

She squeezed her lids tightly, gritting her teeth as she silently willed him to touch her harder.

He blew across her overheated skin. "I like it."

She froze, everything inside her going still. She jerked up. "What are you doing?"

His head lifted and he stared at her from beneath her splayed thighs. "I told you I was going to lick you."

Panic edged out her lust. "Please don't."

One brow arched. "No?"

She shook her head vehemently, trying to scramble up the bed.

A hard clamp over her thighs ceased her frantic movement. "Why?"

"I don't like it," she said, completely embarrassed. She'd worked up the courage to ask Steve once, and it had been a disaster. She'd lived in fear of him ever trying it again, but thankfully, he'd never brought it up.

She shook her head. No! Not now! She didn't want to think about *him*.

She collapsed onto the bed and threw her arm over her face. All that greedy, dizzying desire was gone like a puff of air. Ruined.

He licked the length of her slit, shocking her.

"No!" She tried to close her legs, but his large palms pressed her down to the mattress.

Another swipe of his tongue.

She glared up at the ceiling, clenching her hands into fists. "I thought you'd said you'd stop."

His mouth danced over her flesh, lips grazing her inner thigh before his teeth gently scraped over her sensitive flesh. Despite her unease, her thighs trembled in response. She gritted her teeth.

"You're nervous, not turned off." His warm breath blew over her skin, tickling her.

It was an effort, but she stayed completely still. "I don't like it."

He sat up, and powerful relief stole through her as she let out the air she hadn't realized she'd been holding. "Thank you."

He smiled and entwined their fingers together. "Don't thank me yet." He brought their joined hands to rest between her thighs. "Touch yourself."

"Wh-what?" she sputtered. Was he crazy?

He changed his hold, gripping her wrist so that her hand rested against her opening. "Touch yourself."

"I most certainly will not." Her tone was as prim as a schoolmarm. This was turning into the disaster she'd been afraid of. "You're ruining this for me."

He shrugged, as though totally unconcerned. "Do it, or I'll do it for you."

"No," she said, and looked around for something to cover herself with. "This was a mistake. I'm leaving."

He laughed. Actually laughed!

Anger spiked, cooling the last remaining heat in her blood. She tried to wrench away, but he held her tight. Over the years she'd taught herself to repress her temper. All the consequences of unleashing it roiled to the surface, but she pushed them away as she kicked at him. "I'm never going to forgive you for this. It was going so well, and you had to go and spoil it."

"Ruined you for sex forever, did I?" His tone was amused instead of concerned.

"Yes!" She glared, her fury as hot as her lust had been moments before. "It looks like I have to join the convent after all, thanks to you!"

"I see," he said, looking her over with a lazy glance. "Such a shame."

"Are you making fun of me?" Her foot shot out as she aimed for the center of his chest.

He batted her away as though she were a pesky fly, his hold on her wrist not loosening even a fraction. "You are so irresistible when you get all riled up."

"I hope you're happy. This is exactly the disaster I imagined." She wanted to kill him. Everything had been perfect, exactly what she'd been wanting, and now it was her worst nightmare.

Without letting her go, he moved up her body and loomed over her. "You have only yourself to blame."

With her free hand, she pinched him.

Laughing, he shook his head, then captured her free hand and manacled her wrists together. "I knew I was going to have to restrain you."

"Jerk!" The insult did not leave her mouth with the vehemence she'd intended.

He planted one of those hot, open-mouth kisses over her pulse, calling her attention to the frantic beat under her skin.

"That's not excitement," she said, her tone petulant. "It's anger."

"I don't care." He scraped his teeth over the spot and her body betrayed her by stirring to life. "I like the way it feels under my tongue."

"Don't you care about my pleasure at all?" Ugh. She sounded whiny. She hated that.

He sucked at her neck and her vision dimmed as he licked and tortured the soft skin. Some of the lust-filled haze returned, dulling her mind.

No. She would not get distracted. She had a point to make.

"Yes," he said, his breath hot against her neck. "But if you're determined to talk yourself out of what you want, there's nothing I can do about that."

"I'm not." She wasn't. She just didn't like it and he wouldn't listen.

He shifted to the side, and to her annoyance she missed the heat of his body pressing into hers. He clasped one of her hands and brought it down over her head to rest between her legs. This time, his palm covered hers and forced her middle finger to slide inside her core, right along with his. "Feel that?"

She gulped. She was hot. Wet. Too wet.

Something must have shown in her expression because he pressed harder, pushing her deeper as her own excitement slicked her skin.

He leaned down and licked a circle over her nipple, and

her inner muscles clamped down, practically milking her finger in enthusiasm. He nipped at her nipple, causing another undeniable ripple before he blew across the aching tip. "You don't know what you like, Maddie."

"And you do?" She panted out the words.

"Not yet, exactly," he said, flicking the hard bud with his tongue. "But I've got a damn good idea."

"I don't like *that*," she said stubborn.

He moved their fingers inside her, a slow lazy pump that heated her blood. "You could have fooled me."

"I said no."

He slid them out of her body, releasing her and swirling a thumb over her clit. She jerked, a soft gasp escaping before she could push it back.

"Yes, that's what your head says." Mitch sucked her nipple into his mouth, pulling deep and strong, and the sensation shot straight to the bundle of nerves between her legs where he stroked with feather lightness. He lifted his head. "But you keep rocking your pussy into my hand just the same."

A shocked, heated flush spread over her entire body. "No."

"Yes. You were just too busy talking to pay attention." With eyes dark as burnished gold, he met her gaze. "Let's try a little experiment, okay?"

She didn't like the sound of that, but was so embarrassed she couldn't do anything but squeak.

He kissed her, a short, fleeting over-too-soon kiss. "I'm going to go down on you for fifteen minutes. If you still don't like it at the end, I'll never do it again. Sound reasonable?"

Well, when he put it like that, she'd look foolish to refuse.

After all, he wasn't hurting her, and at the end of fifteen minutes, she wouldn't have to endure any more humiliation over this again. She nodded.

He gave her one of those trademark sinful smiles that

never failed to make her weak in the knees and pointed to the bedside clock. "You can watch the time. Just tap me on the shoulder when the fifteen minutes is up."

"Okay," she mumbled.

He laughed, sliding down her body. Muscles taut, she braced herself, gaze glued to the red digital display. She'd expected him to go right to ground zero, but instead he brushed his lips along her inner thigh, first one and then the other. Nerves she'd believed numb quivered to life.

She watched the clock.

He licked the soft flesh. Nipped. Sucked.

Her core contracted. She bit her lip as her blood stirred.

His lips moved so softly over her skin, the pressure so light that she couldn't help but crave more.

The red numbers on the clock changed. One minute.

He treated the other thigh to the same attention.

Her lashes fluttered and she stubbornly forced them open.

The urge to close her legs was impossible to resist, but he tightened his grip the second she tensed, not allowing her to move.

Two minutes.

He nibbled his way to the crease of her thigh, his breath hot against her folds. She braced herself, her eyes clinging to the red numbers as though they were her lifeline. But he didn't go in; instead, he scraped his teeth against the taut tendon on her inner thigh, and she sucked in her stomach as desire shot through her.

Four minutes.

Her breath came a little faster as anxiety grew, tinged with pleasure. Her hips twitched as she fought the desire to force him to deepen the contact.

Six.

Finally, he licked, flicking his tongue along her slit. Involuntarily, her body arched, but she pressed her spine along the mattress, determined not to give in.

He chuckled, and she knew he hadn't missed the movement.

He *was* mean. She'd make him pay. Later. Much, much later.

He dipped inside. Just a fraction.

Her nipples beaded once again into hard, almost painful peaks. A dark, wayward thought entered her mind. She wanted to stroke them, pull them, and pinch them as he'd done earlier. But she couldn't do that.

Sure, she'd touched her breasts before, but never in front of anyone.

An image of his mouth between her legs and her playing with her nipples filled her mind with such erotic vividness that her inner muscles clamped down.

He moaned, causing a sinfully delicious vibration against her skin.

Her breath grew faster, and her lids grew heavy at his heady exploration.

Eight minutes.

He licked her clit and the nerves there jumped to life. She bit her bottom lip, fighting the cry that filled her throat.

He increased his pressure.

She grabbed a fistful of the sheets and hung on for dear life.

His tongue swirled.

His mouth was hot on her skin.

No longer able to stand it, her eyes closed as an impossible, undeniable pressure coiled tight.

Two fingers slid inside her as he lapped at the hard bud. Oh God.

His tongue was too talented: impossibly, wickedly talented. Unable to fight her body's urges any longer, her hips rocked.

The sensation built.

He hooked his fingers deep, right over her pelvic bone, and rubbed in hard, sure circles.

Her body jerked. Her hands clenched the cotton. The cry tore unbidden from her throat.

His lips sucked her clit. The rhythm increased on that one maddening spot.

Everything clenched.

He became relentless, demanding—no longer coaxing a response, but forcing one. Every nerve she had flamed.

A sharp, exquisite, almost painful pleasure twisted and coiled.

He persisted.

The orgasm hovered just beyond her reach, taunting her, teasing her. She moaned, partly in frustration and partly from how unbelievably his mouth and hands tormented her.

Unable to stop, her hips moved. Strained to get closer. This was nothing like what she'd experienced before. She forgot all her reservations, her protests, and her stubborn stand, and reveled at his talent.

Inside, his fingers twisted. His teeth scraped along her clit.

She exploded. The climax ripped from her body as wave after wave of almost violent contractions wracked her body. She cried out when he pressed harder, not letting go, not letting up. The sensations were so intense that they'd be unbearable if they hadn't felt so damn good.

Another wave of pleasure shook her frame, tossing her about. "Oh God!"

The orgasm went on and on until she finally went limp, her muscles slack.

His fingers slid from her body, and he pressed one last kiss to her mound before moving up her body. Beside her, he trailed a path over her belly, and she jumped, her over-sensitive skin ticklish. He brushed his mouth over hers. He smelled and tasted of her. She thought she should be mortified, but instead she lay there, too boneless and satisfied to kick up a fuss.

"You forgot to tap me and tell me the time was up," he said, his voice the epitome of smug, arrogant maleness.

"Don't brag," she murmured, eyes still closed.

He chuckled, cupping her breast and rubbing his thumb over the peak. "You only came once. It's not much to brag about."

She opened one eye. "Only once?"

"If I had more time, I could have done better."

The other lid popped open. "You did fine." Understatement of the century.

He rolled her nipple, leaning down to kiss her neck. Her pulse stirred to life, even though she'd been sure she'd never move again. "Wake up, Maddie. I'm not nearly done with you yet."

He shifted, and lying on his back, he reached into the nightstand to pull out a handful of condoms. He tossed them onto the table.

Her eyes widened. "Ambitious."

He chuckled. "I've been hard for three days straight. It's going to take more than once."

"I'm not sure I have the energy."

With a smile, he unzipped his jeans, shucking them off along with his underwear, his eyes never leaving hers. "You do like to challenge me, don't you, Princess?"

Was that what she was doing? Was she throwing down the sexual gauntlet? She let her eyes roam, taking in his golden skin, those hard muscles, and the flat of his abdomen before resting on his erection.

He was steely hard, the head of his cock brushing his belly.

Her fingers twitched. She wanted to touch him. She reached out tentatively at first, stroking over his stomach. The muscles jumped under her touch. She trailed a path over the plains, marveling at the way he responded to her.

Growing bolder, she circled his flat brown nipple, much like he'd done to her.

With a hiss, he gripped her hand. "Don't do that right now."

"Why?" She scooted closer, bent her head, and licked.

"Fuck!" He nearly crushed her fingers. He rolled her over onto her back, covering her.

"We'll play later. Right now, I just need inside."

She loved the way his body felt on hers: the hard length of his frame, his lean muscles, and the press of his thighs against hers.

He covered her mouth in a crushing, brutal, passion-soaked kiss. Stealing her breath along with any conscious thought, he sucked her underneath that drugging, all-consuming passion. He ate at her mouth, played her body like a violin until she moaned and twisted. Need coiled tightly in her belly.

His erection slid between her wet folds.

She forgot everything.

Her past. His. Her family. Steve. The wedding. Every-thing. For the first time since she was fifteen, she lost her-self in the abandon of emotion. She wrapped her legs around his waist, wanting him so badly she'd kill for it.

"Please," she whispered, not caring if it sounded like begging.

He groaned, shifting his weight, thrusting the head of his cock over her clit.

The sensation jolted like electricity down her spine.

He repeated the action, shaking his head. "Goddamn. You feel so fucking good."

She arched to meet him, desire ratcheting up at a fevered pitch. "Please, please."

She forgot to be embarrassed. Forgot about how she sounded or looked. Forgot about God's watchful, disapproving eye as she clawed her nails down his back. She needed more.

He growled a low, primal sound from deep in his throat. He shifted his hips. He aligned the head of his cock at her opening, then thrust hard, filling her completely, only to freeze.

"Damn it." He pulled out, and she tried to keep him within her, but he was too strong. "Princess, give me a second. I forgot the condom."

Her lids were heavy; it was an effort to open her eyes. He reached over to the nightstand and grabbed a foil packet, rolling to a kneeling position between her legs. His lids were heavy, and his cheekbones looked carved from granite.

He was so beautiful: a work of art she wanted to capture on paper. The thought came from out of nowhere, surprising her, but before she could latch on to it, Mitch tore the package open with his teeth, then handed the condom to her.

"Put it on."

His voice was a steely command, and she didn't even think to refuse.

With trembling fingers, she took the latex ring. She sat up and positioned it over the head of his erection. Watching his face, she rolled it down his shaft inch by slow inch, reveling in the stark hunger etched over his strong features.

He hissed out a breath. Flipping her onto her back, he pulled her splayed legs over his thighs and thrust into her.

She was filled by and stretched tightly around him, and he didn't move, letting her adjust to his length and girth. When her muscles loosened, he shifted, filling her impossibly further. She arched, stars crowding her vision as he ground his hips in a slow, mind-altering circle.

Then he started to move, each thrust setting her nerves on fire.

He didn't make love to her. It was no gentle wooing. No,

it was a claiming. He took her. Hot. Hard. Primal. Pumping into her with brutal thrusts.

"So." He slammed into her. "Fucking." With another drive home, his hips swiveled so the base of his cock hit her clit on the up stroke. "Good."

She cried out. Relentless, burning desire threatened to incinerate her.

"Tight." His voice low, he pushed her back onto the mattress. "Wet."

"Harder," she pleaded, the blinding need for release engulfing her.

He rose onto his hands and rocked into her, brutally, beautifully hard.

Over and over.

Faster.

Desire coiled deep in her belly.

Just a little more.

He reached between them and rubbed a finger over her clit.

She exploded, coming so hard that her vision dimmed to blackness as she nearly passed out from the fury of her climax.

Seconds later, he followed, pumping fast, with a loud roar that nearly shook the rafters.

Finally, the mad rush and thrust of their bodies stilled and the world slowed down. He rolled off of her, and they both stared up at the ceiling, gasping for breath.

"That was . . ." Mitch panted out, running a hand through his already impossibly messy hair.

Maddie giggled, another piece of that invisible weight she carried on her chest chipping away. "A total disaster."

"Little brat." He laughed. "You know what that means?"

"What?" She risked a glance at him, only to flush the second their eyes met.

"We'll have to try again."

"Until we get it right."

He rolled over and kissed her. "I have a feeling it's going to take quite some time before we're even remotely proficient."

Forever. The word slipped into her mind so smoothly, so effortlessly, she'd had to be thinking it on some visceral, unconscious level. The thought shook her. A slice of panic cut through her bone-deep relaxation.

She'd just met Mitch. She'd run out of her wedding precisely because she'd never been alone. Now, not even a week later, she imagined "forever"?

No. She refused to think about that. It was only her Catholic upbringing playing tricks on her mind, wanting her to be proper. That was all.

Mitch gripped her chin, pulling her away from her thoughts. "What is going on in that head of yours?"

"Nothing," she said, far too quickly.

He searched her face. "You know, Maddie, you can tell me anything."

"Yes, I know," she lied. She flashed a blinding smile.

His eyes narrowed doubtfully.

"I'm fine," she said, fluttering her lashes at him. "Except for how awful the whole messy ordeal was."

He rolled over, trapping her and pinning her under him. "I knew you liked it mean."

Yes, this was what she needed. More sex. More Mitch. More blinding passion and explosive orgasms. She had no intention of confessing her unbidden thoughts of fairy tales. She'd stopped believing in happily ever after on that afternoon back when she was fifteen.

No amount of Catholic guilt was going to convince her otherwise.

Chapter Sixteen

Muscles Maddie hadn't known existed ached as she padded down the back staircase to the kitchen below. Heat flooded her cheeks at the vivid memories of her night with Mitch.

The man was both inventive and deviant.

She stepped into the bright kitchen, the sun blinding after the dark hours in Mitch's bedroom. She held her hand up to shield her face. "Ugh! Too bright."

"Not a morning person, is she?" a lazy voice drawled.

Maddie dropped her hand to stare into Sam Roberts's amused face. He sat across from Mitch, long, denim-clad legs stretched out, one hand hugging a coffee cup.

Of course. What was breakfast with Mitch if not another new humiliation? This town was custom-made to put her in awkward situations. She glared at Mitch, who grinned like the cat who ate the canary. "Do you ever have breakfast alone?"

He shrugged. "They're big fans of the drop-in."

"From the looks of her, she should be in a much better mood," Sam said, clearly entertained.

Maddie crossed her arms over her breasts. She might as well be naked in her skimpy tank top and cotton shorts.

"No need to be shy." Sam winked at her. "I saw you last night, although you were considerably less rumpled."

She rolled her eyes. "Isn't it polite to allow a girl some dignity?"

"What do you mean, last night?" Mitch asked at the same time, eyes narrowed on Sam. A muscle jumped in his forearm as his fingers tightened around his mug. "Don't even tell me that's what you were wearing."

"I was sitting on the front porch when he came home." She ran her hand through her disheveled hair, getting caught in the wild mass of tangles.

Sam gave Mitch a sly, devious smile. "Not my fault you left her alone for just anyone to come take a peek."

Mitch's attention snapped to Maddie. She refused to fidget under his scrutiny. One golden brow rose.

Maddie huffed. "I don't need to explain myself to you."

"Hmmmm . . ." Mitch gave her a through once-over.

Maddie's chin shot up. "This is your fault, not mine!"

Sam scrubbed his blond, stubbled jaw. "She's got a point."

"I suppose she does," Mitch said, but his tone spoke of a different story. Those amber eyes told her without words that she'd be paying later with his own delicious brand of torture.

She shivered at the thought, toes practically curling in anticipation. She was going to hell.

And it was totally worth it.

Mitch flashed a cocky, knowing smile.

Maddie wanted to stick her tongue out, but that'd only make her look petty.

"Need some coffee, Princess?" Mitch asked. The chair scraped against the floor as he got up from the table. He stood in front of her, staring down at her with that look on his face.

She swallowed.

Then he was on her, kissing her. His hard body pressed against hers.

Right in front of Sam.

She squirmed, but he held her still, hands firm on her hips so she couldn't move. All she could do was fight to not get sucked under. Desire made her head spin as memories from the night before mixed with the heat of his lips. She gripped the counter in back of her, refusing to twine herself around him.

When he pulled away, she chased his mouth, jerking when she realized what she was doing.

Mitch grinned. "I get final outfit approval."

She straightened with as much dignity as she could muster and said haughtily, albeit breathlessly, "You most certainly do not."

"We'll see about that, won't we?"

"Yeah, we will."

The phone rang. Laughing, he reached around her and picked up the receiver. He smelled mouthwatering, like soap, spice, and man. She wanted to take a bite of him. Instead, she ducked under his arm and ran for the coffee machine.

"What?" Mitch said to his caller, running his hand through his hair.

Maddie grabbed a mug and poured some coffee before scooting into the chair at the table.

Sam's smile was all innocent, his cornflower-blue eyes guileless as those of a newborn foal. "Nice night?"

She scowled, narrowing her gaze. "You don't fool me."

"I don't know what you're referring to." His lips quirked as though he was trying not to laugh.

She waved a hand over him. "Your choirboy act."

Now he chuckled outright. "Honey, I'm about as much a choirboy as you are a good girl."

Heat flooded her cheeks, and she distracted herself by

taking a sip of coffee. When she was more composed, she said, "You and your sister are cut from the same cloth."

"I'm the more subtle of the two."

"More devious," she muttered under her breath.

"That's another word." Sam grinned.

"And shameless."

"I've never seen the point in shame," Sam said, and pointed to her. "You've got mud in your hair."

She laughed. The sound came from out of nowhere, surprising her. These people were truly crazy.

"Are you fucking kidding me?" Mitch's hard voice broke through her enjoyment.

Maddie whipped around in time to see him slam down the phone. His gold eyes flashed with what looked a lot like fury, but before she could ask what had happened, he stalked out of the room.

She exchanged a glance with Sam. He shrugged, but strangely, didn't look surprised.

Maddie nibbled on her bottom lip. Did she follow Mitch? Give him space? What was the protocol? She blew out an exasperated breath. Screw protocol. She got up and headed in the direction he'd disappeared.

She found him a second later in the library, booting up his computer. "What happened?"

His jaw tense, he ignored her, drumming his fingers on the desk as he waited for the machine to work its way through the startup.

Sam wandered in and sank down onto the leather armchair as though he didn't have a care in the world.

Mitch's lips firmed into a hard line. "Don't you have anything better to do?"

"Not particularly," Sam said, linking his hands over his stomach.

"Did you know about this?" Mitch asked, eyes narrowing. Once again lost in the conversation, she glanced back and forth between the two men as if she were at a Ping-Pong match.

Sam nodded. "I was about to tell you, but then you got distracted."

"You should have warned me."

"I was trying." Sam flicked a glance over at Maddie. "She looked like a nice distraction and bad news can wait."

A sliver of dread snaked down Maddie's spine, causing a chill to break over her skin. "What is going on?"

Mitch's gaze went to the computer, and he started typing. Thirty seconds later, he shook his head. "That son of a bitch."

Since neither guy volunteered any information, she walked around the desk and peered at the computer screen.

In big, bold, black letters the headline screamed CAUGHT. A picture of an older man and a young, too-beautiful-to-be-believed chestnut-haired woman filled the frame. Wide, brilliant blue eyes stared into the camera, while the man's hand was up to block his face. The door behind them showed the telltale numbers of a hotel room.

Maddie frowned, not understanding. What did this have to do with Mitch?

She read the caption and took in a quick breath. It couldn't be. That was impossible.

Stunned, she said, "I never connected the names."

"Why would you?" Mitch scrolled down the page and shook his head. "It's a common name."

Plus, why would she ever think that a member of one of Chicago's oldest, most elite families would be hiding here, in some small little town of barely twenty-five hundred?

But somehow, it made perfect sense. It explained so much about him. All the questions rambling around in her head clicked into place until the pieces completed an overall picture. "You're . . ."

"Yes, Maddie, I'm Senator Riley's son." He turned back

to the pictures filling the monitor. "As you can see, the apple doesn't fall very far from the tree."

"How is he?" Gracie asked, concern, darkening her sky-blue eyes.

Maddie ran a finger around the rim of her coffee cup, staring into the mud-brown puddle pooling in the saucer. "I don't know."

Mitch had been distant for most of the day. He'd finally made an excuse and headed to the bar around two, and she hadn't spoken to him since. She'd tried to broach the subject of his father's scandal one time, and that had been enough. His expression had shuttered closed and the glint in his eyes had made it clear that the topic was off limits.

"He doesn't want to talk about it. He never told me about his family, so it was a shock."

Gracie's blond brows drew together as a frown formed on her lips. "He's a guy. I doubt he wants to talk to anyone." Gracie's hand covered hers. "But he wants you here, I promise."

A bad feeling had settled in the pit of her stomach. The real world had closed in. She could feel it in her bones. "I hate reality."

Gracie's head cocked as she watched Maddie with speculation. "Sam says you need to stay."

Maddie had no idea where that little tidbit of information might be going. "How would he know?"

Gracie shrugged and looked out the window overlooking Main Street. "He just knows things. I don't know how, but he's always right."

Surprised, Maddie laughed. "And did he say why?"

The blond curls on Gracie's head bounced as she shook her head. "No, only that's the way it needs to be."

Maddie studied the woman across from her, taking in her set jaw and troubled eyes. "Wait, you're serious."

"Yes. If Sam says so, you need to listen."

Maddie thought back to last night, with his dead-on assessment of the situation between her and Mitch. It hadn't exactly been a stretch, so it hadn't seemed odd at the time. "What, is he psychic?"

"Ssshhh, don't say that!" Gracie glanced around Earl's Diner, suspiciously eyeing the other customers. "He hates that word."

She was serious. Maddie shook her head. "What are you saying?"

Gracie tucked a stray curl behind her ear. "I'm saying I trust my brother, so you're staying here until he says otherwise."

Again, Maddie laughed. "What? Are you going to kidnap me?"

Gracie's lips lifted at the corners. "If I have to chain you to my bed, I will."

"Now that's a fantasy come true." A low voice had Maddie's head shooting up. Sheriff Charlie Radcliff, with his midnight hair and fathomless eyes, smiled down at them. "How are my favorite girls today?"

"Why, we're just fine, Sheriff." Gracie's tone took on a thick Southern drawl as she batted her eyes. She moved to the far end of the booth, and Charlie slid into the space next to her.

"What are you doing here?" Gracie asked.

"I was cruising down Main Street and saw your car." He gave Maddie a smile so filled with charm and sin that she felt her cheeks flush. The silver star on his tan work shirt glinted in the sunshine streaming through the large window. "If we're talking chains and beds, I see stopping was a wise move."

Before Maddie could think of a thing to say, the pretty

teenage waitress, who had long blond hair with hot pink streaks, hurried over. It was the fastest Maddie had seen her move since they'd sat down. Ignoring the women completely, she beamed at Charlie. "Sheriff, what can I get for you?"

"Just a Coke, honey," Charlie said, grinning at the girl with a wink.

"I'd like a refill." Gracie waved her cup in the air. "Like I asked you for ten minutes ago."

The girl's doe eyes flicked over Gracie like she was a pesky fly. "Yeah, I, like, forgot."

Gracie snorted, and Maddie covered her smile behind her hand. Charlie managed to be sexy, scary, and downright charming all at the same time, and Maddie couldn't blame the teenager for being smitten. The girl practically ran in the direction of the soda fountain.

Gracie shook her head. "That was disgusting. This is why I hate going out in public with you."

"Not my fault, darlin'.'" Charlie swung an arm around her and tugged her close. "I don't have to do a damn thing."

"You were encouraging her."

"I asked for a Coke." Charlie eyed Gracie with a cop's suspicion. "Are you jealous?"

"God no, you egomaniac." Gracie patted his cheek. "This is one more example of why I like to keep you in the bedroom where you belong."

Charlie laughed and kissed her temple.

Maddie didn't understand one thing about Gracie's relationship with Charlie, but she had enough problems without trying to figure them out. She took a sip of coffee, cringing at the weak taste.

What was she going to do? Maddie turned to look through the window, and a surge of panic coursed through her like heroin. The fine hairs at the nape of her neck rose, and she put the cup back in the saucer with a shaking hand.

Oh, Jesus, no. Please no.

She put her hand on the window and sweat beaded her temples. She'd known it. Since she'd read the article about Mitch's father, she'd known the momentary slice of heaven was over.

Reality was coming to get her. A wave of nausea rolled through her.

"Maddie, what's wrong?" Gracie said, sounding alarmed.

Steve. How had he found her? Maddie closed her eyes and scrubbed her fists into the sockets, hoping the vision would vanish. She opened her eyes and blinked.

He was gone.

She waited for the rush of relief at finding that the apparition had disappeared, but it didn't come. In fact, her fear increased. Cold with dread, she leaned closer to the glass, peering up and down Revival's Main Street.

Nothing. She saw only a lone bike rider and a few families out for a stroll.

"Maddie!" Charlie's sharp voice snapped her out of her daze.

"Sorry," she mumbled. Had she imagined Steve? Was she hallucinating? Did she need to go to confession?

"What's wrong?" Charlie asked, his tone suddenly taking on a hard edge that gave Maddie a chill.

She shook her head. "Nothing. I, um, just thought I saw someone."

"Who?" he pressed, his strong square jaw firming.

"No one." Nerves skipped through her.

"You look pale," Gracie said, sliding a glass of water under Maddie's nose. "Drink this."

"I'm fine." She nibbled on her lower lip.

Across the street, Mary Beth Crowley stepped outside the garage door, followed by a customer. They walked over to a black SUV and started talking. Mary Beth waved her hand over the body like a spokesmodel.

Maddie cleared her throat. "Maybe I should see how my

car is doing." She hadn't given it one bit of thought since they'd left the shop, and it would give her something to do.

That sense of foreboding slithered over her skin again like an oily snake. She peered up and down Main Street again.

Steve was here. She could feel it. She might be crazy, but she didn't hallucinate.

He was out there.

She turned away from the window to find Gracie and Charlie watching her as if she were a bug under a microscope. Maddie flashed them a bright, cheery smile, and twin frowns formed on their faces.

Gracie leaned forward. "Is everything okay?"

"Yes, fine." Maddie tucked a lock of hair behind her ear, realizing that Charlie had gotten his Coke and she hadn't noticed. "I saw Mary Beth across the street, and it reminded me I should go check on my car."

Gracie flashed Charlie a glance that Maddie couldn't even begin to decipher.

Charlie shook his head. "No need. Tommy and Mary Beth have everything under control."

"I don't see the harm of checking. Maybe they'll get done earlier than planned."

Gracie's blond brows drew together. "I saw Mary Beth at the grocery store, and she said they've been real busy."

Why did these two care if she checked on her car? Maddie shrugged. "Doesn't hurt to ask."

Gracie opened her mouth, but Charlie squeezed her shoulder and she snapped her lips shut.

Maddie didn't know what the hell was going on and, at the moment, didn't care. She had Mitch to worry about.

And Steve.

A slow throb pounded at her temples. Unable to help it, she looked out the window, her gaze roaming up and down Main Street. Searching.

"Hello, Maddie," a deep male voice said behind her.

Her stomach dropped like a lead weight. She slowly turned. "Hello, Steve."

While she felt like she'd lived a lifetime since she'd last seen him, he looked remarkably unchanged: composed as ever with his blue-eyed, sandy-haired boy-next-door good looks. His tall, lean frame was immaculately dressed in a white shirt and khakis. No stress showed in either his face or stance. "I have to admit, I didn't expect to find you so easily, but here you are. It must be my lucky day."

Bile rose in her tight throat and she didn't dare look at Charlie and Gracie sitting across from her, far too quietly. "What are you doing here?"

Steve smiled, a calm, easy smile. "I'm here to claim my runaway bride."

God, reality was a cold, cruel bitch.

Chapter Seventeen

There was no more hiding. No more running. Fate had taken the choice out of her hands and now she had to do the right thing. Maddie glanced over at Charlie and Gracie.

Maddie could not, would not, have this conversation in front of them. She cleared her throat. "Can you excuse us? I'll go outside with Steve."

"No." Charlie's voice had a flat, do-not-fuck-with-me tone.

"I'll be fine," Maddie promised. She wiped her sweaty palms on her jean shorts and jutted her head toward her ex-fiancé. "I owe him."

"I've been taking care of her since she was fifteen. She's perfectly safe," Steve said, his tone calm and reasonable, as though she'd misbehaved at the church picnic instead of running out on their wedding.

Gracie shot a nervous "do something" look at Charlie, who assessed Steve like he was a murder suspect. Long, tense moments passed before he shifted his attention to Maddie.

She nodded slightly in response to the clear question in his black eyes.

"All right," Charlie said, as though he had every right to

the final say. He turned his body so Steve could not miss the silver star on his chest. "Stay where I can see you."

"I'm not here to cause any trouble, Officer," Steve said pleasantly. "I only want to speak to my fiancée."

Maddie cringed at the word.

"Sheriff," Charlie corrected. "And stay where I can see you."

"Not a problem."

He was so agreeable that Maddie experienced an almost irresistible urge to smack him, which was completely childish and wrong.

Steve smiled at Charlie. "Her family and I have been worried sick. I'm sure you can appreciate me wanting to make sure she's safe, can't you, Sheriff?"

Charlie's only response was stern, narrowed eyes.

Guilt at the mention of her family sat like a rock in her stomach, and Maddie cursed herself for taking the easy way out yesterday by not calling them. She rubbed her temples. She had to stop this avoidance. It solved nothing. Taking a deep breath to steady her nerves, Maddie scrambled from her seat. "Let's go, Steve, and we can talk."

He took her elbow. She walked toward the front door and at the same moment he pulled her toward the back booth. They stopped and stared at each other. The clatter of dishes and din of patrons was too loud, making her hyper-aware of the spectacle they made and reminding her that she was the subject of gossip. She pointed at the door. "Let's go outside."

"It's ninety degrees and humid. I'm not going to have this conversation on a sidewalk," Steve said, his grip tightening slightly on her arm.

He was right. The sidewalk wasn't the place, and while the middle of a crowded diner wasn't either, the only other option was his car. And there was no way in hell she wanted to be alone with him.

She went.

Once they'd reached the empty back-corner booth next to

the kitchen, Steve let go of her arm and she slid into the red vinyl bench seat.

Maddie's stomach churned the black coffee she'd been drinking.

The pink-streaked-haired waitress ran over. "Hi, like, what can I get you?"

"Nothing," Steve said, not bothering to give Maddie a chance to answer. The girl's face fell and she walked away, albeit much more slowly than before.

When she was out of earshot, Maddie folded her hands on the table and looked directly at Steve. She'd known him almost half her life, and yet, in some ways he was a stranger. She cleared her throat. "Steve, I'm sorry for what I did and how I left. It was unforgivable, but as I told you on the phone, I don't want to talk."

"Do you honestly think I'm going to let you walk away without a word?"

"There's no *letting* me," she said. Her temper sparked and she shoved it back down. "I told you I need time alone."

He shook his head. "For what? So you can talk yourself into some notion about how you'd be better off without me?"

"Steve, pay attention," she said, her voice a too-loud whisper. "I ran out of our wedding. Call me crazy, but that's a problem."

His lips pressed together. What might have been anger flashed over his expression before a veil of calm slid over his features. "Pre-wedding jitters."

"It wasn't jitters."

Flat blue eyes fixed on hers and a muscle ticked in his jaw. "This isn't productive."

Irritation jabbed like a knife in her stomach. She took a deep breath, crossing her arms. "How did you find me?"

"Is that important?"

"Ah yes, the credit cards." Earl's was the last place she'd used the card before it had been declined. She wanted to rage at the blatant manipulation, but didn't see the point. He'd never admit it. She squared her shoulders. "I want my files back. I'll ask Penelope to pick them up as soon as possible."

He clasped his hands on the Formica table. "Did you expect me to not fight for you?"

Maddie looked away, staring fixedly at the framed nineteen-fifties advertisement for ice cream. "I don't know what I expected. I only know this isn't right."

"It's fine, Madeline. You're being dramatic."

"Steve, look at me." She waited until he met her gaze before she continued. "I'm not fine. Please, I don't want you here. I'm sorry."

"Don't I deserve a chance to talk to you?" There wasn't one thing about him that looked out of sorts. He didn't even have dark shadows under his eyes.

"Yes, you do." Needing something to do with her hands, she grabbed a napkin. "We can talk when I get back, but not now. I need time to think."

He shook his head. "I can't believe you're acting like this after everything I've done for you."

She twisted the white paper around her fingers, tugging tightly. "What exactly have you done for me?"

He raised a brow. "You want a list?"

"No, forget it." He didn't understand. She wasn't talking about taking care of her or picking up her dry cleaning. She was talking about *her*. She hugged herself, wishing for Mitch. "I was selfish and I'm sorry. That's all I can say."

"Let's put it behind us."

Stunned, she could only stare openmouthed at him. "Steve. Listen. I left you in the worst way possible and you're not even asking why. Don't you think there's something wrong with that?"

He sighed and pinched the bridge of his nose. "All right, why?"

"You don't even care, do you?"

"Of course I care," he said, his voice conveying the ultimate patience. "But I already know why."

She could not believe this. "And tell me, what are my reasons?"

"You were nervous. Plain and simple. You would have been fine as soon as you walked down the aisle. You were stressed out and overwhelmed because of all the wedding details. As soon as we were married, all the pressure would have been off and everything would have been fine. If you'd only stopped to think it through, I'd be on a beach in Hawaii instead of being forced to chase you down at some crappy diner in the middle of nowhere."

He didn't know the first thing about her—not the real her. That had been her fault for letting things go for so long. She tore the napkin in two. "It was more than nerves. I couldn't breathe. I was suffocating."

"It was a panic attack. With your history, you should know that."

She'd suffered the attacks the first year after the accident, and they weren't the same as what she had gone through on her wedding day. "No, you're wrong. And even if you're not, I don't think having a panic attack on your wedding day is a good sign."

"It happens all the time," he said, reasonably.

"Shouldn't I have been happy?"

"You were fine until that day."

"I wasn't. Every day, my anxiety got worse."

"If you were so distraught, why didn't you talk to me?"

It was the million-dollar question. If only she hadn't been so afraid, so worried about everyone else, she wouldn't have gotten into this mess in the first place. She'd been wrong and she owed him the truth. "I didn't think you'd listen."

"I always listen to you."

She shook her head. "No, that's the point. You don't."

"Give me one example." His lips formed a thin, hard line before he took a breath and seemed to visibly compose himself.

She could give him a hundred, but settled on the most compelling. "I told you I didn't want to get married."

"You needed a push," Steve said, the first threads of irritation lacing his tone.

She started shredding the napkin. "I specifically told you I wasn't ready. There were things I wanted to do, but you shrugged me off. You didn't listen. You pacified my feelings, then proposed to me a month later in front of God and everyone at my aunt and uncle's anniversary party. You called me up on a stage, got down on one knee, and gave a speech guaranteed to make every woman in the room cry."

He shook his head, staring at her as though completely dumbfounded. "I gave you a memorable proposal that women live for. How is that wrong?"

She balled up the ripped-to-pieces tissue. "You made it impossible for me to say no."

His brows furrowed as his jaw hardened into a stubborn line. "You had us stuck in dating hell, what did you expect me to do?"

"You emotionally manipulated me."

"No. I took control of the situation. What difference does six months or a year make?"

The temper she'd been containing for years rose to the surface. Through gritted teeth, she said, "The difference was I wasn't ready."

"We weren't getting any younger and you were stalling." He smoothed a hand over his blond hair. "I pushed you. So what?"

She closed her eyes and counted to five before opening them again. "So nothing. It's over. We're over."

His gaze narrowed, the blue glinting. "You'll have to do better than me nudging you down a path we were already on."

She blew out a breath and said softly, "I wasn't happy. Isn't that a compelling enough argument?"

"You should have come to me when you started having doubts. You know sometimes you get depressed."

She wanted to scream at him that she'd only been depressed when her father had died, but that wasn't the point. "And what if I'd come to you? Then what?"

"I could have fixed things."

With those five little words, everything about their relationship became crystal clear. He didn't love her any more than she loved him. He'd needed something to fix and she'd been broken. Only she was tired of the pattern and he still wanted to force her into the mold. "I don't want to be your project anymore."

"Don't be silly." A muscle ticked in his jaw.

"I don't think you even like me." Like most profound revelations, it was painfully obvious, once one was smacked in the face with the truth.

"That's preposterous. I love you."

"Name one thing you love about me."

His knuckles whitened as he clasped his hands tightly together. "You're acting crazy. I love everything about you."

"You can't do it, can you?"

"Of course I can. If I didn't love you, why did I stick with you all these years?"

"I don't know. You'll have to answer that for yourself." That was his job to figure out, but she knew it was true, deep down in the pit of her stomach.

"What are you saying?"

"I can't marry you. Not now. Not ever." She spoke the

words with so much conviction that they rang with a truth even Steve couldn't deny. "It's not your job to fix me anymore."

"I'm sure we can work this out," he said, but his voice had lost its strength and its smug certainty.

"No, we can't."

"Why?"

She met his gaze. "Because I don't want to."

All the background noise dimmed and the diner seemed to still as several long moments passed.

He lowered his eyes and stared down at the table.

"I'm tired of playing it safe," she said, the words gentle with compassion.

He gave a frown, followed by a twist of his lips. "You know better than anyone the danger in that statement."

It was the first mean thing he'd said to her, and it was like a stab in the heart. It rocked her to the very core, resonating with everything she had understood about herself since her dad had died.

But it didn't break her, didn't change her mind.

"I'm not afraid anymore." To her shock, she realized it was true.

"So that's it? No more discussion."

"I'm sorry."

He took a deep breath, slowly exhaling. "When are you coming home?"

"I don't know," she said, picking up another napkin and blotting under her lashes. "But it's no longer your concern."

"There's nothing I can do, is there?"

She looked into the eyes of the man who'd been a part of her life for so long that she couldn't remember a time without him, and she saw it: resignation. Acceptance.

A weight lifted from her chest and she spoke the words that would set them free. "There's nothing left to do but say good-bye."

Chapter Eighteen

Mitch watched Maddie walk out of Earl's with a tall, good-looking blond man.

The fiancé. Mitch didn't know what he'd been expecting, but it sure as hell wasn't the guy standing on the sidewalk not twenty feet away from him.

Her red hair blew in the breeze as she looked up at the man and nodded. The man frowned and raised a hand as if to touch her.

Mitch gripped the steering wheel so tightly that he was surprised it didn't shatter under the pressure. Raw, turbulent emotions rammed through him like the fiercest of storms, threatening to engulf him until he was all reaction and no logic.

The fiancé's hand dropped away.

Charlie's words came rushing back at him: *You never fucking learn.*

Mitch fought the urge to jump out of the car and break every bone in the guy's body. Possessive, almost feral, jealousy unlike anything he'd ever experienced before in his life locked around his throat and wouldn't let go.

Jesus. He was going to lose her.

The reality of the situation was like a punch in the gut.

She was only his until she wanted to leave. He had no claim on her—nothing real.

The fiancé turned away. Maddie watched him with an indescribable expression on her face as he walked around the corner and disappeared.

Despite the cold air blasting at him from the vents, Mitch's brow beaded with sweat. As soon as he'd gotten the call from Charlie, he'd rushed to the diner like a bat out of hell with the notion of rescuing her. Now he wasn't sure she'd welcome the intrusion.

He wasn't sure if she'd want him.

The insecurity made him so furious that he jumped out of the car, ran across the street, and grabbed her before he had time to even process his actions.

She swung around, blinked, and burst into tears.

Mitch gathered her up, cuddled her into his chest, and shuffled her into the car. A minute later they were on the road, but he experienced no sense of relief, no victory. How could he, with Maddie bawling her eyes out?

He wanted to comfort her, take her into his arms and tell her everything would be okay, but he had to get control of his emotions first.

So far, he was losing the fucking battle.

Panic, jealousy, and fear rammed through him like the most violent of storms. He managed a strained, "Princess, are you okay?"

"I did it," she said in a shaky voice. "It was hard, sad, and scary, but I did it."

Mitch took her hand, squeezing her fingers. He was afraid to hope, afraid to even breathe. "What did you do?"

"I said good-bye."

The completely irrational possessiveness burned in his lungs. Adrenaline still pumped in his veins, not caring whether the immediate threat was over. "Are you okay?"

"Yes," she said, still staring out the window. "I'm . . .

just . . . I don't know. It was almost half my life. And now it's over."

"I'm sorry." He pulled to a stop at Revival's only traffic light. "I hate that you're upset."

Maddie looked at him, her tear-streaked cheeks and watery gaze making her look beautiful and tragic. "I'm relieved."

The light turned green and he floored the gas pedal. Possessive, primal urges pulsed inside him, beating at his chest. At the first corner he saw, he jerked the car right and pulled onto the side street, swinging the car into the first available spot.

"What's wrong?" Her voice trembled.

He needed her. Right now.

Her eyes widened, her pink tongue darting out to wet her lips. She gave him a slight nod.

He lunged.

She met him halfway, their mouths coming together in a hard, brutal rush of lust that stunned him.

Pushed to the very edge of control, Mitch kissed her as though he were a starving man. He gripped the back of her neck. Slanting his lips to deepen the angle, thrusting his tongue into her mouth far too aggressively.

She groaned and curled her fingers into his shoulders, her nails biting into his skin despite the cotton separating them.

With a low, guttural sound, he yanked her T-shirt up and rubbed his thumb over her nipple through her bra. With no patience and zero finesse, he ripped the cup down and pinched and rolled the hard bud with a force that had her gasping.

He ripped away and sank his teeth into her neck, biting her, marking her.

She jerked against him.

He growled, covering her lips again with almost savage need. He took, demanded, fucked her mouth with his tongue and teeth. Impatient and fumbling, he pulled at the button on her shorts, sliding the zipper down. Their arms and elbows flailed and bumped. The horn went off as he smacked it with his elbow while stripping her shorts down her legs.

Frantic hands undid his jeans. His cock sprang free, and her hot fingers encircled his length. She stroked, and his balls pulled tight. He pushed her away, tearing his mouth from hers and sitting back against the seat. He gripped her waist, pulling her on top of him and positioning her legs over his thighs.

It was too fast, too rough, but he couldn't wait.

He grabbed her hips, lifted her up, and drove into her.

She cried out, forehead hitting his as she shifted to accommodate his size. A distant part of his brain warned him to slow down, but he couldn't. He thrust high, fingers digging into her hips and ass as he impaled her.

Harsh, ragged breathing filled the car. Her hands tore at his shirt. Their mouths fused together, almost fighting. Primal and primitive.

He tore away from her. "Mine."

"Yes," she whispered against his mouth.

"All mine." They came together in a fast, furious pounding of flesh. He looked down and watched his cock slide in and out of her, claiming his ownership.

Mine, mine, mine. The visceral violence of his emotions scared the shit of out of him, but he couldn't stop.

He slammed into her, almost brutal in his desire.

She met him stroke for stroke, increasing her pace to keep up with him, her lips parting in a gasp. "Oh, God."

"Say my name." His balls tightened, but he couldn't slow down. He needed to be closer.

Faster. Harder. Higher.

"Mitch," she whimpered, nipping his bottom lip and scratching his forearms with her nails.

He couldn't take her hard enough. Couldn't get close

enough. All of his thoughts dissolved into two words. More. Mine.

Her inner muscles clenched around his cock like a vice.

"Tell me." The words were practically a growl.

"What?"

"Tell me how much you want it." That primitive part of his brain demanded surrender, and he pushed harder than he would under normal circumstances.

"I want it. You. Please." The words were half moan and filled with need, sending feral satisfaction through his blood. She threw her head back, riding his cock like her life depended on it, and he loved every single second of it. "Mitch, please, I—"

"Are you mine?" The dominance was clear in the guttural tone of his voice.

"Yes," she said in a panting gasp, her muscles rippling along his erection in confirmation.

He reached up and grabbed her jaw, forcing their gazes to lock together. "You're damn right you are."

She came in a mad rush, and he thrust into her one last time, his orgasm pounding through him like a stampede. He emptied into her, coming so hard that his vision blurred and dimmed.

She collapsed against him.

His arms settled around her and he squeezed her tightly, trying to work air into his burning lungs. She nuzzled closely, panting for breath as their heated bodies pressed together.

He trailed his fingers over her bare lower back, loving how she shivered and trembled at his touch.

The car windows were fogged and he realized they were sitting somewhere less than private in broad daylight. He punched down the air conditioner.

She heaved a sigh. "Wow."

"Wow is an understatement."

She sat up, and when he met her eyes, she blushed. A

smile curved over his lips and he pushed a damp lock of hair behind her ear.

A subtle awkwardness permeated the thick air as the silence grew. What was there to say after sex like that? Sex that transcended time and place. Sex that hid nothing and revealed everything.

He trailed a thumb over her swollen lip. "Want to agree we'll talk about it later?"

Shoulders relaxing, she laughed. "Maybe that would be best."

He curled his hand around her throat, stroking the spot where he'd bitten her. It was red. It marked her, made her his.

She trailed a finger over his forearm, inspecting the damage she'd inflicted. "I, um, scratched you."

He kissed her. "Don't worry about it. I bit you, so I think we're even."

She flushed again and started to tug at her clothes.

He pulled out of the warm, wet haven of her body and froze. "Fuck."

"What?" she asked, tension clouding her features.

"I didn't wear a condom." He dragged a hand through his hair. "Goddamn it, it didn't even cross my mind. I never forget. Ever. I'm sorry, Maddie."

"Oh," she said, climbing off him and reaching to the floor to retrieve her abandoned shorts. "I'm on those birth control shots."

He wasn't relieved. He frowned. Why wasn't he relieved?

He cleared his throat and focused on zipping his jeans. "There's more than pregnancy to worry about these days."

She adjusted her bra, staring at the floor instead of looking at him. She shrugged. "I'm not worried."

He should give her some sort of lecture about safe sex, but damned if he had the energy. He was too fucking confused at the torrent of unnamed emotions storming through him. "Good, I'm not worried either. But I promise I'm safe."

"Me too," she mumbled.

Something he didn't want to think about gnawed at him. "We could get blood tests to put your mind at ease."

She fixed her shorts, fumbling with the button while she stared at the dashboard. "If you want."

Quiet ensued as they worked on putting themselves together. The air was still charged with tension as he put the car into gear and turned out onto the road. Needing to break the awkwardness, he grasped her hand and brought her fingers to his lips. "Let's not worry about it right now, all right?"

She stared out the window for several long moments before blowing out a breath and looking at him. "Are you worried about it?"

They weren't talking about sex without protection, and both of them knew it. Something had changed between them, something far too intense for two people who'd only known each other a short time. "Yeah, I am. You?"

"Yes," she said, but squeezed his hand all the same.

"We'll figure it out." Somehow. Although he didn't know how.

"Have—" Voice croaking, she cleared her throat. "Have you ever, um, done anything like that?"

"No." He glanced at her. They weren't talking about the act itself. "Never. That was the most intense fuck of my life."

Her expression eased, and she grinned. "You do have a way with words, don't you?"

The air lightened considerably, putting them once again on sure footing. He grinned back at her. "Princess, I talk like that because you like it."

She poked his thigh. "*You* like it. I go along."

He pulled up to a stop sign, checking in the rearview mirror to make sure there were no cars. He leaned over and nuzzled her neck, sliding his fingers down her shorts, sinking into her pussy, which was flooded with his come.

"What are you doing?" She grabbed his wrist, trying to pull him away even as her body quickened.

The pulse beating fast against his tongue didn't lie. He licked, scraping his teeth over her skin. Lifting his head, he whispered in her ear, "Tell me the truth, and I promise to put you over my knee and give you a proper spanking."

Inner muscles clenched and rippled along his fingers, and he laughed wickedly. "Oh, someone definitely likes that idea."

"You're the worst." She groaned and clutched the door handle as she rocked into his hand.

His cock hardened as he pumped into her hot, tight core. "Admit it—"

A horn blared and he reluctantly pulled away, but not before he planted a hard kiss on her lips. "You are in so much trouble when we get home."

She shivered, her eyes flirting up at him. "Drive."

He drove the next couple of blocks to the farmhouse, turning up the drive. The tires crunched over gravel, and he frowned to see an unwelcome car in the driveway.

He pulled behind the Mercedes and his stomach tightened. He glanced at the porch and flipped off the ignition. "Oh, hell."

"Who's that?" Maddie asked.

Jesus Christ, could anything else go wrong? "It's my mother."

Chapter Nineteen

"I don't want to meet your mother," Maddie said, completely horrified. She stared at the attractive older woman with champagne-blond hair, wearing a pale tan linen suit and standing on Mitch's porch.

Mitch laughed. "Yeah, well, today isn't exactly going as planned, is it?"

Maddie bit her lip. "I know. It's a mess. We didn't even get a chance to talk. . . ." She felt herself flush ten shades of scarlet as the images filled her mind of them, wild and abandoned in the front seat. "In the car."

Mitch tightened his grip on her hand. "I didn't give you much of a chance to do anything but get your brains fucked out."

With brows slamming together, she angled her head at the woman watching them from the porch. "Your mother."

"She can't hear me," he said almost absently as he contemplated the woman who'd given birth to him as though she were a stranger.

Neither mother nor son rushed to meet each other.

"Are you okay?" Maddie asked. It had been a stressful day, and she wasn't sure how much more either of them could take.

"Let's get this over with." His voice was like the hard blade of a knife.

Their fingers unlaced, and they exited the car. They walked around and he took her hand, striding up the stairs so quickly that she had to rush to keep pace. When they reached the top of the steps, he nodded to the older woman. "Mom, this is a surprise."

"Mitchell." She inclined her head. "I'm sorry for arriving unannounced, but you know your father. He's probably having my calls monitored."

Mitch smirked. "He's turned into a paranoid son of a bitch, hasn't he?"

Amber eyes that matched her son's flickered, then turned to rest on Maddie.

Mitch slid his arms around her. "Maddie Donovan, meet my mother, Charlotte Riley."

Maddie held out a hot, sweaty palm and said primly, "Mrs. Riley, it's a pleasure to meet you."

Charlotte's hand glanced over hers, polite but remote. "You too, dear."

Mitch hugged Maddie more tightly. "What can I do for you?"

Maddie cringed at his words and gave him a little nudge with his elbow. "I'm sure your mom has had a long ride. Maybe you should invite her in."

"Yes, thank you," Charlotte said, her expression warming a smidgen when her lips curved in the barest hint of a smile.

Mitch sighed and went to the door, tugging Maddie along as though she might try to run away if he let go. When they walked into the foyer, Maddie's gaze immediately fell on the mirror. She blanched.

She looked horrible. With flushed cheeks, rumpled clothes, and hair a rat's nest, she looked like she'd been doing, well, exactly what she had been doing. Unable to help herself, she examined her neck, and found a red spot, glowing like a neon sign, where Mitch had bit her. Pulling free from Mitch's grasp, Maddie fussed with her hair to hide the mark.

He threw his key on the accent table, the clang of metal against wood too loud in an already tense room. The three of them stood, warily watching each other while they waited for someone to break the ice.

It sure as hell wasn't going to be her. Maddie pressed her lips together as she fought the urge to babble.

Finally, Mitch put her out of her misery by pointing to a suitcase near his mother's expensive tan pumps. "Are you planning on staying?"

"May I?" Charlotte asked. Her tone was cool, but something flickered in the older woman's gaze. Something sad and hurt.

Why wouldn't she be? Her husband's alleged affair with another woman had been splashed over every media outlet in the modern world. Maddie's heart warmed in sympathy and she asked, "Do you want some lemonade? It's home-made."

Charlotte gave her a hesitant smile. "That would be lovely, dear."

Maddie practically ran to the kitchen, pulling out glasses and filling them with ice. She busied herself while Mitch and Charlotte walked through the swinging door to sit down at the table in stony silence.

The glass rattled as she placed the fresh lemonade in front of them and stared at the empty seat. She glanced at Mitch, smoothing her shorts. "I'm going to take a shower."

Mitch shook his head. "Sit."

She backed away. "Really, I'm a mess and I don't want to intrude."

Mitch scowled at the chair.

Maddie slid a glance at Mitch's mother.

"Please," Charlotte said, gesturing gracefully at the chair.

With a sigh, Maddie grabbed her glass and sat.

Mitch's shoulders relaxed and he turned his attention to his mother. "So, you're staying?"

"Is that all right?" she asked politely, as though they were strangers instead of family.

"Are you asking?" Mitch's long fingers encircled the glass.

An expression of longing flittered over Charlotte's expression before it smoothed over into a bland mask. "Yes, I'm asking. I need some peace as I work things out and didn't know where else to go."

"It's your house," Mitch said, his eyes filled with a coldness that was hard to reconcile with the man who'd practically incinerated her with heat not thirty minutes ago.

"Not anymore. You bought it from me fair and square, even though I insisted on giving it to you." She raised her glass and took a delicate sip.

Mitch rested his elbows on the table and gave his mom a hard-eyed stare.

Appalled, Maddie nudged his knee under the table, but he said nothing to put the older woman at ease. Maddie scowled at him, but when it was clear he wasn't going to speak, she turned a bright smile on Charlotte. "I'm sure Mitch would be happy for you to stay."

A deep sadness filled Charlotte's eyes. "Mitchell, I'm sorry."

Under the table, his leg slid next to Maddie's, pressing close as though seeking her comfort and warmth. "It's over. Forget it."

"I was wrong." The older woman's long, tapered fingers clasped tightly in front of her.

"Doesn't matter," Mitch said, his tone indicating that it certainly did.

Whatever had happened was a private and painful matter,

and as curious as Maddie was, she could no longer sit here and listen. Maddie shifted in her chair. "I, um, should go—"

Mitch's hand shot out and gripped her wrist. To the casual observer, his tanned fingers entwined over her pale skin looked loose, light—a gentle hold between lovers. Except it was like a vice, making it impossible to get away without struggling out of his grasp.

She risked a glance at his mom. Charlotte stared at her son's hand, then raised her gaze to meet Maddie's. The questions were clear under the Junior League mask of banality.

Maddie took a deep breath. Okay, they didn't want her to go. Maddie settled in the chair, prepared to wait out the uncomfortable conversation. Mitch loosened his hold but didn't release her.

Mitch's chin jutted out. "How long will you be staying?"

"I don't know." Charlotte's eyes slid away. "I don't want your father to know where I am."

Mitch laughed, a harsh bitter sound. "God knows he'll never look for you here."

Charlotte pressed the tips of her fingers to her lips, and Maddie thought she detected the barest tremble.

"So, did he do it?" Mitch asked.

"I don't know." Charlotte looked over her son's shoulder and out the window. "He says it was some crazy setup."

"For what?" Mitch's fingers stroked Maddie's inner wrist.

"For money, what else?" The older woman pressed a hand to her chest. "He wants me to pay her."

Mitch shook his head. "That's crazy. The pictures are already out there, how much more damage can she do?"

"Those pictures are only the tip of the iceberg."

"Start from the beginning, and don't leave anything out." The voice he used was one Maddie had never heard before, and in that moment, she had no trouble picturing him as a shark of a lawyer: ruthless and powerful.

Nothing like the man who'd made love to her like she was his salvation.

"She said the media must have been tipped because she wasn't going to release anything until she'd made her demands. An unfortunate coincidence, if you will. If we pay her, she'll go on record and say the picture was a misunderstanding. Yes, his reputation will be tarnished, but not unrecoverable. If we don't pay, she has other pictures that are much, much worse."

"Have you seen them?" Mitch let go of Maddie. He sat forward, resting his elbows on the table.

She nodded, the dipping corners of her mouth the only evidence of her distress. "They're very damaging."

"How'd he explain those?"

"He can't. He says she called because she had insider information on a senator opposing one of his bills. He invited her to his room to discuss the matter. They had a drink and it was the last thing he remembers until the next morning."

Mitch's eyes narrowed. "Convenient. What did the pictures look like?"

"You can't see his eyes, he's mostly in profile. It's hard to tell if he's awake or not." She shook her head. "Not that the papers will care about those details."

"Do you believe him?" Mitch asked.

Charlotte's expression crumpled for a split second before she regained her composure. "I don't know. She's young and very beautiful. Maybe this time he gave in to temptation."

Mitch got up from the table and walked to the sink, peering out into the backyard for a good two minutes before turning back. The calculation was clear in the set of his jaw and glint in his eyes. "How much does she want?"

"A million," Charlotte said, stating the number as though she were rattling off an item on her grocery list.

Maddie tensed.

"That's a lot for a senator caught fucking his intern," Mitch said in a hard tone.

"Mitchell!" Charlotte blanched, her gaze fluttering down.

"What else?" Mitch asked. "There's got to be more to this story."

Charlotte reached for a napkin in the middle of the table and started to wipe an invisible spot like Lady Macbeth.

"Spit it out." Mitch's voice was so cold that it sent ice water splashing through Maddie's veins.

His mother blinked, all the color draining from her face. "It seems she's uncovered the whole sordid story."

"What. Story." Mitch fired the words like torpedoes.

"She knows what you did."

Maddie's stomach dropped, and her eyes flew to Mitch's. He raked a hand through his hair. "Son of a bitch."

"What?" Maddie spoke for the first time, unable to stop the word from flying from her mouth.

Charlotte eyed her son as though looking for direction.

Mitch crossed his arms and shook his head.

"Mitch?" Blood rushed through Maddie's ears. She knew something bad was going down.

He gripped the counter with both hands and leaned back. If he was trying to look casual, he failed miserably. He blew out a long breath. "I didn't tell you the whole story the other night."

"And what is the whole story?" Maddie asked, forgetting all about his mother sitting there, watching them.

"When I was trying to find evidence to clear my name I hired an MIT hacker friend of mine to break into Thomas's files. We didn't find anything, but we stumbled across something else, a deal Thomas and my father had done. A highly illegal deal that would ruin them." Mitch met her stunned gaze. "I destroyed the evidence."

Maddie turned back to Charlotte, still not making the connection.

"Somehow, she found out, and if I don't pay her she'll go public," Charlotte said, suddenly looking twenty years older. "Not only with the affair, but with details about the deal. Somehow she knows what Mitchell did to save his father's career. A sordid Riley family exposé, if you will."

Mitch's expression shuttered over into a cold, blank mask. "How could she possibly know?"

"We don't know," Charlotte said, pressing her lips together for a moment before continuing. "But she provided enough details to confirm she's not lying."

She pressed a perfectly manicured hand to her chest. "If it was only your father, I'd let him clean up his own mess, but I failed you once and I don't want to fail you again. It's not too late for you. In my heart, I know it. I haven't always been a good mother, but I still have a chance to change that. I can't let her bring you down with him. Not again. Not after what you sacrificed the last time."

The headache started in the back of his skull and worked its way over Mitch's forehead.

Jesus, could this day get any worse?

He dragged his fingers through his hair as he stared at the river meandering slowly downstream. He'd bailed after his mother's dramatic announcement, needing time alone to think and ponder the state of his meager future.

He sucked in the humid summer air, picked up a stray pebble, and tossed it into the water. It plunked into the center, sending ripples through the smooth surface.

Obstruction of justice was tricky; the sentence ranged anywhere from fines to jail time. The case was old, half of the parties were dead, and the spotlight would be on his father, not him. While it was too hard to predict the penalty of his actions, one thing was certain: he'd be disbarred.

There'd be no getting around that.

The word twisted in his gut like a knife. It shouldn't matter. He didn't practice anymore.

But it did.

To realize he harbored hope was like a kick in the gut. All this time he'd convinced himself that he didn't give a shit about his nonexistent career. But it was a lie. Complete bullshit. Deep down, hidden where he wouldn't have to examine it, he'd wanted to start again. He hadn't avoided Luke's case out of some misguided sense of honor. He'd avoided it so he wouldn't have to confront the truth. That he had hope.

It was Maddie's fault. Until she'd come along, slipping past his guard, he'd been content with the numbness. Content to believe he didn't care about anything or anyone. He'd been fine, happy even, drifting along in oblivion. But then she'd walked into that shithole bar he hated and made him remember what it was like to be alive.

And hope had snuck in.

He skipped another rock into the river, watching the smooth gray pebble bounce over the water's surface before sinking to the bottom below.

This time, losing everything would be worse. Back in Chicago, he'd had a lifestyle but not a life. Sure, people had surrounded him, but no one had *known* him, not even Sara. Yes, they'd had sex and passion, but despite the stories they'd told each other, they'd never really been in love. It had been a game. They'd been two bored, unfulfilled people who had needed the challenge and lure of the forbidden to add excitement to their lives. She'd never crawled inside him.

Not like Maddie.

"Here, I brought you a drink." Maddie's soft voice came from behind him as though he'd conjured her, blowing over him like a soft summer breeze—a calm, soothing presence in the increasing chaos of his life.

He peered at her over his shoulder and his breath lodged in his chest. Deep red hair blazed like licks of fire in the early evening sun as she smiled down at him. Unnamed emotions pressed in the corner of his mind, wanting to take hold and be named.

He resisted. It was too much, too fast.

She pushed the pale glass of lemonade toward him. "I spiked it with vodka."

He laughed, surprised he still could. "Thanks, Princess.

She sat next to him on the blanket, and he took the drink, downing half of it in one gulp. It was sweet and tart, with a hint of a kick lurking underneath, just like Maddie.

She dropped her head onto his shoulder and her warm little body snuggled close.

"Wait." Mitch placed the glass carefully on the grass and lay down. With a tug on her wrist, he pulled her next to him.

The scent of her honey-and-almond shampoo wafted up as her long hair brushed over his skin. She nuzzled close, sliding one smooth thigh over his. His fingers trailed a path over her arms, and he smiled in pleasure when goose bumps broke over her skin, despite the heat. He took a slow breath and the knot that had been coiled tight in his chest unraveled as her small frame curled close. He kept up his rhythmic stroking. Up and down, over and over, until the turbulence eased from his mind. She burrowed more deeply, tracing a path over his stomach. She said nothing, asked no questions and shot no probing glances. In her silence, in her complete understanding of what he needed, another barrier crumbled from between them.

A bone-deep satisfaction and an odd sort of contentment loosened his muscles. His body relaxed. With Maddie lying beside him under the trees, the late afternoon sun peeking through the leaves, and the sound of the river trickling downstream, his eyelids grew heavy and closed.

Some time later, he drifted back to consciousness to find her propped on one elbow, watching him. He blinked, bringing her into crisp focus. "Did I fall asleep?"

She nodded. "You were out like a light."

He dragged a hand through his hair. "I'm sorry."

"Don't be," she said, trailing a finger over his jaw. "I could watch you for hours."

Warmed by the sun and dazed from his nap, he felt lazy, like he never wanted to move again. He yawned. "I'm sure you'd get bored eventually, Princess."

"No way. You're an artist's dream. I hope you don't mind." She reached behind her and picked up a piece of paper, which she held out to him.

He took the sheet and was instantly awake.

To his embarrassment, his throat grew so tight he was unable to speak. She'd drawn him in pencil. His lashes brushed his cheeks as he'd slept. The crisp, strong lines accentuated his jaw and bone structure. Somehow, even in black and white with shades of gray, she'd managed to show the cast of the sun on his body, making it look as if he were lit from above. It was uncanny. Her talent was unmistakable.

He cleared the lump sitting behind his Adam's apple. "Is this how you see me?"

She traced a path over the scrolls of his tattoo. "I see you as you really are."

He shook his head, unable to think of anything profound. "You are incredibly gifted."

She plucked the paper from his fingers and scrutinized it with narrowed eyes. "I can see the flaws."

"I can't."

She put the paper down. "It's the first thing I've drawn since my dad died. I'm rusty."

"I'm honored." The words were grossly inadequate; he was in awe. "But why are you wasting your talent?"

She frowned, shrugging. "I haven't wanted to."

He brushed a stray lock of hair behind her ear. "Why?"

"I guess after the accident," she said, her chin trembling enough to tell him that she held back tears, "I didn't feel like I deserved it. Quitting was my penance. Silly, I know, but I was a teenager. I think my rationale was that he loved that about me, so it was only right it died with him."

"But why would you think he'd want you to abandon something you're so good at?" He'd never met her father, but he'd learned enough about him from Maddie to know that he'd never want his child to waste such a gift.

She swallowed, and her eyes closed momentarily before her lashes lifted once again. "He's dead because of me."

"Maddie, it was a car accident. It wasn't your fault."

"I was driving."

Shit. He should have guessed. All that guilt, all the bending over backward to make everyone happy. It made perfect sense, but he'd never put two and two together.

The first tear slid down her cheek. "I had my learner's permit, and I wanted to drive so badly. He was working. He didn't want to go. But I wouldn't stop." She gave a broken sob. "I knew if I kept asking I'd get my way."

Mitch moved to take her in his arms, but she jerked back, shaking her head. "No."

He lay back down and didn't speak.

She drew in a shaky breath. "Sometimes I wake up with the sound of the dangling keys echoing in my ears. The memory of how I waved them in front of his face burned in my brain. I still can see his exact expression as he put down his pen, sighed, and got up from his desk. Do you have any idea how many times I've played that scene in my head? How many times I wished I'd taken no for an answer?"

Her shoulders shook as she began to cry in earnest. Mitch

wanted desperately to comfort her, but he didn't reach for her again.

She brushed away the tears with an angry swipe. "I wanted to go to the store to get lip gloss. It was the only makeup my mom let me wear. I had a date with Steve that night. I was driving and laughing. I didn't like the song on the radio, and I went to change the station. He warned me to pay attention, but I kept flipping. He got mad and yelled at me, pushing my hand away. I looked down, only for a second, but it was too late. I ran a stop sign and a truck plowed into us. Next thing I knew, I was waking up in a hospital room and my whole life had changed."

She sat up, her movements angry and jerky. "And you know what the worst part of it was?"

"What?" Mitch said, feeling sick to his stomach for what she'd suffered.

"Everyone felt sorry for me. So sorry. God, I hated it. Hated them. They looked at me with pity in their eyes and each time I died a bit more inside. I'd ruined their lives. I changed them forever. And *they* feel sorry for *me*."

"Maddie," Mitch said, putting his palm over her knee and rubbing.

She buried her head in her hands. "They never say it, never let on, but every time they look at me they have to think about what I did to them. They have to hate me."

"No." He'd never met her family, but of this he was sure. Their closeness and unity was clear in the way she talked about them. He knew estranged or strained families, and the Donovans weren't like them. "They don't, I promise you."

She looked at him, her eyes watery and her nose red. "I hate me. Why wouldn't they hate me too?"

Not caring if she protested, he picked her up and put her on his lap, wrapping his arms around her. He swayed back and forth, the gentle rocking motion meant to soothe away a pain that he couldn't even begin to erase. "Maddie, you were a kid. Every teenager has worn their parent down. The only difference is that you had horrific, irreversible consequences. I'm sorry—I wish there was something I could do to change that for you—but since I can't, I can only promise your dad would hate for you to blame yourself like this. For you to let it eat you up inside."

"I know that here." She pointed to her head before placing her hand over her heart. "But it's hard to believe here."

He lifted her chin and brushed a soft kiss against her lips. "What can I do to make you believe?"

"I don't know," she said. "But I'm working on it."

"I'm sorry, Maddie."

"I miss him." She rested her cheek on his shoulder.

He rubbed slow circles over her back. "I know you do."

She quieted, relaxing into his hold. "You help."

"I'm glad," he said. "What else can I do?"

She raised her watery gaze to meet his, and her eyes were so impossibly green, so full of something he didn't want to name, that he sucked in a breath. "Fight."

Chapter Twenty

In the dead of night, Mitch stared out the bedroom window. It had been a grueling day. He should be exhausted, but sleep eluded him. He dragged his fingers roughly through his hair and peered over his shoulder at the woman sleeping in his bed. The full moon streamed in, casting Maddie in its white, iridescent light. With her hair fanning out onto the pillow, she looked serene, so peaceful that it was hard to believe she'd cried in his arms until she'd had no more tears left.

Embracing the storm of her emotions that had been pent up since her father's death had seemed to release something inside her. When she'd emerged on the other side, her expression had held a softness that hadn't been there before. But her eyes held the biggest change: they'd been filled with a steely, determined certainty. Not only an elemental understanding of the path ahead of her, but a desire to walk it.

He'd known what needed to be done, what he could no longer ignore. He turned away from the image Maddie presented to stare once again out the window.

It was time to put hope away.

Chapter Twenty-One

The following morning, Maddie strolled into the kitchen feeling like a new woman. Something had happened last night, something years of therapy hadn't been able to accomplish: She was finally free.

"Good morning, dear." Charlotte's cool voice sounded from behind her.

Maddie almost jumped out of her skin, then spun around. "Mrs. Riley."

"Please, call me Charlotte." The older woman was already dressed immaculately in a white linen, button-down top complete with pearls. "Mitchell left to do some errands. He'll be back shortly."

Maddie tucked a stray lock of hair behind her ear and straightened. There was something about Mitch's mother that inspired good posture.

Charlotte pointed to one of the empty chairs. "Please sit." The words were quiet and unassuming, but the subtle command lurked right under the surface. Like mother, like son.

Maddie didn't even think to protest. She slid into the seat across from the older woman. An uncomfortable silence filled the room as they looked at each other.

Charlotte traced a path around her coffee cup and offered Maddie a small, polite smile.

Figuring that was an invitation to speak, she cleared her throat. "Did you sleep well?"

"Yes, thank you." The older woman raised a cup to her lips and took a dainty sip, pinky raised. Impressive.

Maddie pressed her lips together, desperate to fill the space with small talk, but her mind was a complete blank. All she could think about were the elephants in the room. Finally, she gave up and opted for sincere. "Are you doing okay, Mrs. Riley? Is there anything I can do?"

"Charlotte." Cool, golden eyes the exact same shade as her son's met hers. "You mean, for a woman whose family is in ruins?"

Maddie swallowed. So they were jumping off into the deep end. "Yes."

"I'm as well as can be expected. I had a difficult time sleeping, and this house is filled with so many memories of a happier time. I miss my mother. She was wonderful."

"Mitch has told me a lot about her and the summers he spent here as a child."

"A grandmother isn't supposed to have favorites and she'd never admit it to a soul, but she had a special soft spot for Mitchell."

Maddie raised her eyes to the heavens and said a prayer of thanks to Mitch's grandmother. She blinked, surprised. It was the first prayer of gratitude she'd given in a long time.

Realizing Charlotte watched her, she said, "I'm sorry for your loss. She sounds like a very special woman."

"Thank you, dear," Charlotte said, folding her hands neatly in front of her. Her expression shifted from sorrow to scrutiny. "May I ask how you met my son?"

Maddie had no intention of divulging the whole story. Simplicity was best. "I met him at the bar."

"What were you doing in that dreadful place?"

This part was easy, and Maddie relaxed fractionally. "I was lost. My car broke down and the bar was the first place I came to."

Charlotte nodded. "So you're not from around here?"

"No, I'm from Chicago."

"I see. What brought you here?" Somehow the older woman managed to make her questions sound like polite chitchat instead of the interrogation they really were.

The truth screamed in her head. She shrugged. "I ran away from home."

A small smile stole onto Charlotte's lips. "Aren't you a little old for that?"

"Yes, but sometimes you have no choice but to run for your own sanity." With the similarities too obvious to ignore, Maddie let the words hang in the air.

The smile died, and Charlotte's face once again clouded over. "You must think we're a dreadful lot."

"No, not at all." Maddie didn't know what to think of the Rileys, but who was she to judge? Things weren't always as straightforward as they seemed.

"I'm a horrible mother," Charlotte said, almost absently. "I don't even have a good excuse. I got used to the politeness. I got used to being on guard, until I was cut off from my own children. My mother would be so disappointed. She was married to my father for sixty years and never let that world change her."

Maddie softened toward the other woman. She was clearly hurting. "You don't have to explain yourself. It's not like we plan these things out."

Charlotte shook her head and pressed her fingertips to her lips as though trying to press the words back in. "It's ironic. I married Nathaniel because he was nothing like the boys I grew up with."

Not knowing what to say, Maddie kept quiet.

Charlotte's hands fluttered to her neck, where she sought

out the pearls and twisted. The fine lines, etched with strain and worry, made her look older than she'd appeared yesterday. Suddenly, as though realizing she was mangling the necklace, she released the beads and her hands disappeared under the table. "We met in college. He was a scholarship student and filled with all these grand ideas. He was all raw energy and vitality, and he swept me off my feet."

Maddie nodded. "I've seen him speak. He's very compelling."

"Yes, he is." With a sly glance, Charlotte's lips quirked. "Mitchell is the spitting image of his father."

A surprised laugh bubbled from Maddie, and a hot flush crawled up her throat. "Yes, well, that does explain a lot."

"Indeed," Charlotte said properly.

Maddie grinned, but before she could say anything else, the back door opened and Mitch walked in. His gaze shifted back and forth, narrowing on his mother before resting on Maddie. "Morning, Princess."

Despite the tone, the fine hairs raised on the back of her neck. His eyes, normally warm when they looked at her, were as flat as dull pennies.

He nodded at Charlotte. "Good morning. Did you sleep well?"

"Fine, thank you." A mask of formal politeness slid over Charlotte, leaving behind no trace of the woman Maddie had been talking to.

Mitch propped his hips against the counter and crossed his arms. "Since you're both here, we need to talk about the situation. I've given this a lot of thought and see only one option: you cannot pay her."

"But—" Charlotte began, but Mitch held up his hand.

"Everyone knows blackmailers come back. The best thing to do is let the chips fall where they may."

Horrified, Maddie could only stare at him. "There has to be another way."

"There's not," Mitch said, with no inflection in his voice.

"No, Mitchell," Charlotte said, shaking her head. "You'll be disbarred."

"Not your problem."

"It is. You're in this situation because of him."

Mitch's jaw hardened, turning stubborn. "No. I'm in this situation because I was arrogant and stupid. Now it's time to pay."

Charlotte's chin began a fine tremble. "The price is too high."

"That's the thing about mistakes: you never really know what they'll cost you." His gaze flickered to Maddie.

The parallels weren't lost on her. Still, his mother was right: there had to be another way, one they hadn't thought of yet.

Before she could speak, Charlotte stood and turned toward her son. "You were never convicted, you never even went to trial, and there's no reason you can't go back to practicing."

"The point is moot," Mitch said. "It's too late."

"I'm paying." Charlotte's voice took on a stubborn edge. "I can afford it."

"You are not." Mitch straightened to his full six-three as though he could force his will by sheer size.

No. This was wrong. All wrong. He was supposed to fight for his future, not give up.

Maddie snapped out of her stunned silence and turned to Mitch's mother. "Could I have a moment alone with Mitch, please?"

Charlotte frowned and pointed to Mitch. "This is non-negotiable."

Mitch's face turned stony. "I'll expose her myself if I have to."

Mother and son squared off, and Maddie placed a hand on Charlotte's arm. "Just let me talk to him."

"All right, dear." Charlotte gave a slight nod, then turned and strode gracefully from the room.

His posture a rigid, inflexible line, Mitch scowled. "I leave you alone for five minutes and you've already gone over to her side?"

Maddie's head snapped back at his accusatory tone. "No, I'm on your side. But I don't see the point in being rash."

"There's no other way."

"How do you know? You don't even have all the facts."

"What facts, Maddie?" His hands clenched, and his black tattoo rippled as his muscles flexed. "She has to have proof. Only four people besides myself know about the evidence. Thomas is dead. My parents and sister sure as hell aren't going to set the record straight."

"What about the guy who hacked the system?"

Mitch shook his head. "No."

"How do you know?" Maddie demanded, her frustration level rising.

"Because I got the guy's brother off on a fraud charge."

"But—"

"It's not him, Maddie." It was plainly not open to discussion.

Maddie's shoulder slumped. "So you're giving up?"

"No." His arms crossed again and it felt like the shut-out it was. "I'm getting out from under their thumb. I don't want to live like this anymore, Maddie."

"Isn't throwing away any chance of a career to spite your father still living by his rules?"

His jaw tightened, and Maddie realized that he contained a healthy dose of rage. "What career?"

If she were smart, she'd back down. He was being unreasonable and not thinking things through. But today she was more brave than smart. "What about Luke's case? I don't think the people of Revival care about your past as much as you do. You could have a future here."

A muscle ticked in his jaw. "I gave the files back to Tommy this morning."

"You did what?" Maddie stood up from the table, suddenly furious.

"I've made my decision and that's final." He drew a familiar set of keys out of the pocket of his jeans and held them out to her.

Her heart slammed against her ribs as a steady, irate temper flared inside her. "What are those?"

"Your car keys."

It was like a slap in the face.

When she didn't reach out and take them, he tossed them on the counter, the metal making a too-loud clatter against the white and blue ceramic.

"I paid Tommy two grand to stall the repairs, and to buy Mary Beth's silence I had to take Luke's case."

She clenched her hands into fists. "Why?"

His jaw jutted, making him look impossibly stubborn. "I wanted to keep you here and I wasn't above using underhanded tactics to get what I wanted."

"That's not," she said through gritted teeth, "what I meant. Why are you doing this now?"

His expression hardened, and he looked remote. Unreachable. "I'm doing the right thing."

Anger, the white-hot kind she'd shied away from for years, filled her. But this time, instead of repressing, she unleashed the fury. "You coward!"

"I am not being a coward," he said, his voice rising for the first time.

"What the hell do you call it?"

"Setting the record straight."

She stared at him, unable to process the turn of events. She met his stormy gaze. "Liar."

"I'm coming clean with the truth, Maddie." His tone was a rough scrape over her nerves.

"That's bullshit!" she yelled, taking two steps to stand in front of him. Even though he towered over her, she jabbed him in the chest with her finger. "You're so scared to take a risk, so sure you're going to get screwed over, that you'd rather set up the failure yourself than roll the dice."

He grabbed her wrist and wrenched it away. "You don't know the first thing about it."

"Then why did you pick right now to give me those keys?"

"Because, goddamn it." His golden eyes flashed. "I don't want you to stay because you've got no fucking choice."

All of her anger deflated. She said softly, "Mitch."

He dropped her hand and stepped away, moving around her to walk to the back door. He peered over his shoulder, his golden eyes distant and resigned. "I've got things to take care of. I'll be back later."

With that, he walked out.

He was shutting her out, both literally and figuratively.

She stood in the empty kitchen, staring at the closed door. His desertion signaled everything wrong with her life and his. But she wasn't going back. Never again was she going to curl into a ball and roll over.

Screw that.

If Mitch Riley wouldn't fight for himself, she'd damn well do it for him.

Chapter Twenty-Two

Mitch sat in the back booth of his crappy bar and took another swallow of beer. His fifth. The alcohol had done nothing to quell the anger burning a hole in his stomach.

"Just hear her out." Across from him, a calm Sam spoke, using the casual tone that grated on Mitch's every last nerve.

"What is she up to?" Mitch narrowed his eyes. God, this day had gone to shit. After his fight with Maddie, he'd come here and spent the day in his dark, miserable office scouring the Internet and obscure legal references for ideas on how to handle the aftermath of his father's scandal.

It had been depressing business that had only increased his bad mood. Maddie's escapades around town were the icing on the cake.

"Don't worry about it." Sam scrubbed a hand over his blond-stubbled jaw.

"Fuck you, Sam." Mitch had had about enough of his vague, cryptic shit. He slammed the bottle on the table much harder than he should have, and foam spilled over the top. "I'm not in the mood."

Sam shrugged and returned to the paperwork in front of him. "All right, then."

Several minutes passed and Mitch waited for the ragged

edges of his frustration to melt away, but it didn't happen. If anything, without Sam to snap at, his aggravation increased.

Hell, after this morning, he'd half expected her to high-tail it out of town, but as usual, she hadn't done what he expected. Instead, she'd made her way from one end of the town to the other—stopping at the garage, visiting Charlie at the police station, and, strangest of all, taking his mother to buy flowers.

She was getting into trouble. He could feel it.

Sam rifled through papers, the sound distracting Mitch from his thoughts. Mitch glowered at the invoices and blurted, "I hate this place. Every time I step in here, I want to hit something."

Sam nodded. "Yeah, I know."

"I think we should consider a partnership," Mitch said. Sam did half the shit anyway.

Sam cocked his head to the side and studied Mitch in that annoying way he had. "Things will be clearer after every-thing goes down."

Logic dictated that he shouldn't believe in premonitions, but he'd given up on that when he was twelve and Sam warned him not to play baseball one summer's day. Mitch hadn't listened and had ended up with broken arm, ruining the rest of his summer. "What's going on?"

"I thought you weren't in the mood," Sam answered with a smirk.

Mitch practically growled.

Sam held up his hands in surrender. "All right, this is what I'll tell you: it's supposed to be this way."

"What the hell does that mean?"

"You need to let it play out," Sam said, getting a faraway look on his face. "Stop trying to control everything."

Control? Fuck. His hand tightened on his glass, threaten-ing to shatter it to pieces. He had control over nothing. "What good are you if you won't tell me anything concrete?"

Sam shrugged. "Sometimes things need to play out a certain way, and this is one of those times."

Mitch couldn't help rolling his eyes, but Sam kept talking, ignoring the sarcasm.

"You're getting in the way, stopping the natural progression. If you knew the game, you'd only make it worse."

"What the fuck is that supposed to mean?" His aggravation grew by leaps and bounds. How was this helpful?

"It means I'm not going to tell you shit, because if I do, you'll screw it the hell up." Sam peered at him, his blue eyes knowing and filled with an inner understanding that eluded the rest of them. "Despite being an asshole at the moment, it's time for you to have some happiness, but that won't happen until you give in."

Happiness seemed too far out of reach to be a tangible outcome. And how could Sam say this was his fault? What bullshit. His head pounded along with the too-fast beating of his heart. The panic he'd kept at bay by immersing himself in research all day threatened to boil over. He felt completely helpless, with no clue which way to turn.

Sam chuckled. "You're not supposed to, dickhead."

Startled out of his tumultuous thoughts, Mitch blinked. "What?"

"The path is never clear to the one who's on it."

Mitch snorted and took a sip of his beer. "Where you do get this stuff? A fortune cookie?"

"Nah, I get them off the Internet." Sam grinned. "There's a list."

Mitch laughed, a hard bark. "Well it's annoying as fuck."

"That's why I do it." Sam went back to looking at his paperwork.

Silence descended over the table once again, and Mitch watched the Cubs lose while Sam did whatever it was he did.

Mitch downed the rest of his beer and shook his head,

admitting what he'd known deep down since the scandal broke. "It's not going to work out."

"It depends on you," Sam said, not looking up.

"How does it depend on me?" Mitch asked the question but he didn't expect an answer.

"Stop fighting it and you'll find out."

Sorry he'd even asked, Mitch slid from the booth and walked to the bar to grab another bottle of beer.

A hand clamped over Maddie's mouth, jolting her awake in an instant. With her heart pounding so hard she could hear it in her ears, the strangled scream died in her throat. A large figure loomed over her. She gripped the hand at her mouth, but it wouldn't budge.

"Maddie, it's me." Mitch's whispered voice had her going limp with relief.

He let her go, and she sucked air into her burning lungs, willing her heartbeat to slow. "You scared me."

"Sorry." The word was gruff and raw. "I didn't want you to scream."

With her vision adjusting to the darkness, she said, "You left me."

"I know."

She wanted to be mad, to work up some righteous indignation, but she couldn't. Every time she remembered that look on his face, it died away. She slid up the back of the headboard. "I stayed."

"Good." He stripped off his shirt and undid the button of his jeans. "I need you. Now."

"What—"

"Later." His tone was sharp.

Maddie reared back. She opened her mouth to speak, but before she could, he grabbed a handful of her nightshirt, yanked her to him, and covered her lips with his.

She gasped in surprise, and he took full advantage, angling his head to devour her like a starving man. Her thoughts scattered, fragmenting into a million little pieces as his kiss consumed her with raw, unchecked intensity.

He tore away. Teeth scraped along her jaw and over her neck. Pleasure throbbed between her legs as he nipped and licked.

She should stop him or slow him down so they could talk, but then he bit her throat, right over her pounding pulse, and she lost her ambition to do anything but sink into him.

He ripped the nightshirt over her head. With rough hands, he cupped her sex, rubbing his fingers over her cotton-covered clitoris. She moaned, slithering down the headboard and onto the mattress, parting her thighs to give him better access.

He growled, a low sound from deep in his throat. He grabbed the strings that held her panties together on either side of her hips and ripped, leaving her bare.

She started to pant when he stroked his fingers through her moist folds. God, she was so wet. So hot.

This was wrong. They had important things to say. They needed to talk.

His thumb brushed the bundle of nerves, and she bowed off the bed. "Mitch."

He delivered a hard, almost punishing kiss, then pulled away to grip her chin. Her eyes fluttered open to meet his stark gaze.

"Are you going to tell me what you've been doing today?"

She blinked, fighting her way back from the drugging lust to focus on his question. "Errands." It was not a complete lie; they were errands. Kind of.

He got on the bed and straddled her naked body, making her very aware of her vulnerable position while he was fully clothed. "What were you doing at Charlie's?"

She couldn't tell him the truth.

"I'm waiting." Mitch's voice was like the blade of a knife.

"I got a parking ticket." It was her first lie, but he'd lied too, so they were even.

"You're lying." He shook his head, dropping his hand from her chin. "And you know what? Right now, I don't even care. Right now, all I care about is sinking into that hot, tight pussy of yours so I can fuck the hell out of you."

Instinct warned her to step back. To stop this and force them to deal with everything left unspoken between them, but she couldn't. She needed to wait until she could answer his questions. Then, maybe, he'd understand.

Instead, she followed his lead and reached for him. "Yes, please."

The following morning, after Mitch had finally satiated his desire to claim Maddie in every physical way possible and become saner, he asked Maddie again about the day before. Like the night before, she refused to comment. Instead, she looked guilty and avoided the questions by giving his mother her undivided attention.

Mitch had no choice but to take matters into his own hands.

The first stop on the list had been Gracie, who'd been coy, full of smiles, and ultimately unhelpful. Sam had been there, watching him in that speculative way of his, probably filled with some mystical bullshit that would only confound Mitch. Gracie had pushed him out the door with a plate full of pink frosted cupcakes and a "Have a nice day."

Now, he opened the door to Tommy's garage and spotted the mechanic sitting in his glass-enclosed office with his attention fixed on a computer screen. Mitch scanned the rest of the place, relieved that Mary Beth was not in sight. Good.

Tommy was always more forthcoming when his wife wasn't around. He pushed his way into the office without knocking, and Tommy whirled around.

When he saw Mitch, his mile-wide shoulders relaxed. "Hey."

Mitch didn't see the point of preamble. "I heard Maddie came for a visit yesterday."

"That's right," Tommy said, returning to the computer screen with rapt attention.

"Why?"

Several seconds ticked by. "To pay her bill."

"I already paid you." The trained lawyer skills that he'd abandoned long ago stirred. He crossed his arms.

Tommy scratched his head, his face glowing slightly from the monitor. "Yeah, that's what I told her."

"And?" Mitch pressed.

The chair under Tommy creaked as he swiveled back and forth. "End of story."

"I don't buy it."

"You don't have to." The female voice behind Mitch made his stomach sink.

Mary Beth skirted around him, putting her hand on her husband's shoulder. "She came to pay her bill, we told her you'd already taken care of it, and she left."

Mary Beth's cool blue eyes were implacable, unreadable. Mitch felt like a dog whose fur had been rubbed the wrong way. "What are you hiding?"

She smiled, a bright, cheery expression. "Nothing, but for the record, Counselor, I told her how you bailed on Luke's case."

Mitch ground his teeth and spat, "I didn't bail. I'm doing the right thing."

"Ha! By being a coward."

There was that fucking word again.

"Shit!" Mitch dragged a hand through his hair. Why was

this concept so hard for everyone to grasp? "Do you want your nephew defended by someone who's going to be disbarred?"

One blond brow rose up her forehead and she huffed. "I want Luke to be defended by the best lawyer I know." She pointed straight at him. "You."

"You're crazy." He glanced at Tommy, appealing for help, but saw nothing but speculation behind the feigned dumbjock look. "You don't know the first thing about my skills as a lawyer."

Mary Beth huffed. "Sam told me you were the one."

"Oh, for fuck's sake!" Mitch yelled.

Why was it that after three years of numb solitude, living on the fringe of this town, everyone now felt they were free to meddle in his life? "Are you going to tell me what's going on or not?"

"Not." Mary Beth's chin shot up.

Mitch wanted to roar, but he kept his composure, clenching his hands into tight fists. He looked at Tommy. "You?"

Tommy shook his head, and once again, his wife laid her hand on his shoulder: the picture of solidarity.

"Fine." Mitch stormed out.

Ten minutes later, he sat in front of Charlie, frustration clawing at him like a caged jungle cat. "What the hell do you mean, nothing?"

Charlie's hard black eyes narrowed. "I mean, nothing."

"You're full of shit." Mitch got up from the plain wooden chair and started to pace in the small, cluttered space. Charlie, more than anyone, should be on his side, but that wasn't happening. "Something is going on."

"Relax," Charlie said, leaning back in his chair with a small smile on his face.

"What the fuck does that mean?" Mitch pointed at him. "And why are you grinning?"

"Maybe you should concentrate on your real problems," Charlie suggested mildly.

"The list of my real problems is growing by the hour."

"Fix the most important one."

"And what would that be?" He was irritated that no one would tell him what was going on.

Charlie studied him and Mitch snapped, "Don't try that cop shit on me."

"Fine." Charlie shrugged. "You can go now."

Mitch jerked to a stop. "That's it?"

"I've told you everything I'm going to."

"You haven't told me anything."

"Your point?"

What was the point? Guys like Charlie didn't break. "Fuck you."

Charlie grinned and gave him a salute. "Have a nice day."

Stalled and out of options, Mitch left and headed home.

How had she gotten them on her side? She'd only been here less than a week.

Shit. Was it any wonder? She'd had him in a couple of hours.

Minutes later, he pulled into the driveway, tires crunching as he rolled to a stop. He stared at the scene before him.

Maddie and his mother were both on their knees, digging in the dirt, surrounded by little plastic containers of flowers. Maddie wore a white tank top and jean shorts and hair was in a ponytail.

His mother, dressed in a tan top and matching long shorts, shook her head. The normally sleek chin-length bob was a wild mess of windblown tangles around her cheeks.

Maddie nodded vigorously, picking up a small plastic crate of flowers in a variety of bright colors and holding them out for inspection.

The cold air from the air conditioner blasted him in the face as something hard caught in his chest.

All of a sudden, his mom threw back her head and laughed—a real, hearty belly laugh that dropped ten years from her age in an instant. Mitch could see her as a young girl, full of life, reminiscent of the way his grandma used to talk about her.

In thirty-four years, Mitch had never seen her look so carefree.

Maddie beamed. Even from a distance, her enjoyment was clear.

In a couple of days, Maddie had broken through years of repressed politeness and made Charlotte Riley laugh like a teenager.

What was he going to do with her? More importantly, what would he do without her?

Maddie stared blankly at the TV and shifted restlessly on the couch. She couldn't sleep; couldn't get comfortable. She'd been restless all evening and had gone for a run earlier, hoping it would settle her down, but it had been a temporary fix. After the endorphins had worn off, her unease had returned.

Was she doing the right thing? She thought so, but at what cost?

Refusing to tell him what she'd been up to had created a divide that hadn't been there two days ago. Every time he looked at her, his golden eyes glittering with questions she didn't answer, it grew wider.

In her defense, he wasn't much better. He'd shut her out the second his father's scandal had broken.

She needed to talk. She needed to get all of this incessant chatter out of her head so she could think straight. She purposefully hadn't told her friends anything about where she was or what she'd been doing when she'd made her promised daily calls, but now she reconsidered her stance. She needed confession in the way only her best girlfriends could deliver. She glanced at the clock: it was eleven-thirty. Too late to call Penelope. She went to bed after the ten o'clock news to ensure that she got the full, recommended eight hours of sleep.

But Sophie would be up, and if she wasn't, she wouldn't care. Sophie was the friend you called when it was three in the morning and you got arrested for public drunkenness.

Plus, Sophie loved details: the juicer, the better.

Maddie picked up the phone from the end table next to the couch and dialed. Sophie picked up on the second ring and said a groggy hello.

"I'm sorry I woke you."

Maddie experienced a momentary touch of guilt, which evaporated when Sophie said, "If you're calling to talk about all the hot sex you've been having, you're forgiven."

Maddie's cheeks heated a good twenty degrees. "Oh my God, how'd you know?"

"Wait! What?" Sophie's voice held none of the sleepiness from moments ago. "I was kidding!"

Oops. "Oh."

"Well, as I live and breathe, Maddie Donovan, you little slut."

Maddie laughed and was hit by a wave of homesickness out of nowhere.

"Spill," Sophie said, always willing to be her cohort in crime. "And don't leave anything out."

Maddie spilled.

After forty-five minutes of nonstop talking, she felt much better. "So that's it, the whole sordid story."

"Wow," Sophie said, blowing out a deep breath. "You always did go for the gusto when you decided to raise hell, but it's been so long I'd forgotten."

"Do you think I'm doing the right thing?" Maddie picked at a stray thread attached to the couch cushion.

"I don't know." Sophie paused and something rustled over the line. "What do you hope to accomplish?"

"It can be fixed. I know it."

"Maybe, but what about you?"

"What about me?"

Another long silence. "Do you think it's a good idea to get attached?"

Maddie frowned. Sophie wasn't supposed to be the voice of reason. That was Penelope's job. Sophie's job was to tell her to go for it.

"I'm not that attached." *Liar.*

"Your life is here. Your family and friends, we're all in Chicago. You have to come home soon. Are you sure you're not getting involved in his life so you can avoid your own?"

Was that was she was doing? No. There was something keeping her here. Something she needed to finish. "I'm not avoiding. I'm just not ready yet."

"This guy sounds like he has a lot of baggage."

Maddie's voice raised an octave as defensiveness twisted in her stomach. "I'm hardly baggage-free."

"But you were getting married last week. You've been with one guy since you were a teenager. Hell, between your mom, Steve, and your brothers hovering over you, when's the last time you've even been alone?"

"I don't understand what you're getting at." Actually, she was pretty damn sure. "Why are you being like this? How long have you been telling me to bungee jump off a cliff? And now I have and you're giving me shit about it?"

"I don't want you to get hurt." Sophie's voice turned soft, laced with concern.

Maddie's throat dried up. "I thought you'd be happy I hooked up for hot, dirty, no-strings-attached sex. It's not a big deal."

A noise caught her attention, and she jerked her gaze to the hallway to look directly into Mitch's stormy expression.

He leaned against the wood molding with his arms crossed and his jaw granite-hard. She'd been so wrapped up in her conversation, she hadn't heard him come in.

Her heart sunk to her stomach.

Please, God, no. She hadn't meant it. Hadn't meant to minimize what they'd shared.

"Soph, I have to go," she managed to croak out.

"Wait, I'm sorry," Sophie said. "It's just that you sound different. And I'm worried."

Mitch hadn't moved. Hadn't taken his eyes off her.

"I have to go," Maddie said again.

"When are you coming home?"

"Soon," she said, hating her now-working car, sitting in the driveway. "I'll call you tomorrow."

She clicked off the phone and licked her dry lips.

"Who was that?" His voice was cold enough to freeze ice.

"My friend, Sophie." Unable to stand the tension any longer, she blurted, "I didn't mean it."

"Guess she's not happy about your post-wedding sex romp."

Maddie wanted to cringe at the words and the menace in his voice, but she stood and walked to him, putting her hand on his chest. Other than the muscle that jumped under her touch, he didn't move, and his hard expression didn't waver. "I'm sorry. I swear I didn't mean it. I was upset and defensive. I spoke without thinking."

"Sure, forget it." He shrugged as if it were no big deal.

This pretending was worse than if he'd raged in fury. But the truth was, with things so fragile between them, she was too scared to push.

It would break them.

She closed the physical distance, resting her cheek against his heart. It beat strong and fast against her ear while he stayed ridged as stone.

She whispered the truth and hoped he believed. "You're important to me. I need you. Please believe me."

His arms closed around her, but he didn't squeeze as tightly as he usually did. "Did she ask you when you were coming home?"

"Yes."

"What did you say?"

"I said soon."

His muscles tensed. "What does soon mean?"

"I don't know." She tilted her chin looking up into his handsome face. "Do you want me to leave?"

His gaze met hers, and he gave her a sharp shake of the head.

She traced the line of his hard jaw. "I can't leave yet."

His golden eyes flashed, then shuttered closed. His hand slid up her back to curl around her neck. "Let's go to bed."

She knew what he was doing and let him. She'd hurt him and couldn't deny him. She needed to make it right.

Only in her heart, she knew it was wrong.

Chapter Twenty-Three

A week later, sitting at the kitchen table, sandwiched between his mom and Maddie, Mitch gritted his teeth and tried not to think about smashing his fist into a wall to let off some steam.

They couldn't help it if they were driving him crazy. The two of them had been talking nonstop since they'd sat down to dinner, carrying on about gardening, shopping, and other such nonsense. Today the subject appeared to be the restoration of his house.

He hadn't been consulted on their decisions.

It was uncanny the way the two women had taken to each other.

It grated on his last nerve.

His mom laughed at something Maddie said, a warm, rich sound. Mitch wanted to snarl, but instead he took a bite of the grilled Cajun chicken Maddie had made. He chewed very slowly.

Charlotte put her glass of iced tea on the table. "Madeline, I was thinking we could go over to Shreveport tomorrow. There's a lovely antique mall off the highway."

"Her name is Maddie." He hated when his mom called her that. It had become a childish point of contention.

Maddie shot him a scowl and waved a dismissive hand in his direction. "Ignore him."

Nothing new there.

Maddie went on, "That sounds like fun. I love antiques and this house is full of them. I found this great, old-fashioned telephone table down in the basement covered in ten layers of paint. I thought about trying my hand at restoring it."

"Oh my." His mother placed her hands on her cheeks. "Is it pink?"

Maddie bounced a little in her chair. "Yes!"

"I painted it when I was twelve. It used to be in my bedroom."

Pink? Mitch pinched the bridge of his nose. He needed to get the hell out of here. Maybe Charlie or Sam could play pickup. A game of vicious, no-holds-barred basketball would help to alleviate his agitation.

"Do you mind?" Maddie asked. "Since it's technically yours."

"It's technically mine," Mitch said dryly. He'd increasingly started to resemble a petulant six-year-old, but no matter how much he tried he couldn't seem to stop.

"What is your problem?" Maddie snapped, then shot Charlotte an apologetic glance. "I'm sorry."

"No need, dear." Charlotte raised a brow, her face cool and polite, with none of the warmth she reserved for Maddie. "He is being quite a bear."

"Don't apologize for me," he said in a growl.

The phone rang, and he got up, happy for an escape. The chair scraped over the linoleum floor harder than he'd intended.

He snatched the receiver.

"Yeah?" he barked.

"Geez, someone got up on the wrong side of the bed," Gracie said.

Great, just what he needed. The only person who possibly loved Maddie more than his mother was Gracie. "What can I do for you?"

"Is Maddie there?" Over the line, the sound of dishes clattering was like nails on a chalkboard to Mitch's ear.

"Yeah." He made no move to hand the phone over to her. Now she was getting calls?

"Can I talk to her?" Gracie asked, sounding like a teenage girl talking to her father.

"One second." The words were spoken through gritted teeth he turned to Maddie. "It's for you. Gracie."

Maddie jumped up and grabbed the phone.

He glowered at her.

She scowled back. "What is wrong with you?"

"Not a thing, Princess."

For the past week they'd talked about their days, bickered, and had fan-fucking-tastic sex, but they'd avoided anything real. She was there, right in front of him, but he'd already lost the thing he'd loved best about her. He wanted it back, but couldn't figure out how to bridge the gap.

With a glare, she pulled the corded receiver into the dining room, leaving him alone with his mother.

An uncomfortable tension filled the room.

They hadn't seen each other in three years, and they still had nothing to say.

Charlotte ran a long, tapered finger over her iced tea ring. Finally, she lifted her chin. "I really like Maddie."

"I can see that," he said, for lack of anything better.

"She's wonderful." Charlotte looked up at him. "I wouldn't have made it through this ordeal without her."

"She's got that way about her." Mitch propped a hip on the counter.

She cleared her throat. "You're different with her."

"I'm different. Period." He was trying to make it clear that she didn't know jack shit about him.

She nodded, and a sadness that had not been present a couple of minutes ago clouded her eyes, the same color as his own. "You know, I wanted to call."

"And what stopped you?"

"I didn't think you wanted to talk to me." The fine lines deepened at the corners of her eyes.

"Yeah, that's a good reason," he scoffed.

"You don't exactly make it easy."

He shrugged. "Doesn't matter much now, does it?"

She opened her mouth to speak, only to snap it shut when Maddie came into the room. With her hand covering the mouthpiece, she held the phone out to Mitch. "You have a phone call."

"Who is it?" Mitch wasn't in the mood to talk to anyone.

Maddie swallowed, her gaze darting first to him and then to his mother.

Dread had his stomach dropping. What now?

"He won't say, but I'm pretty sure it's your father."

Tequila hummed through Maddie's veins as the beat of a country song blared too loudly. The patrons of Big Red's Bar & Tavern did a complicated two-step in the middle of the converted barn, and Maddie could almost convince herself she was having a great time.

Almost.

Those Rileys were pieces of work. Not fans of the emotional outburst.

Mitch had talked to his father for two minutes, handed the phone to his mother, and stalked off without a word. Concerned, Maddie had gone after him, but he'd claimed there was nothing to discuss and shut the office door in her face. Pissed as hell and determined to find out what was going on, she'd sought out Charlotte, only to find that she'd locked herself in the bedroom.

That had left Maddie to wander a house filled with closed doors, which was how she had ended up at Big Red's with Gracie, downing margaritas as if she were aiming for first place in a drinking contest.

Gracie whacked a guy on the back. He was wearing a wifebeater and a trucker's hat. "Sure, Billy, we'd love another round." She smiled at him as though he were Brad Pitt in *Fight Club* and shoved him toward the bar.

Maddie yelled over the noise, "Did it ever occur to you to say no?"

"Why on earth would I do that?" She looked Maddie up and down as though she might have a screw loose. "See, that's your problem."

"I don't have a problem." Maddie waved her hand in the air as the buzz in her head pounded in time to the beat of a country rock song. "But how much can we drink?"

Gracie rolled her eyes. "We'll dance it off later."

Maddie narrowed her eyes as Gracie removed another round of cocktails from some other guy's big, beefy hands.

Later, she hoped to be passed out next to Mitch after he'd exhausted her into sexual oblivion. No matter how distant they were in the light of day, at night they went after each other like starvation victims being given their first meal.

At the thought of Mitch, it occurred to her that she hadn't told him where she'd gone.

She'd just left. That was kind of rude. It was common decency to let him know where she was. As the next fishbowl margarita lined up in front of her, she shouted, "I need to call Mitch."

"Don't worry about him. Have fun." Gracie pushed her half-empty glass toward her.

"Are you trying to get me drunk?"

"I'm trying to give you a good time."

She wanted to have fun, too, but now that she'd gotten it

into her fuzzy head that she wanted to talk to Mitch she couldn't get it out. "Can I borrow your cell?"

Gracie slid an arm around her shoulder. "Nope."

She fidgeted in her stool, playing with a damp drink napkin. "I want to call Mitch."

"If he wants to know where you are, he'll find you."

"But we're in the town over."

"Would you relax and have a good time?"

"I will, but first I want to tell him where I went so he won't worry." Swaying in her seat, she took another sip of margarita. It would be nice if he realized she was gone.

Again, Gracie rolled her eyes. "Just shut up and have fun."

Maddie stuck out her tongue, and a giggle erupted from out of nowhere.

Billy sidled back up to their table, drinks in hand. He frowned when he noticed the full drinks that had made an appearance during his short absence. Gracie patted him on the arm and gave him a megawatt smile. "Thanks, Billy. A girl can never have too many free drinks."

Maddie's head was feeling like a cotton cloud, and she wondered if there was a potted plant she could start dumping the cocktails in. She'd be sliding under the table soon if they kept going at this rate.

"How do you like Revival?" Billy asked, his gaze sliding down her body.

"Great," Maddie said absently, and eyed Gracie's phone on the table. "I'm going to call."

"What?" Billy glanced over his shoulder. "Who?"

She grabbed the cell, pressed the menu button, and scrolled through the names until she found Mitch.

The phone was snatched from her grasp. She let out a screech, her fingers clasping at air. "Hey! Give that back."

Gracie slipped it down the V of her tank and into her ample cleavage. "Come and get it."

Billy plopped down on a vacant stool, eyes bugging out of his head.

Maddie stared at Gracie's chest and contemplated. She could stick her hand down a woman's top. It was no big deal—just skin, for God's sake. She jumped off the stool and straightened to her full five-foot-three inches. "What is wrong with calling him?"

"It's a girlfriend's responsibility to stop her friend from the dreaded drunk dial."

Maddie scowled. She was not drunk dialing! "Telling him where I am isn't a crime."

Gracie planted her hands on her hips. "Sorry, honey. I'm doing this for your own good."

"You don't understand." Maddie picked up her drink and took a slow sip. Her gaze was fixed on the stretch of fabric across Gracie's ample chest. She wanted that phone, and with way too many margaritas in her system, she wasn't above groping another woman to get it. "I'm getting that phone."

Billy's mouth dropped open, and Maddie was surprised no drool hung down his chin like a rabid dog's.

"You'll thank me later." Gracie didn't appear the least bit threatened. If anything, she thrust her breasts out farther, as though daring Maddie to come and get it.

"Give it to me!" Maddie stomped her foot.

"Like I said, come and get it." Gracie batted her thick lashes, cornflower-blue eyes sparkling. She tucked her hand into her top and shoved it lower into her bra.

"All right, but remember, I know how to fight."

Gracie laughed and Billy whooped like he'd hit the jackpot.

Maddie charged.

Gracie's eyes widened in surprise, and she let out a holler, crossing her arms over her chest for protection. Maddie refused to be thwarted. She squeezed her lids together so she wouldn't have to look and flung her hands out, praying she'd get hold of something. When her palm brushed against soft, pillowy cotton, she squealed.

Pay dirt.

"Maddie!" Gracie grabbed her hand, twisting her body to block Maddie's progress. "That's my boob!"

Maddie reached again and this time her hand curled around the cotton neckline. She pulled, squirming down the deep V of the top. Her fingers brushed the phone and a surge of adrenaline pounded through her.

"Now, why doesn't this surprise me?" Mitch's voice made her knees go weak.

Before she could swing around, she was hauled against his warm, strong body.

She sagged in relief. He'd come for her after all.

"You girls are giving everyone quite a show." Charlie stood next to Mitch, looking lethal in all black.

Maddie could picture him with an FBI armband over his bicep. Wait . . . was that the FBI? Or was it SWAT?

"With all these disappointed faces, I'm sorry we broke them up." Mitch's tone rang with amusement, and Maddie realized it had been too long since she'd heard him sound like that.

"I wanted to call you, but she wouldn't let me." Her pulse raced from her girl fight and the buzz of tequila.

His palm spread wide over the expanse of her stomach, his thumb brushing the bottom of her breast. "Well, here I am."

"See!" Gracie pointed and shook her hips in a little booty dance. "I told you so!"

Yes, she had. She shivered as his arm tightened around her ribs and she sucked in the delicious scent of him. God, she'd missed him. She craned her neck to peer into his face. "I want to talk."

His fingers tightened at her waist. "Later."

Gracie let out a happy screech and ran, flinging herself into Charlie's arms.

He laughed and gave her a big kiss, licking her lower lip. "Margaritas."

Maddie rested her head on Mitch's shoulder. "How did you know I was here?"

"Charlie called me and told me you girls were up to no good." His mouth twitched at the corners as though he was holding back a smile, but she didn't miss the worry etched in the lines in the corners of his eyes. "You didn't tell me where you'd gone."

The loud music and buzz of chatter dimmed as she focused on Mitch. "I know."

"I didn't like it."

She frowned and squirmed out of his arms, turning to face him. "And I don't like getting a door slammed in my face."

Mitch's gaze met hers, his eyes narrowing. Several moments ticked by and the rest of the bar became a blur, dancing around them in fast motion while they stayed still.

Finally, he gave her a slight nod. "I guess we need to talk now."

She felt a burst of triumph. "Yes, I think that's best."

"All right then." He took her hand and turned to Gracie and Charlie. He motioned toward the door. "We'll be back."

Charlie gave them a salute and slid his arm around Gracie's waist. "Let's go find a booth."

Mitch led her toward the bright red front door, weaving through the crowd while saying hello to people Maddie had never seen. He pushed outside, and she was blasted by a gust of warm, humid air.

He paused, scanning the parking lot, which was littered with patrons relegated to smoking outside by Illinois law. Off in the distance, a woman squealed, laughing as a man swung her up over his shoulder and started off toward a flatbed truck.

Mitch tugged her to the side of the building. They strolled past the parking lot and onto the grass, in the direction of an abandoned picnic table. Millions of stars littered the sky, and a momentary pang of loss made her chest go tight.

In Chicago, she could hardly see the stars. Right now, with the tequila buzzing through her veins, she didn't think she could live without this view every night.

They climbed onto the benches and sat down on the worn wooden table, their bodies close. He always felt so warm and strong against her. His jean-clad thigh pressed against her bare skin as they stared out into the trees. She wanted to reach out and touch him, stroke her hand over his leg, but didn't.

Ten minutes passed. Maybe they both wanted to prolong the inevitable start of a conversation neither was ready to have but could no longer avoid.

"I'm sorry," Mitch finally said, surprising her. "The last thing I want to do is shut you out."

She chanced a glance in his direction. "Then why do you?"

"I'm not used to letting anyone in." He placed his elbows down on his knees. "I'm not used to anyone caring."

She searched out the Big Dipper, remembering the first night they'd lain down by the river, a ritual they'd repeated many days and nights since. "Your mom cares."

He looked at her with an unreadable expression. "Our relationship is strained at best."

"But she wants to change that." Maddie saw the way Charlotte watched Mitch when she thought no one was looking. The longing and pain was unmistakable. "She just doesn't know how to change things."

He shook his head, a wry smile forming on his perfect mouth. "I'm jealous."

She frowned. "Of what?"

"Of you."

She shook her head. "Why in God's name would you be jealous of me?"

"Hell, Maddie, how long have you known her?" He turned away and looked out into the distance. "Anyone looking from the outside would think you were her kid, not me."

Ah, it was clicking into place now: his bad moods, his hostility toward Charlotte. Maddie put her head on his shoulder. "She wants that with you, but you're so cold she doesn't know how to break through the layer of ice."

"The Rileys aren't big on emotional scenes," Mitch said flatly.

"It doesn't have to be one. You don't have to get all gooey. Start by not slamming the door in her face the next time she tries to talk. Or answer her next question like she's not a telemarketer."

He didn't respond.

Maddie placed a palm over his thigh. "She talks about you all the time, you know."

His muscles bunched. "You're saying that so I'm nicer to her."

She raised her head, and when he refused to look at her, she placed a finger on the side of his jaw and forced him to meet her eyes. "I know about Mr. Snugglebottoms."

His eyes widened, and in the glow of the moon and lights lining the perimeter of the parking lot, he blushed.

It was so unexpected, so completely adorable, that Maddie rushed headlong into a realization that left her stunned.

She was in love with him.

It was no gentle breeze of understanding. No whisper in her heart. It was a freight train barreling toward her with unstoppable force. The knowledge was so scary, so overwhelming, that she had no idea what to do, so she leaned forward and kissed him.

The second their lips touched, it was an inferno threatening to consume them both. His fingers curled around her neck, his thumb tilting her chin to allow him better access. She clutched at his shirt as he devoured her mouth, taking control and threatening to drive her out of her mind with desire.

The temptation to slip under his spell was strong, but they had to stop talking with sex. As crazy as it sounded, the knowledge that she loved him gave her the strength to pull away.

She brushed a finger over his lips. "We need to face reality soon."

"I know." It was a harsh, ragged whisper.

"I haven't forgiven myself for what I said to Sophie. You are so much more than that to me."

He met her gaze and his expression was hard. "But you're still leaving."

She blew out a deep breath and said softly, "Every morning, I wake up and ask myself if today is the day. And every day, the answer is no."

"I'm not sure how much longer that's going to be enough." He pulled away from the intimacy of their embrace and sat forward with his elbows on his knees, and clasped his hands in front of him. "I don't want to live in limbo anymore, Maddie."

"I know. What do you want me to do?"

He shook his head. "No. I'm not going to decide for you. I won't."

She bit the inside of her cheek. Old habits died hard. As much as she hated it, sometimes it was so much easier to let someone else make her decisions for her. "You were the last thing I expected to run into on that night. Even when I went home with you, I never thought it would turn this complicated. But I'm twenty-eight and I've never been on my own. Never had my own apartment. I've never lived my own life. Everything has been taken care of for me: my house, my job. Everything."

A flash of emotion crossed over his face like a summer storm cloud, passing as quickly as it had come. "And what makes you think I'd stand in your way?"

"I don't know what you mean."

His fingers gripped her jaw. "You're more yourself with me than you've ever been with anyone."

She blinked. He was right. It was why she loved him. But could she stand on her own? "Maybe."

"Yes." He released his hold, his hand falling back to rest on her thigh.

"I can't keep drifting along." The more she talked, the more she knew her words to be true. "I need a purpose beyond being someone else's daughter, sister, or girlfriend."

"I only want you to be Maddie."

"That's what I want too."

"Then we have the same goal."

Realizing she'd been diverted from the subject, she nudged him with an elbow. "Hey, how'd we start talking about me? We were supposed to be talking about you."

"I'm a law—" He broke off suddenly, not finishing the sentence, his mouth etching back into that hard line.

"You're a lawyer," she finished for him. "That's what you need to be doing, not running some bar you hate."

"I can't. Not anymore." The words were flat and toneless.

She wasn't going to be able to budge him on the subject, at least not yet. A plan percolated in her mind, but she wasn't quite ready yet. She took a deep breath and broached his family situation instead. "How was the call with your dad?"

He shrugged. "Short. I told him I wasn't going to let my mom pay. He blustered. I handed the phone to her. He didn't call for me, he called for her."

"What did your mom say?" she asked.

Mitch jumped off the picnic table and started to stalk back and forth across the grass. "It's a stupid plan. He should know better."

Maddie agreed. The chances were good it wouldn't work. "Your mom thinks this is her chance to make things right for you."

His long legs ate up the ground as he circled like a caged lion. "Bullshit. She wants to save *him*."

"She wants to save *you*."

He shook his head. "She's always been a sucker for him. No matter what story she's selling now."

Maddie shrugged. "I can't say I blame her."

Mitch whipped around to face her. "Why do you say that?"

"She says you're a lot alike."

"I'm nothing like him." Hands clenched into fists.

"As I said, we've been talking a lot. She told me who he was before he got caught up in the power of politics, who he was when she first met him. I think you're more alike than you think."

"I'd never screw over people like he does." Anger emanated from Mitch, aggression in the set of his legs and arms. He was ready to attack.

She raised one brow. "Are you sure about that?"

He reared back as though she'd struck him. "How could you think that?"

"You've said yourself you weren't a very nice person. Have you ever thought about what would have happened if you hadn't lost your career?" She straightened her shoulders and looked him straight in the eye. "You didn't have the best track record. You walked a shady line. You were sleeping with another man's wife. Destroying evidence. Who knows what you would have become if the whole house of cards had never fallen around you?"

He stopped walking as though snapped by an invisible leash. With his expression transforming into a thundercloud, he crossed his arms over his chest. "So what are you trying to say, Maddie?"

He needed some cold, hard truth. Tough love, as her dad used to say. "Have you ever thought that losing your career and reputation was the best thing that ever happened to you? Maybe the tragedy wasn't that everything went to hell, but that you never picked up the pieces and put them back together again."

Chapter Twenty-Four

The following evening, Mitch sat in his back office at the bar, contemplating the chaos of his life. Maddie's words had struck a chord last night, and now he couldn't stop thinking about them. Was she right?

Before he'd lost his respectability, he'd been tearing up the partner track, defending rich, oily assholes more guilty than innocent. He hadn't cared about screwing anyone over, hadn't thought twice about sleeping with another man's wife. Was it really a stretch to assume he'd have followed in his father's footsteps?

The truth rocked his foundation.

Late last night, after Maddie had fallen asleep, he'd realized something. This whole time, some part of him had secretly pined for his old life. He hadn't put down roots here in Revival because deep down he'd believed he didn't belong. He belonged back in Chicago, living a life he'd someday reclaim.

But that was a lie. He *didn't* want to go back. The man he'd been was a distant memory belonging to someone else, not him.

In the quiet peace of his farmhouse, he'd finally shrugged off the past and allowed himself to wonder whether his future was as black and white as he'd thought. It was time he did some good in the world instead of sitting on his ass in a bar he hated, living off his trust fund.

It was time to man up.

A soft knock sounded, and Mitch pinched the bridge of his nose with his thumb and forefinger. "Come in."

Maddie walked into the dreary, rundown room like a ray of sunshine, beaming a megawatt smile.

"I hope you don't mind me stopping by." She carried a box he recognized and put it on the desk in front of him.

He stared at the white cardboard box containing all of the pertinent details of Luke's case. "What's that doing here?"

With her cheeks flushed and her eyes a bit glassy, she didn't say anything. She'd been at home when he'd left for the bar, and as far as he knew she hadn't been hitting the margaritas again.

He raised one brow in a question.

Her pink tongue darted out to wet her full lower lip and his cock stirred. One finger traced the line of the box as she walked around the desk. Her hips were a seductive sway in a little white flip skirt he'd never seen before. It matched the short-sleeved button-down that managed to look both innocent and drop-dead sexy in a combination only Maddie could pull off.

Her green eyes gleamed with something predatory.

Suddenly, the urge to flip her over the desk and take her swept over him so strongly and powerfully that his hand twitched on the pen he'd been absently holding.

He pushed back from his desk and gave her a slow, thorough once-over. "You look like a woman with something on her mind."

"Oh, I am," she purred, in a voice he'd never heard before.

"And what would that be?"

The only answer he received was a slow smile filled with

such lascivious promise that his cock went from stirring to rock hard. She stopped between him and the desk, standing before him with her legs slightly splayed, looking like a warrior princess despite her petite stature. She picked up both of his wrists and put them on the arms of his chair, her fine-boned fingers looking small and fragile against his skin.

The need to take control of the situation spiked hard and furious, racing through his blood and making his heart kick up a notch, but he reined it in. He was too curious about what she intended to put an end to her game.

She leaned over, not touching him except for her hold on his arms, and licked at his bottom lip. The simple touch was like a lightning bolt straight to his balls, and he curled his fingers around the edge of the chair arms to keep from throwing her onto his desk. She traced the seam of his lips with her tongue. Then, slowly and confidently, she melded her mouth over his. A low groan escaped when her tongue slipped inside to caress his.

It was like no kiss he'd ever experienced before. Slow. Deep. Almost dreamlike. She weaved a spell around him until he forgot everything but the drugging sensation of her mouth.

That was, until a cold metal cuff clicked onto his wrist.

He jerked back, tugging, only to find that she'd somehow managed to lock the other end to the chair. "What the hell?"

She straightened, looking oh so pleased. "Now I've got you right where I want you."

He made a grab for her, but she jumped back, sliding onto the desk and out of his grasp. Although he could reach her, he wasn't able straighten enough to get a good hold on her. He said in his most deadly voice, "I hope you have the key, little girl."

She batted her lashes, slipped a hand into her bra, and extracted a key. "I've got it right here."

What was she up to? He narrowed his eyes. "You know,

once I get free, I'm going to turn you over this desk and paddle that ass until you can't sit for a week."

"Sounds like quite a punishment," she said, not sounding scared at all.

The little vixen.

Despite his position, he wanted her like wildfire and his cock pressed insistently against the zipper of his jeans. "What are you planning?"

"I thought we could play a little game." She ran her hands up her legs, stopping at the hem of her skirt. "You know, I'm not wearing any panties."

He stifled a groan. "I don't believe you."

She laughed and flipped the edge of the skirt up, flashing bare skin before smoothing the hem back down. There was no trace of the shy, guilt-ridden woman he'd met in his bar that first night.

He levered up off the chair, only to sit back down when the whole chair jerked with him. These were no play cuffs. "Where'd you get these?"

"Charlie lent them to me. He had a spare set."

"I'm going to kill him," he said darkly. Was that why she'd gone to see him?

"He mentioned that." She reached for the buttons on her top and slowly popped each one, exposing her flesh, inch by torturous inch. "I want something."

"Anything," he answered.

"Anything?" Her tone was so sly the hair rose on the nape of his neck. She pulled forward the cardboard box. "I want you to take Luke's case."

So that's what this was about? He met her gaze. "I'm not going to take it." Not until he had his life straightened out.

She parted the draping fabric of her blouse and traced a path over the white lace of her bra. "Are you sure?"

He stared transfixed at her breasts spilling over the demi cups, but managed to croak out, "Yes."

With trembling fingers, she ran her hands along the edge of her bra before stroking over silk-covered nipples.

He ground his teeth and kept quiet.

She circled the hard peaks over and over, her breath catching. "Why?"

"Because despite his troubles, he's a good kid and deserves a lawyer who's not on the verge of getting disbarred."

"Mary Beth thinks you're perfect." She played with the front clasp of the bra, running one finger up and down until he wanted to rip it off her. But he couldn't, because she'd cuffed him to a fucking chair.

"Plenty of qualified attorneys can handle it."

"Sam told me you're the one."

He closed his eyes, shaking his head. He could not believe this. "What, is he your psychic advisor now?"

"I was informed he doesn't care for that word." Her fingers played over the swells of her breasts, taunting him.

Though dangerous and edgy, he managed to keep his voice controlled. "I'll find Luke someone and pay for it. Will that make you happy?"

The clasp popped. "No. That will not make me happy."

"It will have to do."

"We'll see about that." She peeled the cups off her breasts and rested her hands on the desk. Pink-tipped nipples begged for his mouth. "I asked Tommy and Mary Beth about the case."

That confirmed his suspicions about her trip to the garage.

She thrust her chest out, arching her back. "You're acting like he's up for murder, not teenage delinquency. I think you can handle it before any concrete action would even be taken against you."

She was probably right. Not that he'd tell her. She didn't understand. He didn't want to get a taste of the law again only to have it ripped away. "I don't want to take the chance."

"On him, or on yourself?"

Before he could retort with something scathing, she straightened and ran her thumbs over her nipples.

His argument fragmented. He remembered their first night together, when she'd been so hesitant to touch herself.

There was no hesitation now.

He had to get out of these cuffs. Using the only weapon he had available, he started to talk. "You'll need a lot more pressure to get yourself off, Princess."

"You don't think I know how to give myself an orgasm?" she shot back, still playing gently over her nipples.

"I hadn't realized you needed to since I came along."

"I haven't." She licked her lips. "But I still know how."

"You might know how to give yourself a nice come, but you need the bite of a little pain to really get you going." His gaze flicked to her breasts. "Pinch them for me."

Her lids drifted closed, and she squeezed the hard buds between her thumbs and forefingers, head tilting.

Jesus Christ. His cock pulsed, and his breathing increased as he watched her. "That's it. Harder."

She followed instructions well, moaning as she increased the pressure of her hold.

He growled low in his throat like some feral beast. "Don't stop, but reach down and flip up your skirt."

She raised her head and gave him a smile so carnal that he wondered if it was possible to rip off the arms of the chair and get free. Her hands fell away from her breasts to once again rest on the desk. "I will, as soon as you agree to finish the case."

Stunned, all he could do was blink at her.

She sucked in a breath. "I'm prepared to do this all night."

"Are you sexually blackmailing me?"

She laughed, a low husky sound from deep in her throat. "What was your first clue, Counselor?"

Hazy lust clouded her green eyes, but so did conviction. Perseverance. The quiet fortitude had only gained in strength since the night she'd cried her heart out down by the river.

"It's against my better judgment," he said, through clenched teeth.

She shrugged one shoulder. "I don't care about that right now. I just want you to agree." She slid one hand up her skirt, making sure to keep herself hidden. She was a damn tease. Her head fell back as she stroked, keeping what he wanted out of sight. He knew what all that smooth flesh felt like.

Hot. Wet. Silky smooth.

Her chest rose and fell in an increasingly rapid rhythm, and he gripped the arms of the chair so tightly that he was surprised the wood didn't shatter. "When I get out of this, I'm going to bend you over that desk."

"Yes, I want it," she said.

"Then let me go."

Her skirt fell farther up her thighs, giving him a glimpse of her fingers circling over her clit. The whole room was permeated with sex and desire.

"If you keep going that fast you're going to come." Her hips lifted and the white fabric fell away, no longer obstructing his view. "Jesus, Maddie. Open your legs wider."

She complied, one hand behind her as she braced herself on the desk.

"Slip those fingers inside."

"Tell me you'll take the case." Her voice took on a needy, desperate quality. If he were inside her, he'd either go harder or stop, depending on his mood and hers.

He needed inside. Now.

"Please, Mitch."

"Fine," he said harshly.

Fingers slipped into her core. "Do you promise?"

"Yes." He needed to feel the way her tight muscles clenched around his cock, milking him. "Take off the cuffs."

She moved fast, grabbing the key and sliding off the desk as though she was scared he'd change his mind. She fumbled as she tried to work the key into the lock, telling him how nervous she'd been.

He waited with the stillness of a predator, knowing not to jump and scare his prey. The second he was free, he grabbed her wrists, twisting them behind her back and catching them both in one hand. "You are in so much trouble."

She trembled, her nipples peaking at his words. "I don't care. It was worth it."

He took her mouth, a hard, brutal melding. She rocked into him, helpless to do anything but squirm against his on-slaught.

With his free hand, he pinched her nipple, pulling and squeezing as he rolled the hard tip. He dragged his mouth away, roaming down her neck, licking over the pulse pounding at her throat, scraping his teeth over her sensitive flesh.

And then he broke.

He couldn't stand it one more second. He released her hands, whipped her around, and pushed her flat over the desk. He flipped her skirt over her hips and smacked her naked ass. Once. Twice. Three times.

Color bloomed pink over the round cheeks. She let out a scream that had to permeate the paper-thin walls. He kicked her legs apart and reached between her legs.

Soaking wet, his fingers glided over her. He rubbed her clit until she moaned and thrust her hips back. He snapped his fingers over the flesh, and she let out another strangled cry. "Oh, God, yes."

Jesus, she was made for him.

She bucked under his touch. "Again, please do that again."

"Some punishment this is turning out to be." He delivered

a series of rapid beats as she went wild under him. At the first swell of her orgasm under his fingers, he backed off.

Unzipping his pants, he freed his aching cock, bent at the knees, and drove hard and high inside her.

She clutched at the desk, nails scraping along the worn wood as her red hair fanned out over her back. "Mitch, please."

He gripped her hips and impaled his cock so deep that he kissed the tip of her womb.

There was a knock at the door.

"Go. Away." He gritted out, not missing a stroke, closing his eyes as her muscles rippled down his length.

"Mitch, you need to come out here." It was Sam.

Under him, Maddie stiffened, but he paid no mind, pulling out and slamming into her again. Her hips rocked back.

"Mitch," Sam said again. "It's important."

"Go away," Mitch yelled back. Whatever it was could wait.

The door rattled as though coming off its hinges as someone's fists slammed against the wood. "Maddie Donovan, open this fucking door."

Mitch froze at the unfamiliar voice.

Maddie went shell-shock still, squeaking, "Oh no."

More pounding and banging. "I'm giving you thirty seconds, and then this sucker is coming down."

Mitch pulled out, leaving the hot, wet heaven of her body. "Someone you know?"

With flushed cheeks, her expression had turned from lustful to horrified in a fraction of a second. "It's my brother."

Chapter Twenty-Five

Maddie tried the best she could to straighten her clothes, clumsily buttoning her top as Mitch zipped his pants. His face was unreadable as he smoothed out his hair and pulled at the T-shirt he wore.

She felt naked. Exposed. Shaken. With her heart skipping a beat, she sent up a silent prayer that all hell wouldn't break loose.

Why was Shane here? When she'd called him over a week ago, she'd asked him to stay away, and she'd truly believed he'd follow her wishes. Tears threatened, but she squeezed her lids tightly to push them away.

Mitch walked to the door and flipped the lock.

"I'm sorry," she said. It was woefully inadequate preparation for what was to come.

A second later, the door crashed open.

Shane stormed into the room, eyes narrowed on Mitch. She'd seen that look before: he was out for blood. "What the hell is going on here?"

"Shane! Stop!" she yelled.

He ignored her, his green eyes filled with ice. He breathed in deeply. "What were you doing to my sister?"

Mitch crossed his arms, looking like an immovable object as they faced off. "Do you really want me to answer that?"

The scent of sex seemed to infuse the room. Maddie flushed, her thighs rubbing together, reminding her that she wore no underwear. "Shane, that's none of your business."

"You said he was a friend." With his expression fierce, Shane braced his legs as though preparing for a fight.

She might have skirted the truth. Guilty, she shifted her attention to peer over her shoulder. Behind Shane and Sam stood her middle brother, James.

"James." She smiled at her quietly handsome, six-foot-two-inch professor brother. With his expression a study in wry amusement, his cool, rational aura enveloped her like a comfortable blanket in the face of Shane's aggression.

Behind his wire-rimmed frames, green eyes that matched her own settled on her. "Maddie."

She ran over to him, throwing her arms around him and giving him a hug, whispering in his ear, "Help me."

He squeezed her tightly. "You got yourself into this mess, baby sister. You'll have to get yourself out." He kissed her on the top of her head. "But it's good to see you."

It wasn't much, but it was enough to give her a sense of calm as she turned to face her oldest brother's wrath. With as much dignity as she could muster while wearing no panties, she straightened. "Shane, I asked you to stay away."

Mitch turned cool eyes on her. "You didn't tell me you'd talked to your family."

Guilt knifed through her. "Um . . ."

"And you didn't tell me you were screwing a perfect stranger," Shane said flatly.

"Um . . ." She gulped.

"Shit, all your talk about independence." Shane's expression turned thunderous. "Fucking the first random guy you happen across so he'll give you a place to stay doesn't count, Maddie."

Even as anger flared bright inside her, she winced at the words. She opened her mouth to give him hell, but before she could, Mitch turned on her brother, moving faster than she'd ever seen him. Before she could blink, Shane was up against the wall with Mitch's hand around his throat.

"Don't. Ever. Talk to her like that." His tone shook with rage and barely contained violence.

"Mitch, please." Maddie ran over to him, gripping his arm to pull him off. It was like trying to move granite. He didn't even budge.

James walked up behind her, sliding his arm around her waist and pulling her back as Sam grabbed Mitch's shoulder.

"Let him go, Mitch." Sam's voice was calm and controlled. "This isn't the way to handle the situation."

"Fuck. Off." Mitch's tone was like ice.

Sam's fingers tightened. "Trust me on this."

Shane's face reddened, and Mitch's hand tightened. Shane gripped the wrist that had him pinned to the wall, but he didn't attempt to free himself. This struck Maddie as strange. Her oldest brother was a known ass-kicker. Half of Chicago was scared of him.

"If you ever talk to her like that again," Mitch said, in a deadly tone, "I will rip your fucking throat out."

The air shifted, swirling with tension and far too much male testosterone. Maddie's heart thumped hard against her chest.

Shane sputtered.

"Mitch, this isn't going to solve anything," Sam said.

Mitch increased the pressure around Shane's throat, turning his complexion another shade darker. "Do you understand me?"

Shane tugged at Mitch's wrist, his gaze flashing with what Maddie could only suspect was fury. There was going to be bloodshed soon.

James ran his hand up her arm, giving her a squeeze. She

pulled away and touched Mitch's forearm. The muscles were taut under her touch. Inflexible. She said softly, "Mitch, please let him go."

Mitch turned his head to her, unnamed emotion flickering in his eyes. She pleaded silently, and finally, he gave a slight nod. A second later, he released her brother.

Shane coughed, bringing his hand up to rub at his neck.

Cool as ever, James shook his head as though dealing with a bunch of unruly toddlers. "Maybe we should start again."

Mitch's attention fell on Maddie. "Maybe you should start explaining yourself."

The coldness in his voice shook Maddie to the core. She bit her lip. "Can we have a moment alone?"

"No," Shane said.

James sighed. "Let's go outside."

Sam cocked his head toward the door. "She's been alone with him for weeks. Five more minutes isn't going to matter."

The office fell quiet, tension thickening the air as Shane and Mitch watched each other with the narrowed eyes of jungle cats waiting for the first flinch to attack.

"Shane," she said sharply. "I'm not asking. I'm telling. Leave."

Without taking his eyes off of Mitch, he nodded. "Fine, you've got five minutes."

How dare he? She flew at her oldest brother, jabbing her finger into his big chest as his expression widened with surprise. "Listen, I'm twenty-eight years old. Your job of taking care of me is done. Got it? Finished. I'll take as long as I damn well please." She pointed to the door. "And you'll sit outside patiently and wait for me."

Shane's lips quirked and he raised one brow. "Geez, no need to throw a fit."

She let out a shriek and stomped her foot, pointing once again to the door. "Out!"

His expression softened, and a slow smile spread over his mouth. He gave a little tug to her hair. "I haven't seen that temper in quite a while." He looked up past her to Mitch standing behind him. "I suppose you have something to do with that?"

There was no answer from behind her, and Shane sighed. "All right, we'll be outside."

Maddie let out the breath she hadn't realized had been lodged in her chest.

The three men moved to the door, filing out. Shane turned back and gave her the hard-eyed stare she remembered from her days of being a teenager. "I'd better not hear any more screaming. Shit, I'm going to have nightmares for months."

Her whole body flushed. Why couldn't the floor open and swallow her up? She jabbed a finger at the door and yelled, "Get. Out."

He chuckled and shut the door behind him.

With a heavy heart, she turned to face Mitch. His expression was a blank mask. "Your brother seems prone to mood swings."

She waved a hand in the air. "That's just the way he is. I stopped trying to figure him out ages ago."

Mitch's mouth flattened into a hard line. He walked to the couch and sat down. "To what do we owe the pleasure of his visit? And why didn't you tell me you'd talked to them?"

She shifted on the balls of her feet, looking down at the floor. If only that were her worst transgression.

She couldn't evade the truth any longer. She understood her brother's MO. He had information, and it had been the perfect excuse to come and check things out.

"I'm waiting." Mitch's tone held the hard edge of impatience.

With her throat constricting, she blinked back sudden tears. *Please God, help me make him understand.* "I called Shane over a week ago."

"Let me guess: on the day you made your rounds around town?"

She couldn't look at him. She fixed her gaze on the coffee table, which was filled with newspapers, a couple of biographies, and stacks of magazines. She swallowed hard. "Yes."

"So what aren't you telling me? Because you're sure as hell hiding something."

She twisted her hands.

"Look at me," he said, his voice sharp and commanding, although this time it didn't send tendrils of desire snaking through her.

Reluctantly, she raised her eyes.

His face was unreadable and remote. "Answer me."

She bit her lip. "My brother has a friend."

"And?" The word was delivered like a single bullet.

"His name is Logan Buchannan. He's some ex-military, black-ops type of guy who owns a security and investigation firm."

Mitch's face transformed to stone, growing more distant by the second. She didn't have to go on: he knew. When she'd dared to think about this moment, she'd pictured anger, not coldness.

Her own blood chilled. Dread twisted in her stomach, making it hard for her to breathe. But she'd made her bed and now she had to lie in it and hope he'd understand.

When he didn't speak, she went on. "I asked Shane to call in a favor. We asked Logan to look into your situation and the current situation with your father's blackmailer."

Those golden eyes, always so warm on her, turned to flat,

dull amber. "You told your brother and some guy I don't even know the things I told you in confidence."

"Yes." She dropped her gaze to the floor. "I'm not sure this helps, but Charlie knows Logan."

"You talked to Charlie?"

"Yes, he helped us with the details I didn't know."

"So you went behind my back, talked to my friends, and told your brothers and some guy everything."

She pressed her lips together. "Yes."

"And you told them things about the blackmail that's not public knowledge."

Maddie swallowed hard as her throat constricted. "I did."

"I trusted you with information about my family that nobody knows."

"Mitch, I'd never jeopardize you or your family. I'd never tell them if I didn't trust them implicitly. You know that." She had to make him understand.

He leaned forward, putting elbows on his knees. "I want you to leave."

"What? No. Let me explain." The blood rushed in her ears as a wave of hot dizziness engulfed her. Fear and desperation warred inside her. "I'm sorry, but you wouldn't listen."

"You didn't ask." Flat.

She wrung her hands. "You would have said no."

"I see," he said, so coldly that it was like being doused with a bucket of ice water. "So that makes it right? You didn't think I'd agree, so you went behind my back, talked to my friends, your family, and some black-ops guy, revealing the things I've told you in private, because you know best?"

She bit the inside of her cheek. "Yes, the same way you went behind my back and stalled the repairs on my car so I wouldn't leave."

His head snapped back. "That's not the same thing, Maddie."

"You lied, just like me. You went behind my back. Just like me." She hoped he could see reason, but his expression said otherwise.

"I told you those things," he said through gritted teeth, "because I thought I could trust you."

"You can." Her stomach clenched.

"The evidence says otherwise, now doesn't it?" Cold, cold words.

Tears sprang to her eyes. "Please understand, I did it for you."

"No, you didn't. You did it for you," he scoffed, shaking his head. "Tell me something. Why are you so interested in meddling in my life when you have your own to worry about?"

She reared back, stepping toward the door, unable to figure out how to handle this dead, cold Mitch who treated her like a stranger. "I wanted to help you."

"You know how you could have helped me?" There was a cruel twist to his lips. "By being the one fucking person who didn't betray me."

"I didn't. That's not what . . ." She trailed off, feeling helpless. She hung her head and said softly, "I'd never betray you."

"Bullshit. If you thought what you were doing was right, you would have talked to me. "

This ice. She'd prepared for fire, for burning anger, not this. She had no defense. No plan. She walked over to him and fell to her knees, taking his hands in hers. He didn't even flinch. It was like he was made of stone, and she met his eyes. Hard chips of gold. "Mitch, I'm sorry, I wanted to help."

He studied her as though she was a stranger. "You need to leave now."

The words were a crushing blow, threatening to break her. She did the only thing she could think of and confessed the truth. "I love you."

His mouth firmed. Eyes flashing, he pulled away and stood, moving around her and going over to the window that overlooked the nearly deserted parking lot. "I need you to leave."

Her heart shattered into a million pieces and desolation swept over her. She hadn't felt anything like this since her father had died and she'd woken in a hospital bed. That same heavy weight crushed her chest, numbing her limbs. Tears spilled onto her cheeks and she wiped them away. Her voice trembled as she spoke, already knowing the answer but unable to keep from asking the question. "Is there anything I can do?"

"Yes." His tone was distant and unreachable. "Leave."

There wasn't any other choice left to be made. She got up and left. She walked like a zombie out of the office and down the hall. Out in the bar, Shane called after her, but she ignored him, breaking out into a run until she reached her car. With frozen fingers, she managed to insert the key into the ignition and start the engine.

Sobs shook her frame as the gravity of her mistake washed over her.

Her brothers and Sam rushed into the parking lot. She gunned the engine and spun out of the spot.

Everyone in Mitch's life had lied to him. Betrayed him. Nobody, not even his mother, had stood by him. He'd risked his own career by destroying evidence, and his family had deserted him. When his life had fallen apart, he'd had no one.

Mitch didn't trust anyone.

But he'd trusted her.

She threw the car in drive, tires squealing as she floored it out of the lot.

And what had she done? She'd gone behind his back and

shared his deepest pain with strangers. It didn't matter if her intentions were good. It didn't matter she'd only wanted to help. All that mattered was that she'd done the one thing he could never forgive.

She could beg and explain until she was blue in the face, but it wouldn't change anything. She'd violated his trust. Confided things that she'd had no right to reveal.

It was over.

The only thing left to do was go home.

Chapter Twenty-Six

Sitting alone in the depressing office, Mitch took another long drink of scotch. The burn in his chest matched the burn of the alcohol in his stomach. He stared into nothingness as he contemplated his wasteland of a life.

How could Maddie have done that? She'd betrayed him. Maybe not in the traditional way, but somehow this was worse. He'd told her things, things he'd never told anyone, and she'd told strangers. She'd involved his friends behind his back and hidden it.

The sound of her softly whispered "I love you" still rang in his ears, deafening him so that the rest of the world seemed muted.

Ironic. In that moment, when all trust had been broken, he'd known that he loved her too.

A real love. Deep and soul twisting, capable of bringing him to his knees.

She'd made him whole. Feel. Laugh. Burn.

With Maddie, things made sense. She made sense. Even now, he had to resist the urge to find her and hold her close.

She was his anchor in the ever-turbulent storm of his life.

A knock sounded on the door. He ignored it.

The last thing he wanted was company. He poured another

two fingers of scotch. The liquor did its work, helping him return to the numb place he'd existed before Maddie had shown up in his life and turned the world upside down.

It would do for a while. It would have to.

Another knock, louder this time and more insistent. Before he could tell Sam to go away, the door opened and Maddie's oldest brother walked in.

Mitch scowled. "This isn't a good time."

"No shit," Shane said, sarcasm clear. Without waiting for an invitation, he sat down on the chair opposite Mitch's desk. "What'd you do to my sister? She ran out of here without a word like a kicked puppy."

Mitch took a slug of scotch, his stomach twisting. She was gone. Panic clawed at him with sharp nails.

He took a deep breath.

She'd be at home. His home.

Shane scrubbed the stubble lining his jaw. "Turns out that five minutes can do some damage after all."

"How can I help you?" Mitch needed this guy out of his fucking sight. Now.

Silence. Shane jutted his chin toward the bottle of scotch. "I'll take a drink."

Mitch picked up the bottle and placed it in front of him. The blond man studied it, shrugged, picked up the bottle, and took a long, deep swallow. With a satisfied hiss, he placed it on the desk and slid back into the chair as though he didn't have a care in the world.

"Maddie is gone." The words sliced through the thin veil of Mitch's alcohol-induced haze, bringing unwelcomed pain with them. "We've got nothing to say."

"I don't like the way you look at my sister," Shane said, as though Mitch hadn't spoken. "And I sure as hell don't like the sound of what was going on in here before I barged in."

The sharp sudden image of her round, pink ass in the air while he drove his cock deep inside her filled his mind. The sound of her screams and the scent of her arousal making him dizzy.

Shit. He shook his head, running a hand through his hair.

Shane's mouth twisted into a sardonic grin. "Yeah, I kind of thought it was like that."

Mitch cocked a brow. "Do you really want to discuss this?"

"Fuck no, and I'm not sure I approve," Shane said, with green eyes so familiar that Mitch wanted to look away. "But you know what? In all the years Maddie was with Steve, I've never seen him look at her like that. Hell, he's a decent guy. He's nice and orderly. But there's no way he'd try to take me down, no matter what I said to her."

"Sounds like a real prince." The last thing Mitch wanted to discuss was Maddie's ex-fiancé.

"In fact, he would have sided with me." Shane assessed Mitch, sizing him up. "If Maddie hadn't asked you to stop, you'd have tried to tear me apart. You wouldn't have gotten far. Jimmy looks calm and harmless, but the guy's lethal, and I've kicked my fair share of ass, although I'm a lot less pretty about it than he is."

Mitch had no idea what the guy was going on about and didn't give a shit. "Are you done?"

"No," Shane said flatly. "You're in love with my sister. And she's in love with you. As much as I don't like it, I'm going to be a nice guy here."

"You're being a nice guy?" Mitch laughed and took another drink.

He loved her, needed her, wanted her right this instant.

"I'm going to be stuck with you, aren't I?"

"No." The word tasted like dirt in his mouth.

"Yeah, I am." Shane put a file folder that Mitch hadn't even noticed onto the desk. "You're pissed as hell, but you'll get over it."

"No," Mitch said again.

Shane pushed the manila folder over to him. "Maddie did what she thought was right. That's the way she is, even if she goes about it in a backassward way. Don't fuck up what's obviously a good thing because she went behind your back."

Mitch stared at the guy. "Less than an hour ago you were out for my blood, and now you're playing matchmaker?"

Shane shrugged. "Yeah, well, I saw a little red when I, um"—he cleared his throat—"heard what was going on in here. She's my baby sister. I've raised her since she was fifteen, and you don't have the best past when it comes to women. Although you have been fairly monk-like for a while."

Mitch stared at the folder, curiosity getting the better of him as he wondered what information it contained. "Your point?"

"I love her too and want her to be happy. I've been worried as hell about her. She was lost. Drifting along but not really living. I assume she told you about the accident?"

Mitch nodded.

Shane's expression flickered, then cleared. "She never got over the guilt, no matter how many therapists I dragged her to. No matter how many times we talked to her, she couldn't get it into her head that we didn't blame her. Over time, she just became more and more compliant."

"Yeah, I know," Mitch said, because he understood Maddie. "But she's better now."

Because of him. Them. The way they were together.

"I can see that." Shane smiled. "She used to be quite a little troublemaker. It drove my dad crazy, even though he loved her like mad. It was good to see some of her old spark."

Mitch took another long swallow of liquor, waiting for the slow burn down his throat to hit his stomach before he spoke. "I don't want her to be anything other than what she is."

Shane leaned back in the chair and laced his fingers over his stomach. "I don't think she ever really loved Steve."

"Of course she didn't," Mitch interjected, compelled to make sure the record was straight. "The guy was all wrong for her."

Shane nodded sharply. "I'll deny it, but the day we opened the vestibule and found her gone, I silently cheered her on. That's why I let her be. She needed freedom, a chance to breathe away from all the pressure. I've known where she was almost from the beginning."

It wasn't a surprise. Guys like Shane didn't leave things to chance.

"When she finally called, she seemed like the old Maddie. The one I thought I'd buried along with my dad." Shane picked up the bottle of scotch and poured another healthy dose into Mitch's nearly empty glass before taking a long gulp from the bottle. "I figure you have something to do with that."

Mitch's throat constricted, already regretting sending her away.

"So here's the deal," Shane continued, opening the file. "My friend has methods of uncovering information, and he was able to find some things to help your father, and by default, you. He wasn't able to find much on the embezzlement case, which basically confirms what you already know and what Maddie and your friend Charlie told us. Without Thomas Cromwell and whatever he took down with him in that plane crash, the evidence against you was circumstantial at best. Not enough to convict, but enough to taint your reputation and put you out of the Chicago power set."

Mitch nodded, not at all surprised. Like Shane, he'd known people, too.

"Your father's blackmailer is a different story." Shane flipped through a couple of pages before coming to the picture. "She's quite a looker."

Mitch studied the photo. The woman with her raven-black

hair was impossibly beautiful. "If you can overlook her tendency for blackmail."

Shane chuckled. "We can't all be perfect. Does she look familiar?"

"No." Mitch picked up the photo and examined her brilliant blue eyes and snow-white ruby lips, but there was nothing familiar about the set of her face or expression. "I've never seen her before."

"She didn't get her good looks from her father."

Mitch blinked. "What?"

"Your good friend Thomas had a long-term mistress in Greece. Rachel Brown, a.k.a. Kassandra Apostolis, is their daughter. Logan couldn't find any link to you tampering with evidence." Shane smirked. "Your MIT guy did a good job. If Logan can't uncover it, no one can. Even if she has a paper trail of your father's deal, there's no way to tie it back to you."

Relief swept through him, so powerful it would have knocked him over if he hadn't been sitting. Something inside him eased.

Sam's words came rushing back to him: *Stop trying to control everything*.

In that second, Mitch finally understood what he meant and gave up the fight. He stopped pretending that he didn't care; stopped pretending that he was fine.

Maddie had been right, and he'd sent her away.

"Kassandra has a boyfriend," Shane said, snapping Mitch back to the subject at hand. "He was staying in the same hotel. He filled a prescription for Ambien a couple of days before the trip."

"How is this possible? My father's handlers would have uncovered this all by now."

"She had excellent fakes. She picked a common name. It's harder to wade through all the red tape when you're stuck using proper channels. All eyes are on the senator. He has no choice but to be careful. Logan doesn't have those restrictions. Not saying it will amount to anything, but it's enough to go on. Enough to cast suspicion and send the press digging into her background. But at the end of the day, you won't end up disbarred. I'll have Logan keep digging. He's only been at it for a week."

Mitch raised a brow. "He's really that good?"

"Yeah, he is. He's the guy they call when they want things off the record."

People that talented cost money. Big money. Mitch's gaze narrowed. "How was this information paid for?"

Shane steepled his fingers, his expression inscrutable. "She wants to save you. Let her. But it might not be a bad idea for you to take over with that trust fund of yours."

Mitch's lips tightened. "Have him give back her money and send me the bill."

"Figured you'd feel that way."

"I'm going to get her."

"I told you I was going to be stuck with you."

Mitch stood up, the alcoholic haze evaporating as adrenaline kicked in. "Don't come looking for her anytime in the next couple hours."

Shane's eyes narrowed. "I'm not much of a take-orders kind of guy."

"Tough. Where Maddie's concerned, get used to it."

"Understand that if you hurt my sister, there's not a place on earth you'll be able to hide. I'd better never see her cry like that again."

Mitch ground his teeth as a muscle jumped in his cheek. He'd made her cry. He nodded. "Understood."

Shane looked him up and down. "You want a job? I'm not as picky as those high-priced, old-school firms about reputation. You can't get far in life without bending a few rules. I'm sure my legal team could put you to good use."

Mitch laughed. There was no way in hell he'd be under this guy's thumb. "Fuck, no."

Shane shrugged. "Yeah, that's probably stretching it."

Mitch drove with record speed, pulling into his driveway and screeching to a halt. He was out of the car before the dust settled. He barreled through the door, yelling Maddie's name, even though he hadn't seen her car in the drive.

If only he hadn't refused to talk and told her to leave. He'd been so damned sure that she'd be at his house. He hadn't even contemplated being too late. His heart pounded as he yelled, "Maddie!"

His mom came rushing in from the kitchen. "What's wrong?"

"Where's Maddie?" Panic already clogged his throat.

Charlotte's eyes widened. "She said she was going to see you at the bar."

"And she hasn't come back?"

"No," she said, shaking her head "Did something happen?"

"I've got to find her."

Charlotte put her hand on his arm. "What happened?"

He stiffened and looked down into his mother's eyes. They were filled with concern, with loss and sorrow. They were sad, troubled eyes. He took a deep breath and said, "We got in a fight. I told her to leave."

"Oh, Mitchell," she said, whisper soft.

"I have to find her, Mom." His voice shook. "She can't be gone—all her stuff is here."

"You'll find her. Everything is going to be all right."

It didn't ease his anxiety. "What if she went home?"

His mother's fingers trembled on his arm. "Then you'll go get her."

His throat grew so tight that he thought he might choke. "What if she won't come back?"

"You'll find a way to make it work. I promise."

"How do you know?"

Her eyes grew bright and she blinked rapidly. In thirty-four years, he'd never once seen his mom shed a tear, even at her parents' funerals. "Because you love her and she loves you."

He couldn't speak. Couldn't even breathe. He managed a sharp nod.

She gave him a watery smile. "Now go and do whatever you can to fight for her."

"I will," he croaked out. Maddie Donovan was a woman worth fighting for, and he'd move heaven and hell to get her back.

His days of giving up were over.

Chapter Twenty-Seven

Her mom opened the front door of Maddie's childhood home, looking like she'd aged ten years. Her faded strawberry-blond hair curled messily around her ears, ending at her chin. Fine lines etched her mouth and worry creased her forehead. Her blue eyes, rimmed with dark circles, widened. "Maddie."

Maddie had cried the whole way from Revival to Chicago and thought she'd had no more tears left. She was wrong.

She burst into sobs that shook her body and caused the hiccups to start all over again.

Shannon Donavan took her daughter in her sturdy arms and pulled her close. "Baby girl, I've been worried sick about you."

This caused a fresh batch of hysterics that left Maddie a weeping mess as her mom shuffled her into the seldom-used formal living room and nestled Maddie into the couch. She sat down next to her, and once again wrapped her into a warm embrace.

With a wrenching cry, Maddie said, "I'm s-so s-s-sorry."

Shannon hushed her and rocked back and forth as she had when Maddie had been a child.

Maddie cried.

Her mom held her.

She sobbed uncontrollably for her father, her past mistakes, her abandoned wedding, and most of all, for Mitch.

Clutching her mom, she opened her mouth to apologize for running away, only instead, she said, "I'm sorry about Daddy. I don't blame you for hating me."

She'd never admitted what she'd feared all these years, and hadn't meant to admit it now, but the words had tumbled out in her uncontrollable fit of hysterics.

Her mom pushed Maddie's hair off her face. "Where did you get such a crazy idea?"

"You have to hate me. I'd do anything to take it back. Anything."

"Madeline. Now, you listen to me." Her mother took Maddie's chin in her hand and forced her head up. "I do not hate you. Not now. Not ever. You are my daughter and I will always love you."

"But it was my fault. If I never—"

"Life is filled with if 'I nevers,'" Shannon said, cutting her off. "He could have said no. He was supposed to pick me up, but I got a ride from Judy Kline down the street. It rained and the sewers flooded the field so Evan's practice, which he'd been planning on watching, was canceled. The list goes on and on. There were a thousand moments leading up to the minute that you two were in that car."

Maddie's heart felt like it was being squeezed too tightly as thirteen years of repressed emotion came pouring out of her. "But—"

"But nothing." Her mom kissed her temple. "I'm going to tell you something I've never told a living soul. When you were lying in that hospital bed, so silent and still, the doctors told me they didn't know if you were going to make it. If your father wasn't already dead, I would have killed him."

Maddie blinked, stunned by the admission. She jerked back to look into her mother's face.

Shannon nodded. "Yes, that's right. I wanted to kill him. I have never been so angry with anyone in my whole life. I was furious with him. Not for dying. For dying, my heart was broken with grief. But I blamed him for putting you in that bed."

"I was the one driving."

"He should have known better. I told him you weren't ready to drive on busy streets. We'd argued about it, and he said I was being too overprotective. I was right. He should have said no."

"But I ran the stop sign. It doesn't make sense to blame him."

A tear slipped down Shannon's cheek. "No, it doesn't. When your child is lying in a hospital bed and you don't know if she'll make it through the night, you don't have to make sense."

"I'm sorry." Maddie's voice trembled.

"I never blamed you. And I assure you, your father doesn't either."

"I think I might be starting to believe that."

"It's about time." Shannon stroked her hair, just like she'd done when Maddie was a child and hadn't been able to sleep.

Maddie hung her head, clasping her hands in her lap. "About the wedding . . ."

Her mom tucked a stray lock behind her ear. "You shouldn't have run away, but I'm sorry you felt like you couldn't talk to anyone."

"I was lost and I didn't know what to do," Maddie said, clenching her hands in her lap. "I didn't want to disappoint you all."

Shannon sighed and shook her head. "What am I going to do with you?"

"I don't think I ever really loved Steve," Maddie spoke

what she'd ignored for so long. "I'm sorry I couldn't marry him. I know how much you wanted him for a son-in-law."

Shannon sighed, nodding. "I did. You scared me. You were always a little wild like your daddy. Steve was a nice, safe boy. He wanted to protect you. And after the accident, I couldn't keep you safe enough."

Maddie sniffed and hiccupped, and confessed, "I met someone. A man."

"I figured that out as soon as I opened the door."

"How?"

"I might be old, but I'm no fool." Shannon patted her hand. "There's only one thing that makes a woman cry like that. What happened?"

"I love him and I wanted to help. I broke his trust and he told me to leave."

Shannon clucked her tongue and pulled her close. "This seems like a girlfriend problem. Do you want me to call them?"

"Yes, please."

She moved to stand, but Maddie clasped her hand. When her mom looked down, she spoke the words she'd hidden for so long. "I wish, when I was growing up, I could have been the daughter you wanted."

Shannon squeezed her fingers, then pulled away to gently cup her chin. "Madeline, you are the daughter I needed."

Eyes once again filling with the never-ending supply of tears, Maddie curled into a ball and waited for Penelope and Sophie. They'd bring the standard breakup-care kit of chocolate and ice cream and a tragic movie collection. Maddie hadn't used it since she was fourteen and Nick Cablese had dumped her for Katie Meyer.

Somehow, Maddie didn't think it would be as effective as last time.

* * *

Mitch had combed all of Revival before giving up and admitting that she'd left. Nobody had seen her. Nobody had talked to her. She'd disappeared, without even stopping to pick up her things. Ironically, he'd experienced a twinge of sympathy for her ex-fiancé.

Then the waiting had started. Endless hours had been filled with worry and irrational fear that he'd never find her again. When Shane had finally gotten the call that she was home, Mitch had picked up his car keys and driven like a bat out of hell to get her.

Now, parked in front of the house she lived in with her mother, Mitch realized that it was two-thirty in the morning. If Maddie had lived by herself, he'd have no qualms about banging on her door, but he wasn't sure this was a wise start with the woman he hoped would be his mother-in-law one day.

He stared at the brick bungalow, which was nearly identical to the rest of the houses on the narrow street, and contemplated his options.

Maddie was in there, thinking he hated her and wanted her gone.

He couldn't stand the thought that he'd made her cry. He couldn't stand her believing that he didn't love her. Even if she hated him for being a coward and not fighting for them, she needed to know the truth.

And he couldn't wait another second to give it to her.

Fuck it. He wasn't sitting back anymore. He pushed the ignition button and the engine died. He'd find another way to get on her mom's good side.

He was going in.

Five seconds later, he was up the steps and ringing the doorbell. When no one answered, he rang it again, and then a third time.

Finally, he heard the click of the latch and the door

opened. Instead of Maddie or an older version of her, two women stood in the doorway.

They were around Maddie's age, both dressed in comfortable sweats with their hair pulled back into ponytails. They wore identical scowls on their faces.

Mitch glanced at the address on the side of the house. It was the right number.

"Yes?" the brown-haired girl with the black-framed glasses asked.

The blonde glared. "Do you know what time it is?"

Mitch couldn't help checking out the address again. This was definitely the right place. "Is Maddie here?"

"No," the blonde shot at him. "Go away."

Mitch's brows rose. "Is this her house?"

The blonde opened her lips, but the brunette put a long, tapered hand on her arm and shook her head.

The blonde's mouth snapped closed.

"This isn't a good time," the brunette said, coolly.

"But is it her house?" Mitch asked again, wanting to be absolutely sure before he made a scene. "Shane told me she came home."

The brunette's eyes flickered before she nodded. "Yes, it is, but this isn't a good time. Maybe it's best if you left."

"I'm not going anywhere," Mitch said in a hard, do-not-fuck-with-me voice.

"Do you know how many hours she's been crying?" the blonde demanded, jabbing a finger at his chest.

Mitch's already frayed emotions shredded at the knowledge that she'd been crying all this time. "Yeah, I know, which is why I need to talk to her."

"No," the blonde snapped.

Mitch took a deep breath and tried to hold on to his temper. He turned to the brunette, clearly the more pragmatic, less temperamental of the two, and held out his hand. She scrutinized it for a moment, then slowly shook it. As reasonably as he could muster, he said, "I'm Mitch Riley. Maddie's been staying with me since she ran out on her wedding. And you are?"

"Penelope," the brunette said.

Mitch turned and forced a smile on the blonde. "You must be Sophie. Maddie has told me a lot about you both."

"You're not going to charm us," Sophie said.

Okay, she wasn't his biggest fan. Mitch nodded. "Understood. But I'm not leaving until I talk to Maddie."

"Maybe it's best if you come back in the morning," Penelope said.

Mitch shook his head. "No. I can't. I need to see her now."

Sophie began to speak, but Penelope cut her off and asked, "Why?"

Because he loved her and he couldn't live without her. But the first time he said those words wouldn't be to her friends. He tried to look past them, but the two women blocked the door like professional linemen. "I care about her and I need to tell her I'm sorry."

"Not good enough," Sophie said, bracing her legs as though he was about to rush her.

"She's had a long night," Penelope said, rationally. "She's finally gone to sleep and needs her rest. I'm not going to wake her."

Mitch wanted to scream in frustration.

But before he could say anything else, another female voice came from behind the women. "What is all the commotion out here?"

For a second, Mitch's heart surged with the hope that it was Maddie, only to realize a second later that the tone and cadence was all wrong.

Penelope and Sophie parted like the Red Sea to reveal an older woman wrapped in a white robe.

"Sorry, Mrs. Donovan," Penelope said. "We're taking care of it. You can go back to bed."

"So you're the one," Maddie's mom said.

"Yes, ma'am," he said, hoping politeness would override banging down her door in the middle of the night. "I need to talk to Maddie."

"You made her cry."

"I'm sorry." He cursed himself for the thousandth time for kicking Maddie out. He'd been upset and he hadn't thought. "I want to make it up to her. Please."

The older woman stepped forward and studied him for a long, long time. He resisted the urge to shift under her gaze.

"Come back tomorrow," she said, and her words held not even a hint of sympathy.

Mitch's chest tightened. "I'm sorry, but I can't leave."

Something flickered in the woman's blue eyes. She pointed to the steps. "Feel free to have a seat on the stoop and wait out the night."

Mitch knew a test when he saw one. If he had to spend all night on a concrete step to prove his worth, so be it.

"All right." He turned and sat.

Five seconds later, the door slammed behind him.

Thirty minutes later, his ass had gone numb from the concrete steps and his eyes were gritty from lack of sleep. He was contemplating the slope of roof and whether he could scale the house to find Maddie when a black SUV pulled into the driveway.

Shane, James, and, to his surprise, Gracie got out of the Range Rover.

Shane took one look at Mitch and grinned. "What happened?"

Mitch dragged a hand through his hair. "They won't let me in."

"I see you've met the Wonder Twins."

"And your mom." Mitch waved his hand over the steps. "They were nice enough to give me a place to stay."

Shane rolled his eyes. "Sounds like them. They can be mean as snakes, but you'll get used to them."

Mitch frowned at Gracie, unable to take one more female coming to Maddie's rescue. "Did you come all this way to yell at me?"

She planted her hands on her hips, encased in tight jeans that hugged every one of her curves. "No. I came for you. You big jerk."

"Why?"

She blew out a breath. "Because, dummy, somebody needs to be on your side."

A swell of emotion swelled and his throat tightened, but he pushed it back down. "Thank you."

"You're welcome." Gracie smiled. "If I've got to take down a couple of rogue city girls for you to get your happily ever after, I'll do it."

Shane scrubbed a hand over his jaw and gave her a slow once-over. "She might actually be able to take them on."

"She's very persistent," James added dryly.

Gracie scowled. "You're not still mad about *that*, are you?"

"I don't get mad," James said, but a muscle in his cheek jumped, belying his words.

Gracie snorted, waving a hand. "Whatever, Professor. I still think you're being a baby."

James cocked his head to the side and studied her. "You just don't know when to shut up, do you?"

Mitch glanced at Shane, who shook his head. "It's been a fun drive."

"Hey—"

Gracie started to speak, but Mitch cut her off. "Can you save it for another time?"

The front door flew open and Sophie came storming out. "What is all the racket out here?"

"Hey, Soph," Shane said. "It's three in the fucking morning and I'm not in the mood."

Penelope wandered out, much more slowly. "This is giving me a headache."

Shane shifted his gaze on her. "We're coming in."

Penelope smirked. "I don't take orders after work hours."

Maddie's mom crowded onto the porch. "Jesus, Mary, and Joseph—get in here or the neighbors are going to have a fit."

Mitch felt a surge of triumph. He was one step closer.

The whole lot of them filed into the house, overflowed the living room, and started talking at once.

He let the chaos rein as he waited for his chance to escape.

Maddie woke to the sound of loud, angry voices. Her head pounded, her nose was stuffy, and her swollen eyes hurt. She'd finally gotten to sleep, and now this. What was going on down there? She climbed out of bed and ran down the stairs to find her living room filled with people.

They were all yelling.

"Hey!" she called out, but nobody heard. She squinted. Was that Gracie? She must be dreaming.

Suddenly, she was grabbed at the waist and a hand was clamped over her mouth. "Don't distract them."

Mitch. She sagged with relief. He'd come for her. She hadn't thought he would, but couldn't deny that she'd hoped.

With one big hand still pressed against her lips, he dragged her to the first closed door he saw and pulled it open, letting out a snarl when it was a packed closet. He shut it and moved down the dark hallway. She pointed to the left and he yanked them into the powder room, slamming the door closed behind them.

He spun her around, hauled her to him by the shoulders and kissed her. It was a hot, wet, desperate kiss that left her dizzy. She grabbed for his shirt, tugging him close, sinking into his embrace. She savored each moment, not knowing if it would be their last.

He tore away and shook her. "Don't you ever do that to me again. Do you understand?"

She blinked at him, then shoved him away. "You told me to leave."

"You weren't supposed to listen!" he yelled, wrenching her back for another punishing kiss.

When he released her, she said breathlessly, "How was I supposed to know?"

There was a loud banging on the bathroom door.

"Maddie, open up!" It was Sophie.

Mitch growled. "For God's sake."

"Go away, Soph!" Maddie yelled, pressing her finger to her temple.

"Are you okay?" came Penelope's soft but firm voice.

"Something tells me I'm not their favorite person." Mitch plastered a hand against the bathroom door as if he expected them to break it down.

Maddie shrugged. "I might have cried a little."

"I'm sorry, Princess." He brushed a finger over her cheek. "Forgive me."

"Leave them alone," Shane said, his words muffled through the wood.

"No. She's been up half the night," Sophie said.

"We want to make sure she's okay," Penelope said.

"What is your problem?" Gracie demanded.

"Would everyone calm down?" Even through the door, James sounded exasperated.

Mitch opened the door to a sea of faces hovering in

the hallway and bellowed, "Would you all just shut the fuck up?"

There was a moment of absolute quiet before they all started pointing fingers and talking over each other.

This was getting ridiculous. Maddie put her thumb and forefinger in her mouth and let out a loud whistle. The sharp, piercing sound filled the air and all of the chatter dropped off. She turned to her family and friends. "I love you all, but enough is enough. I appreciate that you want to protect me and I feel grateful to be so cared for, but I assure you I'm quite capable of making my own decisions. I can speak for myself. My life is not a democracy. You all don't get a vote. From now on, if I want your help, I'll ask for it. Understood?"

Collective nodding.

"Good. This is between Mitch and me. Leave us alone."

She glanced at Mitch to find him looking at her mom. He cleared his throat. "Sorry for swearing, Mrs. Donovan."

"I expect clean language in this house." Her mom did her very best to look disapproving, but Maddie didn't buy it—not with the twinkle in her blue eyes.

"It won't happen again," Mitch said, sounding so polite that Maddie would almost believe he was a choirboy.

Then he slammed the door on all of their faces.

A bubble of laughter welled in Maddie's chest and she pressed her lips together.

Mitch eyed her. "Are you laughing?"

She shook her head.

The chorus of voices began again and the first chuckle spilled out. What did she expect? It would take months of constant reminders before they stopped meddling.

Another snicker escaped.

"Jesus, Maddie," Mitch said, shaking his head. "I love you, but they're crazy."

She exploded with laughter and couldn't stop. She howled until her sides hurt, until tears streamed down her cheeks. Every time she thought she was under control, another attack of giggles shook her until she gasped for air.

Somewhere within the chaos of her outburst she realized what he'd said.

Her laughter died away, and she wiped the wetness from her cheeks. "You love me?"

"Yes, Maddie." His reached for her, his hand curling around her neck. "I love you. I adore you. I can't live without you. Please don't make me."

Her heart filled with joy, erasing the last hours from her mind in an instant. "I thought you hated me. I didn't think you'd forgive me."

He gave a sharp nod. "I was angry. I was hurt. And it didn't matter. I loved you anyway."

She wrapped her arms around his waist and pressed her body close to his. "I'm sorry. I didn't feel like I had any other choice. I was wrong. I will never go behind your back again."

He shook his head and trailed a path down her spine. "You're right, I didn't give you a choice. I shut you out. I didn't fight for you. I don't have a good excuse. Only I fell for you so quickly and I was afraid to let you go, for fear I'd ruin you."

Confused, she searched his gaze. "Ruin me?"

"Every day that passed, I became more of a mess. Every time I turned around, something else was falling apart and I had no answers. Everything in my life was going to hell: my family sucks, I own a bar I hate, I couldn't go back to the career I loved, and my father is being blackmailed. And worst of all, I couldn't figure out a way to keep you. I have never felt so helpless."

Tears flooded the corners of her eyes. "Mitch, why didn't you tell me?"

"Because." His voice cracked and he cleared his throat as his fingers tightened on the back of her neck. "You were becoming the woman you needed to be. Every day, you got stronger. More confident. More sure of who you were and what you wanted. I couldn't ruin it for you."

She went to her tiptoes and kissed him, a soft brush of promise. "Don't you understand?"

He shook his head. "I've never been so clueless in my life."

She rubbed her thumb over his jaw. "You saved me. And I will love you forever."

Chapter Twenty-Eight

Three months later, Maddie stood in the doorway of the bathroom, resting her shoulder against the wood molding, now gleaming, beautiful, and polished. Mitch fixed the knot of his tie, adjusting it in the mirror.

Their eyes met in the reflection and Maddie smiled. "You look very handsome, Counselor."

It was an understatement. He looked downright gorgeous in his custom-made charcoal-gray suit, crisp white dress shirt, and blue patterned tie. They'd gone shopping downtown a couple of weeks ago when they'd gone back to visit her family and his mom.

They'd talked about moving back to Chicago, but in the end the decision had been easy. Revival was home now.

For both of them.

They visited a lot, spending time with her family and friends, who'd adopted him as one of their own the night he'd come to claim her. Maddie had met the senator and Mitch's sister just once. It had been a strained affair, full of polite conversation and undercurrents of tension.

At least things had slowly improved between Mitch and his mom. Last week, they'd even called each other without using Maddie as an excuse to talk. It wasn't perfect, but this was real life, and sometimes perfect was too much to ask for.

"Thanks, Princess." Mitch flashed the crooked grin that had stolen her heart the first night she'd walked into the bar.

It was Sam's bar now.

"How do you feel?" Maddie asked, taking a sip from the coffee mug she was holding.

"Strange," he said, shrugging.

Maddie figured that was as much an admission of nerves as she was going to get. "You'll be great."

He gave another shrug as he once again started working at the knot of his tie. "It's not a complicated hearing."

Maddie said nothing and took another sip of coffee. The hearing might not require a lot of technical challenge, but she knew exactly how big a deal it was to Mitch. He'd attacked Luke's case with a vengeance. The man had taken to sitting on the couch and reading law books, for God's sake. How boring was that?

The great thing was, once word had made its way around town, people had started coming to him for legal work and Maddie had been able to flaunt that she'd been right all along. The citizens of Revival didn't care about some scandal in Chicago among a bunch of rich people.

Her cheeks flushed as she remembered all the deviant things he'd done to her last night in retribution for her gloating.

He chuckled, drawing Maddie's attention back to his reflection in the mirror. He cocked a brow. "Is someone having impure thoughts?"

"Not me," she said in a voice filled with feigned innocence. "I went to confession yesterday. I can't ruin it already."

"Princess, we're living in sin. You ruin it the second you step out of the church."

"Yeah, well." She waved a hand in the air. "You can't expect me to be perfect."

She'd started going to church again, as well as to a therapist over in Shreveport, who was helping her through the rest of her guilt over her father's death.

It was getting easier.

Slowly, she was figuring out what she wanted out of life. She'd started restoring the farmhouse. It was hard work, but she'd found she liked working with her hands, liked the sense of completion when the job was done exactly to her specifications. Completing the vision she'd dreamed up in her mind.

And she'd started painting again.

After the first stroke of a brush across canvas, she'd had no idea how she'd stayed away from it all these years. It had been like coming home.

She'd even received a commission for her first work of art, entirely by accident. The other day at Earl's Diner, Maddie had struck up a conversation with a five-year-old girl named Jessica, who was obsessed with fairies. Delighted by her enthusiasm, Maddie had drawn her a picture on a napkin. That evening, Jessica's mom, a longtime friend of Gracie's, had called to say that her daughter loved the picture so much, and asked Maddie if she was willing to paint a mural in the little girl's bedroom. Maddie had jumped at the chance and had already sketched a couple of design ideas to go over with the family.

"I've been thinking," Mitch said, pulling her away from her thoughts of brightly colored fairy walls.

Maddie met his gaze in the reflection.

"I appreciate people asking me for help, but wills and divorces aren't exactly a challenge. Maybe this is a long shot, but what if I switched sides and tried my hand at being a prosecutor?" He turned to face her, his expression guarded.

She walked to him, putting her coffee mug on the counter before running a finger over his jaw. "Sounds like an excellent idea."

"They might not have me." His tone was gruff. Unsure.

She stood up on tiptoes and pressed a kiss to the curve of his neck. "If they don't, you'll think of something else."

"You're not worried?"

"Not even a little bit." And she wasn't. The signs were clear now, and all roads pointed to Mitch and Revival and the life they were building together.

He wrapped his arms around her. "Have I told you today how happy I am that you gave up the good fight and moved back in with me?"

"Not today," she said, sucking in his sex-and-sin scent. "But last night you mentioned it quite a few times."

She'd tried for six weeks to live by herself in the apartment over Gracie's garage, thinking she needed to experience life on her own before living with Mitch.

She'd hated every minute of it.

When she'd taken to sneaking into the farmhouse and crawling into bed with him in the middle of the night, he'd finally put his foot down.

She sighed. Contentment had her curling deeper into his embrace. She didn't care if it was wrong: Mitch and this farmhouse made her happy.

"Maddie," he said, his voice catching in a way that had her lifting her chin. "You know I love you."

"I know. I love you too."

His fingers brushed a lock of hair behind her chin. "Come with me."

He clasped her hand and led her into the bedroom before motioning her to the bed. She sat, and he walked over to the antique dresser and took a box out of the dresser. He walked back to the bed and sat down next to her. "I wanted to give this to you tonight, but then I saw you standing in the doorway and I knew I couldn't wait."

Maddie looked at the box, it was wooden, etched with

an intricate fleur-de-lis design on it and words in another language. "What is it?"

"It was my grandmother's. They bought it on their honeymoon. It's French. It says, 'There is only one happiness in life: to love and be loved.'"

"It's beautiful." That he would give her something so treasured brought the threat of tears to her eyes.

He handed it to her. "Open it."

She took the box and suddenly her heart started to pound. She lifted the lid and gasped, blinking as her vision blurred.

Mitch grasped her left hand. "I know it's only been three months, but in my family, meeting the night your car breaks down is a sign of a long, happy marriage."

Maddie couldn't take her eyes off the ring. It was a gorgeous, simple platinum band with two small emerald stones flanking what had to be a three-carat rectangular diamond.

She looked at Mitch.

"Maddie Donovan, will you please marry me?"

"Yes." She kissed him, a soft, slow, drugging kiss filled with hope and promises. There was no hesitation. Not a seed of worry or shred of doubt. Her heart belonged to only one man, and he was right in front of her. "It would be my honor."

He slipped the ring on her finger. "My grandma would be thrilled that you have her ring."

"It's hers?" It sparkled in the sunlight. It looked important on her hand.

"It's been in the family vault since she died. My mom sent it a couple of weeks ago. She's been a little pushy about the whole thing. I think she's worried I'll do something to screw it up and she'll lose the best daughter-in-law ever."

Maddie laughed. "I love her, too."

He ran his finger over the platinum band. "I changed the side stones to emeralds because they match your eyes. Do you think I made the right choice?"

She put her hands on the sides of his face. "It is the most gorgeous ring I have ever laid eyes on. I love it. I love you. You know I'd take you with a plastic ring from Wal-Mart."

"I know."

She kissed him. "But I'm not going to lie: this is a kick-ass ring."

He grinned. "You know, I think that's what my grandma used to say."

"She was obviously a smart woman."

"For the record, don't even think about running." Mitch pushed her back on the bed and captured her beneath him. "I will hunt you down to the ends of the earth and bring you back where you belong."

She reached for him, this man who'd been her salvation. "I will run down the aisle to meet you."

Keep reading for
an excerpt from the
second book in
Jennifer Dawson's
Something New series!

"We got the lead story." Nathaniel Riley's voice sounded over the car speaker.

The news didn't surprise Cecilia. Reporters don't shove a story about a senator recovering from a blackmail scandal to the back page.

Cecilia stabbed the speaker's volume button until it lowered to a reasonable level. "Then everything is going according to plan."

"I trust you're happy." Her father's purring tone conveyed that he was one satisfied cat.

She clenched the leather steering wheel.

Happy. Now there's a word. When was the last time she'd been happy? Stop. This was *not* the time to get philosophical. If she wanted a chance in hell at winning the congressional seat come election time this was what needed to be done.

It was the smart move.

And she needed to win.

She'd get over the distastefulness sitting in the back of her throat. She always did.

A green highway sign came into focus. Revival. Fifteen

miles. Where everything was sunshine, laughter, and genuine happiness.

Her skull throbbed.

"Cecilia?" Her father's voice fractured her thoughts. "What did you think of the article?"

She hadn't read it. This morning, she'd thrown the un-opened paper in the trash and deleted the Google Alert links sitting in her email. It was a fluff piece, carefully crafted by the senator's finest. The first of many that would lead to a final press conference where she'd announce her bid for Congress. It was all part of a perfectly planned public relations strategy, designed by her.

A fine sheen of sweat spread down her back. She punched down the air-conditioner button in her understated Mercedes sedan and let the cool air wash over her face.

"Paul did an excellent job." After years avoiding the small truths, the evasion was smooth as silk.

"Since you were unavailable, Miles and I had final approval," Nathaniel Riley said, in his polished, politician's voice.

"Of course." While her tone rang with a practiced strength, her stomach rolled. What was wrong with her? She needed to get it together. This was the price her dream demanded. She wasn't losing anything really important. Nothing that mattered.

Life in politics was all she'd ever wanted. When other little girls had been pretending to be princesses in faraway lands, she had played president in the Oval Office.

She'd been content putting her own career aside for her father's aspirations, but that had ended when his scandal broke. She'd sat at her kitchen table reading that dreadful headline and seen her whole world crumbling under her feet.

The young woman who'd attempted to blackmail the senator had eventually been caught and her schemes exposed, but not without damage. Cecilia had managed the fallout to perfection, minimizing the whole sordid affair, publicizing how he'd been a victim of greed. It had worked—the senator was well on the road to political recovery. But she couldn't shake the worry.

This wasn't the first mess she'd helped him escape. At some point his bad decisions would have to come back and bite him. And where would that leave her?

It had been a slap in the face. A wakeup call delivered by a five-alarm fire truck.

"I'm proud of you, Cecilia," Nathaniel said, and she could practically see him sitting there in his office in Washington, scotch in hand, smug in his oversized, leather chair.

Six months ago she would have lapped up his approval like a grateful puppy, but now she recognized the lie. He wasn't proud of her. This plan helped him. How, she wasn't sure and didn't care, but it had nothing to do with her.

It never did.

The truth only made her more determined.

A speed-limit sign whipped past and she checked her speedometer to see the needle creeping past eighty-five. Easing her foot off the pedal, she started to say thank you for his sparse compliment but instead blurted, "Don't you have any reservations?"

"We talked about this," he said in a patient tone that grated on her last nerve. "This is your best shot."

Clammy sweat broke out on her forehead, forcing her to turn the air down to arctic levels. Wasn't thirty-three too young for a hot flash? She swallowed the taste of the bile clinging to the walls of her throat. "It doesn't bother you?"

"Why would it?"

Because I'm your daughter? The truth pained her. That he hadn't noticed made the cut that much deeper.

She shook her head. It didn't matter. Nothing mattered except getting out from under his thumb. She squared her shoulders. "Never mind. Is there anything else?"

A moment of silence fell over the car, filled with nothing but dead air. She prayed for a dropped connection one would expect in farmland Illinois, but the squeak of Nathaniel's desk chair quelled her hope.

"Are you almost there?"

Her jaw tightened and her ever-present headache beat at her temples. "I'm about fifteen minutes outside town."

"And your mother?" The question was clipped.

Part of Cecilia still wanted to believe that under all his bluster and power trips he genuinely cared for his wife of forty years, but she had no more delusions. "She's already there."

The green mile marker sign came into view. Revival. Twelve miles.

She hadn't been to the small town since her grandma's funeral.

A sudden, unexpected tightness welled in Cecilia's throat, and she swallowed hard.

"I see," he said, and another silence descended.

She dreaded spending the next two weeks in a house filled with strangers, watching her brother fawn all over his bride-to-be. Not that she begrudged Mitch his happiness. She didn't, but witnessing it caused a strange yearning she didn't want to contemplate.

She gripped the steering wheel, tight enough her knuckles turned white. "I still think a couple of days before the wedding would have been plenty."

"Cecilia," Nathaniel said, in his patient tone. "Voters love a wedding and we need the family solidarity. This will help your image."

The logic couldn't be refuted, but she tried anyway. "And two or three days doesn't accomplish that?"

"Under normal circumstances, yes, but with Shane Donovan already at his sister's side and that football player on his way, it doesn't look good if we're not there."

An image of Shane snapped through her mind like the lash of a whip. He was one of Chicago's corporate giants, and his sister's impending marriage to the senator's notorious son had been a hot topic on a slow news day. If it weren't for him, she'd be home where she belonged.

"So you get to stay in Washington, but I have to play nice," Cecilia snapped.

"I'm in committee," her father said.

The whole situation annoyed her, and she spoke without thinking. "And God forbid the voters find out your wife and son aren't speaking to you."

"That's enough. I'm still your father."

Something tightened in her chest. Was he? He didn't feel like it. She straightened her shoulders and modulated her tone to neutral. "All I'm saying is that I'm not sure it's necessary."

"Trust me, it's necessary."

She laughed, a hard, brittle sound. "Trust you? You almost ruined your career."

"But I didn't," he said, his voice cold as ice. "I'm doing what I need to do, and if you want to win, I suggest you do the same."

She fought it—the pull that longed for his approval—but the habit was too old and her anger too new. She took a deep breath. "I understand."

Sometimes it was best to concede the battle to win the war. Or at least that was the political spin she sold herself today.

"Good. Remember the plan."

Ah yes, the plan. She ate, slept, and lived the plan.

Revival. Eight miles.

Two weeks with Shane. Two weeks with his sharp, disapproving gaze. Two weeks of playing the ice queen he expected, pretending he had no effect on her.

She was exhausted just thinking about it. "I remember."

"And on that note," Nathaniel said, his voice rich and pleased.

Her stomach dropped with dread.

"I spoke with Miles and Paul this morning, and we decided right after the wedding we'll announce you're running for office."

She frowned. "What do you mean, right after?"

"At the reception. We'd call in a few reporters to cover the wedding. You could let it slip and have a press conference the next day."

"No," she said, shaking her head. Was *nothing* sacred to him? "It's Mitch's day. Let him have it."

"The timing—"

She cut him off. "No. This is *my* campaign, and I'm putting my foot down."

She might not be close to Mitch, or have the slightest clue what to say to him, but she respected what he'd done and how he'd turned his life around after the senator had gone and fucked it all up. She wasn't about to ruin his wedding to gain a few points in the polls.

"Cecilia, let's be frank. You're a long shot."

Yes, the factors working against her were endless, but she was sick of him pretending he wasn't part of the problem. Venom filled her tone as she spit out, "Thanks to you and that little intern *I* told you not to hire."

He scoffed. "That's easy for you to believe, but we both know your image needs work."

Nausea roiled in her belly. "I didn't get blackmailed. You did."

"The voters forgave me. After all, I didn't do anything wrong."

"Ha! You didn't get caught, there's a difference."

"Perception is reality, my dear. You know that better than anyone."

What did he mean by that? He sounded smug, as though he knew something she didn't. "I'll build my own perception."

A long, put-upon sigh. "You can't connect. You're logical and pragmatic, which can be a benefit, but it doesn't win votes. People don't love you. You don't inspire them to act, or empower them to believe that government is within their grasp. You have no voice. No vision."

The truth. It was like a stab to the heart, but she refused, absolutely refused, to give in to the tears that pricked the corners of her eyes. She did not cry. Ever. Instead, she steeled her spine and said sweetly, "Awww, you always give the best pep talks."

Never show weakness. Never break.

"It's up to me to tell you the truth."

A cocktail of riotous emotions threatened to bubble to the surface, but she pushed them back down. "I will not let you ruin Mitch's wedding so you can play father of the year in front of a few reporters." Her training had served her well because there wasn't even a hint of a quaver in her voice. Her hurt was hidden down deep where it belonged.

And since he was so keen on truth, she'd dole out some of her own. "As *your* advisor, let me return the favor. If you want a chance in hell at winning your wife back before the next election, you'd better stop using your son to gain points in the opinion polls. You're losing her. She's starting to loathe you. Maybe that's why you had sex with an intern younger than your daughter?"

"Watch your mouth." His voice was filled with outrage. Unlike her, he'd never been a pro at hiding anything unless he had an audience. "I did not sleep with that woman."

She laughed, the sound filled with rough, bitter edges. "Do you think I'm an idiot? You think I didn't see how you fawned over her? How you preened at her ego stroking?"

Fifteen seconds must have ticked by before he spoke. "Have you told your mother this?"

She scoffed, shaking her head. This was so like him. All he cared about was covering his ass. Another mile marker sign flew by. "Good-bye, father."

He hung up without a word.

She exhaled a slow, steady breath.

Well, that was ugly.

She'd held her own and scored her point, but the victory was hollow.

Revival. Next exit.

She slowed to fifty-five and changed into the right lane. She had to block out this noise—her family crisis, Shane Donovan, the wedding—everything and concentrate on what was important.

Winning the election.

It was the only dream she'd ever had, and she couldn't let it die along with everything else.

Cecilia had been banging on the front door of her brother's farmhouse for five minutes and still no one answered. She glanced around the front yard filled with the same large oaks and weeping willows, but where her grandma had had shrubs, her future sister-in-law had lush hydrangea bushes in vibrant pinks, lavenders, and greens.

It was like stepping into an alternate universe where time had stopped, but reality had been altered just enough to make the familiar, foreign.

The breeze blew, sending the old porch swing swaying, and a burst of nostalgia filled her chest. How many summer nights had she sat there as a little girl, smelling of Off and the river, curled next to her grandma's side reading *James and the Giant Peach*?

She could still see her grandma sitting there in her house-dress, looking like she was part of the earth. A tightness welled in her chest at the memory.

Would her grandma have even liked the woman she'd become?

She huffed out an exasperated sigh. Where was all this emotion coming from? She needed to shake it off and get it together. She turned away from the past and rang the bell, then rapped hard against the panes of glass.

Met with nothing but silence, she twisted the handle and found it unlocked. Since they expected her, she took a cautious step inside. Her heels clicked against the original hardwood floors, which gleamed with a richness that spoke of the care someone had put into restoring the wood.

"Hello?" she called out, peering around the empty foyer. The walls were different. The rose-patterned paper had been replaced with a soft, dark gray paint she'd never have picked because of the dark wood moldings, but it looked exactly right.

She called out again, "Hello?"

A distant, unrecognizable male voice yelled back, "In the kitchen."

Why on earth hadn't he answered the door? She tossed her bag on the bench and walked down the narrow hallway leading to the swinging kitchen door that had been in this house since its creation.

The kitchen told another story, thrusting her out of the past and into the future. It gleamed with newness. With gorgeous, industrial stainless steel appliances, distressed white cabinets, and polished granite countertops in various shades of cream, gold, and brown.

Under the extra-deep double sink, a man sprawled across the floor, his head under the cabinet. "Can you hand me that wrench?"

That voice. It never failed to send an irritating trail of tingles racing down her spine. She ground her back teeth until her temples gave a sharp stab of protest. Of course, Shane Donovan had to be the first person she ran into.

He bent one knee, pulling the worn fabric of his jeans across powerful thighs. Her throat went dry as her pulse sped.

Why him? Out of every man she'd ever encountered— and in her line of work, she encountered plenty—why did it have to be him? For heaven's sake, he belonged to the wrong political party. She shuddered.

It was all so . . . embarrassing.

But her body didn't care, hadn't cared since the first time she'd met him at Mitch and Maddie's engagement party. The second her palm had slid into his, a disconcerting jolt of electricity had traveled through her fingertips and up her arm. She'd had to force herself not to jerk away and keep her face impassive.

It was a good thing he didn't like her. It was the one thing working in her favor. If she stuck to her current strategy of nurturing his disdain, he'd stay away, and her exposure would be minimal.

She walked over to the box of tools and stood over him.

Half hidden under the sink, Shane fiddled with her brother's plumbing. Annoyed at his pure perfection, she wrinkled her nose.

At six-four, his frame stretched beautifully across the hardwood. His hips were lean. His stomach flat. Shoulders ridiculously broad. Most of the times she'd seen him, he'd been dressed in a suit, but today he wore a pair of beat-up construction boots, faded jeans, and a thin white T-shirt. It was a crime against nature that a man who spent most of his time in boardrooms had muscles like his.

She'd analyzed her attraction, and for the life of her, she couldn't come up with a logical explanation. Sure, he was good looking, but so what? Good-looking men weren't impossible to find. He was nothing like the men she dated. She preferred, well, men like her. Men who were more interested in politics and strategy then carnal pleasures. She enjoyed a relationship in which sex was secondary to their intellectual connection. Not that she had a problem with sex—she didn't. Her past encounters had all been pleasant and civilized.

But nothing about Shane Donovan was civilized. And somehow she doubted sex with him was *pleasant*.

She shouldn't be attracted to him. Period. End of story. Only her libido didn't agree.

A loud clang sounded under the cabinet, followed by a grunted curse. He stretched out his hand. "The wrench."

Without a word she reached down, grabbed the tool, and plopped it in his palm with far more force than necessary.

"Easy there, honey." The warm tone of his voice was clearly not meant for her.

Who was honey? A moment of panic washed over her. Oh, no. Was she going to be tortured by watching him with another woman?

The thought bothered her so much, she blurted, "I'm not your honey."

He stilled for a fraction of a second before sliding out from under the sink, like the teasing reveal in bad porn. His strong jaw tightened as his piercing green eyes met hers. "If it isn't the ice queen herself."

His favorite name for her. He'd never called her honey, not even once.

The fine hairs along her neck bristled as something she refused to name sat in the pit of her stomach. It didn't matter. Even if he tried, she'd have to put him in his place on principle alone. Endearments were dismissive; every good feminist knew that.

She slipped into the role he expected, ignoring the jab to ask coolly, "Where's the happy couple?"

He got up from the floor with much more grace than a man weighing at least two hundred pounds should, turned, and flicked on the faucet with the touch of his fingers. "Your brother's out back."

The muscles under his thin T-shirt flexed as he washed his hands.

She squared her shoulders. Good thing broad shoulders, muscular backs, and lean hips didn't affect her. She was a sane, rational woman, not driven by hormones.

Her eyes locked on his ass.

Good thing she was above all that.

When the water ceased she jerked her eyes away and smoothed her expression into her most remote mask.

He turned around and gave her an assessing once-over. "I didn't think you'd show until the rehearsal dinner."

A muscle under her eye twitched. "I was invited. Mitch is my brother—why shouldn't I be here?"

"You Rileys aren't much for family support." He assessed her with a shrewd gaze. "So there must be another motive."

Her spine bristled, and she had the sudden urge to smack him across his smug face. Of course, she didn't, because that would be revealing and out of character. "I'm sure I don't know to what you're referring."

He scooped up a beer bottle and raised it to his lips, taking a long, slow drink while watching her in that predatory way he had.

How could someone's eyes be that green? They were so sharp and clear, it felt as though they pierced right through her.

The continued scrutiny gave her the urge to tug at her navy suit jacket and smooth her knee-length skirt, but she refused to fidget. "Is my mother here?"

"She went to the store with Maddie." He placed the bottle back on the counter and rested his palms on the ledge of the granite that had replaced the linoleum she remembered. "We're out of Cheetos and Mountain Dew."

She planted her hands on her hips and returned one of his long, disdainful once-overs. Her gaze settled meaningfully on his flat-as-a-board stomach. "Ah, that explains it. I've heard after thirty-five things go south rather quickly."

His expression flashed with what looked like amusement. He straightened from the counter and took a step toward her.

The urge to retreat rose in her chest, but she didn't dare step back.

Never show weakness. Never break.

His eyes narrowed. "How'd you know I turned thirty-five?"

Damn it. See, this was why she ignored his barbs—she always said something far too telling. She shrugged one shoulder. "Oh, I hear things."

"Investigating my background? How sweet. I didn't know you cared."

Of course they'd investigated all the Donovans. Just like Shane had investigated all of them. That's the way it worked. Everyone knew that. *Maybe* she'd spent a little too much time on the oldest Donovan brother, but only because he was the most dangerous.

So yes, she knew all about Shane. Had a list of stats she could rattle off in her head in her sleep.

Occupation: CEO and owner of The Donovan Corporation.

Last significant relationship: one year ago with some tech genius.

High school grade point average: an abysmal 1.65.

College degree: none.

Arrests: one for underage drinking at sixteen.

The list went on, and as many times as she went over the facts, the essence of him was missing. How had he beaten such impossible odds? Overcome such dire straits?

All by his thirty-fifth birthday.

Which she *should not* know was three months ago.

One week after hers to the day.

At the memory of her own birthday, she frowned. It hadn't been a good day.

342 of 350 Jennifer Dawson

She'd spent her birthday in strategy meetings concentrating on repairing her father's tattered image. Other than a small fifteen-minute work break, during which the interns shoved a cake under her nose, her mother had been the only person to call.

That night she'd sat alone in her Gold Coast townhouse overlooking the skyline eating Chinese takeout by herself. After a bottle of wine she'd contemplated her accomplishments, trying in vain to pat herself on the back.

Only to realize the things she'd listed had nothing to do with her.

She'd done nothing for her own life.

Not a single damn thing.

ABOUT THE AUTHOR

Jennifer Dawson grew up in the suburbs of Chicago and graduated from DePaul University with a degree in psychology. She met her husband at the public library while they were studying. To this day she still maintains she was NOT checking him out. Now, over twenty years later, they're married and living in a suburb right outside of Chicago with two awesome kids and a crazy dog.

Despite going through a light-FM, poem-writing phase in high school, Jennifer never grew up wanting to be a writer (she had more practical aspirations of being an international super spy). Then one day, suffering from boredom and disgruntled with a book she'd been reading, she decided to put pen to paper. The rest, as they say, is history.

These days Jennifer can be found sitting behind her computer, writing her next novel, chasing after her kids, keeping an ever watchful eye on her ever growing to-do list, and NOT checking out her husband.